## A STRANGELY TENDER KISS

A satanic smile curled his lips as he stared down at her, and Melissa gulped over the lump of fear that rose in her throat.

"What are you doing here?" she said, hoping to sound more courageous than she felt.

"I was about to ask you the same question," Zack replied. "This is my cabin and you are trespassing."

The fur quilt parted on the side, revealing a bare, shapely leg to Zack's hungry gaze. Melissa covered herself quickly and swallowed hard. It wasn't difficult to tell what he was thinking.

"I will pay you well if you let me go." Her chin tilted to a stubborn angle as she met Zack's unwavering gaze.

"It isn't money I want."

Her eyes widened in alarm as Zack pulled off his buckskin shirt, revealing his muscular physique. As his lips lowered to hers, she pressed determined hands to the hard wall of his chest, avoiding his attempts. Her cry of protest was muffled as his mouth covered hers—in a strangely tender kiss. . . .

# Passion's Vixen

## CAROL FINCH

**ZEBRA BOOKS**
**KENSINGTON PUBLISHING CORP.**

**ZEBRA BOOKS**

are published by

Kensington Publishing Corp.
475 Park Avenue South
New York, N.Y. 10016

First printing: July, 1984

Printed in the United States of America

*To Mom and Dad, for the years you gave me—your time, your patience, and your love. . . .*

*And to my brothers, Larry and Kelly. I am so very proud of both of you.*

# Part One

A delusion, a mockery, and a snare.
                    —Lord Denman

# Chapter One

Kentucky county, February, 1778

Melissa Stoddard ambled toward the rustic cabin that was set among the stately pines. A quiet smile played on her lips as she glanced up at the towering branches that reached up to touch the gray winter sky. The moon glistened across the quilt of snow, making it sparkle like diamonds that were hers for the taking. Her face radiated with pleasure as she followed the dim shaft of light from the cabin window. Melissa paused a moment to lick the fresh snowflakes from her lips and inhale a breath of fresh air.

It was beautiful here, she mused, as she released a sigh. There was no place on earth more majestic than the Cumberland Mountains when they were cloaked in a blanket of white. Her gaze deliberately swept the peaceful setting one last time, memorizing the scene for future recollections, and then she aimed herself toward the cabin and the warmth that awaited her.

Melissa brushed the snow from the sleeves of her fur coat and then drew open the door to see her father sitting by the hearth. The smoke from his pipe curled lazily about his graying head, forming a drifting halo. The cozy scene did much to stir her heart. She was strangely satisfied just watching her father relaxing in front of the fire until William felt the draft of cold air that moved across the floor and glanced in her direction.

"Hunting was good tonight." Melissa tossed the skins at his feet and then shrugged off her coat as she flashed him a cheerful smile.

William Stoddard appraised the hides she had snared and cleaned and then shook his head in wonder as Melissa leaned her musket against the wall.

"You have done well, Lissa," he assured her as he focused his attention on the bright, blue-violet eyes that twinkled with their own mysterious sparkle.

A sudden pang of sadness shot through him as she swept her fur cap from her head, allowing the honey blond curls to tumble recklessly over her shoulders to her waist. Even though she was dressed in buckskin clothes she had made from the hides she had hunted and cleaned, Melissa strongly reminded him of his wife, Laura.

He had fallen in love with Laura the moment he laid eyes on her. Although her older sister, Lelia, had been equally attractive and William had pursued her for a time, he had known from the beginning that it was Laura who had burrowed her way into his heart. He had spent his evenings with Lelia, only to get a glimpse of Laura who had been too young to receive a man's attention. When Laura became of age, William had turned his affection to her and had never regretted his choice. He had felt a sense of guilt after using Lelia and then abandoning her, but Laura had been the light of his life, a flame that had never withered and died, even after he had lost her that cold winter night when she had been so ill.

Every passing day since the loss of his beloved wife, William found the resemblance between Melissa and her mother to be more astonishing. A rueful smile crept to his lips. It was difficult not to think that his lovely Laura had returned to comfort him in the form of his daughter, helping him to remember Laura as she had been in the first years of their marriage.

The shape of their faces, the sun-kissed hue of their hair, and their petite, shapely frames were so very similar. Their dimpled smiles were so innocent and angelic that William had never tired of pleasing either of them. He had thrived on those captivating smiles.

Melissa's eyes were the mystifying combination of blue-violet, the gentle, yet bewitching mixture of Laura's sky-blue eyes and her sister, Lelia's, violet eyes, he mused, as he stared thoughtfully at his daughter. Within those colorful depths William could see both of the other women. The thought of them brought long harbored feelings of both pleasure and grief. A sea of memories swirled about him, and William felt a lump rising in his throat. Now Laura was gone and Lelia, hurt and heartbroken after William had told her that it was Laura he loved, had returned to France to wed a man much older than herself. William had often wondered if Lelia had come to love the man she hastily married. Through her tears she had assured him that she would never love again, but William had hoped

11

that Lelia would survive her disappointment and find happiness with Pierre Mooree. The fact that William had hurt her so deeply had always weighed heavily on his conscience, but he had loved Laura far too much to spend his life with a woman he could never cherish the way he had Laura.

At least he had Melissa to ease his loss, he reminded himself. Melissa was much stronger than the other two women in his life. Melissa was so vital, determined, and intriguing. Many a man had come to court her, but he had never witnessed that special sparkle of love in her eyes, and he was well aware that she would never marry until she discovered the meaning of a love like the one he and Laura had shared. Aye, Melissa was a rare gem, one that he had carefully protected since the day Laura died, and he would see to it that she had all that life could offer.

"Come here, child," Will murmured as he lifted outstretched arms to Melissa.

Melissa had noticed the melancholy expression that settled on her father's face and she rushed to him, climbing upon his lap as she had often done as a child. "We should be able to sell these skins for a handsome price. What shall we buy with all our riches, Papa?" she questioned, hoping to distract him from his troubled thoughts.

It was never difficult to tell what he was thinking when he peered off into space. Melissa could see the pain and sorrow in his eyes, knowing that even after all these years he still mourned her mother's death. And she was aware of her close resemblance to her mother. It was little wonder that William had difficulty putting the past in proper perspective when his daughter was a living symbol of a memory that often came to haunt him.

"I cannot claim any of these hides," he said absently as he stroked the soft gold tendrils that fell across her shoulder. "You trapped the game yourself and you may buy whatever your heart desires."

"Then I should like to buy the rest of my life and spend it here in these mountains with you. And we will insist that Jeremy join us," she added before releasing a contented sigh. "I never wanted to leave this cabin in the first place. 'Tis my home."

"But we had to sacrifice this life. We could not remain here forever. You needed a formal education," he reminded her as he lightly flicked the end of her upturned nose and then smiled wryly. "Someone had to teach you to become a young lady. I had failed miserably at it." His grin broadened when she pulled a face at him. "You still are not completely domesticated and I doubt that you ever will be."

"You and Jeremy taught me all I needed to know," she argued. "I have learned to survive in the wilderness. What more does one need to know?"

William chuckled softly at her defense. "Ah, dear Jeremy. I have often wondered if his attempt to train you to manage in the wilderness would be a help or a hinderance."

Jeremy Drieson was William's long time friend, one who had come and gone into the wilds to live the life that suited him best. Jeremy had never lost contact with William and Laura and had reappeared to settle in Martin's Fork after Laura died. Jeremy had taken an immediate interest in Melissa, filling her head with adventurous tales, instructing her in the techniques of hunting and trapping, calling upon her to share a lonely evening when he was stranded in his cottage during the harsh winter.

Melissa had thrived on Jeremy's companionship as well. At times William had experienced a twinge of envy, seeing them become inseparable through the years. But then, giving the matter further consideration, William had realized that Jeremy was as proud of Melissa as he was, as if she were the daughter Jeremy never had since he had never been prone to settle down and marry. Jeremy had always answered the call of the wild and drifted where the restless wind took him, but he was also lonely. He had reappeared from time to time, fading in and out of William's and Laura's lives, but yet never very far away.

After the accident that left Jeremy crippled, he had put down roots in Martin's Fork and had monopolized a great deal of Melissa's time. William had often wondered, although he had never dared to voice his speculations, if Jeremy had been twenty years younger whether he would have asked for Melissa's hand in marriage. There was a strong bond between them, one that occasionally baffled William. There was a certain magic between them that age could not overcome.

"Jeremy's teachings were an important part of my life," Melissa insisted, drawing her father from his silent reverie. "Jeremy took me under his wing when you were busy with the dry goods store. He taught me to survive and to defend myself in most any situation. Do no criticize him. He is a dear friend."

"How well I know," William mused aloud. He focused his full attention on Melissa and then flashed her his concerned father expression. "But there comes a

14

time when you must learn to be a proper lady as well." He urged her to her feet and gestured toward the back room. "Now off to bed with you. We must leave for the settlement in the morning. I have left Jeremy to attend to my business and his as well. 'Tis time that I see to my own affairs. A week away from the store has made me lazy. I must return to the routine before I lose the desire to do so."

Melissa placed a light kiss to her father's cheek and then sighed whimsically. "Very well, Papa, but I wish we could—"

"I know, my dear," William interrupted, smiling sympathetically. "But we must go back."

William eased back in his chair and stared pensively at the fire while Melissa brushed out her hair and prepared for bed. He was going to miss her terribly, but he had to consider what was best for her. He had planned this trip to the mountains to give them some time alone before she sailed to France.

The letter he had received from Lelia crept in from the corners of his mind. Lelia had offered Melissa a place to stay when she traveled France, insisting that she should visit her family's homeland and become exposed to the sophistication that Europe could offer. Lelia could introduce Melissa into society, allowing her opportunities that she could never acquire in the colonies. Since this young country was at war, William felt obliged to ship Melissa abroad. In two weeks William would escort Melissa to Norfolk and she would sail to France to stay with her Aunt Lelia and her cousin Robert. She would be gone a lifetime, William mused despairingly. Six months would seem an eternity, but he had shared her first twenty years and he could not keep her under his wing forever. It was time for her to fly on her own, and he had to be strong enough to watch her soar like a dove who was experiencing her first taste of freedom.

"You wanted to see me, Papa?" Melissa queried absently as she planted herself in the chair across from William's desk. She had been taking inventory in the store and was still making a mental list of the supplies they needed to purchase when he called to her.

"Aye, child. We will be leaving for Norfolk in four days. Your aunt Lelia has invited you to spend six months with her and your cousin Robert," he informed her and then watched her eyes widen in disbelief.

He could just as well have dropped a cannonball in her lap. It would have brought the same amount of shock and chagrin. William had never mentioned the idea before this moment, and she could not believe what she was hearing. Why in heaven's name would she want to sail to France? It sounded as appealing as standing before a firing squad.

"Six months?" she choked out. "You know I have no desire to visit France, much less spend half a year with Aunt Lelia and Robert." Her nose wrinkled distastefully at the thought. Besides, she barely knew her relatives and she had not seen Lelia since Laura died. It was not difficult to recall her impression of them, even after all these years. Lelia seemed as sour as a lemon, and Robert, although he was adopted, was a carbon copy of his mother, right down to his effeminate gestures. The lad could have dressed in women's clothing and Melissa would not have doubted that he was a member of the fairer sex. "The very idea of living with them distresses me," she muttered.

"But I have already accepted Lelia's invitation and I must insist that you go. You will find opportunities in Europe that I cannot offer you here. And 'tis only for six months. I am sure that you will thoroughly enjoy the adventure once you set sail," Will assured her, his tone more confident than Melissa deemed necessary.

"I am not going," she told him firmly and then rose from her chair to pace the study like a nervous cat that had been confined to a cage. "There is nothing in France that would interest me. I am perfectly content where I am, helping you mind the store. Please don't—"

William waved his hand for silence, his brown eyes flickering with a stern gleam that he rarely bestowed on his daughter. "You *are* going. I have never forced you to do anything in your life, but this is one time that I will insist. You will do as I request and the subject is closed to discussion." His face was set in determination, his gaze unyielding. "Now, you are to pack your belongings and be prepared to travel to Norfolk with me Thursday morning."

His voice reminded her of a judge passing sentence on a condemned man, and she could sympathize with anyone who was facing a prison term. Hers was to be solitary confinement in France with Aunt Lelia and cousin Robert as wardens. Lord help her, the jaws of hell had opened to swallow her up.

"But Papa," she cried in exasperation as if she were throwing herself on the mercy of the court.

"Nay, Melissa. I have made my decision and you

17

will not change it with your melodramatic scenes you use when you want your way with me. You *are* going and that is the beginning and end of it!'' he assured her with a hint of finality in his voice that he frequently used with his bartering customers, but seldom with Melissa.

A long, stilted moment of silence passed while their eyes locked and clashed.

"Very well, Papa, if that is the way you want it," she grumbled as she pivoted on her heels and marched toward the door.

"Melissa," he called after her, his tone softer now. " 'Tis not what I wish, but what is best for you. 'Tis all I have ever wanted, you know. And that is what motivates me now."

Melissa dropped her head and sighed heavily at his words. After a few moments she picked up the front of her skirt and hurried to the hall to take the staircase two steps at a time. She forced back the tears that threatened to cloud her vision. How could he do this to her? She had no desire to leave Jeremy and her father behind. They were all she had ever wanted and needed in life. Her aunt Lelia and cousin Robert were poor substitutes for the love she shared with the two men in her life.

Her father didn't really want her to go. He had said as much, she rationalized, as she gathered her belongings, but not the ones William had ordered her to pack. She would return at the end of week and he would forgive her and reconsider his decision, she thought hopefully. He could have asked anything of her and she would have willingly obeyed . . . except for this. Melissa had no intention of abandoning her father and

18

Jeremy to spend six agonizing months under the same roof with Lelia and Robert. Lelia had always regarded Melissa with a hint of contempt. For some reason the woman did not like her and Melissa could not fathom the reason for her aunt's animosity. Why would Lelia invite her to France, graciously offering to introduce her in court when she could barely abide the sight of her niece?

The light rap at the door interrupted her pensive musings. Melissa stiffened in alarm and then hurriedly stashed her selection of garments under the bed before her father barged in on her.

"Goodnight, Melissa," her father called from the hall.

"Goodnight, Papa." She hastened to the door, stepped into the hall, and reached up on tiptoe to press a kiss to his lips. "I love you," she whispered before slipping from his arms and closing the door behind her.

"And I love you enough to let you go," Will murmured to the lingering image of his daughter.

With a heavy-hearted sigh, he walked to his bedchamber, hoping sleep would come to dissolve his misery. Sending Melissa away was one of the most difficult things he had ever done. But this was best for her, he reminded himself, as he sank down on the edge of the bed to stare into the darkness. Torturous loneliness engulfed him when he lost his beloved Laura. It had taken an eternity for the feelings to fade. Now those tormenting sensations were coming to haunt him again. It would be an endless six months without Melissa. How was he to survive without viewing that bewitching face and those angelic smiles, he asked himself, but found no answer quick in coming.

19

Zack Beaugener gazed down at the settlement that was nestled in the valley and then reined his steed to a halt. The coal-black stallion pricked up his ears, his eyes darting side to side, impatiently waiting the signal to move on. After the steed shifted nervously beneath him, Zack nudged Drago in the flanks. Together they edged along the crest, following the narrow path that wound down the hill to Martin's Fork.

He was anxious to see Jeremy Drieson again. The memory of the past weighed heavily on Zack, recalling the eight years that he and Jeremy had spent together before the tragic accident. The scene flashed before him, as if it had happened only yesterday. A shiver of dread flew down his spine. He could still see the pain and agony on Jeremy's face when the grizzly bear caught him off guard, nearly costing him his life. Although Zack had arrived in camp in time to put an end to the attack, the bear had done irreparable damage. It had been six years since the accident, but Zack hadn't forgotten a single detail. The sight had not been a pretty one and Zack cringed all over again as Jeremy's horror-stricken face materialized before him.

Jeremy had befriended Zack, teaching him the ways of the wilderness, traveling as his constant companion. They had shared an adventurous life of hunting, trapping, and expeditions in uncharted land. Now Drieson had resigned himself to living in the settlement, managing the tavern. Zack regretted that he had been unable to see Jeremy except when he was passing through on his way to meet Boone or to see to his own affairs at home. He always brought Jeremy a bundle of furs, not because Drieson could not live without the extra money he gained from them, but because it was a gesture of friendship and gratitude. He owed Jeremy a great deal, more than he could ever begin to repay. The experience he had gained from Jeremy had proven invaluable.

It had been over eight months since he had seen Jeremy. The ordeal with Boone on the Blue Licks expedition had cost him a great deal of time and he had barely escaped with his life. The Shawnees had played havoc with their exploration and Boone had been captured. A few of the men managed to escape. Zack had been one of the fortunate ones, but a few frontiersmen had lost their lives during the attack.

As Zack swung from the saddle, he dragged the bundle of furs down beside him. When Zack walked into the pub, Jeremy glanced up at the muscular frame of the mountain man who filled the entrance. A broad grin split Jeremy's face while he continued to study the sturdy stature of the man who strolled over to drop the pile of pelts at his feet.

"You certainly took your own sweet time about getting here. Your message stated that you would arrive two days ago. I thought perhaps the hunted prey had finally gotten the best of the mighty hunter," Jeremy taunted as he motioned for the waitress to fetch some ale to the table.

Zack planted himself in the chair across from Jeremy and nodded a silent greeting. "It damned near did this time. I almost lost *my* hide," he assured Jeremy, heaving a weary sigh.

A concerned frown knitted his brow as he peered at

Zack's rough, unkempt appearance. "I don't think we are discussing the same thing. What happened?"

"Boone was captured and we lost a few men. I could have been one of them," he explained, his deep voice raspy from exhaustion.

Zack squirmed on his chair. After riding Drago for endless hours he could have sworn that he was still sitting on his inseparable companion. All those days in the saddle had Zack thinking that they were permanently joined like Siamese twins.

Jeremy leaned across the table, his eyes mirroring his anxiety. "What do you intend to do? Knowing your friendship for Daniel, I cannot imagine your leaving him to suffer the consequences."

"I'll do whatever I have to do," he said deliberately, his steel gray eyes meeting Jeremy's probing gaze.

"But before you do, I have one request. It may take a few days of your time, but I think you will find it a pleasurable challenge. I ask it as a personal favor." A wry smile hovered on his lips as he eased back in his seat.

Zack's heavy brows furrowed as he studied Drieson's mysterious grin. "What is it?" he questioned cautiously.

"I want you to track down a runaway for me. William Stoddard, a close friend of mine, has lost his prize possession and he dearly wants it returned. I told him that I would be seeing you any day now and that you were just the man for the task. He is prepared to reward you for finding his misplaced daughter," Jeremy explained, his grin widening to encompass his scarred face.

"Daughter?" Zack snorted cynically. What could

Jeremy be thinking of? What a ridiculous request. "I have more important business to attend than tracking down some damned woman. Anyone in this settlement could trail the chit and bring her back. You don't need me for that." Jeremy should have known better than to ask for help on such a simple matter. He had just told Jeremy that he had pressing matters awaiting him. Lord, the man had been too long in confinement. It was beginning to deteriorate his brain!

"This woman is extraordinary," Jeremy defended, chuckling as he met Zack's skeptical frown. "She is a woman by birth, but her abilities in these mountains far exceed the average wench. You will find that tracking her will be more difficult than you can imagine." There was an underlying challenge in his voice, a taunt that set Zack's teeth on edge.

"What is she, some combination of witch and wild animal?" he smirked caustically. "I have yet to meet a female who qualifies as exceptional. Any woman crazy enough to wander off alone in this untamed wilderness deserves to perish for her foolishness."

"You haven't met Melissa," Jeremy persisted, a mischievous sparkle dancing in his blue eyes. The sound of her name as it floated from his lips drew another suspicious frown from Zack. "She will not perish, my friend. She and her father lived in the mountains for a time. When she was fourteen, they moved to the settlement so she could pursue a formal education. The lass knows this area better than you do." A thoughtful smile pursed his lips as his gaze swung back to Zack. "I'm not even certain that you can locate her. She will have left no easy trail to follow. You would have to rely on your instincts to track Melissa. Even her father was wise enough to know that he was incapable of finding her when that was not her wont. That is why he searches for someone with your experience. Interested?" Jeremy arched a curious brow and then sipped his ale, waiting for Zack to make his decision.

Zack gave his raven head a negative shake. "Nay. If this woman is so adept in the mountains, she will return when she wishes. Why is her father so concerned about her if all you have told me is true? Or is this some folktale that you have devised in your spare time?" he queried, his tone heavily laden with sarcasm.

"Every word is truth, Zack. She was to travel to Norfolk and then sail to France. Her father intends that she be on that ship. He wants her back immediately. Will you at least talk to Stoddard?" Jeremy prodded. "I'll even bet the furs you brought to me that two days won't be ample time for you to find her." A challenging smile curved the corners of his mouth upward, making Zack all the more curious about the reason Jeremy had singled him out for the task.

After a long, thoughtful moment Zack nodded his acceptance. He would find Melissa in less than two days and deliver her to her father's doorstep. No woman could equal his experience in the wilderness, he thought arrogantly. She was probably some ugly witch who no one really wanted returned, except her own father and Jeremy. But why was Jeremy so intent on finding her, he wondered.

"I'll talk to Stoddard," he agreed, his tone reluctant. "Just as soon as you tell me why this woman is so important to you," Zack added that stipulation to quench his own curiosity.

Jeremy's face paled slightly and the scar on his left

24

cheek tightened as he met Zack's level gaze. "She is—"
He fumbled for the words and then decided to begin
again. "Melissa and I have spent a great deal of time
together these last six years. I'm extremely fond of her
and William and I are good friends," he said solemnly.
"You are the only one I would think of sending to bring
her back."

Zack cocked a dubious brow and scrutinized his
gray-haired friend. Jeremy was not telling him everything. Zack could sense it, but he let the matter ride. If
Jeremy had some fond attachment for Melissa, then
Zack would oblige, not willingly, but nevertheless he
would honor the request.

After Zack chugged the last of his ale, he rose to full
stature and then winced as Jeremy struggled to his
feet, grasping for his cane. Zack would have offered a
supporting hand, but he knew that Jeremy was independent, intent on managing on his own.

"I'll introduce you to Stoddard," Jeremy offered as
he dragged his lame leg from the chair and leaned unsteadily on his crutch.

Zack inwardly flinched as Jeremy limped along beside him. His leg was less useful than it had been when
last he had seen Jeremy. That vicious attack had left
permanent scars, mangling his right leg so severely
that it hardly functioned at all. If Zack could have arrived at camp only five minutes sooner he could have
saved Jeremy from this crippled existence. Five
damned minutes! How could a life change in such a
short span of time, Zack thought to himself. Jeremy
had saved him from catastrophe more times than he
cared to count, but the one time Zack could have come
to his aid . . . Zack would have offered his soul to the

devil if he could have relived those five minutes and handled them differently.

As Jeremy and Zack walked into the dry goods store, William smiled in relief. "Is this the man you were telling me about?" he questioned as he sized up the rugged mountain man.

"Aye," Jeremy replied, a faint smile grazing his lips.

"Come back into the storeroom so we can talk privately," Stoddard suggested as he gestured to the small niche at the back of the shop. When both men were seated, William cleared his throat and mentally prepared his explanation. "My daughter has been gone a full day. You have three days to find her and return her to me so we can travel to Norfolk. You will be well paid for your trouble, sir. Your reward will be doubled if you can bring Melissa to me in only two days. This is at Jeremy's request."

Zack's gaze swung to Drieson and tarried a long moment, but he was met with a blank stare. Jeremy had certainly sweetened the pot, he thought to himself. He was issuing him a direct challenge and Zack could not fathom why, but he could put the cash to good use.

Stoddard nervously paced the floor in front of the two men and then paused, turning his attention to the frontiersman dressed in buckskin. "I trust that Jeremy has made it clear that you will not be tracking some simpleminded twit who is unable to fend for herself in the Cumberlands. Melissa is an expert marksman and is deadly with a knife. She won't come back without a fight," he warned, his eyes narrowing on Zack who seemed to be paying very little attention.

Zack's shoulder lifted in a lackadaisical shrug. "Drieson had already informed me that this will be no easy task. However, I must admit that I cannot imagine any woman being so difficult to trail," he added cynically as he eased back in his chair and crossed his arms over his broad chest.

A stern frown made fast work of settling on Williams' wrinkled features. "Your arrogance may cost you precious time, Mr. Beaugener. You may find that you have to swallow your words." He tossed the stack of pelts to his doubtful companion. "Lissa trapped and cleaned these furs only two weeks ago . . . all by herself. She will not go hungry while she carries her musket. She will be tempted to skin you alive if you threaten her freedom. Do not underestimate her abilities, sir, or you may find yourself in a most embarrassing predicament," William insisted firmly.

Zack rose to his feet, his steel gray eyes cold. He was unimpressed by Stoddard's heralded praise of his daughter. "Forgive me if I am not as convinced of her resourcefulness as the two of you are. I have tracked more dangerous prey than women. Do you have a portrait of her?" he questioned blandly.

William reached into his coat pocket and retrieved a small picture of Melissa. Zack had already imagined the wench to have long, stringy black hair, a hooked nose, and dark, beady eyes. An incredulous laugh burst from his lips when he glanced at the picture of a very attractive young woman. How could she be as clever and conniving as Drieson and Stoddard would have him believe?

"This is an old picture and she has changed greatly," Stoddard explained, a fond smile touching his lips as he looked around Zack's broad shoulder to view the picture of Melissa once again. "She was only seventeen then and the portrait did not do her justice. She is more lovely than an artist could capture on canvas."

Zack smirked skeptically. Only a father would make such a remark, he mused.

"I'll need some supplies for my trip," he requested as he handed the picture to Stoddard.

Within thirty minutes Zack had his belongings loaded on Drago's back. He stood outside the pub with Jeremy for a few quiet moments after William had left them alone. With a tired sigh, Zack swung into the saddle and nodded farewell to Jeremy. He had intended to stay the night with Drieson since both he and his horse were weary from their journey, but it seemed that he was not to have his wish.

Zack settled himself more comfortably on his stallion, his attention narrowing on Drieson. "When I return with this valuable wench, I will expect a full explanation as to why she is so damned important to you," he demanded sharply. "You know I wouldn't agree if it wasn't for you. And I go with reluctance. I want to know why I should put this little misfit before Boone. You better prepare a good story because when I drag her home, I will damned well expect a truthful explanation."

A sly smile crept to Drieson's lips as he wrapped his arm around the supporting post to steady himself. He watched as Zack reined his steed toward the road. "I think you will know why sooner than you expect, my friend," Drieson assured him, his grin spreading from ear to ear. "But if you don't, you will be given your explanation as soon as Melissa is returned."

Zack growled disgustedly at Drieson's remark and

threw a frown over his shoulder as he nudged Drago into a canter. What the hell was Jeremy up to, Zack wondered as he left the settlement behind. Why was this woman important to him? The questions continued to plague him as he rode. The fact that he could come up with no answers did much to darken his black mood. Women were nothing but trouble. This witch he was tracking was probably one of the worst. Damn, why hadn't he told Drieson to find someone else to track her?

Boone was being taken to the British headquarters in Detroit, the colonies were up in arms, defending themselves against the redcoats, and here he was, playing nursemaid to some little termagant for Drieson.

"You better have a helluva good reason," Zack grumbled under his breath as his gaze lifted to the mountains that towered above him.

## Chapter Two

"Dammit," Zack growled when he came to the end of another useless set of tracks that led up a rock bluff.

He had spent the entire day trying to pick his way through a myriad of dead-end footprints and hoof tracks. Infuriated by his futile attempt, he decided to do his temper a favor and call it a night. After lighting a campfire he prepared himself a meager meal. As he leaned back against a tree, his gray eyes swept the narrow clearing. He pulled his buckskin jacket tightly about his neck as the cool mountain air settled down around his shoulders.

The sun was shedding its last rays of light through the tall trees of the Cumberland Mountains, and Zack watched its slow descent with annoyance. The cunning wench whom he tracked had eluded him all day. The thought of being outfoxed by this young vixen incensed his pride. With a frustrated sigh, Zack kicked dirt over the fire and dumped the last of his coffee on the smoldering coals.

"Let's go home, Drago," he grumbled as he swung

up on the stallion and reined him toward the shack that he and Jeremy had shared for several years. It was only a few miles from the area he had been tracking. Thinking of returning to it once again helped to ease his ruffled ego. At least his single-handed scouting expedition, as futile as it was, would have some small consolation. He could return to the one place he called home for a decent night's sleep.

Stoddard had given him directions to the cabin in which he and Melissa had stayed earlier that month. Zack had located it late that afternoon, hoping that the woman had gone there to hide out, but it showed no signs of recent occupancy. She was far too clever to seek refuge in the one place Stoddard would have expected her to go. Zack had wasted the better part of the day searching the area around the shack, all for nothing. The damned witch was more skillful than he had imagined, he mused sourly. She had marked trails that were not overly obvious, a broken twig here and there, a set of footprints. He had hunted carefully for signs that would lead him to her and still he had come up empty-handed.

Darkness had settled over the majestic mountains as Zack picked his way through the brush to see the dim silhouette of the cabin he had called home before the accident. The shack had always warmed his heart when he spied it from a distance. For eight years he and Jeremy had hunted, trapped, and explored together, but they always returned to the cabin. Drieson had built it with his bare hands, planning to bring a wife with him to the mountains. But something had happened to spoil his plans and he had occupied it alone until Zack wandered in, three-quarters frozen and half starved.

Discarding his pensive musings, he focused his full attention on the shack. A faint glow illuminated from the borders of the window, and a thin curl of smoke rose from the chimney. Zack's brows furrowed, wondering if someone had claimed the abandoned cabin as his own. And then a wicked smile caught one corner of his mouth as another thought crossed his mind. Perhaps Melissa had stumbled onto the cabin. If she was there he would love to clamp his hands around her neck, strangling the life from her for sending him on as many wild goose chases as he had followed that day. Dragging that conniving wench back to her father would be pure delight, he thought vengefully.

Zack had been hounded with the strange feeling that Jeremy had somehow set him up, but he wasn't sure how or why. For some reason Drieson wanted Zack to see how cunning and resourceful this woman was. There had been a sense of pride when Jeremy spoke of Melissa. At first Zack had wondered if perhaps Jeremy was in love with her, but the more Jeremy said about her, the less likely Zack thought it to be. Nay, it was something else, he decided as he urged Drago toward the shack. Jeremy was fifty-three and the lass was only twenty. He was old enough to be her father. He had heard of May-September romances, but Jeremy had never seemed the type for one of them. Besides, there had been that mysterious woman who continued to haunt Jeremy. She had some strange power over him, and yet, he had never mentioned her unless he had been drinking heavily. Even then he had never uttered her name.

That was one of the reasons Zack had never allowed himself to become entangled with a woman, except for brief interludes to appease his desires. Jeremy was tied to the past, unable to enjoy what a woman could offer. His friendship with women had remained platonic, as far as Zack knew. Although Zack preferred to carry a relationship further than Jeremy, he was determined to remain unattached. When a woman possessed something he desired, he took it and then left, feeling nothing more than the passion that had passed between them. Zack had spent thirty-two years foot loose and fancy free. He had no intention of living the way Jeremy had—lost to some elusive dream that could never become reality.

Zack's thoughts circled back to the present as he swung from the saddle and tethered Drago in the trees. As he crept toward the cabin, he halted and then turned back for the musket he had left on his horse. If the occupant was not the woman he had been tracking, he might find himself face to face with an intruder who would be more difficult to handle than a mere wisp of a woman.

After he climbed through the window in the back room of the shack, Zack picked his way through the darkness and eased open the door to the main room. The scene that lay before him did much to arouse his interest. Zack had to pinch himself to ensure that he wasn't dreaming. It was as if he was peering through the door of heaven. His gaze deliberately swept the shadows, finding no one to pounce upon him. No lantern lit the room. There was only the warmth of the coals in the fireplace for heat. A leather hide had been draped over the front window to keep light from illuminating from it.

When his flinty eyes came to rest on the fire, his breath froze in his throat. Before the hearth lay two fur quilts. From within their plush matting protruded a silky mane of flaxen-blond hair that sprayed across the blankets like a shimmering cape of gold, as if the sun rose and set within the confines of his own cabin. Bare arms and soft, creamy shoulders glowed like honey against the background of smoldering coals. An angelic face that was gentle and relaxed in slumber held him spellbound for a long moment. So tempting was the sight that Zack had to force himself to stand his ground when he found himself creeping closer.

Melissa was far more beautiful in the flesh than she was in the portrait he had seen of her. But then Stoddard had told him that the picture did not do her justice. And indeed it didn't. Zack had cynically concluded that it was father's pride that had spurred his remark. Obviously, Stoddard had an eye for beauty and had spoken the truth.

Zack crept toward the table and eased down on the edge, carefully surveying the exquisite features of the young woman's face. Her dark, sooty lashes lay against her cheeks. Her complexion was flawless, her skin so silky and smooth that it seemed to beg for his touch. Now he could understand why Jeremy had insisted that he track this vixen. She was all Jeremy had claimed: cunning, adept, devastatingly beautiful, easily surpassing the comeliness of any woman he had yet to meet. He had stumbled into the lair of a lioness and had no regrets for doing so. As a matter of fact, he would heartily thank Jeremy the next time he saw him.

A crooked smile touched one corner of his mouth as the image of the hooked-nosed, wild-eyed witch whom he had expected to confront came to mind. His first impression had been all wrong, he mused, his smile widening into a rakish grin. Jeremy had offered him a diversion before he set his mind to freeing Boone from captivity. And he would indeed take advantage of the situation, he decided, as his gaze lingered on her tempting flesh.

Melissa squirmed beneath the fur quilts when an eerie sensation tapped at her consciousness. When her eyes fluttered open, she gasped as the shadow fell over her. She inwardly flinched when her lashes swept up to view the dark form who rested one hip on the edge of the table, only four feet from where she lay. Instinctively, she reached for the musket beside her, but the ominous figure quickly closed the distance between them, placing a moccasined foot on the barrel of her rifle. A satanic smile curled his lips as he stared down at her, and Melissa gulped over the lump of fear that rose in her throat. Apprehensively, she raised her gaze to the heavily bearded face above her.

From where she lay, the massive frame of a man towered over her like a foreboding shadow of doom that could devour all in its path. The man was dressed in tight-fitting deerhide breeches, revealing the finely tuned muscles of his thighs. His shirt gaped at the neck, displaying the dark matting of hair on his chest. His buckskin jacket, which looked the worse for wear, was trimmed with fringe that dangled from the sleeves. When Melissa finally found the courage to meet his gaze, she peered into a pair of cold, narrowed eyes that reflected the dim light from the fireplace. She felt a shiver of dread trickle down her spine. His piercing glance pricked her like burning, silver daggers, and she wondered if she had just met the eyes of death.

The man's features were camouflaged behind a heavy black beard and mustache. The lines of his face that were revealed to her seemed to be chiseled in stone. The mountain man could have easily posed as Satan himself, and Melissa would not have questioned his identity. There was nothing tender or compassionate about the looming figure who hovered over her. Melissa tried to draw a breath, but it was difficult with Satan, his eyes as harsh and gray as an angry winter sky, ready to pounce on her. Once more, her gaze swept from the top of his fur cap to the toes of the moccasins that mashed her musket to the floor. She prayed that this was a bad dream. But it wasn't. She was awake. Lord, how she wished she hadn't been.

"What are you doing here?" she ground out, hoping to sound more courageous than she felt. She was amazed that her voice hadn't quivered with fear since she was trembling inside and out.

"I was about to ask you the same question, wench," Zack countered, in an intimidating tone. "This is *my* cabin and you are trespassing."

"Oh . . . well then . . . I will leave," she offered lamely, attempting to mask her nervousness, but it was becoming more difficult. She was shaking like a potted plant that had been abandoned in the Arctic. "I was not aware that this shack was being used, and I needed a place to lodge for the night." She wrapped the blankets around her and carefully sat up to face the dark demon who continued to watch her like a hawk that

36

was poised to swoop down on his prey.

The fur quilt parted on the side, revealing a bare, shapely leg to Zack's hungry gaze. Melissa quickly covered herself and swallowed hard. It wasn't difficult to tell what he was thinking. His flinty eyes were unnerving, and she was in one hell of a predicament, she thought to herself, as her gaze circled the room to find a means of escape. She had bolted the door and she would need a running start to open it and flee before he caught up with her. If she were to survive this ordeal and remain unscathed by this evil-looking scoundrel, she would be lucky indeed.

Zack squatted down on his haunches to lift a silky strand of gold from her shoulder. "You are not leaving here, Melissa," he assured her, his gaze roaming over her in a bold caress.

Melissa quaked when she peered into his craggy face. The tousled hair that lay under his cap and the dark beard that covered his features glowed like ebony as they absorbed the light of the coals. Again, she was reminded of the comparison she had made between the devil and this gruesome soul. And then a curious frown furrowed her brows. How did he know her name? Had her father sent a merciless bounty hunter after her? Was he furious that she had fled to the mountains?

"I have spent the whole damned day following your carefully marked trails that led into streams and up the side of rock cliffs." He chuckled lightly, remembering one particular trail that had him cursing her name before he had even laid eyes on her. "I especially enjoyed the tracks that led up the pine tree. You would have had me believe that you scaled it and then took to the air to wing your way over the mountains. You left

37

enough broken limbs to convince me that your horse had clambered up behind you," he added, an amused sparkle dancing in his eyes.

The faint smile that hovered on his lips eased her tension. He did not seem so malicious when he grinned. Perhaps he was not as dangerous as she had first suspected. At least there was a ray of hope in his smile, she thought, as she bravely returned his grin.

"I rather liked that one myself," she admitted saucily. " 'Twas my best effort. The other tracks were dull and unimaginative, don't you think?" Her delicate brow arched quizzically.

"I was impressed with your abilities," he confessed as he pulled up a chair beside her and took a seat, cautiously lifting her rifle onto his lap. He had come to respect her cunningness, but his respect warranted no trust. "Your father and Jeremy told me that I would have a difficult time tracking you, but I didn't take them seriously. You presented more of a challenge than I had expected."

"Then how did you find me?" She pulled the quilts tightly about her neck when Zack's steel gray eyes left her face and wandered over every inch of exposed flesh.

"If I hadn't given up for the night and come to my own cabin, you would still have your freedom. Your only mistake was hiding in my shack. 'Tis a shame that such a deceptive lass has been trapped by her own cleverness," he mocked dryly.

Melissa lowered her gaze, her hand brushing over the fur quilt that covered her thigh. "I suppose you are going to take me back to my father now," she speculated, heaving a defeated sigh.

"Nay," he replied, as he squirmed in the hard wooden chair that seemed to have petrified over the years, making a most uncomfortable seat for a tired body. "We will leave in the morning. I have ridden enough for one day."

She slowly raised her gaze to meet the glistening pools of silver. "I don't want to go back. My home is here in these mountains, not in France. I don't intend to be separated from Papa or Jeremy," she assured him determinedly.

Zack winced when he heard Drieson's name. Perhaps this woman did share some type of romantic relationship with Drieson. His attention narrowed on her, studying her thoughtfully for a long moment, visualizing Melissa and Jeremy together.

"Why is Jeremy so important that you cannot leave him?" he questioned point-blank.

Her shoulder lifted in a leisurely shrug. "He is my dearest friend. Jeremy taught me much about the mountains, even more than my father often wishes I knew," she added, a mischievous smile curving the corners of her mouth upward. "When we first came to the settlement, Jeremy told me stories about himself and his companion. I was so fascinated with them that I asked him to teach me all he could. He is the one who taught me to mark trails." Melissa's brows knitted into a curious frown. "Who are you? You are not from the settlement or I would have seen you before."

"My name is Zack Beaugener," he answered, as he swept the fur cap from his raven head and bowed from his hard, wooden throne.

Her eyes bulged from their sockets, her jaw gaping. "You are Jeremy's partner?" she choked out. "I feel as though I have known you all my life. Jeremy has talked of you so often that I would have recognized you on sight." Melissa surveyed his sturdy form. In all her wildest dreams she would never have imagined this to be Zack Beaugener.

She had pictured Zack as a knight in shining armor, but nothing could have been further from the truth.

Casting aside her wandering thoughts, she focused her full attention on their conversation. "Surely you will not return me to my father if you are Jeremy's trusted friend. Jeremy does not want me to travel to France. Don't you see? He sent you because he knew you would allow me to keep my freedom. When my father suggested traveling to France two years ago, Jeremy discouraged the idea. You cannot hand me over to my father." She appealed to his sense of decency, wondering if he had one. Actually, she doubted it.

His brow raised acutely and then returned to its normal arch. What the hell was going on? Either she was lying through her teeth or Jeremy was up to something, but what? Damned if he knew. And Zack had promised Stoddard that he would deliver Melissa to his doorstep. He was obligated since he had given his word. Why the devil would Jeremy insist that he track Melissa if he didn't really want her found in time to deport her?

"Your father wants you back and I'm taking you to him in the morning," Zack assured her, a hint of finality in his tone that made Melissa stiffen defiantly.

"I will pay you well if you let me go," she offered. "I am *not* traveling to France. I am not going anywhere until I have decided to do so." Her chin tilted to a stubborn angle as she met Zack's unwavering gaze.

"Perhaps you will, but that will be none of my concern. You can flee from your father when I'm not around to hunt you down." A confident smile played on his lips. "Otherwise you would meet with the same fate again."

"I can make it worth your time to allow me to escape from you," she baited, hoping to sway him from his firm stand.

Zack released a derisive snort as he peered down at the attractive young woman who was making it difficult to keep his thoughts on the conversation. His mind was wandering in the wrong direction, his arousing thoughts overshadowing her plight. "I don't need your money and I doubt that anything else you could offer would be worth the humiliation of facing Jeremy and your father empty-handed . . . except one."

A bemused frown settled on her features. "And what is that?" she questioned innocently.

Zack crossed his arms over his broad chest and eased back in his chair, a ghost of a smile hovering on his lips. "You."

"Me?" she said dumbfoundedly. As soon as the word floated from her lips, she caught the implication and then choked on her breath, her cheeks coloring beet red.

As he laid the rifle back on the table, he chortled amusedly. "Or perhaps your claim to remain in the colonies is not as important as you would have me believe." Zack leaned toward her, the fringe of his jacket dangling over his muscular thighs. "Is this another crafty ploy to keep your freedom, Melissa?" Zack was cautious by nature and suspicious by habit. He did not trust women. This cunning minx, with the flaxen mane and bewitching face, only confirmed his conclusion that a woman was dangerous if she were taken for granted. "Yea or nay, is it worth the price?" He arched a heavy brow, a satanic smile curling his lips as he bent his gaze to the alluring form at his feet.

Melissa swallowed with a gulp and glanced uneasily about her, searching for a means of escape. Somehow she would find a way to elude this frightening rogue. She just needed time to think. Reluctantly she met the flinty orbs that drilled into her. "It is worth almost any price," she admitted begrudgingly.

"Almost?" he mocked, another smile touching his lips as he cocked his head to the side, studying her from a new angle. When Melissa made no reply, Zack became persistent. "Well?" His voice hinted at impatience, his eyes as hard as granite.

Another long moment passed between them as Melissa discreetly surveyed the room and then she nodded slightly. "Very well . . . it is worth *any* price." The words were hard to force out, and the mere thought of the bargain made her fidget nervously.

Had she lost her mind? Why would she agree to such ridiculous terms. The answer was slow in coming, but she knew what it was. The adventure stories she had heard about Zack had long been a part of her dreams. Jeremy had described him to be some phenomenal creature that defied nature and knew no man as master. There was something intriguing about his confident manner. Zack lived the daring life that she would have loved to pursue, but, as a woman, was only hers in fantasies. Jeremy had made Zack her champion long before she had even met him. And there was yet another reason. She was buying precious time. If he let down his guard with her, she would flee into the darkness.

"You are an unscrupulous scoundrel, Mr. Beaugener. If Jeremy knew that you had backed me into a corner and offered such unprincipled terms for this bargain, he would slit your ruthless throat, friend or no," she assured him, flashing him an icy glare.

Zack inwardly flinched at her remark. Jeremy knew Zack better than anyone. Why would Jeremy want him to track down Lissa instead of some man from the settlement? Drieson knew damned well what could happen between them. Zack had always taken what he wanted from women, and yet, Jeremy had issued no warning about keeping his hands off this one. What the hell did Drieson expect him to do? What game was Jeremy playing and why?

His thoughtful reverie was interrupted when Melissa squirmed impatiently before him. He wanted her. That realization came at him again as he stared into that lovely face. Damn, he ached for her. Just gazing at her was enough to drive a sane man mad. She was beautiful, cunning, and available. It had been an eternity since he had held a woman in his arms. He had spent the winter in the wilderness with Boone, having little time to seek his pleasures. He would have Melissa, he decided, and he would deal with Jeremy later. His lusty gaze swept her with open hunger, imagining what awaited him.

"If those are the only terms you will offer for my freedom, then let us settle them . . . and quickly," Melissa snapped, flinging him a reproachful glare.

A devilish smile parted his lips, showing even white teeth. "I am a bit surprised to find you so eager and willing," he mocked.

"Willing to meet the bargain and eager to see it end, *not* begin," she shot back, her tone laced with bitterness.

"I did not offer the bargain. *You* did," he reminded her flippantly. "I simply stated the terms that might make me consider facing your father's wrath. 'Tis your decision. Since you have agreed, I expect you to come without a fight." He shrugged off his jacket and carelessly tossed it over the back of the chair, his devouring gaze never wavering from Melissa.

Her eyes widened in alarm as Zack pulled off his buckskin shirt, revealing his muscular physique. He appeared as rugged and powerful as the bear she had heard described that had mauled Jeremy. How could she have fought Zack? It was obvious that he could crush her bones with one hand.

When he moved, he reminded her of a sleek panther. His muscles rippled as he walked back to her, his massive chest rising and falling with each breath.

"I have more to gain in my freedom that I can lose to you. I will not fight you," she assured him and then added bitterly, "But do not expect me to enjoy fulfilling the bargain. Only for an important cause do I submit, and *only* for that cause." Her defiant eyes locked with his, blue-violet clashing with silver.

Zack cocked a dark brow as he knelt down beside her, leisurely brushing his hand over her bare shoulder. "Perhaps you should wait until later to decide if you find any pleasure in my embrace. Opinions should be based on experience. Do you have a basis for your conclusion?" he questioned, his voice low and husky.

As his lips lowered to hers, she pressed determined

44

hands to the hard wall of his chest, avoiding his kiss. "Nay, but then I do not need to be bitten by a snake to know that it would be an unpleasant experience. You will not change my mind, no matter what you think of your abilities to convince me otherwi . . ."

Her last word was muffled as his mouth covered hers in a strangely tender kiss. It was in direct contrast to his devilish appearance. She had expected to be mauled, but to her surprise, the feel of his lips playing gently on hers wilted her resistance.

The quilt was drawn away from her bare flesh, and Melissa jerked back as his hand cupped her breast. A strange sensation drifted over her, and Melissa didn't like what she was feeling. It was frightening to realize that her body had responded to his intimate touch when she was determined to dislike the experience.

A wry smile threatened the corners of his mouth as his gray eyes roamed brazenly over her flesh.

It was obvious that she had no experience with men. With Stoddard and Drieson to protect her, Zack doubted that she knew the meaning of passion. Zack had always kept his distance from such women, but now he found himself in a situation that he could not refuse.

A thoughtful frown settled on his features, remembering the last words Jeremy had given Stoddard before they parted company. Suddenly, he backed away from Melissa.

"Have no fear of your daughter's safety," Jeremy had said, sending Zack a subtle wink. "Melissa will be in very capable hands, the best of company, and she will be returned to you. Beaugener is trustworthy to a fault."

He had no time to contemplate that remark when his eyes strayed back to Melissa's perfect body. Her arousing effect on him sent logic fleeing. His hands roamed over her breasts, loving the feel of her satiny skin beneath his caress.

Melissa suddenly bolted to her feet. Although Zack grabbed for her, he found himself holding the empty quilt she had abandoned in her haste to escape. In an instant he was in pursuit. Melissa stumbled against the furniture in her panicky attempt to reach the door, but Zack clamped his arm around her waist and swept her off the floor, as if she were as light as a feather.

"We made a bargain and I expect you to keep it. I accepted your word as a lady," he growled, as he stalked across the room in hurried strides.

"I am not a lady. If I were, I would not have agreed to this damned bargain!" she hissed. "And you are no gentleman." Although she beat her fists against his chest, he held her chained to him, as if her attack was no more than a playful pat.

When they were in front of the hearth, Zack set her to her feet, keeping a tight grasp on her elbows. His wicked chuckle floated about them as his eyes devoured her in one, all-consuming gaze that made her wince fearfully. "I am no gentleman," he agreed. "Nor have I ever made that empty claim, my lovely vixen."

"I have heard it said that a gentleman is one who does not inflict pain on others. Am I to suffer degradation at your hands?" she queried, raking him scornfully. "I doubt that you can be gentle. You are like an animal of the wild."

Jeremy may have thought Zack to be the picture of perfection, she thought resentfully, but she had discovered Beaugener's major flaw. He was calloused and heartless!

His hand crept beneath her chin, forcing her to meet his rakish smile. "I have been many things in my life, Melissa. Gentleness has occasionally been among them. Do not fight me and you will have nothing to fear from me."

His head came deliberately toward hers as his gaze swept over her exquisite features, not missing even the smallest detail. Melissa stared at him wide-eyed as his lips brushed lightly over hers. It was a tender, inquiring kiss that patiently awaited a reaction, one that she refused to give. His amorous assault would have no effect on her, she told herself. Her body was rigid, like a stone post that felt nothing, responded to nothing.

A wry smile tugged at one corner of his mouth as he drew away just far enough to stare into her wary eyes. She was offering a challenge, daring him to find pleasure while she remained aloof and unmoved by his kiss. She did not fight him, but she was making him try to evoke even the smallest of emotion.

Zack gathered her tense body in his arms, making her painfully aware of the contrast between the hardness of his male frame and the softness of hers. His breath was warm against her skin as his lips fluttered over her eyelids and then feathered across her cheek to recapture her mouth. Involuntarily, her eyes closed and Melissa realized that she had lost the sense of sight in her battle to reject him and force him to admit defeat. A wild tingle darted up and down her spine as his tongue traced her lips and then gently parted them to search the recesses of her mouth. She was struck by the strange notion that someone had released an entire butterfly collection in her stomach when his kiss deepened. Her heart was playing an odd tune against her ribs as its pace accelerated. His breath intermingled with hers, slowly drawing it from her lungs and then gently returning it the moment before she was certain she would find herself gasping for breath like a swimmer who had been too long beneath the surface.

Again, his lips left hers to seek her earlobe and nibble against her neck. A knowing smile hovered on his lips when he felt the rapid pulsations that his kisses had aroused, and he took advantage of her when he realized that her resistance was beginning to crumble.

His hands splayed across her hips and then ascended to her back, tracing lazy circles along her spine until her skin quivered beneath his exploring caress. Melissa felt herself losing the second skirmish with this skillful rogue. Her sense of touch was abandoning her in midbattle, leaving her quivering as an odd sensation coursed her veins. It was like a small fire that had been left to burn somewhere deep inside her, one that could become a blaze if it was left unattended. She was melting like butter set by a stove. Once more Melissa called upon her defenses, but Zack was chipping away at them as his index finger continued to trace her spine, tickling and teasing her until she submitted to the arousing feel of hand on her bare skin.

Melissa kept reminding herself that this man was a threat to her existence, but her body was paying no attention to her warning. As his mouth covered hers, she felt her heart thumping in triple time, and she wondered wildly if it would pop out of her chest. This was insane, she told herself over and over again. She cared nothing for this man.

Zack drew her down to the plush fur quilts and then stretched out beside her, his caresses roaming over her flesh that had begun to shiver uncontrollably beneath his inquisitive hands. There was something intriguing about her innocence and her determination, he mused, as his eyes followed the trail his hand blazed across the shapely curve of her hip. Perhaps he and Jeremy would come to blows because of this, but at the moment, he didn't care. She had captivated him. He wanted to caress every perfect inch of her, learning her by touch. Jeremy had been right about this adorable hellcat. She was all that he had claimed, her body soft and tempting, her kisses like the sweet nectar that a honeybee spent its lifetime acquiring.

His wandering caresses moved along her ribs to cup her breast, and Melissa gulped for air as he bent his head to tease the other taut peak. He had fanned the fire into a raging blaze, one that could never be put out if she didn't put a safe distance between them. But she couldn't withdraw. She was paralyzed by the sweet torture of his hands and lips on her trembling flesh. A quiet sigh escaped her as his caresses retracked their tormenting path to her thighs, leaving her relaxed and responsive. Involuntarily, her arms curled over his shoulders, feeling his sinewy muscles beneath her hands. As his mouth swooped down on hers, becoming more impatient as the fever of desire forged their bodies together, Melissa knew all was lost. He had broken her will with his experienced touch, and she was arching to meet his knowing fingers as they found her womanly softness.

There was a hint of wonder in her gaze as her lashes swept up to see him poised above her, the muscles of his arms bulging as he parted her thighs with his hips. Melissa was on fire with a maddening ache that demanded to be appeased. He had filled her senses, his manly fragrance clinging to her, his touch arousing her to the brink of insanity.

Suddenly the pleasure became a searing pain as he came to her, bringing her back in touch with reality. She braced her hands against his chest to push him away, feeling his heart pounding furiously against her palms.

"Relax, Lissa," he rasped, his voice heavy with desire, his eyes burning with a white-hot flame that scalded her flesh. "Perhaps Drieson taught you to outwit a man, but I will teach you how to please him."

He moved slowly within her and then withdrew, only to come to her again. His lips descended on hers, stealing her breath away, leaving her feeling as if she were a drowning victim going down the last time.

A wild, budding pleasure replaced the pain, and she yielded to the unfamiliar sensations that freed her soul and sent it soaring. Why had she abandoned her defenses? Why was her body arching to meet his hard thrusts? Because Jeremy had seen to it that she idolized the man who possessed her, she realized. Each time she gazed into those silver-gray eyes she was lost to the depths of passion that rippled through them.

Zack clutched her to him, unable to get close enough to the fire that seared his soul and branded her lovely face on his mind. He had climbed from the depths of hell to glide to the gates of heaven with this angel in his arms. He could not sort through the whirlwind of sensations that consumed him. He clung to her, ravishing her mouth, driving into her until he melted in the splendor of making love to this golden-haired goddess who had easily satisfied his passions but who left him hungering for more.

Zack nuzzled against her neck, inhaling the feminine aroma that had clouded his senses, and then rolled away to cradle her in his arms. "You surprise me," he breathed raggedly as he smoothed the strands of tangled blond hair away from her face. "You learn quickly. It seems that again I have underestimated your talents."

Her cheeks flushed with embarrassment and she tried to free herself from the prison of his arms, but Zack held her captive. "I do not think it necessary to discuss it," she muttered, delighting Zack with her modesty. When a rakish grin tugged at one corner of his mouth, Melissa stared at the opposite wall of the cabin as if something had suddenly drawn her attention. "We made an agreement. 'Tis done. Now let me up." Her voice cracked with impatience as she struggled for release.

"The night is far from over, Lissa, and you have much more to learn about satisfying a man before I allow you to leave," he insisted as his hands absently roamed over her flesh.

Melissa glared at him, but her anger evaporated when his touch rekindled the fire that she had been certain could be no more than charred ashes. He had awakened a need that had begun to breathe and grow, one that was totally foreign to her until she had experienced his lovemaking.

He crouched on all fours above her, his lips covering hers so tenderly that she felt her body surrendering all over again. Her arms slid over his shoulders to toy with the thick raven hair that lay at the nape of his neck.

"You have a delicious body," he complimented, as his lips hovered over her face, randomly spreading kisses on her flawless features. "I cannot seem to resist you. And yet something warns me to beware of this bewitching spell you have cast on me. But I fear 'tis already too late. I have thrown caution to the wind."

"And I should hate you for this," she mused aloud, and then lifted parted lips to his.

"And do you?" He raised his dark head, studying the exquisite face that glowed in the dim light from the hearth.

"Not now." Her lashes fluttered down to caress her cheeks, protecting her from his probing gaze. "But I am certain I will later," she admitted quietly.

Zack drew her to her knees and then allowed his hands to trail over her firm breasts. She held his head in her arms as his mouth captured the rosy peak. He was the master of seduction, she mused, as his hand fanned across her thigh, awakening the sensations that she thought had been appeased moments before. She knew the rapture that awaited her, and she became a slave to the passion that his skillful touch evoked.

Time ceased to exist as he showed her the ways of lovers, leaving her hot and cold and trembling with the need for him. His hands and lips splayed across her flesh until she could stand no more of his taunting. Unashamed, she touched him, silently requesting him to take her to the world of heady pleasures. She was living and dying in the sweet sensuous feelings that consumed her as he molded his body to hers. For that one special moment, they were one again, enjoying each other, clinging to each other, giving and taking from emotions that churned and then dissipated like storm clouds that left a quiet contentment in their wake.

As their hearts slowed their frantic paces, Zack cuddled her against his chest, a satisfied smile brimming his lips. He had come in search of a skillful lioness and tamed her feisty temper. Jeremy had granted him this interlude of pleasure before Zack set his mind to important matters. He breathed a silent thanks to Drieson for insisting that he track Melissa and then closed his eyes to drift into his dreams.

What had he said about women being nothing but trouble? Perhaps he had been wrong. Melissa was an angel, a goddess made to love, he mused drowsily, as he curled up against her soft flesh. She was beautiful, enchanting desirable. . . .

## Chapter Three

When Melissa heard Zack's slow, methodic breathing, she carefully inched away from his side and donned her clothes. Zack was exhausted from the traveling he had done the past week and much too content where he lay to realize that Lissa had escaped from his embrace. He had intended to wake occasionally, ensuring that she was still beside him, but he slept too soundly to hear her creeping up behind him.

Melissa raised the butt of her musket and then brought it down on the back of his head. With a muffled groan, Zack gave way from sleep to unconsciousness. The wicked smile that hovered on her lips would have had him growling in fury, if only he could have seen it. But now he was at her mercy, foolishly forgetting his philosophy that taking a woman for granted could mean disaster.

"I'm sorry, Mr. Beaugener," Melissa apologized caustically, grinning down at the lifeless form at her feet. "I don't trust you. If you are all that Jeremy claims you to be, you would have taken me back to my father, no matter what the bargain." Casting one last glance at Zack, she gathered her belongings and escaped into the darkness, her reckless chuckle settling about the cabin. She had deceived him into thinking she was his pawn. Melissa frowned at the thought. Perhaps she had been for a time, but no longer. The love they had shared would have died when the morning dawn filtered into their cabin. What she felt for him was only passion, she told herself. He would have turned on her, if she hadn't turned on him first.

Melissa drew her coat closely about her, her eyes searching the shadows before she became one of them.

Zack awoke as the golden sunrays curled their way around the leather hide that Melissa had draped over the window. He winced in pain as he propped himself up on an elbow, carefully inspecting the tender knot on the back of his head. "Damn that little bitch!" he muttered, as he rose unsteadily to his feet. She had made a fool of him again. He would dearly love to wrap his fingers around her neck and strangle the life out of her. But that would do no good, he mused scornfully. The only way to kill a witch was to drive a stake through her hard heart or burn her in a roaring blaze. At that moment, he was entertaining both ideas as a means of revenge. And he thought she was different from the rest of them, he mused bitterly. She may have appeared to be an angel, but nay, she was a deceitful witch!

After shrugging on his clothes and grabbing his jacket, he stumbled outside to find Drago gone. He muttered another curse and stalked off through the woods, driven by anger and determination. Not bothering with the trails she had marked down the slope, he headed for higher elevations, sensing that she had intended to mislead him. When he got his hands on her, she would regret her deceitfulness, he vowed to himself. Damn that woman! He should have tied her up so she couldn't escape.

It was late afternoon when Zack caught a glimpse of Melissa drinking from the stream that trickled down from slopes where the snow had begun to thaw. She was at the edge of a clearing, and he moved silently around behind her, waiting for the right moment to pounce upon her.

The sun sprinkled through the trees to fondly kiss the honeyed strands that lay recklessly about her shoulders. Zack gazed at her, noting that the palomino stallion beside her had an identical mane. Her tight-fitting buckskin clothes displayed each curve and swell that she possessed, and he well remembered them all. The mere sight of her brought the previous evening to mind. No woman deserved to be so attractive when she was as devious as Melissa was, Zack thought disgustedly. He was trying to despise her, but it was difficult. She was different from the rest, a misfit in a man's world. The fact that she was capable of handling herself in his world disturbed him more than he wanted to admit. It burned him to the quick to be bested by Melissa, especially after Stoddard and Drieson warned him to beware and he paid no heed.

A wicked smile curled his lips as he crouched in the

brush and then sprang out at her, knocking her forward in the stream. Melissa shrieked in alarm before her face was forced beneath the surface. Although she struggled against him, she could not overcome his strength. Just when she thought she had breathed her last breath Zack yanked her up beside him, holding her by the nape of her jacket. He shook her soundly, sending her damp hair flying wildly about her. She wiped the water from her eyes and glanced up to see the contempt in his gaze.

"I wish the hell your father had said it made little difference whether I brought you back dead or alive." A cruel smile thinned his lips as he stared at her. "Would you like to guess which way I would prefer to haul you back to the settlement?"

His hateful tone spurred her irritation. "How did you find me?" she snapped. "I set tracks—"

"Pure instinct and utter rage," he growled furiously. "I came to wring your lovely neck!" Zack clamped his hands around her throat. "I don't appreciate being played the fool, especially by the likes of you!" His voice thundered about them, sending the birds from their perches in the low-hanging branches.

"Go ahead. Kill me." She ceased her struggles, her chin tilting defiantly. "I would rather die than be shipped to France to live with my aunt. She cannot stand the sight of me. No torture could be worse than living under the same roof with that woman."

Zack released his grasp on her throat. There would be no satisfaction in hurting her unless he could see fear in her eyes. Unfortunately, there was none. No doubt, she could stare death in the face and never bat an eye. Zack found himself unwillingly admiring her courage. Melissa was afraid of no one and she didn't back down easily. After lifting her up in his arms, he tossed her on her steed's back, securely tying her hands to the saddle and her feet to the stirrups. Zack swung up on Drago and grabbed the palomino's reins. Without uttering another word or casting her a second glance, he picked his way back toward the cabin.

"I thought you agreed to let me go. We made a bargain," Melissa ground out between clenched teeth.

The hiss in her voice reminded Zack of a snake that was poised to strike. He swiveled his head around, just to ensure that she had not transformed herself into a viper. "That was before you hit me over the head and stole my horse. The agreement is off."

"You weren't going to let me go, were you?" She didn't wait for an answer, rushing on before he could draw a breath. "Don't you think I knew that? I am not as gullible as you seem to think, Beaugener," she informed him, her tone cold and clipped.

"Then why did you agree to the bargain?" he taunted, arching a dark brow as he shot her a quick glance.

A muddled frown gathered on her features. "That is something that will probably continue to haunt me until the day I die," she mused aloud.

"That day could very well have been today. And you were right. I had no intention of letting you go. All I wanted was a tumble in those fur blankets," he insulted, his silver eyes raking her damp attire with a heated glare that should have dried them immediately.

Melissa gasped indignantly and then flashed him a scornful glower. "You miserable blackguard! I despise the sight of you! I wish I would have carved your worthless heart from your carcass and fed it to the wolves." She fired the words at him like a full round of ammunition that pelleted at his ears.

Zack chuckled, undaunted by her spiteful words. "You had your chance, but you let it slip through your fingers. Now you'll never have another opportunity again because I don't intend to take my eyes off you," he assured her, smiling arrogantly. "I'll never trust you, vixen. You've only confirmed my belief that all females are devious."

Her indigo eyes spewed fire, her gaze so potent it would have mortally wounded a normal man, but it bounced off Zack's thick skin, leaving no mark. "Heed my words, Beaugener, I'll find a way to make you regret taking me back to my father," she vowed, her voice wavering with fury.

"The devil take you," he shot back at her, his brows narrowing into a hard line.

"He already has twice and I surely know the tortures of hell," she countered.

That remark found an exposed nerve and Zack's face fell like a rock slide as he twisted in his saddle to glare at Melissa.

A wicked smile crept to her lips. Somehow she would find a way to get even with him, she promised herself. Her only mistake was that she had not taken his clothes the previous night. He could not have followed her at all, unless he dared to risk frostbite. Damn, that would have been the perfect solution. Not only could she have escaped, but she could have humiliated him in the process. She could picture him, stalking the mountains, stark naked.

A dark scowl crossed Zack's face as he noted the vindictive sparkle in her eyes. "I don't know what you're thinking, but I swear, 'tis no good," he muttered sourly.

"Aye, Beaugener," she assured him between chortles. " 'Tis utterly sinful, but it brings me small consolation."

Zack cocked a wondering brow and appraised her smug grin. "You're a witch," he concluded, believing that he had hit upon the truth.

"And you're a heartless devil," she retaliated.

They eyed each other like two wild beasts regarding their foe before they did battle. A long moment passed while they prepared a mental list of insults, intending to fling them at each other if the situation presented itself.

Darkness had settled on the mountains by the time they arrived at the shack. Zack was tired, hungry, and annoyed while Melissa did not seem the least bit subdued by the fact that she had been captured again. After tying Melissa to the supporting beam by the door, Zack began preparing their evening meal.

"If you will untie me, I will gladly help you with the cooking," she offered, her honeyed tone drawing Zack's suspicious glance. "I am an excellent cook. We could be eating something appetizing instead of that foul-smelling pottage you're brewing."

Zack scoffed as he stirred their meager meal in the kettle that hung over the fire. "Another of your many talents, I suppose," he mocked dryly, his eyes straying back to Melissa to rake her form-fitting buckskins.

Her shirt was parted, revealing the full swells of her breasts. Zack had unintentionally left himself a delicious sight to feast upon by tying her arms behind the post. He had to turn his back on her to keep his mind on the meal in the pot instead of the temptation tied to the post. And even then he found his thoughts wandering in the wrong direction.

"I am well aware of all of your talents," he mumbled as he stared at the stew.

"What?" Melissa questioned, straining to interpret his inarticulate utterances.

"Nothing," he grumbled, allowing himself one quick glance in her direction. It was one too many, he decided. Melissa was impossible to ignore. Damn her. Damn Jeremy. This was all his fault. Lord, fighting the Shawnees had been easier than tangling with this spitfire. She had spited him at every turn and still he wanted her, but he didn't want her. Zack didn't like what he was feeling, nor did he appreciate the chaos of his thoughts. How could he concentrate on Boone when the image of Melissa's dimpled smile kept creeping into the corners of his mind.

When the stew was heated, Zack dipped out a bowl of his efforts and squatted down on his haunches in front of Melissa, offering her a spoonful. She turned up her nose at the pungent odor that drifted from the steaming soup.

When Zack forced it down her throat, she choked and then sniffed distastefully. "God, that's horrible! What did you put in it, the bowels of a skunk?"

Zack chuckled out loud and forced her to swallow another unappetizing mouthful. "I know it probably doesn't compare to what you're accustomed to eating, but I'm not going to untie you. And I do not intend to drag you back to your father, dying of starvation."

"Nay, you plan to return a stiff corpse that you've purposely poisoned!" she grumbled, and then pulled a face at the nauseous taste. "If you are so pleased with your concoction, you eat it."

His shoulder lifted in a careless shrug. "Very well, I'm not afraid of eating my own cooking." Zack raised the spoon to his lips and then regretted taking such a healthy bite. It was nothing to boast about, and it was all he could do to swallow it.

Melissa watched him closely, noting his distress. "See, I told you it was awful. I'm not eating another bite of that dreadful st . . ."

As Zack tried to stuff the spoon in her mouth, Melissa jerked her head away, and the hot broth spilled down the front of her shirt. She squealed and squirmed beneath Zack's amused regard until he relented and grabbed a rag to wipe the stew that had trickled between her breasts.

The feel of his knuckles against her bare skin made her quiver uncontrollably. Her lashes swept up to meet the glistening pools of silver that stared through her. A long, silent moment passed before Melissa could drag her gaze away from his. She was annoyed with herself for allowing her thoughts to transport her back to the previous night. It was humiliating enough that she had submitted to him, but it was disheartening to realize that the mere thought of his lovemaking could arouse her.

Zack reached beneath her chin, forcing her to meet his level gaze. He had been doing some serious contemplating while they rode back to the cabin. Melissa might prove to be indispensable if he could depend on her. She was clever and he could put her talents to good use.

His hand brushed across her cheek as he studied her closely in the lantern light.

"How much are you willing to yield *not* to make this trip to France?" he questioned solemnly.

Zack choked on his breath when he peered into those mysterious, indigo eyes that were flecked with gold. Only now had he taken the time to observe the expression in them. *Lord have mercy,* he muttered, as his gaze soared to the ceiling. It was fortunate that he couldn't see his own reflection since he disliked staring into the face of a fool. And that was what he was. He laughed bitterly, completely bewildering Melissa. He knew Jeremy was up to something, but until now, Zack wasn't aware that he had tripped, stumbled, and fallen headlong into Jeremy's trap.

The words Jeremy had spoken rang in his ears and, at last, he grasped their meaning. Jeremy's remark had sounded odd at the time, but now it was all too clear. "Zack is trustworthy to a fault," Drieson had said, winking mischievously. Zack's fault was beautiful women, and Jeremy knew that he would never deny himself the pleasures of a woman's arms. This bold firebrand had been impossible to resist, and he hadn't even tried. Jeremy knew that. And now it was too late to undo the damage, Zack mused sourly. Too damned late! He could well imagine what was in store for him when he saw Jeremy again. Damn that conniving old scoundrel!

Melissa's brows furrowed even deeper as she watched the thoughts flicker in his silver eyes. And then a wry smile crept to his lips, thoroughly confusing her. Why was he acting so peculiar and why had he asked her such a strange question? What else could she possibly yield to keep from sailing to France?

"What are you implying now, Beaugener?" she asked, her tone cautious.

His expression sobered once again. "I might help you if, in return, you will come to my aid. But you must be prepared to do exactly as I ask. Are you willing to take my commands without questioning my motives?"

Melissa surveyed his stern features. "Do I have your word that I will not find myself in Paris with my aunt and cousin?" she questioned point-blank. Was this another ploy to gain her trust? If it was, she would agree, giving him the bold-faced lie. Perhaps she could use this to her benefit, she thought to herself.

"You have my promise," he assured her. "And what of you? Will you do exactly as I command, making no attempt to defy me as you have continued to do since I met up with you?"

"You have my word," she agreed without batting an eye, knowing that she would never believe anything he said.

"Shall we seal our agreement with a kiss?" he murmured as he lowered his head to capture her inviting lips.

Melissa eluded his kiss, a mischievous smile curving the corners of her mouth upward. "I would feel more at ease if I had a written agreement with your signature in blood . . . yours."

A throaty chuckle escaped his lips as he reached behind her to untie the ropes. "I'm sure you would, but I am afraid you must be content to settle for less."

His mouth skimmed across hers, bringing back memories that rose like cream on fresh milk, its taste divine. Involuntarily, her arms slid around his neck and she was amazed by her own abandon. When he touched her so tenderly, her body came alive, as if it possessed a mind of its own. As his kissed deepened, Melissa felt her heart hammering so wildly that she was certain it would beat her to death before she could bring it under control.

Zack unfastened her buckskin shirt and breeches, allowing his gaze to roam unhindered over her creamy flesh. He ached to touch what his eyes hungrily devoured. His wandering caresses trailed across her shoulder and then circled each taut peak of her breasts, leaving her quivering beneath his inquiring touch.

Melissa stood hypnotized by the silvery pools that flooded over her and sought to steal her soul. She reached up to loosen the leather ties of his shirt and slipped her hands against the dark, crisp hair on his chest, wanting to return the pleasure he had given her. There was something sinfully wicked about touching his muscled flesh, but she could not seem to help herself. She was standing too close to the fire, and the spark of passion leaped between them, assuring Melissa that it was too late to escape the emotions that simmered just beneath the surface.

Zack groaned as her light caresses trailed across his lean abdomen, and then he clutched her to him, aching to mold her satiny flesh to his. His mouth slanted across hers, taking her breath away with his urgency.

"You have a beautiful body," he murmured against

the rapid pulsations of her neck. "You were made for love."

"Then love me," she whispered and then wondered why she had made such a bold request. What was there about him that stripped her pride and left her trembling in his embrace?

A rumble erupted from his chest as he smiled down at her. "That has been my intention since we returned. I know I should keep my distance from you, but I cannot seem to help myself." Zack drew her full length against him, seeking her soft lips that melted like rose petals beneath his kiss. " 'Tis too late to undo what has been done, and I am left to wonder what price I will be expected to pay," he mused aloud as he drew her to the fur pallet beside the glowing hearth.

Melissa frowned bemusedly at his words, but she had no time to ponder their meaning. His exploring caresses set her on fire, setting her nerves to tingling as he discovered the sensitive points of her body. The flames of desire that he had kindled sent a raging blaze coursing through her veins. She was consumed by a need that she had never known to exist until she met Zack.

His warm kisses tracked a fiery path along her shoulder and then to the rosy peak of her breast, and a surrendering moan escaped her lips. Melissa pulled him closer, ignoring her pride, reveling in the sweet, torturous sensations that tore at her sanity.

"Take me," she whispered breathlessly. "Take me now."

Zack gazed into her indigo eyes, watching them glow with a passion all their own. He cursed himself a thousand times for this unquenchable desire for her. She would lead him into trouble, and he had enough of it without becoming involved with Melissa. But could he turn away from her? Could he walk out the door, leave her behind, knowing that she was warm and willing in his arms? Only a fool would stay, knowing the consequences that might await him when he returned to the settlement.

Her lashes swept up, seeing the fire that blazed in those liquid pools of silver. Why was he staring at her so strangely? What was racing through his mind? Why was she drawn to this ruggedly handsome stranger? Why had she dared to barter her soul to revel in one moment of ecstasy? The questions were coming too fast and Melissa had no answers. The thoughts whipped through her mind and then fled before she could grasp them.

"Lissa . . ." Her name escaped his lips as his sleek body covered hers, pressing intimately against her.

Their gazes locked, seeing a need that defied reason. And then he possessed her. Melissa knew that he had consumed her body and soul. They were one, soaring above the heated blaze that singed their flesh, gliding away from the blackened clouds that curled and spiraled over the burning embers. Melissa could see the castles in the air and feel the radiating light that blazed like a thousand suns. The warmth sprayed over her, touching her so thoroughly that she trembled with pleasure.

His lovemaking bordered on fantasy and she could not help wonder if it was a dream. It had to be, she thought deliriously. There were no castles above the clouds. She couldn't touch the stars.

And then another round of exquisite sensations consumed her and she knew it was no dream. They were soaring higher, seeing the sights again without leaving each other's arms. She was drifting, fluttering down from dizzying heights, cradled in two strong arms that held her as if they would never let her go. A weak sigh escaped her lips as she peered up at Zack, wondering if he had shared the same fantastic experience. Her hand traced the sensuous curve of his lips and then ascended to the hard lines around his gray eyes that seemed to soften beneath her light touch. She was mesmerized by the potential strength that lay in repose.

"Jeremy would have had me believe that you were God himself who had descended from his throne to walk the earth." An impish grin caught the corners of her mouth, lifting them upward as she continued to trace the craggy features of his face. " 'Tis obvious that his friendship is blind. You, Mr. Beaugener, are a demon."

Although her tone was light and taunting, her dimpled smile wide, she somehow believed her own words. He was a temptation that she knew she should resist, but could not find the will to do so.

Zack addressed her with a lazy grin and smoothed the tangled strands of honey gold away from her exquisite face. "Don't sell Jeremy short," he advised. "He knew exactly what he was doing. I have the uneasy feeling that he used us as his pawns. I never did appreciate being maneuvered." His smile vanished as he looked deeply into those blue-violet eyes that had already begun to haunt him.

Melissa arched a quizzical brow. Again he talked in riddles and she could not decode their meaning. "Jeremy? Why would he—"

Zack cut her short with a kiss that carried enough

heat to melt the moon and leave it dripping on the sky. When he finally dragged his lips away from hers, the faintest hint of a smile bordered his sensuous mouth. "Let's not dwell on Jeremy," he insisted, his voice still heavy with the aftereffects of passion. "I have little interest in him at the moment."

"Do you intend to chain me to the post tonight?" she blurted out, taking Zack's advice to change the subject.

Zack tunneled his fingers through her tangled curls and then clasped his hand around the nape of her neck, drawing her steadily closer to lose himself in the taste of her honeyed lips. "Not until later," he assured her, a suggestive gleam in his smoky-gray eyes. "I am not finished with you yet."

Melissa frowned at him and her bottom lip jutted out in an exaggerated pout. "We made an agreement and still you do not trust me. You are heartless and—"

He silenced her with a scalding kiss that stripped the words from her tongue. As his hands began to work their magic on her body, she forgot all except the rapturous tide that flooded over her. Again they tasted passion's sweet nectar and drifted out with the waves. The world was camouflaged in a hazy blur, and they made love as if there were no tomorrow, as if their time together was the beginning and the end.

Melissa fell asleep on his shoulder, exhausted from her lack of rest the previous night. When Zack heard her even breathing, he bound her feet to his so that she could not escape him again. She would wake in a fit of rage, but he had come to respect her cunningness. His instincts warned him to beware of the lioness who lay calm and trusting in his arms. Zack had tracked her, thinking that she had been his prey, but it was as Jeremy had said. The hunter had become the hunted. Zack needed very little explanation from Drieson. It had all become clear when he took the time to piece the puzzle together. Damn that man. How could he have stooped so low? Was this the same man whom he had come to love as a father? Zack would have sworn that deceit was not one of Jeremy's traits, but now he was beginning to wonder if time had soured what he once considered a perfect friendship. Zack had the eerie feeling that this affair with Melissa was going to cost him more than he was willing to pay.

Melissa awoke with a drowsy smile playing on her lips, eagerly responding to the light kiss. As Zack drew away, Melissa squirmed to a more comfortable position, finding that her leg was bound to his. Her smile evaporated, replaced by an annoyed frown.

"I gave you my word last night and still you didn't trust me," she pouted.

"You, my little firebrand, cannot be trusted. I have learned to be wary of the beasts of these mountains. They all have a tendency to turn on a man when he is least likely to expect it. I trusted you once and I ended up with the butt of your musket stamped on the back of my head," he reminded her.

"You make me sound like a savage, Beaugener," she grumbled.

Zack flicked the end of her upturned nose, chuckling at the childish expression on her features. "You are, and don't try to deny it."

"And so are you," she countered. "You have earned my respect, but never my trust. I learned that last night's bargain was another of your ploys. You won't see my faithfulness to any of your agreements again."

"Damn the bargain. 'Tis it so difficult to see that all I wanted was you, just as I do now?" A seductive smile traced his lips as he reached down to untie the rope that bound them together. He had lost interest in conversation before it had even began. All he wanted was to feel her firm flesh pressed tightly to his one last time before they went their separate ways.

Zack drew the quilts away, his caresses roaming over her body, rediscovering every inch of her flesh, his gaze memorizing the sight of her. Melissa was set to refuse him, but his touch kindled fires that were impossible to ignore. Her lashes fluttered down, shutting out all except the feel of his skillful hands wandering along the curve of her hip. Zack found himself wanting to make their last encounter a memory to be branded on her mind, as if he had touched her heart in some small way. And he would remember Melissa occasionally, recalling the tender moments they had shared in his secluded cabin.

His caresses roamed across her flesh, arousing sensations that left her yearning to appease the need Zack had instilled in her. As his hands retracked their seductive path across her abdomen, Melissa heard the echo of her sigh and then the accelerated beat of her heart drumming in her ears. The feel of his hands on her bare flesh was exquisite torture. She was gliding like an eagle in a cloudless sky, soaring and spiraling, drifting far above reality. Time ceased to exist as he held himself above her and then came to her to appease the maddening ache that his caresses had evoked.

She was living and dying in the same breathless instant, unwilling to let the moment end. There was no past, no future, only the present, and she could think of nothing but the darkly handsome face that came at her from all directions.

Zack thrust deeply within her, striving for unattainable depths of intimacy. He was driven by an instinct that tore at his sanity, and he groaned as another wave of pleasure flooded over him. His passion spent, he shuddered above her, nestling against the curve of his neck as his heart slowed its frantic pace. Zack tried to conjure up the face of a woman who could match Melissa's beauty, one whose passions matched his own, but none came. Why was he so captivated by this blond-haired hellion? What mystical power did she hold over him?

In the aftermath of love, Melissa breathed a ragged sigh and let her gaze wander over the man who had taught her the meaning of desire. She knew enough about Zack to realize what kind of man he was: strong, courageous, invincible. But the moment she had shared in his arms displayed the tender lamb who lingered just beneath that calloused exterior of the powerful lion. Zack was his own man, a man whose alert senses defied the forces of nature. And yet, he could become the considerate lover whose gentleness aroused emotions that Melissa was afraid to name. She was certain she would never be the same again. Zack had touched her heart and soul, stirring sensations that left her oddly content when she was cradled in his arms. When she peered up at him, she was reminded of the sleek black panther that stalked the forest, claiming his prey, always emerging the victor. Soon he would slip silently away to search out another quarry. Aye, he was like the wild beast that could never be content in captivity. He was born to thrive in the wilderness, craving adventure and the freedom to roam.

Melissa smiled ruefully, knowing that this interlude had no place in either of their lives, but she would always cherish the memory and continue to recall the feel of his muscular body molded to hers, the manly fragrance that had infiltrated her senses, and that mysterious sparkle of silver in his eyes when he smiled. She was hopelessly captivated by the man Jeremy had made her legendary hero, and yet she was wary of him. He had tricked her by claiming that he would aid in her escape and then he had turned on her. If the opportunity presented itself, she would flee from him, no matter what the cost. It had already cost her dearly, she reminded herself. What more could she possibly lose to the rugged frontiersman with the charismatic smile and kisses that could intoxicate her like wine?

# Chapter Four

Melissa paused momentarily, her gaze scanning the rustic cabin that she and Zack had shared, memorizing the picture that no artist could ever paint. A sense of loss encompassed her, knowing she would never pass this way again.

"Are you ready?" Zack questioned impatiently.

Her eyes circled back to him and the dramatic change in him was baffling. The gentleness was gone. Only the frosty glaze of indifference remained. It was as if she was staring at a stranger. He seemed so remote and distant as he sat on his black stallion, making her realize that she didn't know him at all.

"I don't want to go home," she breathed disheartedly.

Zack shook his head, his shaggy hair settling over the collar of his coat. "You don't want to go home. You don't want to go to France. Just what the hell do you want?" he snapped. The golden flicker that rimmed her indigo eyes sent a pain stabbing at his soul. "Damn that Jeremy." His last remark did not reach Melissa's ears, nor did he intend it to. He grabbed the palomino's reins, leading the steed along behind him while Melissa remained bound to the saddle.

Melissa heaved a heavy sigh as she watched her stallion edge his way along the winding path. No matter what they had shared in quiet moments of seclusion, Zack would not trust her to follow him, not that she blamed him. If he let his guard down, she would pounce upon him without giving it a second thought. But Zack watched her like a hawk, his gaze swinging back to her to ensure that she was still his prisoner. Her spirits sank as they descended from the mountains. Their trip was long and quiet. It seemed they had nothing to say to each other. They were both lost to their own pensive musings.

Zack reined Drago to a halt, gazing down at the settlement, just as he had four days earlier. But now there was even more on his mind. He drew Melissa up beside him, unfastened the ropes, and leaned across to place a lingering kiss to her lips. His arm came around her waist to lift her over in front of him. Zack tilted her head back, his hand smoothing the honeyed strands over her shoulder. His eyes locked with the blue-violet pools that sparkled with amber flecks, and he inwardly flinched at the expression he saw in them.

"If we chance to meet again, we will be different, you and I. It will be as if we knew nothing of each other," he murmured before his mouth urgently sought hers, savoring the sweetness of her kiss. And then he drew away, his face only inches from hers. "Yesterday never existed, Melissa."

Melissa peered bewilderingly at him. He was talking in riddles again. A confused frown knitted her brow. "But why . . ."

"No questions," he insisted, sending her a stern glance. "If we do meet again, I don't want to see any flicker of recognition in those beautiful eyes. Do you understand?"

"Nay," she breathed in exasperation. "The last two days make little sense at all."

"And for that reason, they cease to exist. If only I would have seen through this before it was too late," he mused aloud. He was still annoyed with himself for carelessly falling into the snare that had been set for him.

Melissa rolled her eyes heavenward. More riddles. What did he mean? What was there to see? Lord, the man was crazed. Living alone in the wild must have shriveled his brain.

Melissa felt herself being swept up in his powerful arms and placed in her own saddle, leaving her feeling alone and confused. She rode in a daze, trying to sort her muddled thoughts until Zack halted in front of the tavern and lifted her down beside him.

William Stoddard hurried from the store, his face beaming when he spied Melissa. Jeremy appeared in the doorway behind him and then moved slowly toward Melissa and Zack, a wry smile playing on his lips.

"I see that Mr. Beaugener's talents are as exceptional as Jeremy claimed," William said, as he gazed at his daughter who was not all pleased to be home.

"Aye," Melissa admitted resentfully, casting Zack a

76

hasty, sidelong glance. "I'm certain he could track a bird through the forest without ever catching sight of it."

Zack swept his cap from his head and bowed mockingly before her. "Thank you, Miss Stoddard. 'Tis one of the most accurate compliments I've ever received," he retorted, his wide grin stretching from ear to ear.

"Your ability to search out your prey is only exceeded by your arrogance," she shot back and then gave him the cold shoulder.

Zack could have sworn icicles were forming on that lovely hide of hers. He smiled to himself and choked back a chuckle when Melissa sliced him another glare that kept the icicles from thawing. Her attitude toward him was frigid, but it was just as well, he mused. It was over and that was the way it would stay.

"It took you three full days," Jeremy taunted as his attention focused on Zack. "I suppose I will keep the furs since you lost the bet. Obviously you didn't heed my warning."

"Here is your reward for returning Melissa," Stoddard added as he extended his arm and dropped a pouch in Zack's waiting hand.

Melissa gasped in disbelief and then glared contemptuously at all three men, spiteful thoughts whipping through her mind. They had played a game with her, every damned one of them! "You paid this scoundrel to deliver me to you?" She spat out the words as if they left a bitter taste in her mouth, her gaze pricking her father like sharp-edged daggers. And then she whirled to face Zack, her golden hair flying wildly about her, her eyes narrowing to hard slits. She clenched her fists on her hips to keep from clawing him to shreds as she itched to do. "You claim to be Jeremy's friend and yet you took my father's money. You are despicable! Tell me, Beaugener, are you always well paid for your hunting expeditions?"

A faint smile threatened the corners of his mouth as he crossed his arms over his chest and peered down his nose at the fuming spitfire. "Nay, Miss Stoddard, but the only way they could convince me to delay my journey and track down some spoiled brat who had defied her father was with a well-lined pouch of coins," he assured her, his voice void of emotion.

"You unscrupulous viper! You worthless mercenary!" she snapped in raw fury. "I should have put a hole through your black heart instead of settling for leaving the imprint of my musket on the back of your head. If I never lay eyes on you again that will be all too soon!"

With that, Melissa spun on her heels and stalked toward the store. When she was but halfway, she pivoted to cast Zack one last murderous glower before disappearing inside. How she loathed the sight of him. What a fool she had been! Melissa muttered under her breath, cursing the mocking image that hovered one step in front of her. It was all a ploy, she thought bitterly. Every word he had uttered was part of his game to set her up for the big fall. And she had fallen hard, shattering her pride. She had thought they had meant something to each other, but Zack had said and done whatever he deemed necessary to bring her back to her father and collect his reward. She was merely another notch on his bedpost and an extra coin in his pocket. Now she understood why he said the two previous days hadn't existed. He had been subtlely telling her that he

had no affection for her, not even an ounce, and tha
she would never cross his mind once he had delivered
her to her father. Melissa choked on a sob, fighting
back the tears of humiliation. No one had ever been
able to break her spirit until now, but Zack had managed, and she despised him for that. No man would
ever do that to her again, she vowed, as she brushed
away the tears with the back of her hand and slammed
the door of her bedroom.

"I would have arrived yesterday," Zack explained
as Jeremy and William turned quizzical glances to
him. Melissa's last remark had singed their curiosity.
"She escaped and I had to track her down for the second time. You were both right. The chore was more
difficult than I had expected." He glanced down at the
powdery dust at his feet, hoping to avoid witnessing
two I-told-you-so grins. It galled him that she had
been so elusive and admitted it was no easy task.

"I'm most grateful, Mr. Beaugener," William replied. "I know Melissa is upset with us and bitterly opposed to this trip, but 'tis best for her. Perhaps in time
she can understand and forgive us all." He extended
his arm to shake hands with Zack, nodded to Jeremy,
and then hurried to the store to attempt to smooth Melissa's ruffled feathers.

"Come inside and have an ale," Jeremy suggested as
he limped up the steps that led to the tavern. "I suppose you want your explanation."

Zack followed behind him, dreading the upcoming
conversation. He already knew what Jeremy intended

o tell him.

As Jeremy sank into his chair and leaned his cane against the edge of the table, he flashed Zack a wry smile. "So, you were not prepared for what you had to confront, were you, my friend?" he speculated, arching a taunting brow.

"You set me up, you conniving old man," Zack accused, his tone bitter, his hard gaze making him appear even more distant and unfriendly.

Jeremy leaned casually against the back of his chair, unaffected by Zack's reproachful glare, and called for two mugs of ale. "I wondered how long it would take you to come to that conclusion," he commented with a chuckle.

"I'm afraid the realization came too late to do me any good," Zack growled. "Why the hell didn't you tell me about her before I left? You knew damned well what could happen when we were alone together." He leaned forward on the table, flinging Jeremy a menacing frown.

Drieson's blue eyes twinkled devilishly. "Of course I knew. And I knew exactly what I was doing. After I received your letter, informing that you were coming to the settlement, I decided it was time for the two of you to meet. That is why I convinced William that you were the only man we could trust to bring back Melissa. If you had not come along at the opportune moment, I would have been content to let Melissa seek refuge in the mountains until it was too late for her to catch the ship in Norfolk." He paused a moment, snickered, and then continued, a wry grin splitting his scarred face. "I had intended to introduce the two of you soon anyway. I have been preparing for this moment for several years. This incident could not have come at a better time. 'Tis a shame I hadn't planned it myself.''

Zack snorted derisively. "It wouldn't have surprised me if you had somehow managed that, too. Damn you, Drieson. You know I don't like being manipulated, not by you or anyone else!''

Jeremy glanced up and nodded his thanks as two mugs were placed before them. When the waitress had retreated, his gaze swung to Zack. "One day you will thank me for it,'' he reminded him, as another uncanny smile spread across his face.

"Not this time,'' Zack snapped, his tone acid with anger. "When I looked into that vixen's eyes to see those specks of gold flickering with the same damned expression I had seen a hundred times before, I wanted to wring your damned neck. I didn't want to believe what I was seeing, but the evidence was there, waiting for me to realize that you had played me for a fool.'' Zack stared down at his ale and then brought it to his lips, hoping the brew would cool his irritation. Unfortunately, it didn't. It would have taken a block of ice as wide as Kentucky.

"I knew that there was only one man to handle Melissa,'' Jeremy stated simply. "And the only way to snare that particular man was to set a trap. When I made the remark about the hunter being the hunted. I was referring to your future, not your past.''

"I realized that a little too late,'' Zack muttered. "And I stood there, listening to that fire-breathing witch rake *me* over the coals for being deceptive. *You* should have been the one standing in the direct line of fire.'' Zack guzzled his ale, giving it a second chance to

81

ease his smoldering temper. Again, it failed miserably. He was simmering like an unattended pot of stew.

"I did what I felt I had to do and you reacted as I expected." Jeremy swished his ale around the rim of his mug and then anchored his blue eyes on his friend. "Since you have compromised a young maiden's virtues, you will pay the piper." He paused before he dropped the bomb in Zack's lap. "You will marry Melissa."

Zack sucked in his breath and choked on the ale that had collected in his throat. Jeremy could have selected a more appropriate moment to spring his surprise, he thought miserably, as Jeremy leaned over to unsympathetically whack him between the shoulder blades.

"I will not marry Melissa, not for any reason." Zack crowed like an indignant rooster once he had located his tongue. "I will not be tied down to that feisty chit for all the furs to be had in the Smoky Mountains. You managed without a wife. Why the hell do you want me to suffer through marriage? You know it would be impossible to build a relationship through correspondence. I never remain in one place long enough to call it home."

Jeremy's face paled slightly, his expression sobering. "I managed without a wife, but not by choice. I would have given the world if I could have shared my name with the one woman I cherished more than life itself." He sighed heavily, staring at the contents of his glass, "Twenty-two years ago I asked Melissa's mother to marry me. Her name was Laura." His hushed whisper crackled with emotion. "I have not allowed myself to utter her name since the day I discovered that she carried our child. It is agony to harbor a love for a lifetime, sharing it with no one, speaking of it, not even to your closest friend.

"Laura was afraid to marry me. I was much like you, Zack. I longed for adventure and I couldn't remain in any one place for extended lengths of time. Laura was fragile, a delicate flower who needed secure roots to be content. Her family lived at Stone Gap, and I had met her when I was passing through on an expedition. I saw her secretly on occasion since her father considered her too young to receive a man's attentions. William Stoddard was also in love with her. When she came of age, he asked for her hand. She accepted, knowing that he would be content to make a home for her in the settlement and remain by her side. All I could promise was a cabin in the mountains where she would spend a great deal of time alone."

Jeremy stared at the opposite wall, haunting emotions livid in his eyes. "One night Laura came to me after she and William had quarreled. She needed comforting and I could not be content with offering mere compassion. She was beautiful: her hair the color of the sun, her eyes as clear and blue as a mountain stream. Laura and Melissa could pass as twins except for their eyes." A fond smile found the corner of his mouth as he remembered Laura. "I had yearned for her too long, too often, and I . . ." His voice trailed off, his gaze spanning the space of time, recalling the tender moments they had shared in seclusion. "I tried to convince her to stay with me, but she was afraid of the unsettled life I lived. Laura returned to Stoddard and I joined another expedition. When I went back to Stone Gap, Laura was carrying our child." His voice was barely above a whisper, his face tortured by the story that he had kept a secret for so many years.

"Does Stoddard know the truth?" Zack questioned quietly, his heart wrenching in sympathy for the man who had suffered more than his share of trials.

Jeremy heaved a sigh and then shrugged. "I don't know, but if he does, he has never shown any animosity toward me. After my accident I went back to find them, just to be near them, to know my child. In the meantime Laura had died during one of the severe winters, and William had taken Lissa to the mountains, away from all that would remind him of Laura. It took him years to accept the loss, but he finally returned to open the store here in Martin's Fork. I had the opportunity to see Melissa and to teach her all I knew about the woodlands and mountains. I wanted her to be stronger than her mother, to have no fear of the unknown. Melissa shares my love for adventure. She is a combination of her mother and me," Jeremy murmured, as his eyes finally settled on Zack. "Melissa is as beautiful and sensitive as Laura, but she is also high-spirited and resourceful. She has always loved a challenge."

"Aye, so I've noticed," Zack interjected before sipping his ale.

"You must admit you have never met one like her," Jeremy persisted, as he raised a dark brow, daring Zack to deny the fact.

With a reluctant nod Zack conceded. "Aye, but she is still a woman and she cannot be trusted. And I have no need for a wife."

A sly smile crept to Jeremy's lips. "You *will* marry her because 'tis my request."

"And if I refuse?" Zack challenged.

"Then I shall tell Stoddard exactly what happened when the two of you were alone together. He will demand it," he predicted, smiling victoriously.

"Damn you, Drieson," Zack had to clench his jaws together to keep from shouting the walls down around them. His silver eyes spewed fire as he turned them on Jeremy. "You have become far too clever in your old age, but you seem to forget that I can be on Drago's back, high-tailing it out of town before you can hobble over to Stoddard and give him your story." He bolted from his chair and whirled away from the table, but Drieson's calm, steady voice halted his footsteps.

"I took you under my wing when you were but a young, inexperienced stripling. I taught you to hunt, trap, and track, just as I taught Melissa to survive in the wild. All that you have done and are capable of doing is possible because I took the time to mold you into the type of man you desired to be," Jeremy reminded him. "In fourteen years I have asked nothing of you until now. Remember that each time you blaze a new trail or raise your rifle to sight your game. And one more thing." Jeremy paused a long moment, letting the silence weigh heavily between them. "I do not want her in France, but I can do nothing more to prevent it. The matter is out of my hands, *friend*."

Zack's back stiffened and he inwardly flinched as Jeremy's haunting words settled about him like invisible chains that held him securely in place. With a determined frown, he fought the confining bonds and stalked toward the door, intent on leaving the settlement before Jeremy did as he had threatened.

"I raised you as my own son, took you into my home, taught you to survive. You have learned well,"

Jeremy added, as he lifted a scarred arm in toast to the muscular form who moved silently toward the door. "Goodbye, Beaugener." His words followed Zack as he disappeared from sight and then he sighed discouragingly, knowing that he had pushed Zack too far.

William paused at the bedroom door, watching Melissa angrily stuffing her belongings in her trunk. Her gowns were piled in a careless heap and he strolled over, lifted them out, and neatly folded them before returning them to the trunk.

"I know you think me cruel, but 'tis best for you to go, Lissa. One day you will realize that this trip was a blessing, not a punishment." William sank down on the edge of the bed and drew Melissa down beside him, affectionately wrapping his arm about her shoulder. "I have something I wish to tell you before we leave for Norfolk. Perhaps it will help you understand," he began in a quiet tone. "Your aunt Lelia and I were very close before your mother and I were married. When her family first arrived from France, she and I spent a great deal of time together. She was in love with me and had expected that we would be wed. I cared a great deal for Lelia, but it was Laura whom I loved. When Laura became of age, I turned my attention to her. I suppose I only used Lelia as an excuse to be with her family and her younger sister." His head lowered and he heaved a sigh. "After Laura and I were wed, Lelia decided to return to France instead of staying in the colonies. I doubted that she would ever forgive me for what I did. She was bitter, angry with both of us. But I think perhaps after all these years she has buried her resentment. When she requested that you come to France, I thought she was ready to accept you as part of her family. You are a liaison between the two of us, Lissa." William stared deeply into her eyes, his gaze solemn and beseeching. "I ask you to go not only for that reason, but also because she can teach you many things that I cannot. Six months will seem like a lifetime for me too, child, but perhaps 'tis what we both need. You have learned to survive in our young, untamed country, and now you will flourish in Europe's society. If I did not want the very best for you, if I did not love you so dearly, I would not make such a request." He hugged her close, placing a fond kiss to her forehead. "Can you begin to understand, child?"

Melissa nodded slightly as the tears streamed down her cheeks. "Aye, Papa," she murmured, muffling a sniff. "But it won't make leaving you any easier, nothing can."

"I know, Lissa," he agreed, as he held her in the tight circle of his arms. "I know."

Jeremy sat in the parlor of his small home, waiting for Melissa to come to say goodbye before she and William departed for Norfolk. His brows furrowed thoughtfully as he traced the jagged scar that ran from the corner of his left eye to the side of his mouth. Perhaps he had misjudged Zack, he mused. It had been six years since he and Zack had traveled the mountains and explored the wilderness together. Zack had changed, but surely the strong bond between them had not been severed by time. Although Zack was an expert at masking most of his emotions, Jeremy had known of the respect and admiration the younger man held for him. And yet, Zack was older now and set in his ways. Perhaps those feelings had died.

It seemed that Zack had not been trapped as securely as Jeremy had anticipated. If Melissa had not intrigued him, there was no woman on God's earth who could wedge her way into Zack's heart. He had been burned at a tender age and was cynical of women. Although Jeremy could understand the bitterness Zack harbored, he hoped that time would heal the sensitive wound, but perhaps nothing could. Jeremy had gambled with Melissa and his adopted son and had lost. He had hoped that when Zack took the time to reflect upon the last few days, he would remember what Jeremy had told him and return to the settlement. But Zack was gone and Jeremy knew he wouldn't be back. And now Melissa was leaving and he could do nothing to stop her. What was he to do, Jeremy wondered, heaving a despairing sigh.

He glanced up as the door creaked open and then he smiled affectionately when Melissa walked toward him. The resemblance between Laura and Melissa could bring a piercing pain to his heart, just as it often did to William. It was as if he were gazing into a window of the past, seeing an image that had long been a part of his dreams.

"I suppose you will be leaving soon," he said softly, as he offered Melissa a chair beside him.

She eased into the rocker and settled her blue silk skirts about her. "Aye. Papa is collecting the last of my belongings," she replied, her voice barely above a whisper. It was all she could do to keep from bursting into tears when she gazed into Jeremy's solemn face.

"I still don't think 'tis wise to travel to Europe, Lissa. I cannot share William's conviction that this is best for you."

"Then why did you send Beaugener after me?" she questioned, her gaze slightly accusing.

His shoulder lifted in a shrug as he averted his eyes from her probing stare. "I wanted you to meet Zack, but things did not turn out the way I had hoped."

Melissa's brows furrowed deeper in confusion. He was beginning to talk in riddles like Zack. Discarding the thought, she hastened to explain. "Papa thinks that Aunt Lelia has finally forgiven him for something that happened many years ago. I still don't believe that she can abide the sight of me, but after what Papa told me last night, I think I can begin to understand why she resented me. Although I have no desire to leave here, I feel an obligation to my father," she added, as she toyed with the gathered yards of silk that lay across her lap.

"And I don't want to see you go. I, like your father, will miss you more than you can ever know," he confessed, his voice wavering with emotion. "Beware of what you might face in France. Perhaps your father has allowed his sense of guilt to blind him from the truth." His tone contained a warning as he leveled her a gaze.

Melissa cocked her head to the side, peering quizzically at him. Did he know about Laura, Lelia, and William? What trouble had Jeremy envisioned for her?

"Trust your instincts, Melissa. You have been

trained to sense danger. See that you make use of what you have learned," he urged, as he clasped her hand in his and brought it to his lips.

With a groan, she threw her arms around Jeremy's neck and laid her head against his shoulder. "I'm so confused. This entire week has set my emotions in turmoil, I don't know where to turn or what to do," she choked out.

Jeremy stroked her golden hair away from her face and tenderly kissed her cheek. "Did you find Beaugener so disturbing? You knew what he would be like. I have often described him to you. I thought perhaps you would be well armed when the two of you met."

Her dark lashes fluttered against her cheek, purposely avoiding his steady gaze. "But you neglected to tell me that he looked like Satan himself and possessed a heart of stone," she muttered.

His chortle did nothing to soothe her irritation. "Perhaps his appearance was frightening, but he is a rare breed, Melissa. Many men would love to claim his abilities."

"But why did you have to send him after me? You said yourself that you had no desire to see me sail to France," she queried. Melissa demanded an answer and she would not release Jeremy from her direct gaze until she had been given one.

Jeremy carefully formulated his thoughts before he responded. "Your father is also my friend. He was a desperate man. Since he was determined to send someone after you, I thought Zack was the best selection." He reached beneath her chin when her gaze fell to her lap, forcing her to look him square in the eye. "And what of Zack Beaugener? What did you think of him?" he persisted, his brow arching quizzically.

"Perhaps he possesses all the qualities that you revere, but my opinion of him was shattered when I learned that he could be bought for a price," she muttered scornfully.

"You cannot completely understand Zack's motives, nor do I have the time to explain. But I will tell you this much. You cannot judge him harshly because of what he did. Although he and I are friends, he gave your father his word, and he was bound to it. If you knew the entire story, perhaps you would see it all clearly and forgive him," Jeremy stated, as a faint smile crept to his lips. "Zack is not as heartless as he would have most people believe." Jeremy urged Melissa to her feet. " 'Tis time for you to go. I will think of you often and count the days until you return. God's speed."

Melissa could not agree with what Jeremy had said about Zack, nor could she control the tears that scalded her eyes. She fought them back, hoping to see Jeremy clearly before she left. Holding on to the memory of the tender expression on his scarred face, she backed toward the door. Pausing momentarily, the looked down to the floor, as if something there had suddenly drawn her attention, and then she cast one last glance at the mangled form of a man across the room.

"I shall miss you terribly, Jeremy," she whispered before closing the door behind her.

Jeremy struggled from his chair, grabbed his cane, and dragged his crippled leg as he limped to the window to draw back the curtain. He watched Melissa take the distance between the house and her carriage in measured strides, her head held high, her face set in determination. A proud smile surfaced on his lips as Melissa stepped into the coach. As it rumbled away, his hand fell loosely to his side, allowing the curtain to shut out the present.

His breath came out in a rush as he moved back to his chair, wishing he hadn't meddled in Melissa's life in the first place. It was foolish for him to tamper with destiny and damned if he hadn't done just that! He cursed himself for misjudging Zack. Dammit, where was he? Melissa was gone and Zack had disappeared. Jeremy had expected him to reappear before Melissa departed. Perhaps his heart had turned to stone as Melissa had said. Jeremy tried to massage away the dull headache that nagged at him. Why hadn't he left well enough alone?

As Melissa eased back in her seat, a sea of fond memories flooded over her, only to be swept away with the breeze that whipped through the open window of the carriage. All that she had known and loved was left in a cloud of dust. She was being carried into another world that she neither understood nor cared to comprehend. France was merely a name that had little meaning or interest to her. Her mother had taught her the language and had often spoken of her homeland. But from where Melissa sat, she could not imagine that it even existed. She had no concept of another world beyond her beloved home, and she could not fathom an existence on the other side of the ocean.

Sympathetically, William patted his daughter's hand and gave her a cheerful smile. "You will have the opportunity that few are granted, Melissa," he assured her, drawing her from her silent reverie. "This will be a new adventure for you. Jeremy has always filled your head with the desire to seek new frontiers and now you have that chance."

"I don't think France could be described as an untamed wilderness," Melissa mocked dryly, casting her father a disgruntled frown. "And Jeremy still does not think that I should be making this journey, despite your insistence."

With a shake of his tarnished head, William defended himself. "Jeremy has grown overly fond of you these last few years. He is a lonely man who was forced to settle for a meager existence after roaming this country like a beast of the wild. You were always there to listen to his stories and to learn from his experiences. You gave his life new purpose. Since he was unable to pursue the adventure he loves, he instilled that dream in you. The two of you were good for each other, I'll admit, but perhaps he has become selfish with you. Maybe he does not want you to go because he is afraid that it will mean the end of your friendship." His speculation only drew Melissa's disagreeing frown." It will be good for him to turn his attention elsewhere for a time. He has come to depend on you for more than he should."

William might have had a point, but he could never convince Melissa that it was mere selfishness that made Jeremy feel the way he did about the voyage. He was a man who possessed a sixth sense, that natural instinct that alerted him to danger. Melissa had developed that sense and she was uneasy about the venture.

"Perhaps part of what you say about Jeremy is true," she conceded reluctantly, as she glanced out the carriage window. "I will go to Aunt Lelia's without making a fuss, but I will count the days until I return home." Her chin tilted stubbornly, taking on the angle that her father had witnessed on a number of occasions.

William chuckled, a wide grin splitting his face. "You may find that you enjoy France in spite of yourself, child. And then you may wish to extend your visit indefinitely. If I receive a letter from you saying that you are not ready to return after six months, don't be surprised if my correspondence reads, 'I told you so,' " he said, teasing with a wink.

Melissa sniffed disdainfully. How could he even pretend to believe such a ridiculous notion? "After six months with Aunt Lelia glaring at me with a permanent expression of dislike stamped on her face and Robert prancing about with his dainty mannerisms, I will most likely be stark, raving mad. I don't have a snowball's chance in hell in staying a minute longer than necessary!" she informed him, her voice rising testily.

"Melissa!" he scolded, slicing her a disapproving glance. "If you use such deplorable language in front of Leila, she will come to the conclusion that I have raised an uncivilized heathen. Her opinion of me has just been raised from the cellar. Don't send it plunging right back down again."

"Oh, very well, Papa," Melissa grumbled, heaving a futile sigh. "I shall attempt to act the lady, but I assure you that I will counting the days until I come home to Kentucky. And you must promise me that when I return, we will spend at least a week in the mountains. We will take Jeremy with us. I'm sure that would greatly please him. Please tell him of my plans when you return at Martin's Fork." She turned pleading blue-violet eyes to her father, her enthusiasm renewed by the thought.

"I'll tell him," William promised, a fond smile playing on his lips. "I'm sure the three of us will enjoy it thoroughly. Now while you're planning every minute of that week, I'm going to lean back and catch a catnap. It will be a long trip." He settled himself on the cushioned seat and chuckled to himself. He was going to miss his vivacious daughter. Without her high spirit, the days would drag on forever. God, how he hoped this trip would go well for her. He would never forgive himself if he caused her grief.

Melissa squirmed nervously beside her father, her thoughts filled with excitement, not of the coming months, but of the week when she returned to Kentucky. At least it kept her from dwelling on the near future. For that she was thankful.

Capt. Damion Montclaire sank down in his chair and propped his feet up in front of him, his gaze sweeping the newspaper he held in his hands. His brows furrowed thoughtfully, his attention lingering on one particular article. Taking a sip of tea, he continued to read over the rim of his cup. When Duncan tapped lightly on the door and entered the room, Montclaire did not bother to acknowledge his presence.

"Monsieur, the gentlemen you requested to see are waiting in your study," Duncan announced, bowing slightly to the master of the house who was still absorbed in his reading.

"I will join them in a few minutes," Montclaire replied. Still he had not glanced up from his paper.

When he had finished the last of his tea, Montclaire rose to full stature and walked downstairs to meet his associates. He exchanged a sober nod of greeting and then paced the floor in front of the five men. Pausing momentarily, his eyes swung to the redheaded gentleman who sat on the sofa.

"Did you find someone dependable to deliver the letter as I requested?" he inquired, his deep voice heavy with a French accent.

"Aye, sir. It will be slipped under the door of the room tomorrow morning. My brother has agreed to deliver the message," the man explained.

*"Bien."* Montclaire nodded thoughtfully, and then turned his attention to the entire group who sat anxiously before him. "We will set sail at dawn. Make certain that you have all the supplies for our journey." His gaze anchored on each and every face, waiting for a nod of assent. "Our mission will be difficult, but you have been handpicked. I expect you to be as capable as my superiors have claimed. I can only vouch for two of you, since we have worked closely together on several occasions." His gaze swung to Heston and Stratton, the faintest hint of a smile touching his lips. Then he focused his attention on the other three men. "I find myself forced to put my trust in the rest of you, but you have yet to prove yourselves to me. Each of you has been advised of your duties and obligations while we are on board the schooner. I expect you to obey my commands without question. *Comprendez-vous?*" he questioned soberly.

Davis thoughtfully surveyed the man who towered over him. He had only met Captain Montclaire, but he was impressed. Montclaire stood before them like an avenging god who did not know the meaning of failure and who would not tolerate it from anyone with whom he worked. The captain had considered every possibility and expected each and every order to be followed exactly as it was given. Davis did not want to disappoint Montclaire or to suffer the consequences of failing. Although Montclaire was strikingly handsome, the cold gleam in his eyes and the rigid set of his jaw warranted respect. It would be foolish to cross him or to confront him when he was angered, Davis thought to himself. It would be wiser to call him friend than to be his enemy.

Montclaire was followed by his reputation, and not one of his associates disputed what they had heard about him. The British had been plagued by his raids along the coast, but they were unable to get their hands on the elusive renegade. The redcoats had no clear description of the masked Frenchman who appeared from the shadows to raid British ships and stockades, depleting them of supplies and ammunition. And then he would disappear for a time. His inconsistency had the redcoats baffled. The price on his head was as large as a king's ransom. His name was quietly exchanged among the colonials, taking care not be overheard by the soldiers of the throne. Montclaire had become the unseen hero who could steal supplies right from under the British Navy's nose.

"Davis," Montclaire said abruptly, drawing the man from his silent reverie. "Did you find a clergyman who was willing to travel to Baltimore with us?"

"Aye," the gray-haired man replied with a nod. He sat erect, raising a quizzical gaze to the captain. "But do you think it wise to have a clergyman on board ship? I have often heard it said that a man of the cloth was bad luck on voyages. And why do we need—"

"Davis!" Montclaire cut him short, his eyes threatening and stormy as he clasped his hands behind his back and whirled to squarely face his associate. "He will serve my purpose and I have little time for superstitious prattle. You are not to question my motives. It seems your memory is short, monsieur." A shallow smile thinned his lips, his gaze mocking. "I hope you can correct that flaw . . . and quickly. In the future I expect you to remember what I have told you. I do not appreciate repeating myself."

Davis squirmed nervously in his seat until Montclaire's brooding gaze released him. He looked to the younger man beside him, sending him a silent warning not to make the same mistake.

"Stratton, did you obtain the page from the ledger?" Montclaire inquired, his gaze swinging to the dark-haired man who sat on the opposite end of the sofa.

"Aye." Stratton produced a folded paper from his vest pocket and handed it to Montclaire.

"Did you meet with difficulty while procuring is, *mon ami?*"

He found the name for which he searched and then smiled to himself.

"Nay. 'Twas a simple task. I can only hope that the rest of the mission goes as well as swiping papers from old men," Stratton added with a wry grin. He had worked closely with Montclaire and was not as fearful of him as the three gentlemen who had only recently made his acquaintance.

"*Oui,*" Montclaire agreed. He sent Stratton a smile that could only be detected in the slight sparkle in his eyes, and Stratton had to look closely to see it. "But what we have yet to face will be more difficult than stealing a parchment from the hotel." He stuffed the paper in his coat pocket and allowed his gaze to sweep over all five men. "I will meet you on board ship at midnight. *Adieu*, messieurs."

When Montclaire exited from the room, Davis glanced at Stratton. "Is the captain as irascible as he appears?" he queried. "I thought perhaps I was in danger of losing my head for asking a simple question."

A broad grin settled in Stratton's rugged features. "Only when the situation demands it. When we have accomplished our task, he will not seem so abominable," he assured Davis. "His main concern is for his country, and he is to be admired and respected for his accomplishments. Never doubt that Montclaire far excels other men in any capacity. He appears to be a cold, unyielding tyrant at the moment, but that is because he takes this mission seriously."

Davis shrugged slightly. "I do not doubt his abilities. I have heard much about him, but 'tis his methods that have me baffled," he muttered, a frown knitting his brows as he arose and ambled to the door. "A clergyman? What purpose could he possibly serve on this mission?"

Montclaire eased down in his chair at the desk. With pen in hand he wrote the name as it appeared on the ledger until he had copied it exactly. When he was confident of his ability to forge the signature, he devised a letter and then wrote the name at the bottom. With a self-satisfied smile lighting his clean-shaven face, he leaned back and chuckled wickedly.

"*Pardonnez-moi*, monsieur," he said to the imaginary face that rose before him. "I am in need of your name, but I have no time to obtain it in the proper manner."

After changing into a blue velvet jacket, Montclaire checked his appearance in the mirror and stashed the note in his pocket. As darkness settled over Norfolk, he made his way to a large home on the south side of town. When he rapped on the door, he was ushered in by a dark-headed woman whose face glowed with unmistakable pleasure.

*Mon capitaine,* I thought perhaps you were not coming. I would have been extremely disappointed," she murmured, a provocative smile playing on her lips.

Montclaire swept his top hat from his head, his eyes raking the woman's wholesome figure. "Madame, only a fool would allow such an attractive woman to spend the night alone," he assured her in a raspy voice.

With a delighted giggle, Marie Benet closed the door and flew into his arms, making no pretense at shyness. Montclaire would be leaving soon, and she had no intention of wasting a minute. As they ascended the stairs to her bedchamber, Montclaire tried to focus his full attention on Marie, intent on putting the thought of the other woman out of his mind. But her vision had haunted him since he had seen her riding in the carriage earlier that afternoon. He was annoyed with himself for dwelling on the bewitching face that kept burrowing into his thoughts.

Melissa exited from the hotel where she and her father had spent the night, prepared to journey to the harbor to have her belongings stored on the ship bound for

France. William had invited the captain to dine with them the previous evening and Melissa had been delighted to find Rorick Stephens such a charming and interesting companion. As she and her father strolled up the plank of the schooner, Stephens produced a warm smile and bowed before Melissa, his gaze reassessing her in the morning light. And it came as no surprise to him that the dim light of the previous evening had not camouflaged any flaws. She was perfection.

"Good morning, William, Melissa," he said, as he extended his hand to Stoddard. It was an effort to drag his eyes off Melissa and focus them on her father.

"Since this is Melissa's first journey, I trust I can count on you to keep a watchful eye on her," William requested as he shook hands with the captain.

A broad grin settled on Rorick's handsome features. "It will be my pleasure, sir. I will see that her voyage is as comfortable and enjoyable as possible," he assured Stoddard, his gaze again betraying him as it strayed back to Melissa, sweeping her in careful inspection.

When another couple came on board, Captain Stephens pointed the Stoddards in the direction of Melissa's cabin and then excused himself to greet the other passengers. When her luggage was unloaded in her quarters, Melissa returned to the main deck to say farewell to her father. Melissa was close to tears when she watched William descend the plank and step into his carriage. She amazed herself when she managed to keep the sea of tears from flooding from her eyes. Her heart was twisting in two, leaving an ache in the pit of her stomach.

After the captain had issued the order to open sail, Melissa experienced a sinking feeling that sent her spirits plunging to the bottom of the ocean upon which she was about to embark. She stilled another urge to burst into sobs as the schooner lurched forward, taking her farther away from all she had known and loved.

"Come to the helm with me, Melissa," came the soft, soothing voice from behind her.

She turned to face Rorick's sympathetic smile. "Thank you, Captain. Perhaps it will take my mind off all that I'm leaving behind," she murmured as her eyes drifted back to the shore.

"Please call me Rorick," he insisted as he placed his hand on her elbow and assisted her up the steps to the quarterdeck.

Rorick talked about the ship, acquainting her with the nautical terms the sailors used. The afternoon passed quickly, and Melissa began to feel at ease, thanks to Rorick, who devoted his time to diverting her attention.

It was going to be a most enjoyable trip, Rorick mused, as he escorted Melissa to her quarters. He had been fascinated by her beauty and charm and was anticipating the voyage with her as his constant companion.

"Will you join me in my cabin for dinner this evening?" he questioned, as his hand brushed across the small of her back in a leisurely caress. " 'Tis seldom that I have the opportunity to entertain such pleasant company." A boyish smile spread across his lips. "I'm afraid I have spent too many hours with stubble-faced sailors. The thought of sharing a meal with someone as lovely as you makes our rations sound appetizing."

"Thank you . . . Rorick. I should like that." She returned a smile that displayed her dimples, and Rorick nearly melted into his boots.

As she turned sparkling indigo eyes to him, Rorick fought the urge to take her in his arms and kiss her. Melissa was an extraordinary woman, he mused, as he gazed down at the petite blonde. Most of the female passengers had stayed below deck, attempting to overcome their seasickness, but this rare beauty seemed to thrive on the open sea. Turning her face to the wind, her honeyed hair had billowed about her like a golden cape. Her gaze had swept the glistening white caps as she inhaled the salty sea air. She had been poised like a dove on her perch, her alert eyes missing nothing.

Melissa had talked of the mountains, her father, and another man named Jeremy. After a time, Rorick had concluded that she had left no young man behind, nor was she traveling to France to meet a fiancé. She was free and unattached, possessing the charm that kept Rorick spellbound. She was different than most women he had met. Rorick sensed that he would have to tread carefully with her or he would lose her before he could sample the taste of her kisses. Each time she glanced at him there was that hint of suspiciousness in her eyes, as if she did not completely trust his motives, leaving him to wonder is she had suffered a bad experience with a man. And yet, Rorick could not fathom any man wishing to disappoint this bewitching young lass.

"I will come to your cabin at seven, Melissa," he said, his voice husky with disturbed desire as he placed a kiss to her wrist.

Melissa gazed into his brown eyes and withdrew her hand from his grasp, making a feeble attempt to smile as she nodded her assent. When the captain's footsteps faded in the companionway, she closed the door and stripped from her gown. After washing herself as best she could in the small bath that awaited her, she stretched out on the bunk and let her mind wander through a myriad of memories that had picked that particular moment to surface.

The image of her father played heavily on her mind and she experienced another pang of homesickness. Then the vision of Jeremy sitting before her, his cane grasped in his scarred hand, his gaze holding some unspoken message that she couldn't decode, came to torture her.

And then a forbidden fantasy overshadowed the other two men. Melissa had not allowed herself to dwell on it until now. Within the quiet confines of her cabin, with no one to invade her thoughts, the dark rogue who had tracked her through the mountains, made love to her before the glowing fire, and had returned her to her father to receive his fee, hovered above her. His laughing, silver eyes taunted her, coming at her from all directions. Melissa could not sort out her feelings for him. He had earned her respect long before they had crossed paths, but her idealistic image of him was shattered when she discovered that he was a heartless mercenary who had made love to her because she was convenient. To make matters worse, he had lied to her and then deposited her in her father's hands before disappearing into the wilderness, making no attempt to see her again.

Perhaps Jeremy thought Zack Beaugener possessed remarkable qualities, but Melissa certainly didn't. Zack was a frontiersman whose natural instincts were for survival and whose lusts were those of a wild beast. He was cruel, Melissa thought bitterly. Jeremy's vague explanation of Zack's motives had done nothing to change her opinion. Jeremy did not know Beaugener the way she did.

Rorick was different from Zack, Melissa mused thoughtfully. She could maneuver him with a simple smile. He would not take advantage of her as Zack had because that was not his way, and she would not allow it. She had made a terrible mistake when she attempted to bargain with Zack. The next time she found herself responding to a man the way she had to Zack, she would smother those emotions and avoid situations that might lead to intimacy. She was no longer innocent of the ways of men, and she would not foolishly surrender. Only when she had discovered a love as pure as her mother and father had shared would she completely give herself to a man. Melissa found herself wishing that her knight in shining armor would appear and put an end to her troubled thoughts of Beaugener. He had disrupted her life, and she felt the need to replace him, to forget what they had shared. A weak sigh escaped her lips, knowing it would be difficult to eradicate him from her thoughts. If only Zack hadn't been entangled in her childhood dreams. If only Jeremy hadn't made him sound like some mystical god. . . .

Perhaps Rorick would be the one to make her forget, she mused, as a faint smile surfaced on her lips. He was handsome, courteous, charming, and she was mildly attracted to him. With that thought milling through her mind, she withdrew one of her more fashionable gowns from her trunk and pressed the wrinkles away as best she could. With her hair arranged in curls on top of her head and the stays of her sea-blue velvet gown fastened, she surveyed her image in the mirror. A mischievous smile crept to the corners of her mouth, as she remembered how she had looked when she returned from her seclusion in the mountains. Her hair had been wild and tangled, her buckskin clothes soiled and stained, and her face smudged with grime. If Rorick could have seen her then, he would have been appalled. He would not have recognized her at all, she thought, chuckling to herself. Would he have bestowed all those compliments on her if he had seen her that day? She seriously doubted it.

The knock at the door shattered the image from the past, and Melissa walked to the door to allow Rorick to join her. His gaze wandered longingly over her creamy breasts that rose and fell with each breath. The dainty gown with its low-necked bodice drew his undivided attention, and it took a great deal of effort for him to raise his eyes to her exquisite face.

"You are by far the loveliest thing I have seen in . . ." Rorick searched his memory, trying to name another who could have compared with Melissa, but he was at a loss. "M'lady, I cannot conjure up a face that equals yours," he breathed, his eyes falling to the full swells of her breasts. "I find it difficult to believe that your father has allowed you to travel unescorted."

Melissa was uncomfortable. Rorick had complimented the loveliness of her face, but his eyes was devouring other parts. It was unnerving to be undressed, assessed, and caressed with his bold gaze. Easily reading his thoughts, Melissa slipped her shawl over her shoulders, noting the disappointment that settled on his tanned features. "Thank you for your compliment, Rorick, but rest assured that my father realizes that I am quite capable of taking care of myself," she added, her brows knitting in an accusing frown.

A guilty smile skimmed across his lips. They both

knew where his thoughts had strayed, and apparently, Melissa did not approve. When he finally digested her words, he arched a skeptical brow. "Perhaps your father has given you too much credit, m'lady. How could anyone with such an angelic face be prepared to defend herself in every situation? Unless it is only a disguise for deception." His eyes narrowed thoughtfully when she produced a deliciously mischievous smile that set her face aglow with a hint of devilishness. "Ah, yes," he mused aloud. "The lady appeared to be an angel, but she is, in fact, a ruthless witch."

Melissa chuckled lightly at his taunting remark and then wrapped her hand around the arm Rorick offered to her. "You would do well to keep that in mind," she suggested as another sweet, innocent expression settled on her features, surprising Rorick with the quicksilver change in her appearance.

He could almost believe that she was goddess and sorceress. After all, he had realized that she possessed unique qualities. He shouldn't be the least bit shocked by anything she might do, he told himself. This was going to be a most interesting trip.

The evening passed so quickly that Melissa was amazed at the late hour when Rorick brought it to her attention. She was disappointed when Rorick suggested that she return to her quarters.

"Could we take a stroll on deck before I go back to my room?" she queried, sending him a pleading glance.

"I would be a fool to refuse," Rorick murmured, as he drew her to her feet and captured her in his arms. His mouth covered hers, and it was a long, breathless moment before he could drag himself away. "I've been wanting to do that all day." His hand trailed along the slim column of her throat to her creamy cheek, his gaze warm with desire.

Melissa blessed him with a blinding smile, innocent and yet, mischievous. "And I have wondered what it would be like to kiss you," she admitted.

"And did you find it pleasurable?" he questioned curiously.

Thoughtfully touching her index finger to her chin, she pretended to ponder his inquiry. "I'm not sure, Captain, it happened so quickly that I scarcely had time to make a decision."

A rakish grin curved the corners of his mouth upward. "I won't rush you this time." His lips lingered on hers, tasting the honeyed sweetness of her mouth as he pulled her full length against him, molding her shapely body to his. "I hope I have given you ample time to form your conclusion." His voice was drugged with intoxicated passion, his gaze focusing her moist lips.

"Aye. And it was as pleasurable as I thought it would be," she assured him, and then suddenly freed herself from the tight circle of his arms. Although she smiled up at him, her emotions were in turmoil. The moment she closed her eyes, it was no longer Rorick who held her in his embrace, no longer Rorick who kissed her so tenderly. A shiver trickled down her spine and she drew her shawl closely about her. "I'm anxious to view the ocean at night. Shall we go?" Melissa strolled toward the door, fighting the urge to break and run.

Rorick's brows furrowed puzzledly as Melissa disappeared in the companionway. She had tempted him, taunted him, yielded slightly, and then dismissed him from her spell. Still he was intrigued, but his instincts warned him to beware. She had sensed his rising passion and had set him at arm's length, subtly assuring him that he had rushed her a bit. He had the strange feeling that Miss Stoddard would not hesitate to put him in his place if she considered that he had stepped out of line. And there would be lines forming, Rorick thought, as he ambled toward the door. Melissa could not go anywhere without men filing after her. The lady was impossible to ignore.

After they had walked from bow to stern, Melissa paused to lean on the rail, her gaze drifting out over the water that glowed with a silver hue as far as the eye could see. Silver, she mused disconcertedly. Why silver? It was as if he was staring up at her, never allowing her to forget the intimate moments they had shared in his cabin. Zack's compelling image sought to claim her soul as it rose from the ocean's depths, reminding her that no man could take what he had first possessed. The thought of Zack's experienced caresses set a fire sizzling through her veins. Melissa determinedly fought the sensation, but it was useless. The feel of his hard body pressed to hers had been branded on her mind. The musky fragrance that clung to him had become entangled in her senses.

"Melissa?" Rorick touched her arm, drawing her from her silent reverie. "Did you hear what I said?"

"I'm sorry," she apologized, offering a sheepish smile. "My thoughts were miles away." Melissa scanned the silver-capped sea again, wishing the image of Zack would disappear in the depths and grant her peace.

"Is something troubling you?" Rorick reached beneath her chin, forcing her to meet his inquiring gaze.

She drew his hand away from her face, holding it momentarily in her own before releasing it. "I suppose it's homesickness," she lied. Well, it wasn't exactly a lie. She was just disguising the truth, she rationalized. "And I feel so alone and far from all that I have ever known." Her eyes strayed back to the vast sea that seemed to swallow her, making her feel small and insignificant.

" 'Tis a different world out here, Melissa," he assured her as he wrapped a protective arm about her waist, his smile warm and comforting. "But I promise you that you will see dry land once again."

"And hanging on to that thought, I shall retire to my quarters."

Rorick gathered her deeply in his embrace and lowered his head, his mouth possessing hers in an ardent kiss. Melissa pressed determined hands to his chest and pushed back as far as his encircling arms would allow.

"Goodnight, Rorick. You have skillfully managed to make time fly, but the hour is late and I must not keep you from your duties. You will not find the distance short if I keep you from plotting your course."

As she walked away, his eyes followed in her footsteps. "You are very distracting, indeed," he mused aloud. "But if I should veer off course, I don't doubt that you could find your way across the ocean by yourself if you decided to do just that."

The fragrance of jasmine hovered about him, encircling his senses. Her image floated about him, calling to him, drawing him into her bewitching spell. As he ambled to the helm, a secretive smile crept to his lips. Before this journey came to an end, she would be his, he vowed to himself. He was not about to allow this tempting maid to evade him. Rorick chuckled when he found himself fantasizing picturing her in his bed, her golden hair streaming across his pillow. And he was beside her, discovering every inch of her silky flesh. Melissa could please a man, he convinced himself. And before long he would know just how well.

# Part Two

Revenge, at first thought sweet,
Bitter ere long back on itself.
—Milton

## Chapter Five

As the sun spread its first light across the waves, the helmsman caught sight of another schooner cutting swiftly through the water, heading straight for them. When Rorick was notified, he hurried to the quarter-deck to stare curiously at the approaching ship.

" 'Tis one of ours," Rorick mused aloud, as he lowered his spyglass and squinted at the vessel. Again he raised the glass to read the signal of the flags. "Their captain requests permission to come aboard." He frowned bemusedly at the helmsman. "I wonder what the devil this is all about?" He ordered a reply sent to the vessel and dropped anchor, waiting anxiously for an explanation.

After finishing her breakfast, Melissa donned her pink silk gown, combed her hair, and tied a matching ribbon at the nape of her neck, allowing the golden strands to flow down her back. With her toiletry completed, she climbed to the quarterdeck to see Rorick poised at the helm, watching another schooner pull alongside them.

"What is going on?" Melissa questioned, as she walked up beside him.

Rorick glanced absently at her before his gaze circled back to the ship. "I don't know, but I suppose we are about to find out. The captain wishes to come aboard."

When a plank was maneuvered between the two vessels, Melissa studied the clean-shaven face of the man who approached them. His ruggedly handsome features were framed with raven hair. His expression was grimly sober. The white linen shirt parted to reveal the dark matting of hair on his chest. His tight brown breeches were tucked into his black boots, displaying his muscled thighs. Melissa let her eyes roam from the top of his head to the toes of his polished boots in final inspection before they met and locked with his for a long, breathtaking moment.

Melissa maintained a carefully blank stare, but beneath her mask of indifference her emotions were in turmoil, and her heart was doing back somersaults. She was shocked and confused by the appearance of the ruggedly handsome captain. Her legs threatened to wilt beneath her as she met his gaze for the second time, amazed at the power the man seemed to have over her.

The corners of Montclaire's mouth curved into the resemblance of a smile as he turned his attention from the captivating blonde to Captain Stephens. *"Je regrette, Capitaine.* Forgive the inconvenience, *s'il vous plait.* My name is Capitaine Montclaire," he introduced himself. "I have been requested to return one of your passengers to Norfolk as soon as possible." His rich voice carried a heavy French accent. "Monsieur Stoddard has paid me and my crew to return his daughter to him." Montclaire's gaze never wavered from Stephens's shocked face. "Stoddard has taken ill and wishes for his daughter to rejoin him. Could you take me to the woman so that I may inform her of her father's request?"

"This is Miss Stoddard," Rorick replied, his tone reflecting his disappointment.

Melissa stood frozen to the deck, her eyes wide in alarm. She was unable to find her voice as she accepted the letter Montclaire thrust at her. She unfolded the message and hastily read its contents. When she had finished, Rorick took it from her, cast Montclaire a wary glance, and then read the message.

"Melissa, is this your father's signature?" he inquired.

"Aye," she murmured, managing to locate her tongue after practically swallowing it. But at best she could utter one word. When Rorick held the letter in front of her again, redirecting her attention to the signature, she nodded affirmatively.

Rorick grasped her trembling hand and gazed sympathetically at her whitewashed face. "I am very sorry, my dear. I hope your father is not seriously ill. I will inquire about you at the hotel as soon as we return to the States. Please leave a message for me. I will be most anxious to hear from you."

After Melissa nodded her consent, still not trusting herself to speak, Rorick sent two sailors to collect her belongings. Wrapping a possessive arm about her waist, Rorick lead her to the plank and glanced back over his shoulder at Montclaire who followed in their tracks.

"I have heard mention of your name, Captain. It seems that you have accomplished many daring feats to aid our cause. Do I dare believe all that has been passed by word of mouth?" he questioned point-blank.

A ghost of a smile hovered on Montclaire's lips. "I am wary of gossip, *Capitaine*. Its hunger demands a greater appetite each time it feeds. It seems that the same rumors have reached the ears of our enemy," he said blandly. "The redcoats have placed such a high price on my head that I have been toying with the idea of presenting it to them on a platter and donating the reward to my fellow patriots."

Stephens surveyed the confident expression on Montclaire's craggy features. It was not difficult to believe what he had heard about the elusive captain who had led the British on a merry chase. There was something awesome about him, an aura that radiated from his muscular frame. Montclaire seemed keenly aware of all that transpired about him, his perceptive gaze missing nothing. And yet, Rorick found it a bit odd that such a notorious rebel would cast aside his duties to fetch the daughter of an ailing man.

"How is it that you have found time for this mission of mercy? I should think that this duty could be accomplished by someone other than yourself." Rorick's gaze held a hint of curiosity as he sized up Montclaire, finding nothing about him to criticize.

"Monsieur Stoddard made me an offer I could not refuse. The fee we will receive for making this detour is

118

worth our time," Montclaire replied without batting an eye.

As the crewman walked up beside them, Rorick dropped his cross-examination and turned his attention to Melissa, who had not uttered more than one word since Montclaire informed her of her father's illness. Rorick placed a light kiss to her forehead and then smiled fondly up at her as Montclaire swept her up to the plank.

"Goodbye, Melissa. I pray that your father will be enjoying good health again soon. And I will be dismayed to lose such pleasant company."

"Thank you, Rorick." Melissa had finally gathered her composure that had come unwound like a ball of twine on a downhill roll after meeting Captain Montclaire. "You have been very kind."

"*Adieu*, monsieur," Montclaire interjected, his tone hinting at impatience as he grasped Melissa's elbow and propelled her across the plank. "I am sure Monsieur Stoddard will quickly recover with his lovely daughter by his side to comfort him."

As they moved toward Montclaire's schooner, Melissa glanced back at the forlorn expression on Rorick's face and then turned her full attention on the man who led her away. "What is the matter with father?" she demanded to know.

"Just keep walking, mademoiselle," he ordered through the smile that was pasted on his face. "I will explain later."

"I want to know about Papa *now*," she persisted, her tone cold and clipped. She did not appreciate being shrugged off like a worn shirt. She had every right to know about her father.

"I said later," Montclaire gritted out, his smile still in tact as he waved to Captain Stephens.

When he lifted Melissa down to the deck, he turned to salute the other captain who hardly noticed the gesture, since his eyes were still glued to Melissa. "Wave to your lover, mademoiselle."

As the vessel moved away, Melissa strode over to Montclaire who was busy giving orders to his crew. She tugged on his sleeve, demanding his immediate attention. "I want to know what this is all about. I have a right to —"

"Dammit, woman. Keep a rein on your tongue," he snapped gruffly, causing Melissa to wince at the harshness of his voice.

She managed to curb her curiosity only a few minutes before her temper reached the end of its fuse. She stepped boldly in front of him, blocking his path.

"Montclaire," she muttered as if the name left a bitter taste in her mouth. "If you do not give me an explanation this instant, I will scream at the top of my lungs and bring that ship right back here." Melissa had recovered from her shock and now she demanded to know what the hell was going on. His answer could not come soon enough to please her.

"And if you dare, I will find a way to make you regret it," he snapped back, his voice rolling over her like thunder, angry and threatening.

Melissa was not to be put off. Her chin tilted a notch higher, her eye sparking defiance. "I want to know what ails my father." Her voice was finely tempered, knowing that at any moment she was going to explode if she wasn't given an explanation.

"Not a damned thing. I only needed an excuse to

retrieve you from that ship without arousing suspicion," he grumbled.

Her gaze flew over her shoulder. "Then signal the ship. I wish to return to it," she insisted. "I am going to France."

"What?" An incredulous laugh burst from his lips. "Woman, do you know the trouble I have overcome to chase after you?"

Montclaire grabbed her arm and aimed her toward the steps that led to his cabin, muttering to himself that this beautifully distracting firebrand was more of a nuisance than he had anticipated. Although Melissa set her feet and struggled for release, Montclaire uprooted her from the spot and shuffled her along with his impatient strides.

"Let me go!" she railed. "I prefer to take my chances with the sharks. I am going to France if I have to swim there!" Her voice echoed across the planked deck, exhausting what was left of Montclaire's patience.

He scooped her up in his arms and carried her, kicking and pounding on him. He managed to clamp his hand over her mouth to muffle her protests, disgusted that the heated exchange between them had drawn the crew's attention. Montclaire would not have permitted such a disrespectful outburst from his men, but he was having difficulty controlling the golden-haired hellion who fought him like a wildcat.

"When I am finished with you, you have my permission to swim every league of this ocean and I will personally toss you overboard," he assured her, a distinctly unpleasant edge on his voice that assured Melissa that he would delight in feeding her to the sharks.

When his grip tightened to keep her chained to him, she grimaced as his fingers bit into her ribs. But the pain he inflicted did not deter her from struggling. Melissa clamped her teeth in the flesh of his hand until he removed it from her mouth.

"Put me down this instant!" she demanded, her indigo eyes spewing fire.

As the captain disappeared below deck, Davis ambled over to Stratton and casually leaned against the railing, shaking his head in dismay. "I realize that I do not know Montclaire as well as you do, but I swear he is a madman. We have set out on a mission of grave importance and we ignore our duties to retrieve a woman. I agree that the young woman is breathtakingly beautiful, and, no doubt, a worthy prize for the captain, but Montclaire has given us strict orders to keep our minds on the business at hand. Yet, he has delayed this voyage to Baltimore to kidnap a fancy piece of muslin to serve his purposes." Davis snorted derisively as he stared at the empty steps. " 'Tis a bad omen to bring a woman on board. The curse is doubled now that we are transporting a man of the cloth and this woman. Montclaire has taken leave of his senses. Or perhaps, 'tis that the crazed men of the world are the ones who rule because no one in his right mind would dare defy them."

Stratton chuckled at that logic. "Friend, you must learn not to second-guess the captain's motives. Whatever the woman is doing on board will somehow serve our purpose." He paused momentarily to glance at the stairway that led to the captain's quarters. "Aye," he agreed with a nod and a wry smile. "He appears to be a madman, but in time you will come to see that there is method to his madness."

As Stratton ambled away, Davis frowned thoughtfully. He could not share Stratton's confidence in the captain, but he would not make the mistake of voicing his concern to Montclaire. He had come close to having his head snapped off for questioning the captain the first time they met.

Montclaire tossed Melissa on the bed and then locked the door. Swiftly, he moved back to her, towering above her, sparks spewing from his silver eyes.

"You agreed to help me. You gave me your word!" he reminded her in a gritted growl. "I have kept my end of the bargain."

Melissa rubbed her wrists that stung with the pain of his deathlike grip, reviving the circulation in her arms. "The agreement is off. My father has explained the need of this voyage to France, and I promised him that I would go, *Montclaire.*" She spit out his name, making it sound like a curse.

"You made me a promise, too. And I intend that you keep it. My mission is more important than your voyage. You play a major part in it. 'Tis too late for me to change my plans. I need your assistance and, by damned, you will give it!"

"Like hell I will!" Melissa bolted from the bed, facing him with stubborn defiance. "I have changed my mind since we last met. I will not take orders from you."

"Women! Damn them all," Montclaire raged, rolling his eyes as if summoning more patience, but Melissa had depleted his already short supply. "They change their minds as quickly as the ill-fated winds change direction." He spun away, muttering to himself, and then glanced back over his shoulder. "You may live in France for all I care, but you will not set foot on foreign soil until you have done exactly *what* I tell you, *when* I tell you."

His razor-sharp tone made her bristle angrily. "And how much are you being paid for your mercenary services this time, Beaugener?" she inquired, her voice dripping heavily with sarcasm as she raked him with scornful mockery. "I know you would not be so intent on your duty if it did not mean a pocketful of coins."

His features turned to chiseled granite as he turned to face her. "I will not receive a penny. And if I thought anyone but you could tackle this task and meet with success I would have made other arrangements."

"If that is to be a compliment, I can do without your flattery," she assured him flippantly.

His irritation dwindled when he assessed the proud tilt of her chin. Damn, but she was still bewitching even when her cheeks were flushed with anger. "The name is *Capitaine* Damion Montclaire," he corrected with a thick French accent.

"Ah, *bien intendu*. It seems you are the master of disguises and jack of all trades, monsieur," she replied, mimicking his foreign accent.

One dark brow shot up in surprise as a half smile caught one corner of his mouth. "*Tres bon*, mademoiselle. It seems that you, too, have mastered the art of disguise." His silver eyes flooded over the full swells of her breasts that heaved with each angry breath she inhaled. His smile broadened to encompass his dashing features. "Perhaps I am a jack of all trades, but I am master of only one."

He hooked his arm around her waist, bringing their bodies in close contact. His touch was like a bolt of lightning sizzling its way to her very core, and his kiss left her gulping for air. And then he released her, sending her stumbling backwards to sprawl on the bed.

Melissa fought the flame of desire that he had kindled, but it was as futile as tossing a bucket of water on a forest fire. The man had the power to make her burn with passion, even when she tried to tell herself that she despised him. She peered up at the handsome rogue whose face was void of a full beard and mustache. He was strikingly attractive, more so than she had remembered. All she could do was stare at his virile frame and rugged features. How could she hate him and desire him all at the same time? Damn that man. He could send her senses reeling and turn her emotions into chaos with one blazing kiss.

Damion swaggered toward her and then reached beneath her chin, holding her steady gaze. "*Ma cherie*, forgive me for taking you from your new lover's arms. I am certain that is the reason you wish to continue your voyage. It seems that once you have tasted passion at its sweetest, you have developed an addiction," he teased, flashing her a smile that belied the sting of his words. His remark stung like salt on an open wound, and she gasped at the insult. With the quickness of a coiled snake she slapped the smirk off his face, leaving a perfect hand print on his left cheek. "Rorick was *not* my lover. I only knew him two days."

Damion grinned into her furious face, his eyes

sparkling with deviltry. "But you only knew me one night, *cherie*," he reminded her.

When Melissa raised her hand to strike him again, he grabbed her wrist, holding it in midair.

"I detest you," she hissed venomously. "The sight of you brings unwanted memories of a time when I made the foolish mistake of trying to bargain with you and lost. I learned my lesson and I will surrender to no man ever again." She jerked her arm away and presented her back to him and his mocking smile.

Damion closed the distance between them. His arms curled about her trim waist, his warm breath tickling her neck, sending a rash of goose pimples multiplying across her skin. His eyes fell to the tempting swells of her breasts and his touch became an absent caress.

"I thought perhaps you had allowed Captain Stephens to take my place, but perhaps you have been unable to cast our affair aside. It proves that passion's first encounter is not easily forgotten," he taunted, his voice thick with disturbed desire.

Melissa stiffened in outrage. The warm tide of pleasure that had begun to flow through her veins suddenly turned to ice. "Let me go!" she ground out as she squirmed in his arms. "Do not expect me to fall into your bed again, Demon. Now I know what kind of man you really are and I want nothing to do with you."

"The name is Damion," he said raspily, his gaze fixed on her trembling lips as his head lowered to hers.

Melissa dodged his intended kiss and turned up her nose. " 'Tis Demon," she persisted. "And you are a devil. I will do as you ask since it seems that you have left me with no choice, but I'll be damned if I'm going to become your strumpet during our time together

. . . and I hope it will brief," she added bitterly. "I will not stay in this room with you. I want my own cabin and my privacy."

With an arrogant chuckle he loosened the ties on the back of her gown and pulled it from her shoulders. "You, my fiery vixen, may be damned, but I will not be denied the pleasure I know you can give. I must admit that I have not forgotten that delicious body of yours. I intend to share my bed as well as my cabin with you." His hand moved to cup her firm breast, teasing and arousing her with his skillfulness. "What I want, I take, and now I want you." His silver eyes flamed with desire as they roamed hungrily over her flesh.

Before Melissa could protest, Damion's mouth claimed hers. Impatiently, he ripped away the gown and chemise. His bold caresses rediscovered every inch of her flesh as he stretched out beside her. A submissive moan escaped her lips as her body responded to the familiar feeling that his touch aroused.

Damion shrugged off his shirt, his gaze penetrating her with sparks of passion. As his kisses traced a scalding path along the side of her neck to her breast, Melissa felt the fire of desire consume her reasoning.

"I shall hate you for this," she choked out.

Damion propped himself up on an elbow and gazed into her indigo eyes, watching the tiny flicks of gold radiate like the sun. "You are doing a poor job of convincing me." His hand slid across her belly to caress the tender flesh of her thighs. "You cannot deny that you want me when your body yearns for my touch."

"Nay, I cannot," she admitted, "but I despise you because of it."

The spitefulness vanished from his features to be replaced by a strange tenderness that Melissa was at a loss to understand. It was unlike the granite facade she had noticed when he stepped aboard Rorick's ship. Her anger evaporated when she gazed up at him, seeing the softer side of the man who had taught her to enjoy passion.

"Sweet angel, have mercy," he rasped as his mouth covered hers. "I want you as I have never wanted a woman."

Raw emotion raised its head, driven by a need that had suffered an eternity without being appeased. The craving was so great that Melissa felt her heart catapult to her throat and then tumble back to her chest to hammer against her ribs. The memories that she had attempted to bury surfaced, one by one, like a steady stream of spine-tingling shock waves that rocked her sanity.

Her hands feathered across the broad expanse of his chest, wandering to the corded muscles of his neck, felling the mass of strength beneath her caress. Her heart shed its wall of ice as he bent to accept the invitation of her parted lips.

An aching need consumed him as he tasted her kiss. It melted against his mouth like summer rain, quenching his thirst but leaving him hungering for more. She was all women, every perfect inch of her, and he longed to recapture the moments when she had left him dizzy with desire.

Her caressess become bolder, and Zack fought the urge to ravish her, but he held himself at bay, reveling in the tingling sensations that seared his skin. And then he could no longer endure the sweet splendor of having her so near and yet so far away. He moved

128

above her, staring into indigo eyes that reflected a need that equaled his own. She arched to meet his hard, driving thrusts, giving herself to him, becoming his possession for that breathless moment that defied reality. They moved in flowing rhythm to a melody that played only for them.

For that time in space it made no difference what they thought of each other. Melissa wanted him, needed him, craved that blissful existence that dissolved the biting words that had passed between them. Her body and soul were his, and she sighed with the pleasure of holding him close and loving him as she yearned to do.

Together they glided to those peaceful mountains where they had first shared love's embrace, soaring over those snow-covered crests, seeing the dawn on the far horizon. And only when the flames of desire had fanned and then consumed all in their path did they return to the sea that cradled them. Their passions cooled, taking with it every ounce of strength. Melissa could not find the will to move or the desire to do so. There was no other world outside his sheltering arms, nothing that could compare to the contentment that swept over her.

As Damion rolled beside her, his hands wandering leisurely over her cheek, his eyes focusing on her kiss-swollen lips, he smiled tenderly. "I missed you more that I thought," he mused aloud, his voice soft and raspy. "When you are close at hand, I am powerless to resist you."

"And when we are apart?" Her brow arched as she carefully observed his angular features.

There was a sly smile draped on the corner of his

mouth as he bent his gaze to her. "You would like to hear me say that I cannot find satisfaction with other women, wouldn't you? 'Tis true that your beauty has me bewitched, but time erases memories, just as the sea washes footprints from its sandy beaches. There will be other women to satisfy me, *cherie*. I do not find it compulsive to be particular about what lovely lass shares my bed."

Melissa tried to squirm away, but Damion held her prisoner. He grabbed a handful of golden curls and stilted her head back, wrapping her hair around his fingers to bring her body into close contact with his.

"I will never trust you with my heart," he insisted, his expression somber. "I have no faith in women and you are the most dangerous of them all because your abilities far exceed the average female. I do not expect your fidelity except when I give a command. In that instance I demand that you carry out my request without question. Do you understand me, mademoiselle?" His tone was brittle, his gaze unrelenting. "From this day forward, you will refer to me as *Capitaine* Damion Montclaire. You will not question my authority, especially in the presence of my men. They are expected to blindly follow my orders, and I will not have them witnessing another tantrum like the one you displayed when you came aboard my schooner."

Although his rugged features had turned to stone and Melissa did not mistake his meaning, a challenging smile surfaced on her lips, assuring him that she was far from submissive. *"Je comprendre*, Damion." Her tone held a hint of mockery.

He loosened his grip on her hair, annoyed with the undercurrent of sarcasm he had detected. "Mark my words, *cherie*. My mission is foremost in my mind, and if you defy me, you will be sacrificed."

Her hands trailed across the dark matting on his chest, lingering on the long scar that curved about his ribs, wondering if it was man or beast that had left its mark on his hide. "I will attempt to hold my tongue when your men are about," she promised, her sticky sweet smile causing his brows to furrow suspiciously. "But when we are alone I shall assault you with questions and you will provide me with answers or I will ruin your well-laid plans, no matter what the cost to my welfare. *Comprendez-vous*, monsieur?"

He met her gaze, amazed by the sparkle of defiance on that angelic face. An odd combination, he thought to himself. She had the features of a seraph, but she had a bit of the devil in her as well.

"*Mais oui*, mademoiselle. I think perhaps I have made an excellent choice by selecting you for this mission. You are a cunning sorceress. With you at my side, we cannot fail." His lips captured hers, drawn like a moth to a flame, savoring the sweetness of her kiss. "But with you in my bed, I may not wish to see the deck of the schooner until it is anchored in port," he breathed, his voice raspy with aroused desire.

As he caressed her pliant flesh, he forgot all of the explanations and instructions he had intended to give her. Melissa was far too tempting to ignore. There would be another time for talking, he mused, as her fingertips roamed over the rippling muscles of his back, tickling and taunting him until he hungered to ease his maddening craving for this enticing beauty.

She had learned much, and all too quickly, he mused. She could trigger his passions with her touch.

131

And she was much too resourceful for her own good. He would have to watch her closely. He could not trust her. She had brought him nothing but trouble. With Lissa in his arms, responding ardently to his caressess, he could not think clearly. His thoughts were distorted, torn between mistrust and desire. Later he would think, but for the móment, he would revel in the plea-sure this beautiful vixen could bring, Damion decided, before he forgot everything that had any resemblance to reality.

Again they tasted passion's bubbly brew and felt the surge of intoxicating rapture that invaded their senses. They drifted on puffy clouds in a dreamlike haze that caught and captured time.

When Damion's head finally cleared, he dragged himself away from Melissa and gathered his discarded clothes. Melissa pulled the sheet about her and held up her ripped gown and chemise for closer inspection.

"If all our arguments are as violent as this one, I fear I will have nothing left to wear. I trust you do not ex-pect me to pursue this mysterious mission of yours without a stitch of clothing." Melissa wrinkled her nose at the long rip on the shoulder of her dress.

Damion chuckled amusedly at her distressed ex-pression, clasped her hand in his, and led her to the wardrobe closet. "If I rip all of your gowns to shreds, I think these will suffice." He gestured to the expensive dresses that hung before her.

Melissa gasped as she ran her hand over the rich silk and velvet gowns. And then a cynical frown knitted her brows. "Where did you get these?" She drew her hand away from the cloth as if it had singed her finger-tips. They were probably the discarded garments of one of his mistresses, she guessed.

"I bought them in Norfolk, especially for you. I could only estimate your size," he said glibly. "If they don't fit properly I hope you are as competent with a needle and thread as you are with a musket and knife."

With a noncommittal shrug she reexamined the dresses. "I'll manage," she replied absently.

His arms slid about her waist, pulling her back against the solid wall of his chest. "I must compliment you, *ma cherie*. When I boarded your ship this morning you never batted an eye. I doubted that Stephens realized that you and I were not strangers. You handled the situation well."

"It took a moment to recognize you," she confessed, her gaze sliding back to him. "Without your dark beard, unruly hair, and your buckskin clothes you looked quite different, almost handsome." Her hand brushed across his smooth cheek.

"And I was not certain I could trust my own eyes when I saw you standing at the helm." He chuckled lightly as he nuzzled his head in the curve of her neck. "The last time I saw you, you reminded me of an enraged tigress. Your hair was wild and tangled, your face smudged, and you wore those tight-fitting deerskin breeches. I'm still not sure which vision arouses me most, the lady or the vixen."

Melissa turned in his arms, keeping the sheet wrapped carefully about her, when she noticed where his eyes had strayed. "I can play the lady if I must, but I will always prefer my buckskin breeches."

"I had already presumed that," Damion muttered hoarsely before he lowered his head, nibbling at the corners of her mouth. "That is why you are so perfect

133

for this task."

Melissa dragged her lips away from his and leaned back in his encircling arms. "And just what is this mission that you have designed?" she questioned pointedly.

"One of danger and adventure. I'm sure you will delight in aiding me since you seem to thrive on both." A sly smile slashed across his mouth, bringing a devilish glint to his eyes.

"But what is—"

Damion pressed his fingers to her lips, silencing her inquiry. "I will explain later. But now I must return to the deck before my crew abandons ship to search out their own shapely treasure."

Melissa watched him go, her brows furrowing bemusedly. What was this all about? Why had he incorporated her into his plans? Why was he portraying a captain, using an assumed name? Or was he really Damion Montclaire? The questions whirled through her mind in disarray, but there were no answers to satisfy her curiosity. She would have to be content to wait until Montclaire was ready to give an explanation, and it could not come soon enough to please her. She was impatient to know what fate awaited her.

## Chapter Six

Melissa paced the confines of the cabin after she had repaired her torn gown and chemise. Her restlessness took her back to the deck. She was aware that all eyes were upon her, and she wondered if all aboard had guessed that she and Damion had shared more than harsh words. Damion or Zack, whoever he really was, had shoved her into an embarrassing situation, and she doubted that he cared what anyone else thought.

He was a calloused man, unconcerned of other's opinions. He had made it clear that she could please him for the time they were together, but when their mission was completed, they would go their separate ways, just as before.

Melissa had entertained the idea of escaping when they reached port, but Damion seemed driven by his purpose, and she was afraid to cross him, knowing that he would not hesitate to extract his vengeance from her hide. If she disrupted his plans, he would show no mercy. She would have to disappear without a trace. She was also concerned about her father, wondering if he knew of her whereabouts. Melissa made a mental note to question Montclaire about it later. William had a right to know where she was and why.

As she strolled across the deck, Damion glanced at her and motioned for her to join him at the helm.

"I see you could not keep to your cabin as I had hoped, mademoiselle," he said dryly, his eyes sweeping the choppy water.

"Come now, *mon capitaine*," she chided. "You know me better than that. I don't like to be closeted."

"And so you have decided to come to deck to make a fool of me again, in front of my crew," he predicted, casting her a suspicious glance.

"I have never made a fool of you, monsieur. You have managed to do so without my assistance," she countered.

A low rumble erupted from his massive chest. "I fear you may be right. I have been outwitted on several occasions. One in particular has cost me dearly." The thought brought a dark scowl to his face, remembering his last confrontation with Jeremy.

Melissa raised a quizzical brow and peered up at the dashing captain whose raven hair whipped recklessly about him in the breeze.

"To what are you referring?"

Damion inwardly cringed when he noticed the golden flecks in her eyes and the subtle way the wind lifted her hair and gently swept it back over her shoulders. She was bewitching. If her mother was as breathtaking, it was little wonder that Jeremy had been so taken with her. "I cannot answer that question. That knowledge must come to you from someone else." He dragged his attention back to the sea.

Her gaze followed his, her expression puzzled, wondering what he was mumbling about. He was always so secretive that she could never be certain of his meaning. More riddles, she thought disconcertedly. Why couldn't he say what was on his mind? It would certainly make it easier for her to understand him.

After they had taken their evening meal, Damion requested that Melissa dress in one of the gowns that he had purchased for her. Melissa was delighted with the suggestion and donned a pink velvet dress that was adorned with yards of ruffles and lace. Never had she owned anything so exquisite. As she stood in front of the mirror, combing out her hair, Damion silently watched her, carefully appraising every delectable asset she possessed. And there were many, he thought to himself.

The scooped bodice displayed the fullness of her breasts. The contour of her waist, which was small enough for him to encircle with his hands, was accentuated by the trim cut of the gown. She was a goddess, he breathed appreciatively. Damion fought the urge to take her in his arms and cancel the meeting with his associates. With Melissa in his cabin he was having one helluva time keeping his mind on business. Perhaps separate quarters *was* the answer. But then again, one of his men might be tempted to take his place if he allowed her the privacy of her own cabin.

The vicious curses that he had muttered to the vision of Jeremy had come less frequently. When the thought did cross his mind, they were not as vivid as they had been in the beginning. Perhaps he had embroiled Melissa in this mission, just to spite Jeremy, he mused, as he continued to watch Melissa. Aye, that was the reason he told himself. It was not because he wanted her with him. He was having his own revenge, using Drieson's daughter for his own purposes. Jeremy had set a trap, but Damion was determined to prove to Jeremy that he should not have tampered with their lives.

And yet, no matter how hard Damion tried, no matter which way he turned, one or the other pair of haunting blue eyes were there to stare him down. Damion was beginning to wonder if he was spiting Jeremy or Melissa. It really wasn't her fault. She did not even realize that she had been the bait of Jeremy's trap. But dammit, the wench had incensed him with her resourcefulness and had aroused him with her beauty.

Damion shook his head, shattering his silent reverie. It made little difference what his reasons had been in the beginning. He was using Melissa as bait for another trap, one that served his cause. Then he would deliver her to Jeremy, proving that no man could have the last laugh on Damion Montclaire. He could well imagine what Jeremy would think if he knew what was in store for his lovely daughter. And if Jeremy knew of the danger she would face, he would be incensed. The redcoats would have to stand in line to have his head when Jeremy learned of this mission. But there had to be a compromise, Damion thought stubbornly. He could only hope that he could return the lass unharmed. That was the one flaw in his well-devised scheme. Damion could not predict that all could go well, but if Melissa could not accomplish the mission, no one could. His thoughts were rambling in endless disarray and Damion was having difficulty putting them in the proper order. When Melissa stepped before him, demanding his attention, he discarded his musings and focused his eyes on the tempting display.

"Does my father know where I am?" she questioned abruptly.

"He knows you are with me and that you will be returned to him when I'm finished with you," he replied, distracted by the low bodice that allowed his gaze to caress the swells of her breasts. Damn, he was acting like a love-smitten schoolboy. It was difficult to concentrate when she was so appealing.

"That I am with you?" she repeated, arching a skeptical brow. "Beaugener or Montclaire?"

"Capitaine Montclaire," he murmured as he bowed, placing a light kiss to her wrist.

Melissa promptly withdrew her hand and sliced him a cold glance. "But Papa doesn't know who you really are. He will be concerned about me," she persisted. "And just who are you? Your double identity is confusing. You play each role as if you were born to both of them." Her eyes roamed over his muscular frame which was wrapped in tailor-made garments of charcoal gray velvet.

"My name is Beaugener, but while we are on this mission you will refer to me as Montclaire, especially in the presence of my associates. Only two of them know who I am. Montclaire was my mother's maiden name. 'Tis the one I use when I captain the schooner to seize British supplies along our northeastern coast." He paused a moment, inhaled a deep breath, and then added, "Don't worry about your father, I explained as much as I could in the letter I left for him at your hotel.

And now about the mission."

Melissa smiled in relief. "I thought you would never tell me what this is all about and my curiosity is eating me alive," she admitted.

"I'm sure it is." A devilish twinkle flickered in his eyes as he ushered Melissa to her chair and then sank down across from her to divulge the details. "During our last expedition Daniel Boone was captured by the Shawnees. He has been taken to British headquarters in Detroit. We are going to effect his escape."

Melissa stared at him bug-eyed, stunned, her jaw sagging.

"From this day forward, until the deed is accomplished, you are Andrea Deuvalle, a French countess who will arrive at the fort with your father—" He was cut off by her surprised gasp.

"My father?" she repeated incredulously. "But I thought you said he was on his way back to Martin's Fork."

A wry smile touched his lips. "Aye, that one is, mademoiselle, but you will inherit a new one shortly. You will have escaped a robbery attempt in which your mother has been kidnapped. You and your father will request the assistance of the British while you await word from your mother's captors. I expect you to sound hysterically convincing, and later, to be very charming and seductive while in the company of the redcoats."

"How charming?" she queried cautiously. She didn't like the sound of his insinuation or the suggestive gleam in his eyes.

Montclaire cupped her chin in his hand as another grin cracked his countenance. "You will catch more flies with honey than with vinegar, *cherie*," he reminded her.

Melissa sniffed sarcastically. "Are you suggesting that I wrestle the soldiers to the ground and smear honey on them?"

"You will do what you must to divert the soldiers' attention so Boone can escape," he commanded, his mouth forming a grim line.

She gasped indignantly as she shoved his hand away from her face. "Nay! I will not!" she protested, her voice rising testily.

"You are very clever, Andrea. You will be able to handle the situation. This is why I have selected you. The British have a anticipated a seige by the revolutionists, but they will be taken unaware by the subtly of this plan."

"I will not play the whore, if that is what you expect," she informed him in no uncertain terms.

His eyes turned to hard chips of granite, his jaw twitching angrily. "You will do what must be done."

"Not if it means that I—"

The knock at the door brought quick death to their conversation, and Melissa swallowed the rest of her sentence and glared at Montclaire. He had not heard the last of this, not by any means, she vowed. Her patriotism was strong, but her pride would not allow her to stoop that low!

As Damion swung open the door, Andrea moved to his side, blessing the men with her sweetest smile. The five men came to a startled halt, their eyes betraying their thoughts. There was no question that she had captured their attention, and Damion was assured that she would have the same effect on the love-starved

141

British troops. Andrea was stunning and not one man in the room could drag his eyes off of her for even a split-second.

With a satisfied smile, Montclaire wrapped a possessive arm around Andrea's waist and assisted her to her chair. "Messieurs, may I present Mademoiselle Andrea Deuvalle. She will play an important role in our rescue of Boone."

Five pairs of eyes swung to the captain, certain that this feminine beauty could not endure the rugged cross-country journey with a guerrilla band. Each man sat silently, wondering if the captain's fascination with Miss Deuvalle had muddled his thoughts. Davis had already assumed that Montclaire was a madman and even Stratton was plagued with doubts. This woman would hamper, not help them. The last thing they needed was to uproot some fragile flower and whisk her off at a reckless pace between Baltimore and Detroit. Aye, he was stark, raving mad, Davis decided, as his gaze circled from the comely blonde to the sly, grinning captain. There was a fiendish look in those gray eyes. Davis squirmed in his seat, an uneasy feeling swimming about him. If he had known of Montclaire's idiosyncrasies, he damned well would have stayed home! Lord, he knew this mission was headed for disaster when he learned that a clergyman and a woman were to be traveling on board ship with them.

Montclaire clasped his hands behind his back and strangled a chuckle when he noticed their skepticism. "I doubt that you gentleman trust my judgment in this matter, but I assure you that I have made no mistake. Once you have observed Miss Deuvalle's talents, as I have, you will no longer question my sanity or her resourcefulness."

His amused gaze settled on Andrea and then he directed her attention to Davis. "Andrea, I would like you to meet your father."

Father and daughter turned curious glances to each other while the other four men peered bewilderedly at Montclaire.

"Andrea and Alexandre Deuvalle have arrived from France to visit Andre's sister-in-law, but Madame Deuvalle will be kidnapped while traveling to Detroit. Our poor, bereaved twosome will call upon the British for assistance," he explained, a hint of mockery in his voice. "The rest of us will portray Madame Deuvall's captors. We will see to it that the redcoats believe their story."

Damion's gaze swung back to Davis. "I have been informed that you speak fluent French. That is why you will play the role of Andrea's father. See that you look upon her as a daughter, *mon ami*," he warned, casting Davis a meaningful frown before turning his attention to Andrea. "Mademoiselle, if you find yourself in a predicament that forces you to speak your native tongue, Andre will prompt you. You can always feign such despair that you cannot find your voice."

"*Je parle Francaise, mon capitaine. Je ne demande assistance*," Andrea informed him smoothly.

Montclaire's dark brow raised acutely and then returned to its normal arch. The little vixen was more talented than even he had suspected. "*Tres bon*. You have made your father's charade simple. The two of you will be able to carry on conversations in your native tongue, convincing the British of the authenticity of your plight. And you, *ma cherie*, are most fortunate

143

to be blessed with more than one father," he added with a light chuckle.

Andrea's eyes narrowed, finding little amusement in his remark, but then, she did not comprehend the hidden meaning.

"When we reach Baltimore, our horses and supplies will be waiting for us. We will depart as soon as I have spoken to my superiors. Are there any questions?" His silver gaze scanned the solemn group.

A stilted silence filled the room. The scheme that centered around Andrea had them all baffled. They had expected to confront the British with rifles and knives instead of this intricate scheme devised by a madman. Could this rare beauty endure the trials that lay ahead of her? That was the one question each of them wanted to ask, but none dared to voice his reservations. Montclaire had not seemed to miss even a minute detail, but his associates thought he had overlooked the major flaw: the lovely Andrea Deuvalle. How the devil could one woman and an aging man effect Boone's release in a fort swarming with redcoats?

"You are dismissed, messieurs," Damion said abruptly. "Monsieur Deuvalle." His eyes focused on Davis. "Bring the clergyman to my room, *s'il vous plait.*"

As the men filed from the cabin, wondering where the man of the cloth fit into the scheme of things, only Andrea dared to ask. When she and Damion were alone, she turned squarely to face him, arching a curious brow.

"Why did you bring along a preacher on this mission? Is he to read the last rites over those of us who will not return?" she queried, her tone dripping with sarcasm and a heavy French accent.

Amusement glistened in his eyes as he looked down at Andrea. "Nay, he only escorts us as far as Baltimore. I require his services on this voyage."

Andrea appraised his striking physique, wondering why this man deserved to be so disarmingly handsome. She could well imagine the number of women who had been drawn beneath his spell. One look in those smoky gray eyes was enough to make her swallow her breath. And when he produced one of those blinding smiles that reflected a gleam of deviltry, she was hopelessly lost. Why must she be one of the many who was drawn into his trance, she mused resentfully.

Andrea shook away her wandering thoughts and continued her interrogation. "If the clergyman is not traveling with us to Detroit, then what purpose does he serve here?"

"Mademoiselle," Damion breathed impatiently, his face darkening as if she had bored him with her prying questions. " 'Tis difficult to conduct a marriage ceremony without a preacher." The very thought of what he was about to do burned him to the quick, and he was in no mood to discuss the matter at length.

"Marriage ceremony?" she repeated incredulously. "What on earth are you ranting about now?" Andrea had begun to share the popular opinion that Montclaire was demented.

"We will be man and wife very shortly," he replied blandly as he ambled over to check his appearance in the mirror.

"We?" her breath constricted in her throat. He *was* crazed!

"*Oui*, mademoiselle," he assured, grinning wryly

145

at her.

Andrea stared at him as if he had suddenly sprouted another head, one that was void of sense, and then sidestepped, putting greater distance between them when he reached for her. "And what purpose does that serve?" she questioned suspiciously. She knew he was a cold, calculating man who rarely surrendered to impulse.

"None. It has nothing to do with Boone's release."

Her brows furrowed deeper. "Andrea Deuvalle is marrying Damion Montclaire? The marriage will be as fake as our names," she scoffed, shooting him a disapproving glance. "If this is your flimsy attempt to salvage my reputation, don't bother. You are not an honorable man when it comes to women. I have no intention of making a mockery of marriage. I know you well enough to realize that a certificate would not make you faithful to me or anyone. I have no desire to be your wife and I will not be a party to such a ridiculous idea." He may as well have requested that she fly to the moon, slice him off a piece, and serve it to him for supper!

"You are going to marry me," Damion insisted, his rugged features turning stone cold. "I told you that you were to obey my orders without question and that is exactly what you will do!" The nerve of that woman! She should have been delighted with the idea.

"I most certainly will not," Andrea stormed back at him, her indigo eyes spewing defiance. "Why should I marry you? You don't give a damn what these other men think. Since when have you become so concerned about the opinions of others?" Sarcasm dripped from her voice as she flung Damion a disgusted glower.

" 'Tis not what they think that is important," he growled into her stubborn face. " 'Tis what *Jeremy* wants!"

His remark knocked the wind out of her sails. "Jeremy? What has he to do with this?" A bemused frown gathered on her brow.

"Everything. He knows what happened between us in the mountains and he insisted that I take you as my wife since I deflowered his virgin . . . " Damion bit back the word "daughter" just before it flew from his lips. "Protege," he finished, for lack of a better description.

Angry red made fast work of staining her cheeks. "You told him that? How could you be so despicable? You scoundrel! How dare you brag to him that I was another of your possessions!" Andrea spun on her heels and stalked toward the door, wishing she were anywhere except in the same room with that miserable blackguard. "The agreement is off. Find yourself another pigeon. I want nothing to do with you or this charade."

Damion sprung on her, yanking her around to face him, his lean fingers cutting into the tender flesh of her arm. "I didn't tell Drieson a damned thing. He knew exactly what would happen when we were alone together. He set me up," he defended, his voice acid with fury. "He sent me to track you, knowing full well that I wouldn't be able to resist you. When we returned, he insisted that I marry you or he would go straight to Stoddard and tell him the truth. I got the hell away from there before he had the chance to do as he threatened." Damion scowled sourly when he peered into her face, seeing that familiar expression that made his blood boil. "Damn that Drieson," he grumbled under his breath. Didn't he have enough on his mind without arguing with this little hellcat?

"Why would Jeremy do such a thing?" Andrea glared at him. "I don't believe you. You're trying to turn me against Jeremy, but it won't work, Montclaire. I love him and I don't believe that he would intentionally hurt me. We have been too close for too many years. I trust him as much as I would my own father."

Damion released a derisive snort. If she only knew the truth, she might change her high opinion of Drieson, he thought to himself.

"You better believe me, *cherie*. He wanted me to marry you because, in his opinion, I was the only man who could keep a rein on you. And if Jeremy wants us married, then by damned, we shall be or I will never be able to face him again," Damion insisted, shaking her so roughly that her hair flew wildly about her. If he thought he could have shaken some sense into her he would have, but the wench seemed hellbent on defying him.

" 'Tis your misfortune, Montclaire," she hissed, coiling like a snake, preparing to sink her fangs into his flesh if he did not release her. When he finally did, she retreated, working the circulation back into her arms. "I don't know what madness would possess Jeremy to do such a thing. Even if you are telling the truth, which I doubt, I will not abide this marriage. I will not have Jeremy deciding whom I should marry. You will have to work out your differences with Jeremy, but leave me out of it. I will not be dictated to by him, you, or anyone else. I have a mind of my own and I will decide when and *whom* I wish to wed!"

"Drieson set me up for a specific reason," Montclaire persisted, his tone razor sharp. "If you knew the whole of it, perhaps you would understand his logic."

"And just what was his reasoning?" She sent him a measured look, wondering if she was about to hear another round of lies.

Montclaire stared at the opposite wall, cursing the image of Jeremy that rose before him. Damn that man. He had made Damion look the culprit, when in actuality, Drieson was the weasel. " 'Tis not my place to tell you. You can discuss this with Jeremy the next time you see him."

"Ha! I may never see Kentucky, Jeremy, or my father again, thanks to this mission of yours," she muttered resentfully. "I will not marry you, Montclaire. I have decided to take my pleasures with whomever I choose, just as you do. And I am not changing my name again. I have just acquired a new one. The third name is less appealing than the second. And besides," she add sarcastically, "I'm not certain that my newly inherited father would agree to this marriage either."

Andrea's defiance made Damion all the more determined to make her his wife, although the idea had not been to his liking. It incensed him that she would protest so fiercely. He could name a dozen women who would like to claim the title, whether it be Madame Beaugener or Montclaire. The one time in his life when he made a marriage proposal he was met with an adamant refusal. How dare she decline his generous offer! But then, why should he care? This was what Jeremy wanted, not Damion's desire, wasn't it? The answer did not come quickly enough to suit him. Well, wasn't it? he asked himself again. He was obliging Jeremy's request even when he had no need of a wife. Was this Jeremy's way of punishing Damion? Had he grown resentful because he could not pursue the life that Damion was living? Was this entire set up for spite? Damion stared into those indigo eyes that sparkled with flecks of outrage. Jeremy must have hated him, Damion decided. And Andrea had already informed him that she despised him as well. Was this some kind of torture Drieson had planned? Did he know what a hellcat his daughter was?

Damion's logic was being twisted and stretched. His pride began to dictate, and he realized that he was indignant that this little firebrand had refused him. He had always stared challenges in the face and had never taken no for an answer, and he was not about to start now! Andrea Deuvalle was going to consent to be his bride if it was the last thing either of them ever did! By damned, she would agree to the wedding or he would use brute force on her! Come hell or high water this golden-haired vixen would take his name. Giving way to that thought, Damion glanced over his shoulder, expecting at any moment to see a wave of fire crashing through the porthole to set their honeymoon suite ablaze.

He grabbed Andrea to him, intending to silence her next protest with a kiss that would tear the words from her gorgeous throat before she could voice them.

## Chapter Seven

The timid rap on the door invaded the brittle silence. Damion, with his arm clamped on Andrea's waist, reached over to open the door with his free hand. He and Andrea continued to glare at each other, burnt indigo clashing with smouldering gray eyes that would neither concede nor compromise.

The clergyman entered the captain's cabin, but with much reluctance. He had overheard the fiery argument and had not dared to interrupt until the heated words that shook the outer walls had ceased. And even then he would have preferred to tiptoe quietly away, avoiding both of them.

He had agreed to travel to Baltimore with the crew, intending to visit his sister and her family. It had seemed like an excellent idea when one of Montclaire's men had approached him on the matter, but now he had his doubts. The captain had steered off course to retrieve this woman and now he intended to marry her because someone else had suggested it. And whoever this woman was, she was using an alias. This was insanity, he thought, as his eyes darted apprehensively from Damion to Andrea. Sweet mercy! What had he gotten himself in to?

Damion grabbed a handful of the clergyman's coat and hauled him out of the way to shut the door. "You are going to marry us. Be quick about it!" Damion commanded harshly, not bothering with a polite greeting.

"Nay, you will not! I refuse," Andrea thundered. "I have no desire to be his wife. I want nothing to do with the marriage."

"That is of little consequence, mademoiselle," Damion bellowed into her face, his patience depleted, his temper boiling like an overheated tea kettle.

"I will not!"

"You will!" Damion flared before he turned angry gray eyes on the preacher. "Get on with the ceremony."

The clergyman tugged at the collar of his shirt that was beginning to feel like a noose. "Captain, this is most unusual. If the lady refuses . . . " It was difficult to remain calm with the two of them glaring at each other as if they despised the thought of marriage and the sight of their intended spouses.

"I said marry us now!" Damion barked before his lips narrowed grimly. When Andrea opened her mouth to protest, he clamped his hand over her face, muffling her words. "I am not a patient man." His words hung like a threat and the clergy man squirmed uncomfortably beneath Damion's fuming gaze.

The menacing glower that radiated from the silver-gray eyes was enough to turn a man's blood to ice, and the clergyman finally nodded his reluctant consent. He spoke the words to bind them together while Andrea struggled for release. Damion held her in place, and she

152

found herself literally bound to him. She was fit to be tied and Damion was doing just that!

Only when Andrea was to speak the vows did Damion removed his hand from her mouth. When she refused to promise, he twisted her arm behind her back until she grimaced in pain. The stubborn wench had very nearly tempted him to break her arm for her obstinacy.

"Damn you," she muttered, only loud enough for Damion to hear, and then sucked in her breath when he wedged her arm further up her back.

He leaned close to her ear, whispering between clenched teeth. "Say yes or I'll break your arm." A wicked smile curled his lips as he glared down at her.

"You do and I will be of no use to you," she challenged, returning his spiteful glance.

"I have no intention of changing my plans about the marriage or the mission," he assured her, his tone carrying an undertone of ruthlessness. "It will be you who has to carry on with your arm in a sling and you who has to suffer the pain and inconvenience. The fact that you were injured while your mother was being kidnapped will only add substance to your story. A broken arm will not excuse you from your duty, my stubborn chit."

Andrea stared at him, searching the hard, chisled lines of his face. He seemed to be carved from stone, solid and immovable as a mountain. Damion would do exactly as he had threatened. The glint in those steel-eyes warned her that not only would he do it, but he would thoroughly enjoy it. After flashing him blatant hatred, Andrea turned her attention to the clergyman who stood anxiously before them.

"I do," she muttered in belated response. Her voice

wavered with bridled fury, and Damion wondered if she would split apart at the seams. She was like a bomb looking for a place to explode.

"I now pronounce you man and wife," the preacher then sighed, as if he had been holding his breath and just released it. "You may kiss the bride." He hurried to the door, his stride swiftly carrying him away before another fiery battle broke loose between the newlyweds.

"The papers," Damion reminded him as he planted a hasty kiss to Andrea's unresponsive lips. "We must sign the papers."

Damion finally released Andrea and walked to his desk to retrieve the certificate from the top drawer. He signed his name and motioned for Andrea to join him, he quickly closed the distance between them and propelled her across the room, thrusting the quill in her hand as they approached the desk.

"Sign it," he commanded sharply. "You are still in danger of losing the use of your arm."

Gritting her teeth, she placed her new signature on the parchment and then stomped to the opposite side of the room while the preacher edged cautiously toward the captain.

He swallowed the lump of fear in his throat, meekly voicing the thought that had him concerned. "We need two witnesses," he squeaked.

Damion hastily signed his given name and then insisted that Andrea do the same, which she did with the same amount of hesitation she had when she first took the quill in hand.

"You are dismissed, monsieur." Damion nodded his head toward the door and then caught the clergyman in his narrowed gaze. "If you breathe a word about this, you may well be delivering you own eulogy."

Andrea raised icy blue eyes to her newly acquired husband and then presented him with a cold shoulder, one complete with icicles. Where he found the gall to threaten a man of the cloth, she wasn't certain, but Damion was inviting trouble. Andrea's only consolation was her premonition that one day he would pay his dues.

When they were alone, she grumbled to herself, flung Damion an angry glance, and then paced the floor like a caged cat too long in captivity. She was trapped. What she needed was to straddle her stallion and escape to the mountains. But here she was in the middle of the ocean, locked in a room with a man she had no desire to marry and who obviously was as thrilled with the idea as she was. What was she to do?

Andrea saw the bottle of brandy and impulsively poured herself a drink. The liquor set her throat afire and burned its way to her stomach. Her face whitewashed as she gasped for breath and then panicked when she found she couldn't breathe.

Damion leaned casually against the edge of the desk, his arms and legs crossed in front of him, an amused smile hovering on his lips. He watched Andrea recover, down her second sip, and then turn green around the gills.

"What do you think you are doing, madame?" he queried, raking her from head to toe and all parts in between.

"Nursing my bruises," she managed to say between coughs. "And I fully intend to drink myself senseless so I will be immune to the fact that I have been caged with a crazed loon," she added bitterly.

Damion cocked his head to the side, his gaze making yet another prolonged journey over her shapely figure, watching her breasts come dangerously close to spilling free as she yielded to the coughing spasms. "And do you plan to drink yourself into a stupor that will allow you to sleep for the next hundred years?"

"It does have its advantages," she assured him caustically as she gulped another drink and waited a breathless moment for the fire to extinguish itself in her stomach. Andrea watched in amazement as Damion filled his glass and guzzled his drink without batting an eye. "How can you do that?"

His shoulder lifted in a reckless shrug as he swished the brandy around the rim of his glass and then took another sip. "I have acquired a lead-lined stomach, *cherie,*" he informed her.

"To match the encasing for your heart," she grumbled sourly.

Damion chortled as he glanced over to see Andrea trying to keep up with him. After she had refilled her third glass, he cast a disapproving frown.

"I think you have had enough, my dear. This cabin will be swimming before your eyes if you don't slow down a bit."

Andrea refused to heed his warning. If the brandy could make her immune to Damion, she would be most grateful. She planted herself in his chair and propped up her feet on the edge of his desk, the brandy bottle sitting on her lap.

"I have only just begun," she told him, her words slurring as they tumbled from her lips.

He chose to let her pout for nearly a half-hour before he tired of watching her drain his stock of liquor. Damion unfolded himself from his chair and strode over to tower above her.

"I think 'tis time to find something else to entertain you."

Her lashes swept up to see his hazy image above her, and she giggled when she detected the disapproving frown that was stamped on his clean-shaven face. "And what do you suggest, monsieur?"

One heavy eyebrow lifted suggestively. "Must I spell it our for you? I think you have played the part of the nervous bride long enough." His voice had an undertone of sarcasm. "All that liquor you have consumed has surely taken the edge off your anxieties."

Andrea raised her arm to toast her new husband, his insult sliding off like water from a duck's back. "I shall drink to you, Monsieur Montclaire . . . or whoever you are. Here is to your happiness and my misery."

Damion's patience was still running on a short fuse and he was losing what was left of his good disposition. "Come to bed, Andrea," he ordered gruffly.

She tilted her head back, looked him square in the eye, and then took another sip. "Go straight to hell."

His mouth narrowed in a sarcastic smile. "I would be only too happy to make the trip, just as soon as you give me directions. I am certain that you have been sent up from the eternal furnace to find new ways to torture me."

Andrea gathered her feet beneath her, but found they failed her when she took a step. Grumbling at the intoxicated beauty, Damion hooked an arm around her waist to steady her, only to have her pry his hands from her hips and fling them away. As she weaved across the room, bracing herself against the furniture to maintain

157

her balance, Damion rolled his eyes heavenward, as if summoning more patience. A muddled frown plowed his brow as she fumbled with the stays of her gown and then rummaged through her trunk to retrieve her buckskin clothes.

"What the sweet loving hell do you think you're doing?" Damion wanted to know.

"I am going on deck," she insisted.

"Not dressed like that you aren't," he told her harshly. Damion wagged a lean finger at her. "You are not leaving this—

The sharp wrap at the door interrupted him, and he pivoted to glare at the crewman who timidly poked his head inside.

"The helmsman wishes a word with you, Captain," he informed Damion while his eyes made fast work of assessing Andrea and her gaping gown.

"I will be up in a moment." Damion dismissed the sailor with a curt nod and then focused his full attention on Andrea. "You damned well better be here when I get back."

As he wheeled and stalked away, Andrea pulled a face at his broad backside and then shrugged off her dress. She was not about to take orders from Damion, she told herself. He did not deserve her loyalty. The cad!

Damion made his way to the quarterdeck to speak with the helmsman about their route and then wandered to the bow, his gaze scanning the water's choppy surface. His features hardened as his thoughts turned to the following weeks and the difficulties that lay ahead of them. Many lives were at stake and there was no room for error. His plans must entail each and every hour of the day, and he had to consider every possibility, preparing himself for trouble. There could be no mistakes, no reckless flaws. Damion was determined to see that there were none.

Thomas Sumter, who led several guerrilla bands against the British, wanted to know the details of Damion's plans before they were put into action. How would Sumter react when he learned that Damion intended to seige the fort with a mere woman? No doubt, Sumter would be as skeptical as his men had been, he mused, a wry smile tracing his lips. It would take some fast talking to convince Sumter, but the simplicity of his plan was also its effectiveness.

The thought of placing Andrea in such a precarious situation had not plagued him until he had kidnapped her from Stephens's ship. Just seeing her again led to misgivings about using her as revenge on Jeremy and for freeing Boone. She was young, innocent, and deserved more than Damion could offer her these next few weeks. And yet, she was the one element of surprise that would baffle the British. If anyone could ensure the success of this mission, it was Andrea. Without her, Damion would have to recruit an entire militia and a wagonload of ammunition.

Somehow he would find a way to repay her, he vowed, as his eyes lifted to the myriad of stars that sprinkled across the black sky. When this ordeal was over she could name her own price. He would see to it that she wanted for nothing when he deposited her in Jeremy's hands . . . *if* he could return her alive and well. Damion heaved a frustrated sigh. The price the

British had put on Damion Montclaire's head would be little or nothing compared to the fury he could expect from Jeremy if his precious daughter was harmed. Lord, Damion would prefer to sacrifice himself to the redcoats rather than face Jeremy empty-handed.

"What the hell . . ."

Damion's head swiveled around when he heard the helmsman gasp, his keen eyes sweeping the deck.

"Damn!" Damion was frozen to the spot, his gaze glued to the silhouette that was waltzing along the railing beam.

Andrea's laughter splattered across the deck as she stared out across the moonlit waves and walked the fine line between falling overboard and remaining safe aboard the schooner.

Damion felt his heart come to a screeching halt as her foot slid off the edge of the beam, and then it began to hammer furiously against his chest as she caught herself and continued on her precarious stroll. He moved toward her, afraid to startle her, and itching to thrash her for disobeying him. Damn that mischievous little minx. Instead of curling up in bed to sleep off her overindulgence of brandy, she was parading across the railing as if she were walking a tightrope. Each step she took left her dangerously close to toppling from her perch to plunge into the sea. Had she lost every ounce of sense she possessed?

Cautiously, he approached her. "Andrea, come down from there before you become the sharks' evening meal," he commanded, attempting to keep a tight rein on his temper.

Andrea tossed her head and stared down to the hard frown on Damion's face. He reminded her of the Rock of Gibralter, cold, solid, and unyielding. But in her present state, his glares bounced off without leaving a mark.

"Nay. Have no fear, *Capitaine*. I can fly," she insisted as she flapped her arms and then giggled giddily. It was as if she could spread her wings and skim across the water like a butterfly, gliding on the breeze and soaring toward the distant stars.

Lord, this was all he needed on top of all else, Damion grumbled under his breath. Andrea was feeling the effects of the brandy, suffering delusions of grandeur, making a fool of herself, and risking a fall into the sea. Jeremy would be hopping mad if he learned about this, Damion thought to himself.

"Then why don't you flutter down here beside me, *cherie?*" he coaxed, trying to keep the irritation from seeping into his voice. "Christ!" He involuntarily closed his eyes when she lost her footing again and waved her arms in an effort to keep her balance. He was certain he would hear the splash as she hit the water to disappear in the murky depths. After a breathless moment, he pried one eye open, relieved to see that she had miraculously maintained her balance. It was obvious that her guardian angel had not taken the evening off; otherwise, she would be swallowing an ocean of water at this very moment.

"Come join me, *Capitaine*," she insisted as she weaved along the rail, making Damion quicken his step to stay beside her.

Damion was a bundle of twitching nerves, certain he was to become a groom and widower all in the same evening if she didn't guard her step and quit prancing about the beam as if no harm could come to her. Finally, his frustrations got the best of him.

"Get down from there, you little fool," he ground out.

Andrea merely chuckled at him and sauntered on her way, but she squealed as his hand snaked out to grasp her ankle, leaving her teetering on the beam. Damion dragged her leg toward him and then braced himself as she fell uncerimoniously into his outstretched arms. He was set to rake her over the coals for scaring ten years off his life, but she was wearing such a silly grin that he chortled in spite of himself.

"You scared the wits from he," he confessed, exhaling a sigh of relief.

Andrea wormed from his arms and aimed herself toward the mast above the helm. "Leave me be, sir. I am enjoying myself. I think I should like to see the world from the crow's nest."

Damion rolled his eyes and hurried his step to whisk her up in his arms before she could scramble up the mast. "Why don't you save that journey until daylight. The view is much better. I think it would be wise for you to sleep off your brandy, madame, before it gets the best of you."

Her lip jutted out in an exaggerated pout." I don't want to sleep and I am not drunk," she assured him thickly.

If she wasn't, he would eat his hat, he muttered under his breath. What had he done to deserve this, he asked himself. All he wanted was to free Boone and deliver Jeremy's daughter to him. He never dreamed he would have to wade through hell first. Damn, but this spitfire was worth her weight in trouble.

Stratton backed against the companionway when he saw the captain marching toward him, carrying Andrea who was still squirming for freedom.

"Are you having difficulty this evening, Captain?" Stratton inquired, an amused smile playing on his lips.

"Aye, an armload of it," Damion assured Stratton as he brushed past him and took the distance to his cabin in swift, impatient strides.

When he had kicked the door shut with his boot heel, he stalked over to toss Andrea on the bed, leaving her head spinning. After her stomach settled she tried to roll to her feet, but Damion pounced on her, pinning her to the cot.

"You are going to bed if I have to tie you in it!" he growled down into her face.

"I refuse to sleep with you." Andrea informed him, undaunted by the black look that was plastered on his face.

" 'Tis our wedding night," he reminded her sternly. "And I demand my husbandly rights!"

Andrea ceased her struggles, becoming relaxed beneath his vicelike grip. "And you will be granted them when hell freezes over." Her voice was quiet, but there was a hint of bridled fury wavering in it.

Heaving an exasperated sigh, Damion sank down on her belly to keep her from eluding him. "I do not understand you. You possess a passion, the likes I have never known, and yet you would deny both of us the pleasure we could share." He shook his raven head and then stared at her. "I have generously offered you my name, half my fortune, and an adventure that most women can only dream about. I have never asked another woman to be my wife, although I could name a few who would gladly claim your position," he added. There was no arrogance in his voice. It was only a bland statement

163

of fact. "What is it you want from me? I have given you all I can possible give?"

Andrea sniffed distastefully and then shoved him away, sending him sprawling. "Your name means nothing to me since you are blessed with several of them. I have no need of your fortune and this mislabeled adventure to which you refer could very well cost me my life. I would eagerly forfeit the title of your wife to the first woman who comes along." Her expression mellowed as she stared across the room, trying to focus on some distant point. "You offer me all that *you* deem important, but you cannot give me what I desire. I would have married for love, that special attachment that my mother and father shared."

"Was it so perfect?" Damion's tone was soft and inquiring as he measured her with his eyes.

"Aye." She was not to be put off. She demanded a response, and he was not going to weasel out by sidetracking her. "Can you offer your love and your heart?"

Damion gave his head a denying shake, his face stone-cold sober. "I will offer passion until you wish no more of it. But love?" He laughed cynically. "Nay, I will not forfeit my heart to a woman like you who would feed it to the wolves. I have seen a woman choke a man's will to live, and I have watched Jeremy wallow in unrequited love for too many years. I will not be the victim of that trap. To bare one's heart invites pain."

Andrea propped herself up, her hand bolding her head, and stared quizzically at Damion. "Who was she?" She had sensed a sadness in Jeremy, but until now, she had been unaware of its cause. "Tell me about her," she urged, casting aside her irritation with Damion to appease her curiosity.

When she looked up at him with those gentle pools of indigo that were flecked with gold, it reminded him of sunrays glistening on the sea. He was seeing Jeremy, reliving a lifetime in a split second. Damion smiled tenderly as he eased back on the pillow and stared up at the ceiling.

"She was a woman of rare beauty, a fragile flower who could not survive the harshness of the wilds. And she knew Jeremy well, realizing that her love would only tie him down to a life that would leave him restless. Jeremy was a wanderer who could never put down roots, and she could not follow him into the unknown, nor could she be content to await his return, spending a few cherished moments with him before he left her again. She was not as daring as you, *cherie*." His gaze slid to Andrea whose eyelids were beginning to droop after her excursion on deck and the numbing effects of the brandy. "All she could share with him was the memory of a forbidden love. They could not claim the future and they both lived, tied to the past. She let him go, knowing that it was best for both of them. Neither could survive in the other's world, but Jeremy has never forgotten her, and her memory will not allow him to find comfort elsewhere. Jeremy never mentions her name, but I know she lives in his heart, haunting him when the lonely nights close in on him."

Andrea was spellbound by the story he related and by Damion's quiet voice. Like a small child seeking comfort, she curled up beside him, resting her head on his shoulder. Jeremy had suffered greatly, she mused. Pity clouded her eyes and she tried to blink it away, but a tear managed to escape and trickle down her cheek.

"Life can be cruel to those who dare to love and

loose," she murmured and then muffled a sniff.

"*C'est vrai*," he agreed, as he laid his arm around her shoulder and frowned thoughtfully. "I have no desire to endure Jeremy's misery, nor do I wish to hurt you. We have much in common, but we cannot expect more than the moment. We are in the middle of a war, and life is too uncertain to depend on tomorrow. We must take each day as it comes, accepting what little happiness is thrown our way and overcoming the sorrow."

Andrea nodded mutely and then leaned back as far as his encircling arm would allow to peer up at him. Her thoughts stumbled as her eyes flooded over him. He was the essence of virility, and there was nothing about him that invited criticism, nor did she take the time to seek out flaws. The craggy featured of his face were hardened by nature's forces, the sun bronzing his skin to a rich golden brown. The wind had given a rough texture to the crow's feet that sprayed from the corners of those captivating silver-gray eyes. The rain and snow had eroded paths along the corners of his mouth, erasing any signs of gentleness. But within that calloused shell was a softer man who could comfort and appease, even displaying tenderness when it met his mood.

That was what had drawn her to him even before she met the man Jeremy had often described, she thought, as she reached out to follow the line of his jaw. He was the lion and the lamb, a powerful man of convictions and a tender lover at times.

The brandy had freed her thoughts and her tongue, and Andrea could not bite back the words that tumbled from her lips. "Damion, I must confess something to you. I love you." When he opened his mouth to protest, she gave her head a negative shake, sending her tangled hair spilling over his shoulder, and then touched her index finger to his lips to silence him. " 'Tis not because you have taught me the meaning of passion, but because of your devotion to a friend, your loyalty to your cause. You are one of one, a guiding light in the darkness, a breath of hope in a void of disillusionment. I love those strong qualities that make you wild and free. I would never seek to hold you for I know that you must answer the call of the wild. 'Tis enough that I have walked in your shadow. I ask for no more than to say that I have known you and have called you friend."

The faintest hint of a smile grazed his lips as he kissed her fingertips and then held her hand in his own. "I am not at all certain I can stoop to calling you friend after we have—"

Andrea cut him off before he reminded her of the times she had surrendered to him. "I have decided to aid in Boone's release. And when the time comes for us to go our separate ways, I will demand nothing from you. It is as you have said. I have been issued a challenge, an adventure that few women are granted. I will not complain, nor will I request more than is necessary to survive. My time and efforts will be yours until I have served your purpose. When it is done, we will go our separate ways."

Damion cocked a heavy eyebrow and observed the intoxicated beauty, wondering if she would remember any of what she said when she roused. But still he was moved by her words and her compliments. "I think perhaps the word you seek is respect rather than love," he corrected. "But do not fall in love with me. I cannot offer love."

Her reckless chuckle floated about him, tickling his

senses. "I am not a fool, Montclaire. I do not expect your love. Aye, perhaps you were right. Respect is the word I seek. I was speaking of admiration and paying homage to the qualities you possess that I desire to claim as my own." There was a hint of deviltry in her glazed eyes as she glanced up at him and grinned. "And do not fall in love with me," she advised, tossing his words back in his face. "I will never be your slave, nor am I subdued by your fiery temper. And when you do turn your back on me, it might be wise to glance over your shoulder occasionally, just to see which way my knife is pointed."

"You wouldn't dare." Damion chuckled at the intoxicated minx.

"If you give me cause I might find that my irritation overshadows my admiration, *Capitaine* Montclaire." Andrea sighed heavily. Her bout with the brandy was beginning to catch up with her. She lost interest in taunting Damion and let her lashes flutter down against her cheeks for a moment's rest.

Damion chuckled again. "Then I am never to know if you are friend or foe, vixen. 'Tis a pity that I do not have a pair of eyes in the back of my head so that I can keep a constant vigil on you."

A long silent moment passed as she nestled against his arm, and Damion found himself bored with conversation. The feel of her shapely body cuddled up against his was having an arousing effect on him.

"Since this is our wedding night, I think we should call a truce," he murmured against her ear as his hand trailed across her thigh.

A frown creased his brows when his caress spurred no reaction. Had he lost his touch, he wondered, as he withdrew to peer at Andrea. Damn, the little imp was sound asleep. His wedding night? Damion grunted disgustedly. Andrea had taken a stroll on the railing of the schooner for her amusement and then fell fast asleep in his arms when he finally got her into bed. As far as he was concerned, wedding nights were not all they were cracked up to be. This day would be one he remembered, but not with fondness. He had dragged her to the alter, twisted her arm to force her to say the vows, and then allowed her to fall asleep before he could ease the hunger that was eating him alive.

A reluctant smile touched his lips as he studied her perfect features that were so soft in repose. She was the combination of Laura and Jeremy, he mused pensively. He could begin to understand the deep feeling Jeremy held for Laura. It was like drowning in a sea of emotions and being unable to catch a breath before being swept into the undercurrents.

Damion felt disappointed that she had laughed in his face when he warned her not to fall in love with him. Aye, he did not want to hurt this lovely lass, but she didn't have to appear so unconcerned. Damion rolled his eyes at the direction of his thoughts. What *did* he expect from Andrea? Why did he feel this fierce urge to hold her close when she had made it clear that she did not want to share his name or his bed? Dammit, he scowled, as he fluffed his pillow and sought a more comfortable position. He ached to satisfy the craving that had gnawed at him since that afternoon, one that had left him content for a time but never pacified.

He heaved an agitated sigh and forced his eyes shut, trying not to think, but the vision of that shapely lass walking on the railing kept creeping into his mind, bringing an unwanted smile to his lips. She was far too daring for her own good and far too tempting for his. Although she had managed to burrow into his heart, Damion was doing his damnedest to route her. He had no time for lasting affairs, he told himself. Their marriage was temporary, as was his lust for her. The feelings that tugged at his heart would fade when she had been delivered to Jeremy. And then he would be free once again to pursue any wench who caught his eye.

Andrea groaned miserably as she lifted heavily lidded eyes to the sunlight that sprinkled through the porthole. Her groggy gaze came to rest on Damion who had edged a hip on the desk and had been watching her sleep.

"Good morning."

His cheerful tone did not brighten her mood. "Is it?" The sound of her own voice rattled about her head as if someone had blown a bugle in her ear and she grimaced at the vibrations.

A low chuckle erupted from his chest as he studied her distraught expression. "Are you under the weather this morning, madame?" he inquired, his tone lacking in concern. "I warned you to avoid overindulging in brandy, but you paid me no heed."

Andrea attempted to force herself into an upright position, but every muscle in her body rebelled, and she sank back to her pillow, the color seeping from her face.

"In the future I will take your advice to heart," she murmured over the lump of nausea that had risen in her throat.

His dark brow quirked as he swaggered toward her. "Since you chose not to rouse from bed, I must assume that 'tis your invitation for me to join you."

Mustering her strength Andrea dragged herself up, assuring him that a tumble in bed was the *last* thing she wanted or needed.

"I don't think any doctor would prescribe lovemaking as a cure for a hangover." She shot him a frown and then hauled herself to her feet, only to find the room swimming about her.

As she wilted, Damion hurried to her side to steady her and then gestured toward the table. "Then perhaps a cup of tea would be more to your liking."

It took a great deal of effort not to chuckle at her misery. She looked a sight. Her blond hair was in tangles, her features were as white as the sheet, and her eyes were as streaked as a map. And yet, she was still the most attractive woman he had ever laid eyes on. How could she be so appealing when she was at her worst?

Andrea sank down in her chair and stared into her cup, vowing to herself that she would avoid liquor entirely. The side effects of drinking were hardly worth the price she was paying that morning.

"Andrea . . . about last night." Damion cleared his throat and then offered her a faint smile.

"What about last night?" she prompted, eyeing him warily. Had she surrendered in a moment of weakness. Andrea gulped hard, hanging on the edge of the chair to hear his reply.

"You don't remember?" Damion braced his arms on the table, his smile spreading to encompass all his rugged features.

She picked up her cup and glanced at him from over the rim, trying to remain calm and aloof. "Of course I remember. I drank myself senseless, you told me about

Jeremy, and then I must have fallen asleep." A thoughtful frown creased her brow as a hazy memory cropped up in her mind. "But I had the strangest dream. For some reason I thought I was flying."

Damion chuckled and then eased back in his seat. " 'Twas no dream, my little butterfly. You fluttered across the railing and for several minutes I wondered if you were high enough to scrape the moon. You were very confident that you could indeed fly."

Andrea choked on her tea and sputtered to catch her breath. "What?" Had she done that? Lord, she must have appeared the utter fool!

He nodded affirmatively as he leaned over to whack her on the back, practically knocking her forward into her teacup. "Aye, my dear, but I think that sharing my bed would have been less dangerous than your daredevil stroll in the moonlight."

Her jaw swung from its hinges as she peered up at his amused smile. When she had collected her unraveled composure, she stared at the opposite wall. "Nay, I think I made the correct choice," she sniffed.

His fist hit the table, sloshing tea down the sides of his cup to soak into the tablecloth. "Dammit, woman. You are my wife and I intend that you share my bed!" he growled, his temper getting the best of him.

Damion had planned to gently coax her into his bed that morning and to smooth out the differences between them, but Andrea infuriated him with her sarcastic remark. Damnation, even all the liquor she had consumed could not mellow that chit's stubborness. She seemed to have her heart set on making his life miserable. Marriage! What a disasterous institution and, like a fool, he had paid his dues and become a member. And for what? he asked himself disgustedly.

"I am your wife in name only," Andrea shouted back at him and then regretted her outburst. Loud noises were agony on her sensitive head.

Damion bolted to his feet and stalked toward the door. "I wish I would have had the good sense to leave you with Captain Stephens," he muttered sourly.

"I wish you would have, too," she agreed in a softer tone.

He wheeled to face her, his gaze locking with hers. "You are avoiding the inevitable, Andrea. You will never be my wife in name only. I will receive more for my troubles than a document of marriage and an empty bed."

As he slammed the door behind him Andrea held her pounding head in both hands, uncertain which was worse: the misery of a hangover or the agony of being married to a man like Damion Montclaire. Both were painful experiences that she wished she could have avoided entirely.

## Chapter Eight

The journey back to Martin's Fork was long and troubled for William. The message he had received from Captain Montclaire was vague. It merely stated that Melissa's services were required for the good of the colonies and that she would be returned when she had completed her mission. Unfortunately, Montclaire's assurance did little to ease his worries. He knew nothing of the man and only had his word that his daughter was unharmed. After inquiring about Montclaire, William had learned that the mysterious renegade tormented the British along the coast. That information had played havoc with his thoughts. What did Montclaire intend to do with Melissa? Why was she singled out and how did the privateer know about Melissa?

William impatiently drummed his fingers on his knees and peered out the window to see the settlement in the distance. He breathed a relieved sigh when the carriage came to a halt. William went directly to Jeremy's home, feeling like a bubble that was about to burst. He had to talk to someone.

William planted himself in the chair Jeremy offered to him, guzzled his brandy, and exhaled, as if he had been holding his breath since he had left Norfolk.

"Melissa will not be going to France," he announced, his voice trembling slightly. William extracted the letter from his vest pocket and presented it to Jeremy. "I don't know what to make of this. I am reluctant to take the word of a man I have never met."

A wry smile crept to Jeremy's lips as he read the message, noting the signature at the bottom of the parchment. "I have met this Captain Montclaire," he informed Stoddard. "I am sure that whatever the mission, he will see to Melissa's safety. I wouldn't worry about her." His gaze lifted to William's distraught frown. "I am relieved that she isn't traveling to France. I was opposed to it in the first place."

"Aye, I'm aware of that, but I have yet to understand your reason. You know Melissa has no future in Martin's Fork." William squirmed uncomfortably in his chair and chased his first glass of brandy with a second. "She would have been away from the skirmishes that are moving in our direction. She could have been safely tucked away until all this fighting is over. And now where is she? Perhaps in the middle of a battle, for all we know. How the hell do I know what is going on?" William bolted to his feet and paced the room, his stride stiff and restless. "A man and his family are no longer safe. Even traveling to Norfolk was hazardous. First I was a Tory sympathizer and then a Whig. I practically had to lie my way across Virginia and back. The next thing we know those damned redcoats will be pounding on our doors, rummaging through our

175

homes. The Indians have been our only concern until now. There is no peace to be had in the colonies." William threw up his arms and let them drop to his sides. "Now 'tis the redcoats! Damn the lot of them!"

"William calm down," Jeremy coaxed as he directed William back to his chair and pushed another drink into his hand. "You are exhausted from your journey and upset about Melissa. The British have little concern for us. They are interested in the coastal cities, Philadelphia, New York, and Boston. They are not trained for the wilderness. Besides," he added with a nonchalant shrug, "they have little use for the backwoods. We have nothing to fear from their troops. We barely manage to blaze trails. Why would a handful of soldiers wish to seize the wilderness that they believe to be colonized by misfits and scoundrels?" Jeremy produced an encouraging smile as he poured them both another drink. "Nay, William, there will be no soldiers loitering in your sitting room. Men like Beaugener, Marion, and Sumter will not allow that to happen. Our greatest fear still comes at the hands of the Indians. The British have persuaded them to push us back from the western territories."

William took a long sip and then carefully scrutinized Jeremy's face which was marred with scars from his narrow escape from death. Jeremy was a man of conviction whose spirit would never be subdued by physical limitations. If it came to protecting the settlement from attack, Jeremy would be standing beside those who were more capable of defending their homes, no matter what the consequences to himself. And throughout their years together, William had come to call him friend because of his noble qualities.

Although Drieson had suffered more than most, he had not become bitter because of his trials.

He and Jeremy had grown old together, and much wiser. It wasn't difficult to understand why Laura had been so fond of Jeremy. She had made William promise that Melissa would have the opportunity to profit from the man's friendship. William had first resented Laura's plea that she had made just before she died, but over the years, his animosity had been forgotten. Laura had been right. Melissa deserved to know what a special man Jeremy was.

"I suppose you have a point," Stoddard replied, nodding thoughtfully. "I don't expect to be feeding the redcoats, but this business with Melissa is upsetting. I'm sure Lelia will also be distressed when she arrives to meet the ship and finds that Melissa is not on it. My letter will arrive too late to keep her from worrying, but there is naught else to do about it." As he rose to his feet, he let his gaze slide back to his crippled friend. "Join me for supper tonight," he requested, forcing a feeble smile. "I have a feeling I will be calling on you for companionship quite often until Melissa returns. The table will be empty without her, as will the whole damned house. Perhaps you can cheer me when my spirits hit rock bottom." William didn't bother to add that they already had.

Jeremy watched William stroll to the door, trying to maintain his reassuring smile. When William was out of sight, a troubled frown creased his marred features. If Zack was planning to free Boone with Melissa by his side, they were both treading on dangerous ground. What the hell could Zack be thinking of? Why would he expose Melissa to such a precarious crusade? Revenge, came the quick answer. It was his retaliation for the trap Jeremy had set for him. Had he been so infuriated that he had taken Melissa for spite? Jeremy's eyes were burning an angry blue flame as he clutched at his cane until his knuckles turned white. If Melissa was not returned unharmed, Zack would have hell to pay. But, of course, Beaugener knew that, Jeremy thought to himself. If anything happened to Melissa, Jeremy doubted that Zack would make the effort to see him again. Zack would know better than to show his face in the settlement. Jeremy would have his carcass on a platter, roasted and carved, if this ridiculous notion met with catastrophy. By damned, he would track Zack down, even if it took the next one hundred years!

Jeremy raked his fingers through his hair, heaving an exaspirated sigh. How could he keep Stoddard from being concerned when he was overwrought with worry himself? Damn! This was all his fault. He should never have sent Zack to track down Melissa. He should have allowed her to return in her own good time. His meddling had caused her misery. That was not what he intended. Jeremy took a large gulp of brandy, but it did not cool his irritation. He stared at the opposite wall, seeing nothing except a pair of haunting gray eyes.

"Wherever you are, Zackery Montclaire Beaugener, you damned well better know what you're doing or I swear I will make you rue the day you were born," he muttered to the looming figure that hovered in his thoughts.

178

Without informing Andrea of his meeting with Sumter, Damion left their hotel room with nothing more than, "Behave yourself. I will be back later."

Andrea had spent too many days on the schooner's confining decks to keep to her room. With her coat tucked tightly about her, she took to the streets of Baltimore, intent on familiarizing herself with the city.

It was late afternoon when she returned to the hotel, her face beaming with pleasure. The enjoyment of the day evaporated when she met Damion's dark scowl. His hand clamped around her wrist, and she found herself whisked up the stairs, shoved into the room, and pinned to the wall.

Damion towered over her like a fire-breathing dragon, the spines on his back bristling angrily. His gray eyes smoldered with rage, his features like molten rock. Melissa was reminded of a volcano that was about to erupt. When the twitch in his cheek rippled across his face like a warning tremor, she knew he would surely explode. She stood wide-eyed, wondering what she could possibly have done to deserve this harsh treatment. But she was not allowed to voice her question because Damion fired one at her first.

"Just where the hell have you been all day?" he growled as he leaned toward her, his face only inches from hers, his gaze piercing her with its intensity.

Andrea peered incredulously at him. Surely he wasn't upset because she had left the room. "I went sightseeing," she answered, her brows furrowing slightly. "What is wrong with you?"

"What is wrong with *me?*" he repeated caustically. Damn, he was tempted to slap that innocent look off her face. "What the hell is wrong with *you,* madame?

179

You do not venture out for the entire day without leaving me a message. I have spent the afternoon trying to find you." His eyes narrowed to cold, hard slits, his lips curling in a menacing sneer. "Did you find yourself a new lover and persuade him to help you escape from me or have you turned traitor and informed the British that Montclaire is alive and well and staying in the hotel?"

Andrea gasped in indignation, his hateful tone bringing her temper to a rolling boil. "I do not need your permission to leave this room. How dare you even think that I would *ask* for your permission! You are not my father and I do not have to answer to you." Andrea drew an angry breath and returned his penetrating glare. "I had no intention of escaping. I gave you my word. You have no reason to doubt me."

"And I have no reason to trust you either," he defended, his tone as sharp as hers.

"I swear you would doubt your own mother. You, Montclaire, are the most exaspirating man I have ever met!"

"You are right," he assured her gruffly. "I don't trust my own mother and I am suspicious from habit. Now where were you?"

Her chin tilted to a proud angle. "If I wanted to search for another man with whom to wallow away the hours while you left me alone, that is *my* business. You said yourself that this marriage was made to appease Jeremy. You also informed me that you expected me to bed every British soldier in Detroit if it served your purpose," she reminded him, her voice resounding about them like a thundering cannon.

Damion clamped his hand over her mouth. "Dammit, be quiet!" he hissed. "Do you want everyone in the hotel to know our plans?"

Andrea tore his hand from her face, flaming indigo locking with smoldering silver sparks that tried to splinter her confidence. "Is that not what you said?" she persisted, gritting her teeth to keep from shouting the walls down around them.

"Aye, I said that but—"

"But nothing." She cut him short. "Those were the terms you offered and the ones I accepted. I owe you no explanation except that I told no one of our mission and that I made no effort to flee. I assured you that I would help you. What do you want, my signature in blood?" Her cheeks flushed in irritation. He was scolding her like a disobedient child and she would not stand for it.

"Then you *did* meet someone this afternoon," he concluded, sending her an accusing glower.

"I will answer to you only when it pertains to the mission. The rest of my life is my concern and you will not pry into it." Andrea tore his hand from her arm and put a greater distance between them. "I think we have said enough on the subject and I would appreciate it if you would stop harassing me." Andrea stalked to the bureau, grabbed her brush, and tried to arrange the neat bun that had tumbled over her shoulder after Damion's rough handling.

"You told me that you would do as I commanded without question or complaint," he reminded her, and then snorted derisively. "So much for broken vows and empty promises. How can I begin to trust you when I am never certain if you are planning to stab me in the back when my head is turned?"

Andrea slammed her brush down and wheeled to face him. "I agreed not to complain and to follow your orders, but I said nothing about backing cowardly away from arguments, especially when I have been unjustly accused of treachery and treason." She leveled him a gaze that would have severed an average man's head from his neck, but Montclaire's remained intact, much to her dismay. "If I choose to carve up your calloused hide, you will see it coming. My mark will be your cold heart and I have decided to cut it from your chest, *not* from your back." She took a bold step toward him, resting her hands on her hips. "I could not stand to be cooped up in this stuffy room, twiddling my thumbs while you were out." Her gaze narrowed, eyeing him accusingly. "And just how do I know that you were not out seeking your pleasure with some wench?"

"Would you have cared, madame?" he queried as he shrugged off his blue linen shirt and cast her a sidelong glance.

"Not in the least," she assured him, her chin tilting higher. "I have no intention of manipulating your life."

"My, my," Damion mocked dryly. "Perhaps I do not fully appreciate my good fortune. I wonder if all men are blessed with such understanding and permissive wives."

"I wouldn't know," she said disinterestedly, her attention focused on one honeyed strand that refused to stay in the bun on top of her head.

"And then again, perhaps I am the one who deserves sympathy. No one else would endure your tirade of insults and violent fits of temper," he mused aloud as he donned a fresh white shirt.

Andrea slowly turned to face him, a sticky sweet

smile glazing her lips. "I tried to avoid this mock marriage and even stooped to making an unexcusable scene in front of that poor preacher. You cannot blame me for your misfortune, *my dear husband*." The title strongly resembled a curse when it floated from her tongue. "As I recall, you dragged me into wedlock, kicking and screaming."

"And I have your . . . " Damion swallowed the next word before it escaped his lips. He had begun to think of Jeremy as her father and again, he had very nearly blurted out the truth without giving it a second thought. He would have to guard his tongue or he would let that information slip out. "Your dear friend and mine, Jeremy, to thank for my suffering," he finished lamely. "Shall we go downstairs for supper now, madame?"

"*Mais oui*, monsieur," Andrea sorted through her repetoire of smiles and presented him with a very mischievous one. "I am starved after my secret rendezvous this afternoon," she purred as she curled her hand around the arm Damion offered to her.

Damion flicked the end of her upturned nose. "Perhaps this vixen is hungry for her husband's attention if her mysterious lover was unable to appease her craving."

"Don't look so smug," she warned. "There are many men who possess your ability to satisfy a woman's desires."

"Are you speaking from experience?" His gaze was more skeptical than curious.

A hint of deviltry sparkled in her eyes. "Give me time, monsieur. I have only begun my search. If you like, I will keep a record of all my excursions and give you a full account of the details."

Damion opened the door, bowed before her, and then gestured for her to step in front of him. "You do that, my dear," he smirked. "I am most anxious to know just where I stand in your long line of suitors."

Andrea paused, throwing a provocative smile over her shoulder. "My suitors will not be standing," she assured him saucily before sauntering down the hall.

Damion rolled his eyes and closed the door behind him. "Touché, madame. I do enjoy fencing words with you. You are as witty as you are beautiful." He hurried his pace to catch up to her, lifted her hand to press a kiss to her wrist, and then flashed her a smile.

Andrea returned his blinding smile with a feminine finesse that swept away Damion's lingering doubts that she could not outmaneuver the redcoats. "And you are as handsome as you are exasperating," she retorted in a honeyed tone.

After they dined, Damion offered to take Andrea for a stroll. As they ambled along the boardwalk, Andrea came to life, dancing gaily about him, tugging on his arm when she saw something in store windows that caught her eye. Damion found himself smiling down at her for no particular reason except that her light-hearted mood was contagious. Andrea was delightful company and the more time he spent with her, the less difficult it was for him to accept the fact that they were man and wife . . . at least for a time. When Jeremy had sprung his little surprise on Damion it burned him to the quick. But the thought had not been so disturbing once the vows were made. The dread of taking his medicine was far worse than actually swallowing it, he mused with a secretive smile playing on his lips. Perhaps it was that he had grown accustomed to the idea, or maybe it was because Andrea had protested so fiercely that made him determined to see the deed done. Whatever the reason, Damion had married her. But at least he had compromised by using his alias. Jeremy would not be pleased, but dammit, he had to compromise, too.

His thoughts circled back to Andrea's disappearance that afternoon. And he could not help but wonder if indeed she had found someone to take his place. The thought of Marie turning to another man did not annoy him. He was aware that she did not spend the long months alone while he was away. But the idea of Andrea accepting another man's caressess spurred a strange jealousy within him. It was his pride that was being twisted, he convinced himself. He would never admit that the image of Andrea in another man's arms distressed him. How could he? He had allowed her that privilege, hadn't he? And he planned to exercise his freedom when another wench caught his eye. Unfortunately, spending time with Andrea, learning her moods, seeing her strengths, and even doing battle with her left other women sorely lacking. The more he discovered about her, the tighter he became entangled in her web. When she was out of sight, she would be out of mind, Damion told himself. It was only that she was convenient and he had been starved for affection after his expedition with Boone. He had paid his dues to Jeremy and after Boone was free, he would take her home, leaving her behind without regret.

With that determined thought milling through his mind, Damion gazed down at the angelic face beside him and then wished he hadn't. Just peering into those perfect features and sparkling indigo eyes sent his mind off on the wrong track, arousing him all over again. She was like an infection that had spread through his body, and he would have to be patient, waiting for his affliction to run its course. But now she was his poison and also his cure. Damion rolled his eyes and muttered to himself. The fever of desire was beginning to contaminate his thinking. If he didn't get a grip on himself, he would be as mad as Andrea had accused him of being.

Andrea puttered nervously about their room, packing and repacking her belongings for their cross-country journey while Damion lay propped in the middle of the bed. He watched her pace the floor until she had him squirming uncomfortably.

"Andrea, come sit down," he ordered.

"Nay, I can't," she informed him as she wrung her hands and chewed on her bottom lip, mentally checking her list of supplies.

"Then come lie down beside me and relax a bit. You are making me uneasy jest watching you wear out the rug." There was a suggestive flicker in his eyes, and Andrea stopped her pacing to cast him a wary glance.

She had not allowed him near her since the day he had taken her from Stephens's ship. She had countered his amorous assaults and had refused to join him in bed until he was asleep. It had been difficult to avoid him, but she had managed, afraid she would surrender to her weakness if she allowed him within ten feet of her.

"We will be leaving soon and . . . " she fumbled in

excuse.

"Come here," he demanded, his brows forming a firm line over his smoky gray eyes. "You agreed to obey my commands."

"Only the ones pertaining to business." She reminded him of the stipulation she had placed on their bargain and eyed him with mistrust. "I have the feeling that business is not what you have on your mind."

Damion rolled to his feet to snuff the lantern and then imprisoned her in his arms. "We will be spending several weeks without privacy, sleeping on the ground, stealing a few moments of rest where we can find them. I do not intend to waste this feather mattress. It has been a long time, *cherie*," he murmured, his lips playing persuasively on hers. "Do not deny me. I have tried to be patient with you and I have not forced myself on you, even though I have been sorely tempted each night."

Hesitantly, she looped her arms around his neck and then found that she was grateful to have something to occupy her thoughts besides the upcoming journey. When the spark of passion leaped between them, she drew a shuddering breath, wishing she had kept her distance from the one man who had the power to stir the emotions she had so carefully held in check. She had feared his touch and now she remembered why. She had a weakness for this silver-eyed rogue, and once she surrendered to those compelling sensations, all was lost. Her body had suddenly acquired a mind of its own, urging her to yield to the taste of his skillful kisses and caresses.

Andrea's initial reluctance made him draw back as a troubled thought struck a sensitive nerve. "Or perhaps once a day is enough to satisfy you," he speculated, his voice tight. "Am I to receive only the leftovers of your affection?"

A wicked chortle drifted from her lips as she toyed with the ebony hair that curled about his collar. "My, but you are inquisitive. I thought you were the man who had little concern about where he quenched his desire or with whom. Now, do you wish to kiss me or interrogate me?" The raspiness in her voice sent an unwanted tingle skitting across his skin.

"You don't plan to tell me the truth, do you?" he muttered as his hand slid from her waist to the back of her gown to loosen the stays.

*"Mon capitaine,* it worries me that you are so concerned about the incident," she taunted, her finger provocatively tracing the sensuous curve of his lips. "Could it be that you are jealous, or does it prick your inflated ego that I might have found pleasure that surpasses your caresses in another man's arms?"

As the gown fell to the floor in a reckless heap, Andrea reached up to draw his face to hers, but Damion pulled her arms away, as if annoyed with the physical contact.

"I demand to know what you did this afternoon and with whom," he insisted, his voice rising testily. Her teasing remarks were creeping beneath his skin. The more he thought about it, the more annoyed he became. "You are my wife and I have a right to know what you were doing."

A seductive smile played on her lips as she lifted the chemise and carelessly discarded it. As she began unbuttoning his shirt, her hands brushed over the dark matting of hair on his chest. "I will be happy to give you a detailed account of my activities, if that is what you wish. But as you said, our time is limited and we shall have very few moments to claim as our own once we leave our room."

As the moonlight stretched across the floor, capturing her in its silvery glow, Damion caught his breath, unable to drag his eyes off the tempting sight. It was as if he were staring at a cherished picture he hadn't seen in years: so captivating, so compelling. At the moment, he didn't give a damn how many men she had taken to her bed. All that he knew was that he wanted her.

"Damn, you ornery little witch," he mumbled, his tone more affectionate than his words. "You are becoming a proficient temptress."

Andrea slipped the shirt from his shoulders, her gaze locked with his. "I had an excellent instructor," she whispered, her voice raspy and alluring. " 'Twas you who taught me how to get what I want."

Damion could not resist the feel of her flesh molded to his. She knew how to make his skin quiver with anticipation, his body ache with need. Andrea could torment his thoughts, making him yearn to lose touch with reality for a timeless moment. He swept her up in his arms and carried her to the bed. As he stretched out beside her, he caressed each tempting curve and swell, memorizing the feel of her satiny skin beneath his hands.

Their time together would become stolen moments, and he wanted to remember this night. Damion was obsessed with taking her with him to sensuous heights of pleasure, making the memory one that would sustain him on the nights when he would have to be content watching her from afar.

"You have a bewitching way of making me forget that Boone requires our assistance," he murmured, his voice drugged with passion as he nuzzled against the hollow of her neck. "And perhaps I was jealous." His admission was so quiet that Andrea had to strain to catch his words. "I want no other man to discover your passions."

Andrea chortled softly as she traced the deeply inbedded crow's-feet around his eyes. "No one has, except you . . . not yet," she added, leaving her remark open-ended. She was too proud to admit that he was the only man who made her burn with desire.

"Witch," he murmured, a teasing smile brimming his lips as he hooked his arm around her waist and lowered his head to taste her lips.

When their breath intermingled as one, the beat of their hearts raced in anticipation. The playfulness was gone, replaced by a need that begged for fulfillment. His kiss became more demanding, roughly insistent, silently requesting and receiving a response. Andrea wrapped her arms about his neck, drawing him to her, unable to get close enough to the fire that burned her inside and out. And then her heart was doing somersaults against her ribs. She felt the world sliding out from underneath her. As his caresses touched and aroused each sensitive point on her body, a surrendering moan escaped her lips. She was helplessly drifting, savoring the sensations that tore at her sanity.

Damion lifted himself above her, his gaze penetrating her with a desire that glowed like smoldering silver. "I need you," he whispered raggedly.

As his mouth devoured hers, the quiet knock at the

door brought them back in touch with reality. Damion muttered under his breath as he dragged himself away from her, his eyes touching her like a caress. He felt as if a team of horses had been hooked to each leg to gallop off in opposite directions, tearing him in two.

With a great deal of reluctance, he rolled to his feet and donned his breeches.

"Who is it?" he questioned quietly.

"Heston. We are ready to leave," came the hushed reply from the other side of the door.

"We will be down in a minute," Damion assured him as his gaze circled back to Andrea.

As she edged up on the bed Damion closed the distance between them and drew her to her feet. "Another time. . . . " He let his words hang in midair as Andrea raised parted lips to him.

Their embrace spanned eternity and yet, it left an aching need that remained unappeased. Andrea heaved a quiet sigh as she donned her buckskin clothes and silently collected her belongings. How many days would pass before she could know the fulfillment of his lovemaking? When she glanced back at Damion, she had hoped to see the flicker of disappointment in his eyes, but she was met with a carefully blank stare. How she wished she could peel away his disguise to see what emotion lay beneath that cool facade. Did he ache with the same desire that continued to tear at her thoughts? Andrea tried to discard her musings as they slipped down the back stairs, but she kept seeing Damion's face above hers, his gaze holding a promise of an intimacy that always sent her spirit soaring. Determinedly, she focused her attention on the trials that lay ahead of her. There was no time to dwell on the past.

Montclaire swung into the saddle and glanced back to see Andrea sitting atop her steed, her head held high. As he nudged his steed, his gaze swept the shadows, ensuring that they were leaving in secrecy.

After several hours of riding they came upon a small British encampment and veered to the north. When they finally stopped for a few hours of sleep, Andrea climbed down from her horse, watered and fed him, before seeing to her own needs. All six men eyed her skeptically, expecting to hear a complaint, but she never uttered a discontented word. All they noticed was a tired smile as she made her bed on the ground.

Throughout the following days, the men realized that Montclaire had spoken the truth. Her ability to survive the hardships was as apparent as her natural beauty. She became an integral part of the guerrilla band, earning their respect and admiration. The meals that she prepared were highly anticipated at the end of the long days traveling. Her skills in hunting and cleaning game were a frequent part of their conversations. But Andrea took their compliments with a simple smile and a casual shrug. Even Damion found himself staring at her in admiration when she tackled some feat that he doubted she could accomplish.

He had intended to treat her just as he did his men, ignoring what they had shared in the past. He made no attempt to spend private moments with her, but the task became increasingly difficult, especially since Andrea didn't appear the least bit disappointed that she had to make her own bed and sleep in it alone.

She was living by the rules he had issued to her. It

was Damion who was reluctant to accept them. He wanted her, and yet, he wanted nothing to do with her. He despised her for being so determined and independent, but then again, he admired her courage. The fact that she was being herself upset him. All that she did began to grate on his nerves. She was so damned skillful, so relentless. Where were the whining wenches who would have begged to turn back? Where were all the fragile women who could not withstand the grueling life he had forced upon her? And where were the simple affairs that he had walked away from the past ten years without giving them a second thought?

Damion was annoyed with himself for comparing Andrea to other women, and yet, at times, he wanted her to be more like them so he could criticize her flaws. He needed to see her weaknesses, but dammit, the wench didn't have any!

Every man in camp had put her on such a high pedestal that if she fell from the lofty perch it would have broken her lovely neck. But Damion was not about to stand around gawking at her while she worked tirelessly over their meals, thinking arousing thoughts that would play havoc with his dreams. He didn't need her. He could do without her even if the rest of his men couldn't. She could sleep with every damned one of them and he could have cared less. Damn that woman! Damn that Drieson! This was all his fault! Why hadn't he refused to track her through the mountains? Damion found himself wishing he could turn back the hands of time and relive the past two months. He was a tormented man, torn by a man's needs and a man's pride, neither of which would grant him peace.

The silent war that Montclaire fought with himself

night and day had worn his patience threadbare. His face darkened with each new dawn until a permanent scowl etched his features. One glance in Andrea's direction had him cursing under his breath, damning her for being the woman that every man yearned to take in his arms and claim as his own, except Damion Montclaire, he told himself. He was invincible, a man who could master his thoughts. Damn that woman a thousand times! Every time he closed his eyes she was burrowing her way into his mind, smiling at him with the same provocative smile that hovered on her lips that night in Baltimore when the moonlight had captured her silhoutte, holding him spellbound.

Damion squirmed on the hard ground, worming his way deeper into his blankets, trying to shut out the memory of a time when he was dragged away from her willing arms.

## Chapter Nine

Within two weeks, Damion had become a tyrant who was plagued with his own twisted logic and strained emotions. Heston, who had traveled on several expeditions with Montclaire and who was two years his junior, had spent a great deal of time with Andrea. Each time she could use a helping hand, Cory was there to offer assistance. That, and the fact that Montclaire had Andrea so close without appeasing his desire for her, had darkened his black moods. Since Montclaire had avoided her, the other men became open with their intentions, although not as obvious as Heston.

Damion respected Cory. His wit was exceptional and his striking looks turned the ladies' heads. Andrea's easy acceptance of Heston's friendship irritated Damion more than he wanted to admit. Although he tried to ignore the growing attachment between them, his gaze strayed to them each time they were together.

One evening after Heston had offered to stand watch

with Andrea, Damion, who had not been able to sleep a wink, watched as they returned to camp. Cory wrapped a possessive arm around her waist and then leaned close to press a light kiss to her lips.

That was the last straw! Damion could not sit quietly by, allowing Heston to make advances toward his wife. Dammit, she had made no attempt to stop him, Damion growled to himself, as he bolted to his feet and stalked toward them.

"Heston!" he bellowed, causing every man in camp to flinch and involuntarily reach for his musket. "Take your hands off of her!"

Heston stared him straight in the eye, reluctantly dropping his arm. His gaze locked with hot silver, refusing to be intimidated by Damion's harsh command.

"What we do is none of your concern," he replied coldly. "You have made no claim on her since we left Baltimore."

"I will not have you making a fool of me," Damion assured him, his calm tone more deadly than his previous bark. "The lady is my wife."

"What?" Cory choked on his breath and then frowned suspiciously. Montclaire married? "How the hell was I supposed to know . . . "

"I give you credit for having a little sense. It seems to have been an oversight on my part," Damion retorted, his French accent dripping with sarcasm. "What is mine, I keep, Heston. Whether she is my wife or not, I expect you to keep your distance from her. She is not part of the reward for this mission."

Andrea stared at Damion, her eyes wide in disbelief. Where did he find the audacity to chastize Cory for befriending her? He was born with it, she decided, as she met his scornful glare.

"No one is playing you for a fool, Montclaire," she flared. "You have always managed to pursue that role with little prodding from anyone else."

Damiom scowled as his hand snaked out to grasp her elbow, his lean fingers applying painful pressure to the bone. "Silence! You probably encouraged him," he accused. "Perhaps you are the one who deserves punishment."

Cory grabbed Montclaire's shoulder, demanding his attention. "Nay, the lady only offered companionship," he insisted. "It was I who wanted more. You of all people should know what a special woman she is. There is not a man among us who would not wish to share her affection."

"But only you dared to make your intentions known," Damion countered, his gaze holding disdainful mockery.

"I had no idea that you had married her. Why didn't you tell us in the beginning?" he pressed, a curious frown knitting his brow. He still doubted that Damion had spoken the truth.

"Because I don't owe you or anyone else an explanation," he snapped harshly, his eyes falling to the hand that remained on his shoulder, silently ordering Cory to remove it.

When Cory backed away, Damion returned his attention to Andrea who stood stiffly beside him, her face red with rage. Damion whisked her with him to the clump of trees by the creek. When the Montclaires had disappeared Heston strolled over to his bedroll and stretched out on the ground, a disgusted sigh escaping his lips.

Stratton paused beside him, laying his musket across his arms. A wide grin split his stubbled face as he bent his gaze to Heston. "Perhaps the captain has a deeper affection for the lady than we suspected," he predicted.

"Aye. So it would seem," Heston muttered sourly as he folded his arms behind his head and stared off into space. "But I find it difficult to believe that he is so possessive of her. He has never been particular about sharing his women in the past."

"That was before he met up with Andrea. And he never married any of the others . . . until now," Stratton reminded him with a chuckle. "I always thought the captain had excellent taste."

"But I have heard Montclaire swear that marriage was not his cup of tea," Cory said thoughtfully. "It never occurred to me that he might have married this one."

"Aye," Stratton agreed with a nod. "But as I said, he did not know Andrea Deuvalle when he made that vow. She has a way of making a man forget that other women exist. I've even found myself visualizing her in my arms and I've already taken a wife."

"I tried to fulfill the same dream," Cory muttered as he rolled to his side and pulled his cap down over his forehead. "Andrea has much to offer a man, but her allegiance is to Montclaire. I knew that, but it didn't stop me from spending every available moment with her. She deserves better than him." The bitterness in his tone drew Stratton's hearty chuckle.

"Can you name a better man?" he challenged. "For once he claims something you want. Tread carefully, Heston." The amusement evaporated from his expression. "Montclaire is not a man to cross swords with.

The three of us have been together too long to end a friendship because of a woman, even one as lovely and resourceful as Andrea."

As Loren strolled away, Heston yanked the quilt around his shoulders. Stratton was right, but it didn't make forgetting Andrea any easier. He would not purposely avoid her. Cory intended to share her friendship, even if that was all it could ever be.

When Andrea was out of earshot from the rest of the men, she flung Damion's hand away and wheeled to face him, her eyes sparking rebellion. "You are despicable! How dare you accuse us of carrying on behind your back!"

"Why shouldn't I?" Damion released a derisive snort. "I saw Heston with his arm around you and I witnessed his kiss. What the hell would you have thought?"

"I didn't think you cared what I did or with whom, but if you must know, his kiss was an innocent display of affection between friends."

"Heston openly admitted that his interest was more than brotherly concern," Damion reminded her, his tone brisk.

"You have ignored me as if I had the plague for more than two weeks. Cory thought there was nothing between us. And there really isn't, you know. After all, that was part of the agreement," she replied, her voice rising testily. "If I would have considered that Cory had overstepped his bounds I would have told him so." Andrea wagged her finger in his face as she took a bold step forward. "And you, Montclaire, are not my guardian angel." Her gaze slid over him, carving him apart as if he were a Thanksgiving turkey. "I have always been able to take care of myself and I don't need you to fight my battles for me."

"Oh?" Damion arched a skeptical brow, his annoyance dissolving into mild amusement.

"That's right." Andrea whipped her knife from her belt and pressed it to his chest in one fluid movement. "Do not doubt me, *Capitaine*." Her tone was as mocking as his expression. "You may judge me by the other women you know who accept any man's attention like a love-starved pup, but I am more particular."

When Damion tried to move, her blade pricked his chest and the look on her face left him to wonder if she was entertaining the idea of cutting his heart from his chest. Carefully he raised his arms in surrender. "I do not judge you as I have other women, *cherie*." he insisted, the faintest hint of a smile hanging on one corner of his mouth. "You, madame, are in a class all of your own."

A smug grin settled on her features, and it galled Damion to see how well she wore it. As she glanced down to return her dagger to its sheath, Damion yanked her to him, holding her captive in his embrace, his wicked chuckle spurring her anger.

"And there are times that even you, as cunning as you are, cannot escape a man's embrace," he taunted. "You are too trusting, vixen. Don't even trust your shadow and you will never find yourself in an uncompromising situation."

The feel of his sinewy arms about her transformed her anger into smouldering desire. Brazenly, she met his gaze. "There may be times when I have no wish to es-

200

cape." Her index finger traced the sinuous curve of his lips. "Now that you have bellowed the fact that we are married to all your men and half the countryside, either release me or prove to me that we are indeed husband and wife . . . before I turn my attention to someone who appears more willing to accommodate me," she insisted, a hint of mischieviousness sparkling in her eyes.

"Heston? for instance?" he inquired as he tossed her fur cap aside and pulled the pins from her lusterous mane, letting it tumble about her.

Her shoulder lifted in a reckless shrug. "I have a choice of five men. Any of them could appease me," she assured him.

"I thought you just said you were particular." His brows had a mocking tilt as his gaze slid from the honey-gold strands and anchored on her face.

"You handpicked them yourself," she countered. "They are all admirable men, *n'est ce-pas?*"

Damion grunted disgustedly, knowing he could not argue the point. "And just what am I to do, my frivolous wife? You are the only woman in camp. Am I to take my place in line?" His measuring look did not miss the twinkle of deviltry in her eyes.

" 'Tis not my problem. I thought you might have become a man without desire since you have ignored me. But as you once said, I have become addicted to passion." She derived great pleasure in turning his words around and tossing them back in his face. "If you have no desire to exercise your husbandly rights, I will look elsewhere."

An amused grin surfaced on his lips. She was baiting him. Rarely had she offered herself to him. He usually had to fight his way through her protective armor to take what he wanted. Now she had become the seductress, tempting and taunting him until he raised the flag of surrender and admitted that keeping his hands off of her was what had caused his mood to turn pitch black.

"If I have appeared disinterested it was only because I wanted to prevent my men from craving a woman's touch. You have left me with little choice." He moved a step closer, only to be trapped by the feminine fragrance that clung to her and had begun to wrap itself around his senses. "The rest of my men must suffer, knowing that I will be enjoying what they cannot possess, but I have endured this celibacy as long as I can stand."

As he reached for her, Melissa darted away. A provocative smile traced her lips as she drew the buckskin shirt over her head and held it in her hand, only to let it drop carelessly to the ground. "So have I," she assured him in a raspy tone.

Damion swallowed his breath as the moonlight sprayed across her bare flesh, leaving him aching to touch what his eyes were eagerly devouring. As she shed her breeches and stood before him, wearing nothing but a deliciously wicked smile, Damion attempted to plug his eyes back into their sockets. Lord, she was breathtakingly beautiful, like a nymph that hovered just out of reach, coaxing him into her spell.

As Andrea pivoted to stroll down to the stream, his eyes followed her, mesmerized by the graceful sway of her hips. Lady Godiva had emerged from the forest and he stood there dumbstruck. As she glided through the water, she glanced back to see that Damion, who had been frozen to the spot a moment earlier, was tearing off his clothes in his haste to pursue her. A wry smile hovered on her mouth, knowing that he had shed his pride as well. Perhaps all he felt for her was physical attraction, but at least she had a meager amount of influence on him. He followed like an obedient pup and she delighted in seeing him drop that facade of indifference, if only for the might.

As he swam toward her, Andrea eased onto her back, staring up at the ceiling of stars that twinkled above her. Damion caught his breath as his gaze fastened on the taut peaks of her breasts, watching the water mold itself to her tempting figure. He had been shivering from the chill of the stream and, although he was treading water, he could feel his temperature rise a quick ten degrees. Lord, but she was enchanting, like a sea siren that had emerged from the depths to lure him away. The instant he reached for her, she splashed water in his face, leaving him choking and coughing as she glided away, her merry laughter wafting its way back to him.

"Witch," he teased as he followed in her wake.

"Aye," she giggled as she headed for deeper water. "Have you no fear of your safety? You will be stewing in my kettle if you do not keep your distance."

"I'll take my chances," he murmured as he lunged at her, only to have her squeal and dart away, leaving him holding an armload of water.

"Stop this nonsense," Damion grumbled, annoyed that, among her other talents, she could swim like a fish. "A midnight swim is a remedy, not a cure for what ails me."

"Nay?" She arched a provocative brow as she swam into the circle of his arms.

"Nay," he assured her thickly. "You are the cause and the cure of my torment."

As he drew her full length against him, Andrea swore

203

she saw columns of steam rising from the water. The feel of his muscular body entangled in hers started a fire that even a stream of cold water could not extinguish.

"God, woman, you are driving me mad," Damion rasped as the peaks of her breasts bore into his chest.

His mouth clung to hers as he clutched her closer. He chided himself for being unable to resist this temptation, but he could not deny his need for her any more than he could prevent the sun from bringing another dawn. She had captivated him with her playfulness and seduced him with techniques that left him to wonder how hot the flame of desire could burn. It seemed an eternity since he had touched her velvety flesh, and he was helpless when her lips melted beneath his.

Damion scooped her up in his arms and waded ashore, his gaze locked with hers. When he set her to her feet, he found his hands roaming over her skin and his eyes following the path that his caresses had weaved over her breasts. He was like a blind man who was seeing the world for the first time, awestruck by a vision that left him breathless. His lips feathered across her neck, loving the taste of her, delighting in the feel of her hands as they glided around his ribs to bring their bodies together like two pieces of a puzzle that made no sense at all until they were fitted together.

Damion groaned with the want of her, his kisses becoming more insistent as he plundered her soft mouth. Driven by a need that defied reason, he came to her, claiming her as his possession until, like a shooting star that blazed across the night sky, they were consumed by the heat of passion. It was wild, sweet torment to lose himself in the fires that coursed his veins and forged their bodies as one.

He cupped her face in his hands as he propped himself above her. His thumbs brushed over her flushed cheeks. "It has been a fortnight in hell without you," he whispered hoarsely. His lips claimed her for a long moment before he found the will to drag himself away. "And I have had little sleep this night. But I will be the envy of every well-rested man. I hold what they cannot have." His expression sobered as he traced her kiss-swollen lips. "Guard your step, *cherie*. I have seen desire in their eyes, and I would hate to kill one of my own men for trying to take what is mine." His mouth descended on hers in a gesture of possession, nothing more.

With the silence of a cat, he withdrew from her arms, grabbed his clothes, and crept into the shadows, leaving her cold and alone in the darkness.

Andrea heaved a heavy-hearted sigh as she collected her scattered garments. He had whispered words of want and need against her skin in moments of passion, but he would never allow her in his heart, she mused discouragingly. She glanced up at the stars that sparkled between the limbs of the low-hanging branches and blinked back the tears. Damion would never feel any true affection for her, she told herself. He was only interested in the pleasure she could offer. No matter how she rationalized, she came to the same conclusion. She was his hand maiden. Soon she would be discarded like a used shirt, her services no longer required, her purpose complete.

She had ignored her pride, shamelessly offering herself to him, silently assuring him that she loved him above all else. If he couldn't see her heart in her eyes when she stared up at him, he was either as farsighted as a mole or he just wanted to see the emotion that transcended passion. A tear trickled down her cheek and she brushed it away with the back of her hand. Being unloved and unwanted was a new experience for her. She had been uprooted from a sheltered world where she had basked in Jeremy's and her father's love to be transplanted in a vacum of emotion. The ache that gnawed at her stomach was unbearable, and she fought back a wave of sobs, determined not to walk back into camp with red-rimmed eyes. She would not give Damion the satisfaction of knowing that she had been crying because of him or that her pride was dangling about her knees. Raising a determined chin, she picked her way through the trees toward camp.

Damion marched over to saddle both his and Andrea's horses and the other men took the silent cue to gather their belongings. As Stratton stuffed the bit in his steed's mouth, he glanced at Damion who had yet to utter a word since he stalked off with Andrea.

"Congratulations, Montclaire," Loren offered dryly.

Damion cinched up the saddle, making his mount shift uncomfortably from the excessive pressure on his belly. *"Merci,"* he replied, his voice showing no evidence of emotion.

"Your announcement took me by surprise. I could have sworn you had vowed never to take a wife," he added, flashing Damion a mocking smile.

"Necessity dictated it," Damion muttered without glancing up from his chore.

"And just what is the lady's last name, Montclaire or

Beaugener?" he pressed as he leaned close, ensuring that no one else could hear his question.

Damion's face darkened as he sliced Loren a cold glare. "Montclaire," he answered.

Stratton chuckled and shook his head. "If I may be so forward, I think you have made a mistake by not making this a permanent arrangement." His brow furrowed thoughtfully, undaunted by Damion's silencing frown. "Did you think to protect her from the rest of us by giving her one of your names?"

"You need not be so forward," Damion snorted caustically. "Andrea is my business and I owe you no explanation."

Lifting one shoulder in a leisurely shrug, Stratton cast the captain a sidelong glance and then tightened the girth strap. "Sooner or later, Heston is going to brave the question about Andrea's last name. What will you tell him?" When Damion made no effort to reply, he continued, "You know how he feels about her. When he discovers that this arrangement is not binding, he will take up where he left off. And he isn't the only one around here who hasn't entertained the thought of wandering off with her."

"I'm not blind, Stratton," Damion said, his tone clipped and angered. "I can read your thoughts, as well as every other man's in camp. Just keep your distance from her and let me handle Heston when the time comes."

"If you don't plan to keep her, let her go now. Cory would be good to her. He knows how to please a woman," he added, his grin taunting.

"Enough!" Damion snapped impatiently. "I'll make my own decisions. Quit prying! I should have never brought her with us in the first place."

Stratton snickered as he swung into his saddle. "Aye, Captain, whatever you say." As he reined his horse around behind Montclaire, a face-splitting grin settled in his rugged features.

When Andrea ambled up beside him, Damion tossed her the reins and turned his back on her, only to meet Stratton's ornery smile.

As Damion stepped into his stirrup, Andrea frowned bemusedly. The chortle behind her drew her attention, and she glanced up to see Loren's wide grin. What was going on? What was wrong with Montclaire and why was Loren chuckling? She found nothing amusing. Andrea felt like screaming at the top of her lungs in frustration, but it would have been a wasted breath. Montclaire had changed moods again. He was cold, distant, and aloof. Determinedly shrugging away the thought, Andrea mounted her steed, knowing she could never read Damion's mind. She must learn to accept him as he was and leave it at that.

The following week was lonely for Andrea, although she had been determined not to be affected by Damion's black moods. A tension filled the air while Damion stalked about, barking orders in his sharp, impatient tone. He had become cold and distant, offering her no more than a slight nod of greeting, assuring her that he knew she was around, but that it made little difference to him. When Damion ordered her to spend her spare time with Davis, her newly acquired father, it came as a welcomed relief to have his permission to carry on a conversation with someone.

Davis's French was excellent and Andrea enjoyed his company. They concocted each detail of the story for the British soldiers, carefully covering every year of her life since the day she had been born. By the time they had worked out their life history, they could almost believe it themselves.

Since Davis was about the same age as her father, it was easy for Andrea to imagine him in his role. He had even become a little protective of her in a fatherly sort of way. Montclaire seemed relieved to have Andrea off his hands so he could spend more time sitting pensively on his steed, staring off into space as he led them toward Detroit. It was as if she no longer existed, except as a necessary means to an end. She was no longer human, but rather a moving part of an efficient machine, one that Damion had created and controlled.

The day before they were to arrive in Detroit, Damion ordered Andrea to gather her belongings and to change into a dress. She eyed him curiously but did not question him. He had developed such a sour disposition that she hesitated to cross him, especially in the audience of his men. When she was prepared to leave, he lifted her into her saddle, his mere touch sending a tingle down her spine. It was the first time in three weeks that he had been close enough to touch her.

Andrea peered down at him, but she could read nothing in those silver-gray eyes. They were masked with indifference. If he felt the same sensations that had shot through her veins, he didn't show it. Who was she kidding, she asked herself, as she heaved a despairing sigh. He had not reacted to her touch because it simply had not affected him. Damion could turn his emotions off and on, allowing them to show only when it suited his purpose.

As Damion led the way through the brush toward the small settlement located a few miles from camp, Andrea stared at his broad backside, the same side she had seen a great deal of the past few weeks. Finally she lost her patience with her closed-mouth companion. The stilted silence was driving her mad.

"Would you mind telling me why we are going to the settlement?" she questioned abruptly.

Damion bent his gaze to her, raking her disheveled attire. "You are going to make yourself presentable before we arrive in Detroit. You look a sight, madame. If you expect the enemy to believe your story, you will have to do something about your shabby appearance. You remind me of a bedraggled ragamuffin who has barely survived the wilderness, instead of a gently bred countess."

The nerve of that man! How did he expect her to look after riding through the wind and rain for weeks on end? She had not gazed into a mirror since they left Baltimore and had given her appearance little thought. Perhaps Damion found her repulsive and had no urge to touch her. And then her gaze swung back to Damion after she had given herself the once-over. Andrea bristled indignantly when she had scrutinized his appearance. He didn't look a damned bit better! His hair was long and shaggy. His beard had not been trimmed and his clothes were as battered and soiled as hers.

"I hope you don't consider yourself to be Prince Charming," she snapped caustically. "You couldn't turn a lady's head unless she was turning *away* from such a disgusting sight." Her nose wrinkled distastefully as she raked him from head to toe and then looked the other way.

"You think not, madame?" he quipped, raising a dark brow.

"I know not," she assured the arrogant cad. "I may look like a filthy ragamuffin, but you remind me of a mangy scalaway who has slithered from the swamps."

Damion bowed slightly from atop his steed. "*Merci*, madame. Your compliments touch my heart," he mocked dryly.

"As do yours," she countered, addressing him with a sticky sweet smile that was so heavily coated with sugar that it dripped from her lips.

"Save that smile for the British," Damion suggested sarcastically. "I'm not sure you have enough of them to go around."

When Damion halted in front of the inn, Andrea put aside her resentful thoughts, her face glowing with anticipated pleasure. She accepted his arms as he lifted her down beside him. After unstrapping her gear, she followed Damion inside and gazed appreciatively at the moderately furnished quarters. Andrea dropped her bags in the corner and then walked over to brush her hand over the soft quilt on the poster bed.

"I had almost forgotten the feel of a feather mattress." A contented smile spread across her lips as she eased down on the edge of the bed. She had intended to ignore Damion, but her malicious thoughts evaporated when she sank into the mattress.

Damion dropped his garb at the foot of the bed and flashed her a disapproving frown. "I would prefer that you did not infest the bed before I have the opportunity to lie upon it."

Andrea bolted to her feet, flinging him a piercing glower that would have pricked his hide had he not been so thick skinned. When she stomped to the mirror, she shrieked aghast at the wild witch who stared back at her.

*"Mon Dieu!* You were right. I look worse than I had imagined."

She spun away to retrieve her comb and brush and immediately set to work to remove the tangles. Damion chuckled as he watched her struggle and grit her teeth when the comb hung in the twisted mass of honey-gold.

"So at last you see that I spoke the truth," he taunted, his gaze wandering over her, wondering why he was still aroused by such a bedraggled-looking young woman. She was no less appealing even when she looked her worst and that galled him, that and all her other exceptional talents.

Andrea pulled a face at him and then motioned for him to join her at the mirror. "Take a look at yourself and then tell me how handsome and charming you are," she suggested, her tone laced with mockery.

Damion stepped up behind her, thoughtfully assessing his appearance. "I do look a bit worse for wear," he admitted, "but as they say, beauty is only skin deep, 'tis what lies in the heart that is important."

His philosophical comment drew Andrea's distasteful sniff. "It would be wise for you to scrub away the layers of grime and filth since you do not possess a heart," she advised.

Damion shrugged off the insult, along with his shirt. "The proprietor promised to have the tub filled. We will both shed this filth." Damion retrieved his razor and wedged his way back beside Andrea to peer in the mirror.

"The sooner the better," Andrea muttered as she tugged at the tangles in her hair.

When the tub was prepared Andrea disrobed and eased down into the soothing liquid while Damion watched attentively, captivated by the sight of her creamy flesh. He tried to shave, but his eyes kept straying over his shoulder to linger on Andrea and he nicked himself thrice. Damion muttered to himself and concentrated on his task, but again his eyes betrayed him.

Andrea leaned back in the tub and held the sponge in her hand, letting the water trickle down her arm, a happy smile blossoming on her lips. It was heaven, she mused with a sigh. How often had she taken the simplicities of life for granted? Never again, she vowed to herself.

Her velvety skin glistened with golden droplets, and Damion could not keep a rein on his arousing thoughts; they were running away with themselves, causing him discomfort, as much as the slices on his chin. Damion hurriedly finished his chore, grabbed a shirt, and hastened toward the door, grumbling under his breath.

"Where are you going?" Andrea questioned curiously. "I thought you were anxious to bathe."

He allowed himself another glance in her direction and then wished he hadn't. The sight was too tempting and it took a long moment for him to find his tongue. "Downstairs for an ale. When you have finished, have the tub prepared for me," he requested, his tone harsher than he intended.

As he exited from the room, Andrea's eyes narrowed puzzledly. Not only did he look like the devil, but he acted like him as well, she decided. He was as sour as a

213

lemon and so unsociable that she was relieved to have him gone. His foul disposition dampened her spirits, and she could do without him and his dark scowls. Andrea sank into the water, submerging her head, thrashing playfully, enjoying her long-awaited bath. Let him burn, she thought to herself. That was what he deserved for the way he was behaving.

Damion planted himself in a chair and then appraised the buxom waitress who sauntered toward him. She cast him a willing smile and he returned her seductive grin.

"Bring me an ale." His eyes made fast work of assessing her attributes, and he made no effort to conceal the fact that he liked what he saw. "When I've finished, I may require your services again."

The waitress sasheyed to the bar and returned with his drink. As she leaned close to sit the mug in front of him her full breasts pressed against his arm. Damion glanced up, his dark brow arching rakishly, his smile widening to show even, white teeth.

"It won't take me long to finish my drink, mademoiselle," he assured her in a husky voice.

"I hope not, sir. I will be off duty in five minutes."

As she sauntered away, her full hips swayed beneath her skirt, and Damion's eyes followed her provocative movement until she threw another smile over her shoulder. Here was a woman who could offer much and take very little from him, except his time, Damion decided, as he continued to study her from over the rim of his mug. He could leave her behind when the time came, feeling nothing more than sexual satisfaction.

But that was not true of the little witch who was upstairs soaking in her kettle. Andrea's silky web would only entangle him. Although there had been a few opportunities to ease his desire for her in the last few weeks, he had refrained himself, testing his resistance to her bewitching charms. It had not been easy and his abstinence had played havoc with his temperment. His men knew what disturbed him, but Andrea seemed unaware of the devastating effect she had on his disposition. The sultry barmaid could appease his lusts, erasing his desire for Andrea.

Damion had been haunted by the thought of what had happened between Laura and Jeremy and the love child they had conceived. He had no intention of allowing history to repeat itself with their daughter. He was doing his damnedest to prevent such an occurrence. Each night, when he finally closed his eyes, he gave way to the thought of Andrea carrying his child, a child who would have a pair of haunting indigo eyes, flecked with gold sunrays. And then he would see Jeremy grinning down at him, assuring him that the trap had snared the prey.

When the waitress ambled toward him, a warm smile playing on her lips, Damion discarded his pensive musings.

"Do you wish me to bring you another ale, sir, or would you care for something else?" she questioned softly.

"My thirst has been quenched, *ma cherie*, but my appetite has only been whetted by the sight of you." Damion reached up to trail his fingertips along her arm in a leisurely caress.

The waitress giggled as she brushed her hand over his cheek. "My room is in the back. Would you care to see it?"

" 'Tis not the room that interests me, but the privacy it will allow for us to become better acquainted," he murmured against her ear as he urged her toward the door.

Once and for all Damion was going to route that honey-haired vixen from his mind. When he held another woman in his arms, he would counter the spell that had haunted him these past few months. Damion gazed into the woman's dark eyes, relieved that they were not flecked with gold. At least he could find peace in the embrace of a woman who wanted to share nothing more than a few pleasurable moments.

## Chapter Ten

After Andrea had washed her hair and braided it up in a bun on top of her head, she dressed in a pale blue velvet gown and ordered Damion's bath prepared. She checked her appearance in the mirror, satisfied with the transformation, and then started downstairs to tell Damion that his bath awaited him.

Before she reached the foot of the steps she saw her infidel husband and the voluptuous waitress walking arm in arm. Her jaw sagged, and for an instant she could only stare bewilderedly at them. And then his eyes darkened to stormy gray, as if *she* were the one who had committed some unforgivable crime. Andrea's cheeks flushed crimson red with humiliation and it took her a moment to gather her composure. It was as if she had the wind knocked out of her. When she finally got a grip on her emotions, she clamped her jaw shut, proudly drew herself up, and stared Damion squarely in the eye.

"I came to inform you that your bath awaits, but I can see that cleanliness is not your foremost concern at the moment. Excuse me, *s'il vous plaît*, I did not mean to interrupt." With that she spun away, lifted the front of her skirt, and flounced up the stairs, fighting the urge to leap up them two at a time in her haste to return to her room.

Damn him! He couldn't wait to be rid of her so he could seek his pleasure in the arms of another woman. Andrea bit back a sob, despising the image of Damion that hovered above her. It was only injured pride, she kept telling herself. She had expected more of Damion, more than he admitted he could give. Why hadn't she heeded his words? She was deluding herself in thinking that he would ever feel true affection for her.

"Who is the wench?" the waitress questioned as she watched Andrea ascend the stairs. A haughty smile pursed her lips, pleased with herself for stealing this handsome rogue from such an attractive young woman.

Andrea heard the question and turned to lean back over the railing at the top of the stairs. She was in an excellent position to look down her nose at both of them, which she did, finding some small satisfaction in belittling them. "I am the gentleman's sister," she lied through her tight smile. "I do hope you find my brother's company as pleasant as all the other wenches who have caught his eye." Her gaze slid over the woman and then focused on Damion as she nodded curtly. "*Adieu.*"

Damion rolled his eyes in disgust and cursed himself for being caught in such an embarrassing predicament. The look of disappointment in those blue-violet eyes continued to haunt him even after Andrea had disappeared down the hall. He could not be content until he had seen that expression erased from her face. Heaving a heavy sigh he started after her. Andrea might be tempted to pack her belongings and ride off with a cloud of dust at her heels. He needed her. It was too late to change his plans. She could not turn tail and run out on him now.

As Damion stalked away, the waitress hurried to catch up with him, clutching his arm to detain him. "What about us?"

"Later, perhaps, mademoiselle," he muttered as he untangled himself from her grasp and then took the stairs two at a time.

Damion was at odds with himself as he walked down the hall. What the hell was he going to say to Andrea, or rather what *should* he say? After all, he mused scornfully, he had told her that they were not bound to each other. And yet, he had been enraged when he witnessed Cory Heston kissing her.

He wasn't certain how to handle the situation. Should he act nonchalant, stroll inside, strip from his clothes, and settle himself in the tub, pretending nothing had happened? Or should he chastise Andrea for spying on him? Although Andrea had claimed that she admired his qualities that set him apart from other men she had known, he had the uneasy feeling that her lofty image of him had taken a headlong dive into hell.

This was all Jeremy's fault, Damion thought bitterly. Jeremy had told Andrea that his partner was flawless. Andrea expected too much of him. And now, every way he turned, he found himself face-to-face with something Drieson had said or done. Damn that man! Why had he meddled in Damion's life?

Damion paused by the door and hesitantly grasped

the knob. He still hadn't decided on the best approach to take with Andrea. Taking a deep breath, he pushed open the door, hoping the perfect remark would find his tongue when he met her gaze.

When Andrea heard the door creak, her eyes spewed fire. She snatched up the closest weapon to her, wishing it could have been her musket or knife. As Damion's masculine form filled the entrance, she wheeled around and hurled the pitcher at him. Damion didn't have to make any decision about his course of action. His role suddenly became a defensive one. If looks could kill, he would have been drawn, quartered, and cured in a matter of seconds, and Andrea would have been content to see his carcass hanging upside down, waiting to become a meal for a pack of wolves.

After ducking away from the oncoming pitcher, Damion stared at her in amazement. The porcelain hit the edge of the door where he had been standing the moment before and then crashed to the floor, shattering in a thousand pieces, splashing water all over him.

"You cur!" she hissed venomously as Damion slammed the door shut. Andrea stalked over to retrieve his bags from the end of the bed and hurled them into his belly, causing his breath to come out in a rush. "Go stay with that friendly bitch, my *dear* husband." She clenched her teeth together to keep from shouting the walls down around them.

"This mock marriage is dissolved. You are free to do as you please, but, of course, you don't need my permission, do you, Captain?" She raked him with disgust before she looked away, repulsed by the sight of him. "You had already decided to seek comfort with that eager doxy. Pardon me for interrupting your little tryst. You have your belongings, now get the hell out of here before I find something more lethal than a pitcher to throw at you!"

As Andrea whirled away, Damion's hand snaked out to grab her arm. His other hand matched the grip of his right hand as he held her at arm's length, despite her protest. Although she was his captive, she refused to meet his gaze.

"Andrea, look at me," he demanded gruffly.

"Nay," she snapped, her chin tilting rebelliously. "The sight of you disgusts me. As if your outward appearance were not offensive enough, you are rotten to the core. You have earned my hatred. The man I thought I admired no longer exists."

He reached beneath her chin, forcing her to meet his level gaze. "I'm sorry," he said simply.

"For what?" Sarcasm dripped from her lips as her chin tilted a notch higher. "Sorry that I caught you with another woman or are you apologizing for being guilty of infidelity?"

He stared at her for a long moment, watching the fiery sparks blazing from her eyes, wondering why he had bothered to apologize. Before he opened the door that had not been one of his alternative plans. As a matter of fact, the thought had never crossed his mind. Why the hell had he said that?

"Well, which is it?" she persisted as she jerked from his grasp, repulsed by their physical contact. "Not that it matters. I won't believe anything you say, not now or ever again."

"Then there is no point in continuing this conversation," he replied glibly. Damion unfastened his shirt, shrugged it from his shoulders, and recklessly tossed it

221

aside. "You once told me that it made little difference to you where or with whom I found pleasure, *n'est ce pas?*" His dark brow arched tauntingly as he cast her a sidelong glance.

"Aye," she admitted bitterly. She had said as much, but uttering the words and witnessing him exercise that privilege were two entirely different matters. "And you once told me that you cared about me." Her eyes narrowed accusingly on him. "But that was another of your lies. If you cared, even a little, you would not have flaunted that wench under my nose. The least you could have done was to have been discreet. I'm surprised you didn't bring her to our room and ask me to leave while you sampled her charms on the feather mattress."

Damion stepped out of his buckskin breeches and slid down into the tub. What the hell could he reply to that? He had indeed confessed that he cared about her and that she could depend on him while they were together. "I did say I cared," he conceded, for lack of much else to say.

Andrea flashed him a contemptuous glower and stomped to the door, slamming it none too gently behind her. Damion's breath rushed out as he eased back against the edge of the tub and grabbed the soap to lather himself.

He hadn't handled the situation well. When he gazed into her blazing eyes he had been tongue-tied, unable to draw upon the words to soothe her injured pride. If it had been any other woman he would have pursued the waitress and dispensed with any explanation, but not with Andrea. He was tied to that little firebrand. She was an important part of the plan, and

222

she was also Jeremy's daughter. Dammit, he muttered, as he vigorously scrubbed himself, wishing he could wash away the memory of Andrea. What was he to do now? Should he find the waitress and ease his needs or stay in the room and drive himself mad, wondering if Andrea would ever return?

The door swung open and Damion glanced up to see Andrea with a broom in one hand and a bucket of steaming water in the other. He waited tensely, wondering if she intended to scald his chest or scorch his lower half. Andrea lingered momentarily, indecision etching her brow. Although she had her heart set on singing the hide right off him she relented, showing the rogue, who sat anxiously waiting to know his fate, a little mercy, not much, but more than she had originally intended. She held the bucket up over her head and poured the water into his bath, letting it splash about him. Damion cringed and sucked in his breath as his temperature rose a quick ten degrees.

When his face had twisted in a sufficient amount of pain, a self-satisfied smile caught the corners of her mouth. Watching him grimace from the excessive heat was gratifying, but she was not content to leave it at that. Andrea added fuel to the fire with her remark. "May all of your baths be as hot as fire and your women as cold as ice, my *dear* husband."

Andrea wheeled and walked away to sweep up the pieces of porcelain without bothering to cast another glance in Damion's direction. When she had completed her chore, she exited and then returned a few minutes later to repack her belongings. Damion hurriedly finished his bath and draped a towel around his hips. When he started toward Andrea, she put more distance between them and then paused by the door, casting him a contemptuous glare.

"I'm going downstairs for supper, monsieur," she informed him, her tone as cold and brisk as the arctic winds. "If by chance I meet someone with whom I can pass a few pleasurable moments, then 'tis my intention to do so. I trust you will do the same."

As she swept from the room, not allowing Damion to work a word in edgewise, he muttered under his breath and hurled the towel at the wall, standing stark naked while a puddle of water formed at his feet. He hurriedly dressed and continued to grumble a long string of curses to the wench who had an uncanny knack for keeping him in hot water. When that woman was under foot there was no peace, Damion thought bitterly. He should have enlisted the aid of the militia instead of depending on Andrea. He would have been a much happier man.

As Damion entered the dining room, his eyes narrowed, spying Andrea who sat at a table with a handsome, young gentleman. She damned sure didn't waste any time, he mused in annoyance. When he had strolled up beside them, he bowed slightly and nodded a greeting to the man who had his eyes glued to Andrea. After standing unnoticed for a moment, he cleared his throat to call attention to his presence.

"May I join you?" he questioned, masking his irritation behind a polite smile.

Andrea sent him a disinterested glance and then smiled sweetly at her companion. Damion seated himself, despite Andrea's obvious attempt to ignore him.

When Nathan finally dragged his eyes off Andrea and focused them on Damion, she was obligated to introduce them.

"Nathan Gibbs, this is my brother, Damion Deuvalle," she began, biting back a smile when Damion nearly choked on his breath at the mention of his new name. "Did the young lady you were visiting earlier have other plans for the evening, *mon frere?*" A pretentious grin hung on her lips, but it evaporated when she met Damion's hard gaze.

"*Je ne sait pas.* I did not bother to ask, dear sister." His tone was courteous enough, but when his eyes circled back to Andrea, she felt she had been pricked with talons that were sharp enough to draw blood.

"You have a most charming sister, sir. I suppose it keeps you busy protecting her from her flock of suitors in the colonies," Nathan remarked as his gaze fell back on Andrea, dipping to the creamy flesh of her breasts that were enticingly displayed by the low-necked gown, one that Damion had selected for her, one that he had begun to regret purchasing. "She has been telling me about your journey from France."

"Oh?" His attention narrowed on her, a warning gleam in his silver eyes.

"Aye, it all sounds so fascinating," Nathan commented before losing himself in the depths of the blue-violet pools that had drawn him into their spell.

Damion felt himself losing ground. He could have been a stick of furniture for all Nathan cared. The man was too busy drooling over Andrea to even notice if Damion was wearing his charcoal gray jacket or his birthday suit. And Andrea, the ornery little minx, was baiting the love-starved gentleman into conversation, leaving Damion to sit and stare at the silverware.

"May I fetch you something to eat, sir?" the waitress inquired as she strolled up beside Damion.

Damion eased back in his chair and nodded agreeably. "Would you perchance be serving crow tonight?" he queried, as his gaze slid to Andrea. "I think there are those among us who think I should be eating it."

The waitress smiled and then gave her reddish blond head a negative shake. "I am afraid the cook did not include crow on the menu. Perhaps you could substitute stewed chicken," she suggested.

"That will suffice," Damion grumbled, while Andrea bit back a mischievous grin.

Finally, after what seemed an hour of being excluded like an outcast weed, Nathan turned to Damion with a questioning smile.

"May I have your permission to show Andrea our community?"

Dammit, of course not! Damion would have preferred that Nathan Gibbs scoop himself up from his chair and run along home. Andrea would have hell to pay when he got her alone, he promised himself. If Damion thought he could have escaped unscathed after clamping his hands around her lovely neck he would have cheerfully choked her. But he expected every man in the tavern to come to the distressing damsel's defense if he harmed on hair on her head. No doubt, he would have found himself stuffed and mounted on the mantel.

"Well, monsieur . . . I don't know . . ." Damion stammered, thoughtfully rubbing his chin, masking his irritation with a concerned frown. "I rarely allow my sister out of my sight and we must be leaving early in the morning. I don't think—"

"*S'il vous plaît*," Andrea pleaded as she sorted through her repertoire of persuasive smiles and then flashed him one of high quality. "I promised not to stay out late." Her gaze circled back to Nathan, her lashes fluttering coyly. "Monsieur Gibbs has been such pleasant company and I would truly enjoy a ride in his carriage."

Spiteful sparks bridged the gap between indigo and steel-gray eyes, arching over Nathan's head, leaving him oblivious to the fact that there was silent war raging between Damion and Andrea.

"I will not be gone long," Andrea assured him, taking advantage of Damion's hesitation. She leaned over to place a sisterly kiss to his cheek and then unfolded herself from the chair. When Damion opened his mouth to protest, Andrea pinched his cheek, a little too hard to be considered playful, and then spoke again before he could locate his tongue and lash her with it. "*Merci*, Damion. I knew you would agree that I occasionally require a *gentleman's* company. *Bon soir.*"

She curled her hand in the crook of Nathan's arm and sauntered away, leaving Damion brewing like an overheated tea kettle that was about to reduce itself to a pot of steam. She was inwardly giggling, gloating over the fact that for once she had outmaneuvered the scoundrel.

Damn that woman! Damion gritted his teeth and uttered several more unrepeatable epithets to her name as she strolled away with her beau hot on her heels. He tossed his napkin on the table and stalked out of the tavern. If he could have found the dark-haired doxy, he would have whisked her up to the room and seduced her on the very bed where Andrea intended to sleep!

Andrea breathed a contented sigh as her eyes swept the peaceful setting. The bright moonlight shielded the stars, except for a sparsely scattered few that twinkled against the black velvet sky. The silhouette of trees left a jagged line against the horizon, breaking the flat landscape. Andrea was entranced. She had always considered Kentucky to be God's country, but from what she had seen of the Northwest Territory, it could have been the Lord's summer home.

"This is a charming settlement, Nathan. It somehow reminds me of home." She had already given Nathan a short, prefabricated history of her life in France and her travels in America. Nathan had digested her explanation without question, much to her relief. If he swallowed the lie, perhaps the British would not be skeptical of her appearance at the fort. "Your corner of the world is most enchanting."

"Do you miss France?" he questioned as he popped the reins, sending the steed into a faster pace.

"*Oui*," she assured him as she flashed him a blinding smile. "But I am enjoying my stay here, especially when I find myself in such good company."

A wide grin split his face and then his gaze fell to her bodice, betraying his thoughts. "And I am most fortunate that we met." He heaved a forlorn sigh and managed to lift his eyes to her exquisite face. "I wish you were staying longer. I was almost afraid your brother would refuse us this time alone together. I must admit I would have been disappointed if all we could have shared was a meal."

Nathan pulled the steed to a halt and laid his arm back on the seat, his hand lightly caressing her shoulder. "You are breathtaking, Andrea. I cannot seem to take my eyes off you." A guilty smile crept to his lips. "Your brother would not have allowed you to be alone with me if he could have read my thoughts."

"And just what are you thinking, monsieur?" she questioned demurely, as if she didn't know.

"It would be easier to show you than to tell you," he murmured raggedly before his lips covered hers in a kiss that spoke of rising passion.

Of late, Andrea had allowed three men other than Damion to embrace her, all for the wrong reasons. Rorick had helped her forget the mountain man who had haunted her thoughts, Cory had eased her longing for the dashing sea captain who continued to ignore her. Now she had used Nathan to spite Damion's afternoon tryst. And to her dismay, she found Nathan's embrace sorely lacking. All three of her companions had been handsome men who would have pleased any woman, except her. She was disheartened to discover that she preferred Damion. There were kisses, and then there were kisses. Damion's had always been fiery enough to melt the moon. Why did he have to be the one man whose heart she could never hope to win? Why couldn't Rorick, Cory, or even Nathan make her burn with desire? Because Damion had taken her soul, she thought despairingly. She could not put him from her mind, no matter how hard she tried. There was no denying the emotion she harbored in her heart. She loved him, even when she knew he would break her heart in two and then recklessly toss it aside.

As Nathan drew away, Andrea smiled ruefully, aware of the flame of passion in his deep green eyes, wishing she could have returned his longing gaze. But all she felt was a fond affection, nothing more. Her entire being hungered for Damion and she had nothing left to offer another man.

"I could spend the entire evening kissing you," he breathed as he inched toward her.

Andrea dodged his intended kiss, holding him at bay as she pressed her palms against his chest. "I fear that my brother would not approve, monsieur. He has a violent temper and if he discovered that we—"

"He doesn't have to know," Nathan whispered as he captured her in his arms.

"But you have taken privileges that would infuriate him," she argued. "We hardly know each other." Andrea pried herself from his grasp and scooted as far away as the buggy seat would allow without toppling from her perch. "I do not wish to face Damion's wrath. He would show neither of us any mercy."

Nathan heaved a sigh. She was so tempting that he could scarcely control himself. "Very well, my dear," he conceded regretfully. "I shall attempt to portray the gentleman, but 'tis not an easy task. You are irresistible."

"Could you show me your home?" Andrea requested, attempting to change the subject and get the carriage moving once again.

"If you wish." Nathan patted the seat next to him. "Come sit beside me. I promise not to frighten you away," he assured her.

Andrea eyed him warily, but then scooted over beside him as the buggy lurched forward. After riding two miles north of the settlement, Nathan pulled the mare to a halt and gestured toward the cottage that was nestled in the trees. It was a quaint, well kept home that Andrea would have loved to claim as her own.

"You have a lovely house," she murmured, her gaze fixed on the silhouette that glistened in the moonlight.

"My sister, Nancy, and I live there," Nathan explained. "She is about your age. I wish you could meet her. It seems we have much in common. We lost our parents several years ago, just like you and Damion. The only difference is that we cannot afford to tour the world," he added with a smile.

"If Damion and I owned such a quaint home, I would never wish to leave it," she mused aloud. "Unfortunately, that is not the case."

"But I thought you said you missed France," Nathan reminded her, frowning curiously.

"France, *oui*," she acknowledged with a thoughtful nod. "But not our home. It is much too large and impersonal. It rather reminds me of the hotel where we lodged in Baltimore—cold, drafty, a nice place to visit, but not to live permanently," Andrea smiled beseechingly. "Please take me back to the inn. Damion will be annoyed with me if I do not return at a reasonable hour."

"If that is what you wish," Nathan murmured, none too pleased with the request.

"Not particularly what I wish, monsieur. Damion will grace me with one of his brotherly lectures. Since we must leave tomorrow I will be forced to endure one of them if I ruffle his feathers. And he can be such a boor when he is angered." Her nose wrinkled distastefully at the thought of confronting him.

"Your brother does seem to be a bit foul tempered," Nathan agreed. "I should hate to upset him." A pensive smile grazed his lips. "But I wonder if tarrying in the moonlight with you would be worth facing his wrath."

Before Andrea could protest, Nathan gathered her in his arms and planted a devouring kiss to her lips. If this was to be their last time together, he intended to make the most of it. When he finally dragged himself away, Andrea readjusted her gown and handed him the reins.

"Please take me back. If Damion is not already breathing fire he will be soon," she insisted, as she scooted to the far side of the seat.

When they arrived at the inn, Nathan lifted Andrea down beside him, holding her longer than necessary. Andrea gracefully stepped away and displayed another disarming smile, one that she had learned to turn off and on when the situation dictated.

"*Merci*, monsieur. You have been charming company."

Damion materialized from the shadows, his brooding gaze anchoring on them. "It appears that you and Monsieur Gibbs enjoyed your overly long ride," he said tightly.

"Nathan and I had a wonderful time," she assured him. "He even took me to see his home. It was quite lovely."

A disapproving frown knitted Damion's brow, wondering what room had occupied most of the time, as if he didn't know.

"I would like to take you to breakfast before you

232

leave in the morning," Nathan directed his request to Andrea, bypassing her brother who seemed as cold and unyielding as a stone mountain.

"We shall be leaving early in the morning, monsieur," Damion replied for Andrea. "I do not think that would be a good idea."

Andrea frowned disappointedly, her lip jutting out in an exaggerated pout. "*S'il vous plaît*," she cooed, intending to make Damion the culprit, tormenting him even when she knew he was having difficulty being polite as it was. It served him right, she thought spitefully. Let him stand there and smolder until he had reduced himself to a bootful of ashes. "Surely it would not hurt to delay—"

"*Non!*" Damion growled, as he clamped his hand on her wrist and hauled her toward the steps. "*Bon soir*, monsieur."

"I hope you're proud of yourself," he hissed as he roughly escorted Andrea up the stairs, making her hurry to keep up with his impatient strides.

"Extremely, dear brother," she assured him sarcastically. "I hope your evening was as enjoyable as mine. Did you find some willing wench to warm your bed?"

Damion offered no answer until the door was locked behind them. "I spent the whole damned evening wondering if you had convinced your love-smitten beau to aid in your escape." His gray eyes narrowed on her, a hint of steam rising from his collar. "If I didn't require your services, madame, I would delight in wringing your neck for that little charade! And I assure you that it would be gratifying to choke the life out of you." His voice was rising testily and he had to clamp his mouth shut to prevent bellowing at her smug smile.

Her shoulder lifted in a careless shrug as she sauntered to the bureau to pull the pins from her hair. "I don't doubt that you would, just as I would have relished carving your heart from your chest this afternoon." Andrea turned to face him, a mocking tilt to her brow. "But as you said, you need me. You will have to refrain from strangling me until we have accomplished our task in Detroit."

"Then I will find some method of torture to appease my vindictiveness until that time comes," he declared as he strolled toward her, a wicked gleam in his eyes.

His arms curled about her waist and then wandered to her breasts. Andrea caught her breath as a warm tingle skitted across her skin. Although she was doing her damndest to remain unaffected, her body was responding to his caresses. She squirmed for release, but Damion tightened his grip on her.

"Unhand me, *Capitaine*," she ordered harshly. "I have had enough loving embraces for one night and yours is most unwelcomed."

Damion crushed her to the hard wall of his chest, his taunting kisses tracing a hot path along her neck. His hand dipped beneath her gown, cupping her breast, teasing its peak to tautness. "And did Gibbs's embrace crumble your resistance, *cherie?*" he whispered against her ear. "Did his kisses stir your blood?"

Andrea tried to pull away, but Damion would not be denied. "I hope you are not so egotistical to think that *your* embraces could arouse such emotion," she sneered, wishing she could have convinced herself that she was repulsed by his touch.

"I am not being egotistical, only realistic. I know they do," he assured her, his tone heavy with disturbed desire. "I can feel your heart beating wildly against my chest at this very moment. You can pretend that I don't arouse you, that you don't want me, but I know better."

Damn him for being right and knowing it! She would have given almost anything if she could have prevented her heart from doing back somersaults each time Damion touched her. She wanted to feel nothing, remaining cold and unaffected.

"Let me go! I—"

His mouth urgently possessed hers, stripping the words from her throat before she could voice them. His forceful kiss took her breath away, just as it always did. He pressed her hips against his solid frame, letting her feel his desire for her before he loosened the stays of her gown, allowing his caresses to roam unhindered over her silky flesh. Andrea found the room spinning furiously about her as his hands worked their magic. She had vowed never to allow him to touch her again, but her body denied her, wilting beneath his caresses, keenly alerted to the virile form that was molded tightly to hers. A surrendering sob escaped her lips when she felt her defenses slipping away. She was responding to his devouring kisses, knowing that she was hopelessly lost to the one man who could force her to abandon reasoning.

Damion snuffed out the lantern and drew her with him to the bed, knowing that he was about to break his vow to himself. He had not intended to take her after her spiteful prank, but the thought of another man touching what belonged to him incensed his pride. He could not be content until he had erased the memory of the other man from her mind.

As he deliberately aroused her to breathless heights, he moved beside her, propping himself up on an elbow to gaze into her shadowed face. "Tell me you want me," he demanded, his caresses roaming over her flesh, loving the feel of her velvety skin beneath his hand.

"I despise you," she choked, averting her eyes from his probing gaze.

A wicked smile tugged at the corner of his mouth. "I think perhaps the lady protests too much."

"I do hate you," Andrea insisted, although her body quivered beneath his experienced touch. "You are a heartless scoundrel."

"So you have told me, *cherie*, but I wish you would refrain from voicing such endearments while I'm making love to you," he whispered, as he traced searing kisses along the curve of her neck, sending a rash of goose pimples skipping across her skin.

"You have no concept of the meaning of love. You are only appeasing animal lust and I refuse to think of it any other way."

"Are you trying to convince me or yourself?" he questioned, as he nibbled against her lips.

"I feel nothing for you," Andrea assured him, wishing she could believe the lie.

"You once told me you loved me," Damion reminded her, his eyes raking her body, memorizing each curve and swell of her enticing figure.

"Once I admired and respected you, but even that is gone. The world and the people in it are merely a challenge to you. You don't seek to win their love, only conquer their hearts," Andrea accused, setting his hands from her. "I will not forfeit my heart to you. You would tear it in two and then return it to me, laughing in my face."

Damion cupped her face in his hand, forcing her to meet his level gaze. "What makes you think I would be so reckless?"

"Today was proof enough. I thought you cared a little about me. I even believed that you needed me for something more than your plot to free Boone. But after I saw you with that wench this afternoon, I knew that I was only convenient. Any woman could offer you what you want, an affair with no strings attached."

"I only turned to her to keep myself from devouring you," he confessed, his tone soft and sincere as he brushed the back of his hand over her cheek.

Andrea was caught off guard by the honesty in his expression. Rarely did he allow any emotion to show on his face except anger. "But why? Are you afraid you might fall in love with me?" She arched a mocking brow, unable to resist the gibe. "You? The man who fears nothing and no one, a man who prides himself in remaining free and unattached?"

"You don't understand, Andrea." Damion heaved a heavy sigh. "I cannot explain my motives. 'Tis more complicated than you know."

"You *are* afraid of me, aren't you?" she teased as her hand trailed over the rippling muscles of his back in an arousing caress.

"Nay," he objected. "You pose no danger to me. I could crush you with my bare hands. You may be an extraordinary woman but you are still no match for me." It annoyed him to see the smug grin on her lips and incensed him that she wore it so well. "You would be advised to remember that."

"Perhaps what you say is true," she conceded, her smile intact. "But intangible bonds are more difficult to sever. I think now that the *gentleman* protests too much." Andrea shrugged carelessly. "But you have nothing to fear. I do not expect your love, nor will I make demands on you. You may find satisfaction in other arms if that is your wish. I will accept your passion when it meets my whim, but I will never request the key to your heart."

Damion sought her sensuous lips, unsure of the strange emotion that tugged at his soul. When she casually spoke of their affair and their parting it disturbed him. He yearned to hear a confession of love, and yet, he didn't really want her to fall in love with him. The fact that she only intended to satisfy her own desires annoyed him. She was becoming too much like him, he decided. Andrea was as much a rogue as he was, taking pleasure, seeking no ties. And yet, she confused him. She claimed that she admired him but despised him. She admitted that she wanted him, but she seemed to be content, knowing that their affair would not last forever. She could have any man who met her whim and he had watched her draw several men beneath her spell, only to cast them aside when she tired of their attentions.

Perhaps he had taught her too well, he mused, as his absent caresses glided across her silky flesh. It would be ironic if he were trapped by his own philosophy. He wanted Andrea to learn to play his game, detaching herself from her emotions, prepared to face the British and meet with success. A skillful woman had emerged from his teachings. But was she after something more? Was her intent to conquer his heart, enslave his soul, and then discard him to search out another victim who would fall prey to her bewitching charms? He had created a temptress that even he could not resist. But he would not be lured into the trap, he told himself. He would not suffer as Jeremy and his father had. They had surrendered to love and it had destroyed both of them. There would be no chains on his heart and no confessions from his lips. He would let the world fade away when he found pleasure in her arms, but he would never attach the name of love to the sensations that gripped him when he shared her embrace.

All of his well-meaning vows escaped him as her lips hovered on his, quenching a thirst that lingered on his mouth. He was drawn like a moth to a flame, unable to get close enough to the fire that scorched him inside and out.

His heart thundered furiously against his ribs as she boldly returned his caresses. Her lips feathered across his chest, expertly arousing him to sensuous heights, leaving him drifting in a haze that blocked out all except his tormented need for her.

Damion twisted above her, unable to curb a desire that had consumed his being. He clutched her closer, plunging deeply within her, groaning in pleasure as she took him higher and higher. Her name was on his lips as they soared among the clouds to reach that lofty pedestal on the far horizon where the blue-violet sky intermingled with silver stars. And for that timeless moment nothing mattered except the exquisite feeling of holding her in his arms, lost to the scent of jasmine that clung to his senses and the taste of honeyed kisses.

Contentment drew a ragged breath as they drifted back to reality like a weightless feather carried on a breath of wind. When Andrea's heart slowed its frenzied pace, she pulled up on his chest to brush her hand through the ebony hair that lay recklessly across his forehead. She gazed down into the glistening pools of silver, captivated by the depths of gentleness that had surfaced on them. She had spent the evening voicing deceitful lies, but she could no longer deny the truth. The word tumbled from her lips, unconcerned with the consequences. Tomorrow was uncertain and she may never see Damion again. For once, she would be honest with him, hiding nothing of her feelings.

"Damion, I do love you," she confessed, her eyes clouding with emotion. "I know I have professed to hate you, but 'tis only anger and injured pride that force such words from my lips. I have come to love you as a woman loves a man." A smile traced her lips. " 'Tis a love that engulfs all reasoning and emotion. Perhaps you are cynical about its existence, but I can feel it in my soul, just as surely as I know I live and breathe." A rueful smile touched her lips as she traced the rugged lines of his face, wondering why he could never understand what she was trying to say. "Perhaps Jeremy was right. Maybe reliving tender memories of time past is a fair price for sharing that one, unequaled moment of love, even if it cannot endure eternity. At least it is a treasure that I can keep in my heart, something that no one can take from me."

"Andrea, don't . . . please . . ." Damion grimaced as he gazed into her perfect face, watching the moonlight glow on the golden cape of hair that sprayed across her bare shoulders. She was like an angel, so delicate, so lovely, and yet so far from his grasp. He had waited for her confession and now that he had heard it, he was plagued with guilt. She deserved more than he could give.

She pressed her fingertips to his lips, silencing his protest. "Allow me to finish. I want to be honest with you and myself. No more games, no pretentions. I have tried three times to put you out of my mind, but other men's embraces do not compare to yours. I found no consolation in their arms, only a longing to be with you, to share your passion."

Her lashes fluttered against her cheeks as she breathed a sigh and then she raised her gaze to his. "I may never see you again after I have served my purpose, but at least my conscience will be cleansed. My admiration has blossomed into a deeper emotion because I have come to know you too well. I know that you cannot return my love and that other women can also give you what you want, but it doesn't matter. My love is given freely and without regret."

Andrea nestled beside him, content in his embrace. "You are a man who craves to be as free as the wind. I have learned to survive in your world, but I still possess a woman's heart. I knew I was treading dangerous ground, but I followed that path and I am not sorry for my choice. I have discovered the true meaning of unselfish love.

"Perhaps in time I will learn to love again," she whispered. "But for now and for a long time to come, I will love you, Damion. At a time when I'm not certain of my own name or who I really am, at least one truth is clear. You possess my heart and I will do your bidding until you no longer need me."

Her quiet words struck a sensitive nerve. A twinge of guilt crept across his soul once again. He had not wanted to break her spirit, and yet, each time another man came between them, he had become obsessed with hearing her admit that no other man had taken his place. He didn't want to keep Andrea chained to him, but he could not let her go, not to some other man. He could release her to soar freely, her spirit touched by only his hand, but he could not relinquish her to anyone else's arms. The thought of sharing her was distasteful and he could not permit it. He had won her wild heart and he had no desire to hurt her. He was trapped. Damn that Jeremy. Why couldn't he have left well enough alone!

Damion sought her lips, afraid to reply for fear of destroying the tender moment. His emotions were in a turmoil and he could not trust his words when she was warm and yielding in his arms. As he pressed her to her back, his silver eyes sparkled with renewed passion. He could read the message in her gaze, knowing her desire matched his.

"Then love me," he murmured hoarselay. "Prove to me that no other man claims your heart and soul. Show me the meaning of this love you offer."

Andrea pulled his head to hers, touching his lips in a kiss that spoke of such tenderness that Damion felt as if he were being held suspended for an endless moment. "I will love you while we are together, each time you want me," she promised, her voice crackling as her breath caressed his cheek. "And when we are apart, I want you to recall this night in your dreams. Although you do not wish it, I will touch your heart for this brief moment. 'Tis enough, Damion."

She took the initiative, using techniques she had learned from him and inventing some of her own, making him desire her as much as she yearned for him. They came together like the clashing of thunder that shook the earth, warning of the tempestuous storm that could devastate all in its path. Her touch was like lightning sizzling across his flesh, leaving him trembling with a need that shook his very core. He was caught up in the whirlwind of emotions that left him tumbling, dizzy with desire and breathless with an urgency to calm the winds of passion that swept him along in their forceful path.

Their bodies glistened with perspiration as they nestled in each other's arms. They had survived passion's storm, but it had drained their strength. Andrea could not muster the will to move, so content and relaxed that she could only sigh weakly and quietly relive the moment when she had claimed this powerful man as her possession.

Andrea choked back a sob of ultimate pleasure as she snuggled in his protective arms. Tomorrow was full of danger and he had no desire to see the sun raise its weary head. It would fling them apart, and all she would have left was a bittersweet memory of a time when she had traveled to the edge of the universe.

"I do need you, my lovely witch," Damion confessed as he stroked the golden tendrils away from her face to gaze into the shimmering pools of indigo. "In my own way I want you. You have cast your spell upon me and I cannot seem to escape. I have tried to ignore you, seeking pleasure in other arms, but I come back to you, knowing I may be burned by the flame, but unable to resist the heated passion that awaits me in your embrace. You don't even know your own power." A faint smile hovered on his lips as he traced the exquisite lines of her face. "The sight of you arouses me, your touch brings a craving that seems unquenchable, and the need to possess you becomes an obsession. I cannot stay, I cannot go, and yet I know I must. I am like a man on the rack, torn between duty and desire. If I stay I'm a coward, but if I go I'm a fool. You have tempted and tormented me. 'Tis I who have lost direction." His hand slid around her throat, feeling the steady pulsation of her heartbeat beneath his fingers. "You have made me your pawn. I am not accustomed to moving upon command. In the past, I have dictated to others, yet you have played havoc with my plans and distorted my dreams to the point that I know not what I want of you or myself. But I grant you this," he murmured as he pressed a kiss to her forehead and then drew away to stare directly at her. "You are not easy to forget and I must have tried a thousand times. More than once I have cursed Jeremy for sending me after you because my life has not been the same since I glanced into those mysterious eyes of yours."

"Nor has mine," Andrea replied, a drowsy smile playing on her lips. "Once I bargained with my soul and I have been unable to buy back my freedom at any price. And when you hold me in your arms, I have no wish to escape."

"I would trust you with my life, my resourceful temptress, although I am still left to wonder if there is folly in that. But I cannot yield my heart. I have seen too many men destroyed. Please don't turn against me because I am cynical of love. I offer you all that is in my power to give. I need you, Andrea. Boone needs you. Without you I would require an army to free Daniel from captivity. We cannot spare the manpower when the redcoats are attacking us from all directions."

Andrea smiled up at him, watching his rugged face soften in a quiet plea. He would never truly believe in her unless she laid her life down for him. "I have never turned against you, Damion. 'Tis you who have turned away from me. You are too skeptical to trust anyone completely."

The resemblance of a smile surfaced as he wrapped a possessive arm about her waist and molded her to him. "I am a creature of habit, *cherie*. I cannot change what I am. Sleep now," he rasped. "Tomorrow requires that you are well rested and prepared to face a dangerous challenge. I want nothing to happen to you. Believe that."

Andrea nodded slightly as she cuddled against his muscular chest. She would do what she could to free Boone because that was what Damion wanted. He was not the pawn, she was. His dreams and aspirations had been incorporated into her thoughts. Damion was a powerful man and she had bent to his will, yielding to the stronger force. No other man could have made her do his bidding, except this one man who had taught her the meaning of passion and had swept her off into an adventure that might very well cost her life. And she was going willingly, serving him as he commanded.

## Chapter Eleven

When the ship docked in France, Lelia and Robert were there to welcome Melissa. After all the passengers disembarked, Lelia walked up to the captain and inquired about her niece.

"I'm afraid Melissa returned to. Norfolk, Madame Mooree. Another schooner flagged us down after we were out of port. The captain delivered a letter from her father, saying that he had become ill and requested that she return to him," Rorick explained.

"William ill?" She gasped, the color seeping from her cheeks, her violet eyes wide in alarm. "What was wrong with him?"

His shoulder lifted in a shrug. "The note merely requested that she return."

"How dreadful," Lelia choked out as she clutched her son's arm for support. "We must travel to the colonies immediately."

"My ship will set sail at the first of next week, madame," Rorick informed her. "If you wish to travel with us, I will make the necessary arrangements." The

246

thought of helping Madame Mooree locate her niece and brother-in-law brought a smile to his lips. He was anxious to see Melissa again. She had been on his mind since he had watched her walk away with Montclaire.

"*Merci*, monsieur," Lelia replied, a grateful smile adding a little color to her ashen face. "We shall be ready."

"But *ma mere*," Robert interjected, his tone bewildered. "I cannot leave France now. I have father's business to attend and there is a war on."

"Then I shall go alone," she insisted, her chin tilting determinedly. "If something is wrong with William, I cannot rest until I have seen him with my own eyes."


Lelia paced her bedroom, wringing her hands in front of her, her brows furrowed in thought. William's illness and the fact that Melissa had not arrived in France had disrupted her well-laid plans. She had intended to take care of that golden-haired snip and once she was out of the way, Lelia had decided to go to William. The chit looked too much like her mother, hauntingly so. Lelia had detested the sight of both mother and daughter. The burning hatred that she harbored for Laura had grown like a malicious cancer, consuming her thoughts. It had been twenty-two long years since Laura and William had wed, but Lelia recalled it as if it had happened only yesterday. She had rushed into a loveless marriage, hoping to put the thought of William out of her mind, but it had only enhanced her hatred for Laura and her love for William. Now Lelia's husband was gone and she was free to pursue the one goal she had desired in life—William Stoddard. But the only way to have him was to dispose of

Melissa, the lovely image of her mother. When William was rid of her, his memory of Laura would be buried with her. Lelia had arranged Melissa's unfortunate death, but now that the twit had returned to her father other arrangements would have to be made.

Her violet eyes turned cold as she mentally prepared her scheme, unconsciously toying with the sable hair that was beginning to show signs of gray. She was still an attractive woman, she thought to herself. She was wealthy and she could make William desire her as he had before her deceitful sister had stolen him away, even after Lelia had aided her sister in sneaking away with Drieson each time he returned to the settlement. Lelia had stooped to lying for Laura if the need arose. Laura had been such a little fool, thinking Lelia had helped her in the name of forbidden love. But Lelia had been doing her damnedest to keep William a safe distance from Laura.

Lelia silently smoldered, remembering Laura's angelic smile, one that would melt a man's heart. How often had she turned envy green when Laura graced her gentleman callers with a blinding smile, and how many times had she cursed under her breath when the man drooled over Laura?

With a determined frown Lelia turned her thoughts to Melissa. If she would have known of Melissa's precarious situation, she would have seen to it that Melissa's guardian angel had taken an extended vacation. She would have preferred that her niece meet with disaster on her own accord, but Lelia intended to take matters into her own hands when she arrived in the colonies. Once and for all, she would be rid of the living memory of Laura. William would be hers after long years of waiting and yearning.

Robert appealed to his mother one last time as he helped her into the phaeton. He had not taken to the idea of traveling to the colonies while the British were attempting to bring the unruly heavens under thumb, and he was too much of a coward to cast himself into such foreboding circumstances. Lelia refused to listen to his pleas, determined to see for herself that William was alive and well.

When Captain Stephens learned that Madame Mooree intended to travel to Martin's Fork alone, he offered to accompany her, much to Robert's relief. Lelia was quick to note the captain's fondness for the twit, and she intended to take advantage of his affection. It seemed Melissa possessed the same wicked ability to attract men, just as her mother did. But this time Lelia would see that Melissa's mystical power turned on her. Stephens would make an excellent escort, Lelia decided, biting back a sinful smile. He might even help her dispose of Melissa without his knowing that he had been used in her scheme.

As Lelia stared at the receding shoreline, another satanic smile hovered on her lips. Before the voyage had ended, she would have planned every intricate detail of Melissa's untimely death.

As Andrea and Damion carried their belongings downstairs, they came to an abrupt halt when they saw Nathan leaning casually on the banister at the foot of the steps, his face-splitting smile fastened on Andrea.

"Good morning," he greeted cheerfully, his gaze missing nothing of Andrea's shapely form. "I couldn't think of allowing you to leave without saying goodbye." He hurried up the steps to relieve Andrea of her heavy bags. At closer inspection, his eyes hovered on her full bodice that was delicately framed with pink silk and lace. She was breathtaking and he could not drag his eyes off her long enough to nod a greeting to her foul-tempered brother. "You are bewitching, even at this early hour."

Damion's brows formed a hard line over his stormy eyes as he watched Nathan practically fall at her feet. He was not accustomed to having so many men show blatant interest in the woman he had claimed. Although he couldn't blame any of them, it still galled to watch them all flounder like a fish out of water. It took every ounce of self-control he possessed to play the charade Andrea had spitefully arranged for him. He had to clench his fists to keep from tossing Gibbs down the steps that he had so hastily ascended.

Andrea produced a gracious smile as Nathan pulled the bags from her hands and wedged himself between her and Damion.

"I'm surprised to see you so early, monsieur," she said lightly. Her smile evaporated when she braved a glance at Damion, noting the angry twitch in his cheek.

"I'm not," Damion grunted disgustedly, flashing a disapproving glare that bounded off the back of Gibbs's head.

Nathan was too entranced to catch the snide remark, much to Damion's dismay. It seemed Gibbs had only one thing on his mind, and nothing could deter his lusty thoughts, except perhaps the pain of a broken jaw.

As they stepped outside to tie their bags behind the saddle, Nathan stared incredulously at Damion. "You are forcing your sister to make this journey on horse-back?"

Damion paused from his chore, heaved an impatient sigh, and threw a cold glare to the man who had fanned the short fuse on his temper. "Monsieur, Andrea may appear to be a dainty flower who might wilt in the sun, but she is made of sturdy stuff," he insisted, his tone harsher than he intended. "I am capable of caring for my dear sister. As you can plainly see, she has survived the journey thus far, and I doubt that the last leg of this trip will endanger her health."

"I did not mean to criticize you," Nathan apologized hastily, attempting to cool the fires of Damion's temper. "I only thought perhaps she would be more comfortable in a coach. It would offer protection from the scoundrels who inhabit the territory."

"And I am beginning to think she has already met one of them," Damion snorted derisively. "When I am unable to care for her, I will let you know!"

Nathan flinched at the bite in Damion's tone, expecting at any moment to see him frothing at the mouth like a rabid dog.

Andrea interceded before the two men came to blows. "Nathan is merely concerned about my welfare. You need not be so insulting," she admonished, flinging Damion a reproachful glare and then blessing Nathan with a smile that miraculously healed his wounded pride. "Damion is quite right, monsieur. I prefer to ride on horseback and I am accustomed to the out of doors. And he is very capable of protecting me. I have no fear for my safety."

Nathan affectionately clasped her hand and brought it to his lips. "I wish I could convince you to stay a few more days." His gaze slid to Damion who leaned against his horse, looking angrier than a disturbed hornet. Nathan would have preferred to plant a passionate kiss to Andrea's tempting lips, but the threatening glower that her brother wore on his chiseled features warned him against it. "Goodbye, Andrea," he murmured as he led her to her horse, knowing that Damion had no intention of tarrying a moment longer than necessary.

Damion wedged himself between them to place Andrea atop her steed, not allowing Nathan to handle her a minute longer. "*Adieu*, monsieur," he said stiffly as he brushed past Gibbs and swung into his saddle.

Nathan watched them ride away, marveling at Andrea's ability to manage her horse. She seemed a part of the steed as she galloped beside her brother. A puzzled frown gathered on his brow as he watched the Deuvalles disappear from sight. How could such a lovely young woman have been plagued with such a sour-dispositioned cad for a brother? Damion had disliked him since the moment they had been introduced and those cold features were permanently stamped with a frown. Damion was over possessive of his sister, scarcely allowing her to breathe, Nathan mused, as he strolled toward his horse, mounted and reined in the opposite direction. He could only hope that Andrea could convince Damion to follow the same route on their return trip. And next time Nathan intended to make his intentions clear to that irascible brother of hers.

"That was a touching scene," Damion snorted. "You had Gibbs wrapped around your finger so tightly that I doubt that he will ever come unwound." His sarcasm drew Andrea's chortle.

"Perhaps you envy the gentleman's manners since you have none of your own, dear brother," she taunted before she spurred her steed and sent him off in a reckless pace.

Andrea felt the urge to turn her face to the wind, to hear the pounding of hooves beneath her. Her nerves were on edge, knowing the for the next few days she would have to keep a tight rein on them. It was a therapy of sorts, she thought, as she leaned against the steed's powerful neck, watching him cover the ground at his swiftest speed. Her tension took flight as she thundered toward the trees where the other men waited in camp.

As Damion watched her race across the meadow, a hint of a smile surfaced on his lips. Perhaps she had been a mite jealous of Gibbs. Nathan treated Andrea as if she were some regal queen and he was her knight. Damion had only been using her, denying her the respect she deserved. But then he was left with little choice, and it tormented his pride to watch Gibbs flutter about her. His mind had been on the mission, not Andrea's comfort. True, Damion had been inconsiderate, and the fact that the love-smitten Gibbs had brought it to his attention did not set well.

He would make it up to her, Damion decided, as he nudged his steed into a canter. When this was over, whatever she desired would be hers: money, gowns, furs. She could name her own price and he would pay it.

When he edged up beside Andrea, he grabbed her reins, bringing the steed to a halt. "Andrea, the time has come," he began solemnly. "The success of this mission rests on your shoulders. I wish I could be there with you, but I cannot, and I know that you don't really need me. You can rely on your own cleverness." His brows gathered over his slitted eyes and he regarded her for a long, thoughtful moment. "I have watched you charm men in Norfolk and throughout this territory. What you have done was practice for what you are about to do. I am counting on you to turn the redcoats' heads in your direction and to use them for your purpose. I will give you and Davis two days to familiarize yourselves with the British headquarters, to survey the stockade where Daniel is being held prisoner, and to become friendly with the guards. They will be your main concern. You must map out the area so that if anything goes amiss, my men and I will be able to sneak into the fort and aid in the escape."

"But how will I get the map to you?" she interrupted, raising anxious eyes to him. This was not helping her nerves. She thought she had gotten a grip on herself, but Damion's explanation had her fidgeting again.

"Let your father worry about that. You have enough to occupy your mind without concerning yourself with delivering the map," he insisted. "We will send a ransom note to you and your father the night before you are to free Boone."

"But how will Davis be able to get the map to you? The British might become suspicious if . . . " she persisted, still fretting over the details.

"Your newly acquired father will make the connections."

"But how?"

"Andrea," Damion snapped impatiently. "Just do as I request and remember, you must be convincing. Every remark, every action must be carefully planned. I designed this scheme around your cunningness. I have every confidence that you can handle the British." He reached beneath her chin, holding her gaze. "Keep your wits about you and do not fail me. I'm depending on you." Damion placed a lingering kiss to her quivering lips and then slowly withdrew to stare off into space. "Another quarter of a mile."

Andrea gulped fearfully as she followed Damion's lead. She was having serious second thoughts about her ability to play the charade, and now it was too late to turn tail and run. She had to master her emotions and quickly. If the British suspected anything, she and Davis would be in grave danger. They would be brushing shoulders with the enemy, and one false move could land them in the cell beside Boone. Andrea had a choice: do it right the first time or spend the remainder of the war looking at the world through a barred window. A determined frown settled on her features as they rode into camp. She would not fail. Too much depended on her, her own life included.

The other five men were sober faced and pensively silent as they traveled toward Detroit. It was dusk when they arrived at their destination, and Andrea was a bundle of nerves. When Damion glanced up at her, his expression was unreadable. Suddenly, he yanked her from the saddle, pushed her to the ground, and fell upon her, capturing her lips in a rough, bruising kiss. Andrea's cry was smothered in another harsh kiss as he ripped the pins from her hair and twisted it about his hand like a rope. And then she heard the rending of cloth, her gown splitting at the shoulder to allow his kisses to trace a scalding path down her neck, his hands roaming over her breasts. The indignant shriek that escaped her lips was silenced as his mouth came back to hers in biting insistence. Andrea struggled against him, but she was no match for his overpowering strength. Had he gone mad? Why was he abusing her, and in front of his men?

And then as swiftly as he had grabbed her, he whipped her back to her feet and tossed her up behind Davis. Andrea clutched the torn gown that left her breasts partially exposed and bit down on her bleeding lips, her gaze spewing fire as Damion laughed dementedly. Damn him! She had confessed to love him and he was treating her like an unwanted whore.

"Ride, Davis," he ordered hastily as he swatted the horse's rump and stepped out of the way as the steed bolted into a run.

Cory Heston stalked up to Montclaire, clamped his hand on Damion's shoulder, and wheeled him around. Cory's face twisted in a menacing sneer. There was no excuse for his treatment of Andrea, and Cory intended to tell him that he had stepped way out of line.

"What the hell's wrong with you?" Cory bellowed, his voice rolling over Damion like thunder. "If that's the way you usually treat your wife you should be shot!"

A wry smile etched Damion's craggy features as his gaze slid down Cory's rigid body. "If Andrea and her father were supposedly accosted by thieves, would you expect that lovely lass to escape without a scratch?" he questioned, arching a mocking brow.

A reluctant grin caught one corner of Cory's mouth as his hand dropped from Damion's shoulder. "You are clever, Captain. You don't miss a single detail."

Damion's gaze sobered. "Not when her life hangs in the balance."

A speculative frown plowed his brow. "But if I were a thief, I would have kidnapped the daughter and released the mother," he commented, tearing a hole in Damion's logic.

."You would have tried." His mouth quirked as his eyes strayed to see Andrea and her new father disappear in the distance. "But you would have met with difficulty trying to subdue that wench. If she managed to escape, you would have been left with little choice, *n'est ce-pas?*" When Corry nodded in agreement, Damion continued. "Mademoiselle Deuvalle is adept at maneuvering men. Just when you think you have the upper hand, you take a second look, discovering that your eyes have deceived you." His gaze circled back to Cory and he freed a smile. "When the British see her disheveled appearance and take one look in those captivating eyes, they will believe her story."

Cory exhaled slowly. "Aye. You're right. I've spent the better part of the day worrying about whether Andrea could handle herself in the midst of the redcoats. I wasted my time. I should have saved my sympathy for the soldiers. She'll make blundering fools out of them." As he turned to walk away, he paused, and then tossed a glance over his shoulder. "Who is she, Montclaire? I doubt that her name is Andrea Deuvalle. You would not have permitted her to use her given name, especially when you know the British will be offering a handsome price for her scalp when this ordeal is over."

He shrugged noncommittally. " 'Tis no matter."

"What is her married name?" Cory questioned pointblank. "Is it another alias?" His brows furrowed as he met Montclaire's carefully blank stare.

Indecision tampered with his thoughts. If he spoke the truth, Cory would be tempted to resume his relationship with Andrea. And if he lied, Cory would find out later. He settled for divulging information that would halt the questions and take Cory off track. "She is Jeremy Drieson's daughter."

Heston choked on his breath and then his eyes narrowed suspiciously. Cory knew Drieson and was aware that he had never married and had no child that he had admitted to fathering. "Drieson never wed."

"Nay, he didn't, and Andrea does not know that Jeremy is her father, nor will she ever discover the truth unless Jeremy decides to confess it," Damion informed him. "She goes by many names, but she is still my wife, my responsibility until we choose to go our separate ways."

Cory eyed him levelly. Whatever Damion felt for Andrea, Cory would never know for certain, but Montclaire was involved because of his ties with Drieson. If and when Montclaire released her, Cory intended to seek her out. She was well worth the wait, he thought, as he spun on his heels and walked to his horse.

Damion pulled himself into the saddle, his expression pensively sober. Heston was a good man, one who would care for Andrea. Another thought jolted him, and he felt the knife being twisted in his back, the one Jeremy had implanted when he sent Damion to track Andrea. He found himself comparing the situation to Jeremy's life. Laura had returned to William Stoddard because he was dependable and would give her a home and security, remaining by her side when Jeremy would have disappeared into the wilderness for months on end. Heston would gladly do the same for Andrea, showering her with love and devotion. That affection was mirrored in his eyes each time he had gazed at Andrea. Heston had fallen hard for that feisty little vixen, just as every other man had, except for Zackery Montclaire Beaugener, he thought to himself. In time he would release her, and he would willingly give Heston her real name and the opportunity to win her heart. Damion shook his head, trying to discard his musings. There was much to be considered and he had no time to predict the future. The present was all that was important. Boone must be released and they all had difficult tasks ahead of them, especially Andrea.

"Be strong, *cher ami,*" Damion murmured to the lingering vision. "Your resourcefulness can make all the difference between life and death."

The words that slipped from his lips had him cursing himself. Why had he involved Andrea in such a risky scheme? It was too easy to visualize her as a prisoner, forced to submit to the soldiers' desires and who would brutally use her after she had tried to make fools of them. Damion blinked back the anger, searching for an encouraging thought to erase the scene that was swimming before his eyes. She must not fail!

# Chapter Twelve

When the Deuvalles galloped to the fort, they were halted by two guards who carefully scrutinized Andrea's torn, stained gown and the wild expression in her eyes.

"Assistance, *s'il vous plaît!*" Alexandre Deuvalle pleaded. "My daughter . . ." His shaky voice trailed off as he glanced sympathetically at Andrea who huddled against him, her head resting on his shoulder. "The scoundrels have kidnapped my wife and . . ." He allowed the soldiers to assume by Andrea's appearance what had been her fate.

Without another word the guard ushered the Deuvalles to the major's office. The major frowned in concern when he noted Andrea's crumbled composure and the condition of her gown.

*"Ma mere!"* Andrea choked over a sob as she nestled in her father's embrace. "They have kidnapped her. Monsieur, please help us." Her hysteric tone brought the major to her side.

"What happened?" he questioned as he watched

Alexandre wrap a comforting arm around his daughter and press a kiss to her bruised forehead.

"We were accosted by four men. They took what few valuables we had and then attempted to . . . " He glanced pitifully at Andrea before returning his attention to the major who could see for himself that Andrea's journey had been precarious.

"I escaped from that horrible man," Andrea muttered. The thought of why Damion had roughly abused her suddenly became clear. He had given her an experience to call upon when she related her story to the major. She was inwardly smiling to herself, quietly thanking Damion for his forethought, even though her eyes were clouded with tears that drew the major's sympathy. "He dragged me from the carriage and—" She stopped short, letting the officer use his own imagination. "It will be some time before that scoundrel will have the use of his right arm again. I hope he bleeds to death!" There was vengeance in her gaze as she turned to the major. "It is what he deserved for what he tried to do."

"Those damned colonial heathens," Major Bedford muttered contemptuously.

"They took our carriage and my wife after Andrea escaped into the brush. After they gave me one of their horses, they told me to gather money or I would never see Celeste again." Alexandre's face twisted and he choked on the woman's name. "I found Andrea hiding in the brush along the road as I came toward the fort. I am so thankful that she escaped, but I am worried about my wife. Monsieur, *s'il vous plaît*. Help us. I am not familiar with this country, and I know not where to turn for aid, if not to you."

Andrea appealed to the major as she raised pleading eyes that spilled a sea of tears.

"I will do what I can," Bedford promised. "I can give you a place to stay and send out a searching party to scout the area."

"*Merci*, monsieur," Alexandre murmured appreciatively. "I cannot thank you enough. Now my daughter must rest. I'm afraid she is in shock."

"I'll find you and your daughter suitable quarters," Bedford offered. "You can join me for supper and you can give me a description of the thieves. We will decide on the best course of action to take after you have had time to collect your thoughts."

Andrea swayed toward her father, her head rolling recklessly to the side, and found herself swept up in the major's arms. Bedford gazed down at her, his attention drawn to the full swells of her breasts that were exposed by the torn gown. She was like a beautiful, lifeless doll. He was tempted to stand and admire her, but common sense tapped him on the shoulder and he swiftly carried her to her room and laid her on the bed.

"I'll stay until she rouses," Bedford suggested, but Alexandre was hesitant. "You have suffered a shock yourself, sir. See to your needs and I will care for your daughter."

Alexandre finally nodded his assent and followed the major's directions to another room. Heaving a sigh of relief, Deuvalle loosened his cravat, shrugged off his jacket, and strolled to the window to survey the activities of the fort.

When Bedford knelt down beside Andrea, her lashes swept up and she struggled to sit up on the edge of the bed. "*Je regrette*, monsieur," she apologized as she smoothed her tangled hair away from her face. "Where is Papa?"

"He is in his room. You must rest." He urged her back to the pillow and fluffed it for her.

"*Non*, monsieur, my mother is in danger!" Andrea clutched at his jacket, her eyes wild and frantic. "We must do something!"

Bedford clasped her hands in his as he displayed an indulgent smile. "We will, mademoiselle. If they are requesting money from you, they will probably send you a message. We must wait until they contact us, unless my men sight them."

"Then search for her immediately. What if they attack her as they attempted to do with me?" she gasped in exasperation. "My father would never be able to live with that. Oh please, monsieur!" She threw her arms about his neck, huddling against his chest as she forced another stream of tears down her cheeks. "We must find her!"

Bedford held her tightly, feeling her body tremble against his. "We will do all we can, mademoiselle," he comforted. "But you will be in no condition to help us if you do not rest. When my men return from their search, we will discuss our plans."

Andrea nodded and muffled a sniff as she stretched out on the bed, clasping her torn gown together. While he continued to watch her, she raised her skirt and drew the dagger from her garter to lay it beneath her pillow.

A faint smile grazed Bedford's lips as he noted her overly cautious action. "Is that what you used to escape your captor?"

"*Oui*, monsieur. If it would have been larger or if I

would have had the time, I would have been tempted to cut out his heart," she hissed, as her brooding eyes took on a faraway look.

When Bedford had quietly closed the door behind him, Andrea let her breath out in a rush. She had been so nervous that her voice quivered each time she spoke. And yet her shaky reactions had added substance to her story. But that was as Damion had expected, she thought to herself. And that was one of the reasons he had decided to use the kidnapping and attempted rape as a ploy. It all fell into place and she smiled to herself, knowing that Damion had considered every detail, weaving a convincing story that the British could swallow. But what of the escape? Andrea began having second thoughts about that. When the time came, the charade would not aid them. It would be she and her newly acquired father against a fort of redcoats. Lord, she must have been insane to agree to this!

After Andrea had spent her time preparing her plan of action and studying her surroundings from the window, counting the number of guards posted in the area, a rap at the door halted her thoughts. One of the soldiers who had been sent on the scouting party had found her bags scattered on the road and had returned them to her. When she had bathed and donned the royal blue gown that Damion had purchased for her, she checked her appearance in the mirror and arranged her hair in fashionable curls on top of her head.

Andrea presented Major Bedford with a blinding smile when he arrived to escort her to his room for dinner. The poor man stood speechlessly appraising the lovely goddess in blue velvet, and he had swallowed his tongue as his eyes ran full length of her shapely figure.

"Mademoiselle, I'm afraid I will have difficulty concentrating on my meal if you are sitting across the table for me," he breathed. Bedford had taken note of her comeliness when she arrived at the fort, but now there was no comparison to the bewitching beauty who stood before him.

"You are very kind, monsieur," Andrea replied coyly, batting her eyes at him with just enough finesse that Bedford didn't realize that he was being taken for a ride. "However, I fear that you exaggerate." A demure smile touched her lips as her lashes swept up to meet his bold regard. "Or perhaps it has been too long since you have seen a woman."

"Nay," he assured her, his gaze making slow descent to linger on her bodice. " 'Tis an honest statement and you are a rare beauty."

Andrea pulled her shawl about her shoulders and tucked her hand in the crook of Bedford's arm. It came as no surprise to him that she attracted attention as they strolled to his quarters. Andrea played her new role as if she was born to it. She was graceful, charming, and very feminine.

Major Bedford found that his remark was accurate. He hardly tasted a morsel of his meal because he was too preoccupied devouring the delicious damsel who had strategically positioned herself across the table from him.

When Alexandre spoke he found himself repeating his comment to gain the major's attention. He bit back a smile as he watched the British soldier drool over Andrea. She already had him eating out of the palm of her hand, he thought to himself. Montclaire was not as mad as he had first suspected. Alexandre retracted every remark that he had made about the captain and even those he hadn't dared to voice. She could have charmed a snake out of his skin, he decided, as he observed the angelic smile that radiated from her exquisite features. Alexandre could position himself behind that smile and no one would ever notice him.

"Major, I must see if I can raise the money the thieves have demanded for Celeste's return. I was hoping that perhaps one of your men could escort me to the lieutenant governor's home tomorrow," Alexandre said, his sober expression masking his amusement.

Bedford dragged his eyes off Andrea and settled them on Alexandre. "A . . . why . . . of course. We will make arrangements in the morning. I'm sure Hamilton will assist you. Did the thieves leave a ransom note?" he questioned, when his thoughts finally circled back to the matter at hand. "Where are you to deliver the money?"

"They will send a message tomorrow night. If I cannot raise the sum they demand, I'm afraid that Celeste will . . ." Deuvalle's trembling voice trailed off into an inarticulate phrase in French and Andrea grasped his hand.

"We must have faith, Papa. Major Bedford has assured me that he will do all he can to find *ma mere*. We must believe that she will be with us again soon," she soothed, her eyes straying to Bedford, silently beseeching him to offer encouragement.

"Aye, Alexandre," Bedford agreed. "We will send out another patrol tomorrow if you wish. My men found nothing but your belongings this evening, but darkness overcame them before they could search for tracks. Perhaps tomorrow. . . ."

"But we must be careful, monsieur," Deuvalle insisted, his tone laced with concern. "I want no harm to come to my wife. If we anger those vultures they might kill Celeste."

"We will take every precaution," Bedford assured him.

"Papa," Andrea murmured, her gaze dropping to her lap. "Would you consent to my taking a stroll? This conversation is making me uneasy. I thought I had my emotions under hand, but apparently not. I feel I need a breath of fresh air."

Alexandre nodded affirmatively and then raised a curious brow when Andrea turned back to him.

"Do you suppose we should send a message to Aunt Monette, telling her what has happened?" she inquired, while Bedford glanced back and forth between them.

"*Non, ma cherie*," Deuvalle said adamantly. "The reason for our journey to the colonies was because of Monette's ill health. The news of her sister might distress her further."

Andrea nodded thoughtfully. "I suppose you are right, but I hope we will not have disturbed her just as much by arriving later than she anticipated."

"Mademoiselle, may I accompany you?" Bedford requested as Andrea strolled toward the door.

Andrea glanced over her shoulder at Alexandre, allowing him to decide which one of them would benefit most by the major's presence.

"I would appreciate it if you would escort her, monsieur," Alexandre replied. "The day has worn on long enough for me. I think perhaps I shall return to my room for the remainder of the evening."

After they escorted Alexandre to his room, the major and Andrea ambled about the area while she made mental notes of the buildings and occasionally questioned her companion when she was unsure of the purpose of a particular structure. She paused momentarily to study a long, sturdy building that had a guard posted in front of it.

"*Qu'est-ce que c'est?*" she inquired, but the major only frowned puzzledly. Chuckling lightly, she apologized. "I'm sorry, monsieur. I forgot that you do not speak French. What is this building?"

"I wish I did," he murmured, his gaze resting fondly on her. "It sounds so soothing when I listen to you and your father speak it." Major Bedford gestured toward the building in question. "This is the stockade."

"Do you have prisoners?" she questioned innocently, knowing full well that the man she intended to free was locked inside.

"Only three at present," he replied before a victorious smile pursed his lips. "One of them is quite a prize."

"Prize?" she repeated bemusedly. "I'm afraid I do not understand."

"We have Daniel Boone in custody. The Shawnee Indians captured him and brought him to the fort. We have been trying to convince him that the settlers must surrender their land and return to the East. Boone has finally begun to bend to our way of thinking. The colonel has spent many hours with him since his capture. I think before long we can trust Boone to return to Boonesborough to evacuate the settlement."

"Where is the colonel?" she questioned, her tone trite and seemingly disinterested, although she was hanging on his every word.

"He has gone to parley with the Indians," he answered. "If Boone refuses to join forces with us, the Shawnees will attack Boonesborough and rout out the homesteaders. The colonel has taken them firearms and he should return in a few days. I am in charge during his absence."

Andrea would have muttered in irritation at that news if she had not been so determined to play her charade. She dropped the subject and raised another question. "What does this Boone look like? Even in France we have heard of him. He has explored much of this wilderness, has he not?" Maybe she should have dragged more information out of the loose-tongued major, she thought to herself, but it was too late. He might suspect something if she brought the conversation back to Boonesborough and the siege.

"Aye, he has established a reputation here and abroad, along with several settlements on land that the Crown has not given permission to inhabit. Would you like to see him?"

It was the opportunity she had hoped for, but she masked her interest behind a skeptical frown. "He is not some uncivilized beast who will attack me on sight?" she queried, her blue-violet eyes wide and apprehensive.

Bedford chuckled at her naivete. The lovely lass had no concept of life in the colonies. Perhaps that was why her family had been accosted by highwaymen. They were not accustomed to confronting such uncivilized heathens. "Nay, mademoiselle. He is not violent," he assured her, a broad grin splitting his face. "Besides, we have a guard posted inside the stockade and another outside. They keep close tabs on him."

Andrea was afraid of that. "Then I would very much like to see him," she responded, nodding firmly as she raised a determined chin. "I would like to see this Boone for myself."

As Bedford opened the whining door, Andrea peered down the dark hallway that was illuminated by two lanterns at either end. The stockade was foul smelling and she covered her face with a handkerchief, offended by the unsanitary conditions. Her senses came alive as she walked past the cells to see the shabby, unkempt prisoners who were caged in confining stalls. These were her fellow countrymen whom the British locked up like animals. She now understood why Montclaire had been so hellbent on his cause. To imagine a man like Boone suffering in these filthy conditions turned her stomach. He was a daring man who craved adventure, like Beaugener. The thought of being restricted to four walls in a stockade sent a cold shiver down her spine. She would go mad if she were forced to endure this existence. And she very well could be, she thought to herself. If their mission went amiss she might be occupying the cell next to Boone.

When Major Bedford strolled up to the cell, he gestured to the shadowed form who sat on his haunches in the corner. "This is the famous Daniel Boone," he mocked.

Andrea squinted her eyes to see the man who thoughtfully chewed on a twig of straw and who didn't bother to acknowledge their presence.

"Boone!" Bedford thundered. "You have a guest.

Where are your manners?"

Andrea shrank away and huddled behind Bedford as Boone rose to full stature and came silently toward them. His face was stern and unyielding, his features rough, reminding her of Zack Beaugener. Boone's hair had been plucked out until there was only a small tuft left on the crown of his head. It was an Indian custom and Daniel's appearance was living proof that he had traveled with the Shawnees. His clothes were tattered and shredded, making him look the bedraggled beast. Andrea squelched the urge to scream in indignation at the sight of him. Instead, she clutched the major's arm, staring at Boone in awe and sympathy.

"Major Bedford," the guard called as he opened the door to poke his head inside. "Mr. Deuvalle wishes to speak with you."

Bedford's brows furrowed as he glanced down at the young woman beside him who could do nothing but stare at the captive. "Excuse me, mademoiselle. I will return in a moment. Will you be all right?"

Andrea nodded mutely, never taking her eyes off Boone. They stood face to face in silence until the major was out of earshot.

"Beaugener has come for you," she whispered. "Make no trouble for the British and you will soon be free. The major has informed me that the Shawnees are preparing to attack Boonesborough if you do not agree to evacuate them."

Boone's brows shot up as he listened to her hushed voice, but he dared not speak with the guard watching them closely.

When Bedford stepped outside, Deuvalle bowed slightly. "Monsieur. I'm sorry to bother you, but I

271

wondered if perhaps I could trouble you for a drink of brandy before I retire for the night. I cannot seem to sleep."

"Forgive me," Bedford said apologetically. "It was inconsiderate of me not to offer you a drink. I will bring you a bottle after I escort your daughter back to her room."

"*Merci.* I would greatly appreciate it." Alexandre smiled faintly and then turned back toward his room, hoping that he had given Andrea ample time to talk privately with Boone.

When Bedford opened the stockade door, Andrea was visiting with the guard and then turned to blind him with her smile. "Is Papa all right?" she inquired.

"Aye, but he was having difficulty falling asleep. I promised to bring him a brandy."

Andrea breathed a sigh of relief. "I hope it will help. I might appreciate a glass of wine if you have some to spare," she hinted as she brushed past both men to step outside.

"By all means. My wine may not be the quality that you are accustomed to drinking, but perhaps it will settle your nerves."

Andrea presented him with another sugar-coated smile and then allowed her gaze to slide to the guard who leaned against the outer wall. If he was paying any attention at all, he would catch her lingering interest.

As they walked across the compound, Andrea returned her attention to Bedford. "Thank you for an enjoyable evening, monsieur. You have helped me keep my mind from wandering to troubled thoughts. I am indebted to you."

" 'Twas my pleasure, mademoiselle." Bedford returned her smile as he held the door open for her. He poured her a drink and then retrieved a bottle of brandy for her father. "I won't be long."

When Andrea was alone, she inhaled a deep breath and then exhaled slowly before taking a healthy sip of wine. She choked on its biting taste and gasped, thinking that Bedford's brew had not aged well. That thought transformed into another and Andrea found herself wondering how well she would ferment in that horrible stockade. Judging by the looks of Boone, all too well, she decided. This ordeal was making her tense and she had little time to relax. She had been preoccupied with her mission. Each time she glanced at something, she had been thoroughly surveying it. Whether it was a building or the stockade, her concentration had been so intense that she had become weary from the mental strain.

If only Damion was here with her she wouldn't be so ill at ease. She felt protected when he was beside her, as if nothing could happen to her. But he was out there in the darkness, waiting for her to complete her purpose. The weight of the world rested on her shoulders, and she was beginning to feel the pressure. The glass in her hand involuntarily came to her lips, as if she could find courage in the wine, knowing that just the opposite was true. She had to keep her wits about her every moment. Determinedly, she set the wine aside and then offered the major a tired smile when she heard the door creak.

"The wine has served its purpose," Andrea murmured the lie without batting an eye. "I feel as though I'm floating on a cloud."

A wide smile stretched from one ear to the other as he shrugged off his jacket and tossed it over the back of a chair. After pouring himself some wine, he sank down beside Andrea on the sofa. "I'm sorry that misfortune has brought you here. I wish we could have met under more pleasant circumstances, but meeting you has been like a rainbow after an angry storm. You are charming company, Andrea," he whispered as he edged closer.

"Do all Englishmen bestow such flattery on women, or is it just a characteristic of soldiers of the Crown? You make me feel like a queen even when I know that is not true," she scolded lightly.

"You are very attractive, my dear." His voice was low and husky. It was all he could do to keep from taking her in his arms and clutching her to him. After her frightening experience, he didn't dare, not yet anyway. Andrea might become hysterical since she had already been mauled.

Andrea had the uneasy feeling that he wanted to kiss her, but after seeing Boone and the conditions of his captivity, her opinion of the British dropped several notches. She did not need to be overly friendly to the major, only the guards at the stockade.

"I think perhaps I will retire for the evening. It has been a very disturbing day," she remarked with a weary sigh. "Please excuse me, monsieur." Andrea rose to her feet and forced a wan smile for the dismayed Major Bedford.

"May I walk you to your room?" he requested.

When they reached her door, Andrea knew that he intended to kiss her, as he had in her quarters, and she was afraid her response would have been a repulsive shiver. She began to wonder if the guards would produce the same reaction. How could she pretend to enjoy their company when the sight of a redcoat nauseated her? Damn, there was nothing easy about this.

As Bedford's head moved slowly toward hers, Andrea sidestepped and put the door between them. "Goodnight, monsieur."

Bedford frowned disappointedly when he found the door in his face. With a frustrated sigh he spun on his heels and stalked back to his room to finish his drink alone.

After Andrea had drawn a detailed map of the fort, she slipped into her gown and robe and moved through the shadows to knock on Alexandre's door. When she was inside, she produced the map from the bodice of her gown and presented it to him.

"How's Boone?" Deuvalle questioned in French as he studied the map. "Did I allow you enough time to talk with him?"

"He is as well as can be expected, under the circumstances," she replied, her nose wrinkling distastefully. "I had time to inform him of the rescue attempt. Before I return to my room I intend to stroll by the stockade and better acquaint myself with the guard." Andrea wrapped her robe tightly about her, reached for the doorknob, and then glanced back at Alexandre. "Keep an eye out for Bedford. I don't need to bump into him after I just told him that I was retiring for the night."

"Alexandre nodded agreeably. "What is the corporal's name who remains inside with the prisoners?"

"Phelps," she replied, arching a curious brow.

"I may need that information if I try to draw him out when we rescue Boone. 'Tis nice to know my enemy by name," he added, grinning wryly. When Andrea trembled nervously he frowned in concern. "Are you all right?"

Andrea nodded slightly. "I will be much better when this is over," she muttered, keeping the conversation in French.

Alexandre smiled sympathetically. "I know this is no easy task, but Montclaire *did* know what he was doing, despite the reservations I had in the beginning. You have handled yourself amazingly well, Andrea. I am very proud of you."

"I only wish I could be as calm and self-assured as you are," she breathed whimsically. " You have played your part so expertly the I could almost believe your dear wife had been accosted." Andrea accepted the comforting shoulder he offered, leaning her head against his chest.

"I am as nervous as you are," Deuvalle confessed as he placed a fatherly kiss to her forehead. "This will all be over soon, and we can sit around the campfire, bragging about our accomplishment."

Andrea withdrew, willfully summoning her composure. "After seeing Boone, I have become even more determined to set him free. He is too much of a man to be caged like some wild beast. It incensed me to see him like that."

"You better go now," he urged, silently agreeing with her remark. "It is getting late."

Before crossing the compound, her gaze swept the area, assuring herself that she would not run headlong into the major. As she walked toward the stockade

Patrick Gates caught his breath. Andrea appeared from the shadows, reminding him of a goddess in her flowing gown of white. The moonlight glistened on the honeyed cape that lay around her shoulders. He was taken with her the moment he laid eyes on her earlier, but now she appeared even more delectable in her gossamer gown, making his lusty thoughts flow like a roaring river.

A sensuous smile hovered on her lips as she paused in front of Gates, her gaze missing not one small detail about him. He looked to be only two or three years older than she was. His boyish face mirrored his thoughts, and Andrea knew she had his undivided attention.

*"Bon soir,"* Monsieur Gates," Andrea murmured. "I couldn't sleep. I was hoping you wouldn't mind keeping me company for awhile."

" 'Tis my pleasure," Gates replied, a pleasing smile splitting his face. After a moment his gaze sobered. "I'm sorry to hear about your mother. I hope she will be back with you soon."

*"Merci."* Her eyes dropped to the ground and then slowly lifted as she gazed off into space. "It is difficult to rest, knowing that she is out there somewhere with those ruthless men. Each time I close my eyes, I can see their faces." She shuddered and sidled a bit closer to Gates, feasting on the sympathy he was quick to offer.

"I know it must be an eternity, waiting, wondering," he breathed as his arm curled around her waist.

As Andrea's hands slid up his chest, she felt him wince nervously. An unseen smile touched her lips as she nuzzled against him, knowing that he was inexperienced with women. "I won't be satisfied until those highwaymen pay dearly for what they have done."

As she raised moist lips to him, Patrick swallowed the lump that had collected in his throat. As her sooty lashes swept up, he gazed into her indigo eyes, losing himself in the sight and feel of her in his arms. Instinctively, he lowered his head to capture her mouth, wondering what possessed him to be so forward with her. And then his thoughts fled, his heart thundering beneath his ribs as he drew her tightly against him.

It was a long, breathless moment before he could drag himself away and glance over the top of her head to ensure that they were not being watched. "Why have you come to me when you have Major Bedford at your beck and call? He is a high ranking officer and I'm only a lowly corporal." Patrick was skeptical of his good fortune. The question flew from his tongue before he could bite it back.

Andrea graced him with a smile that cut a gash in his heart as she leaned back as far as his encircling arms would allow. "Does his title make him more of a man than you, monsieur?"

"Well . . . no . . . but . . ."

"I have made it a point not to judge a man by the clothes he wears or the title he bears. And perhaps I do not prefer older men," she added, as she lightly caressed his neck. "I find you much more attractive than the major. I did not allow him to kiss me tonight." Her confession seemed to please him. "Instead I came to you. Do not sell yourself short, monsieur." Andrea traced the gentle lines around his mouth before her hand fell away, and she dropped her head to stare at the buttons of his jacket. "But if you want me to leave,

I will. It was not my intention to annoy you. I suppose I was being selfish and inconsiderate. *Je regrette.*"

Patrick could have cut out his tongue for questioning her sincerity. How could he have doubted this angel? When Andrea tried to slip from his embrace, he tightened his grasp on her. "I don't mean it that way," he insisted, desire flaming through his veins as her firm breasts brushed against his chest. "It is just that Bedford has much to offer a woman."

Andrea chortled softly. She almost liked Gates, even if he was a redcoat. He was young, cuddly, and not quite as confident as men like Bedford or Montclaire. Damion made Patrick seem like a child. "Are you speaking of money, monsieur?" Andrea questioned, arching a delicate brow. "At the moment that is the farthest thing from my mind." Her smile was an open invitation and poor lovestruck Patrick gave an immediate reply.

Gates could no more resist the temptation of her soft lips than could any other man who found himself holding her in his arms. She had learned much from Montclaire, and she knew how to arouse a man's desires. Perhaps that had been part of his purpose, too, she mused, as she accepted the passionate kiss. It seemed that all Damion had done had a motive, a purpose. Had he taught her the ways of love as preparation for her mission? Andrea was having difficulty concentrating on Gates's kiss when she was so preoccupied with analyzing Damion.

She had been shoved back and forth across the line of love and hate where Damion was concerned. When he was lying beside her, gathering her in his arms, she adored him, reveling in the gentleness he could display, but when she had the opportunity to stand back and study him from afar, she was more realistic. The qualities about him that she admired often became the ones she detested. He was always using people as his pawns, maneuvering them, playing them to his advantage. And now he had trained her to be like him. She was using Gates and Bedford, manipulating them, deceiving them. She was no better than Damion, hiding behind smiles that were only skin deep, offering her affection to gain the end she desired. Her soul searching had taken its toll and Andrea was disturbed by the realization that she was behaving like Damion.

When Andrea squirmed for release, Patrich peered curiously at her. She masked her emotions behind another sweet smile. "I must get back to my room. I do not wish to make trouble for you."

"I have naught else to do but stand here and count the stars. The prisoners cause no disturbance and my duties are dull and tiresome."

"I must go. The hour is late. *Bon soir,*" she whispered, as she reached up on tiptoe to place a fleeting kiss to his lips.

Patrick watched her disappear among the shadows and then rubbed his eyes, wondering if he had been dreaming. The silence that surrounded him was eerie and he shivered, remembering the feel of her trim body pressed to his. It was inconceivable that this goddess would find him more fascinating than Major Bedford, but he decided not to argue with fate. In this uncivilized wilderness Andrea was a shining light in the darkness. He would share the private moments that she granted him. England was a world away and of the few women he had known, Andrea surpassed them all with her beauty and poise.

Gates spent a long, quiet evening lost to pleasant thoughts. When Phelps called him inside for a little conversation to break the monotony, Gates felt slightly annoyed that he was being detained. His imagination had been working overtime, and he was enjoying every minute of a vivid fantasy. When he peered around the door to check his post, he kept hoping to see Andrea floating toward him, praying for another chance to take her in his arms, to kiss those soft lips that melted beneath his. Lord, he was hallucinating! Why would she be interested in him?

# Chapter Thirteen

After the Deuvalles had taken breakfast with Major Bedford, Alexandre was escorted to the home of Lieutenant Governor Henry Hamilton, hoping to raise money for the return of his wife. He was gone several hours and Andrea nervously paced her room, anxiously waiting his return, wondering if he had been able to deliver the map to the other men. When Alexandre finally tapped on the door, she met him with wide, searching eyes.

"How did you fare?" she questioned in French.

"*Tres bien*," he answered with a smile. "The ransom will be delivered tonight. Tomorrow night, while the carriage is being returned to the fort, Montclaire will be waiting outside in case we meet with difficulty." Alexandre motioned for her to take a seat beside him on the edge of her bed, intending to give more details, but Andrea cut in with her curious question.

"How did you contact Montclaire?"

A wry smile hung on one corner of his mouth. "An old man bumped into me. Instead of having my pocket picked, I found a note in it," he explained, and then his expression sobered. "Tomorrow evening you must keep the guard away from the entrance of the stockade. There will be considerable commotion when the carriage arrives and, hopefully, most of the soldiers will be at the main gate to view the scene. You will have to leave all your clothing behind, Andrea. All you will be able to take with you is what you're wearing at the time we release Boone. The rest of your belongings are still at camp. Montclaire will see to it that you manage to salvage a few clothes."

He studied her closely, wondering if she would be distressed about the loss of her expensive gowns, but obviously Andrea could have cared less.

Deuvalle clasped her hands in his, demanding her full attention again, but then, he already had it. Her gaze was boring into him. She was hanging on his every word. "While you are preoccupying Gates I will be outside waiting for you. When Boone is free, we will exit through the back gate with only two guards standing between us and freedom." Alexandre paused a moment and then sighed weakly. "If anything should go amiss, you and I will be left to our own devices, I'm afraid. I hope we will not be sharing a cell beside Boone."

"I do not intend to be held captive by the British," Andrea said determinedly. "Boone must be freed to return to Boonesborough before the Shawnees decide to rout the settlers. I did not travel across this wilderness to fail."

"Nor did I," Alexandre agreed. "But if we should meet with trouble we are on our own. If you can manage to escape, don't look back, just keep running and

283

don't concern yourself with me because I will be following my own advice."

Andrea's eyes twinkled mischievously. "I am not planning to use that advice, dear Papa," she assured him, fondly patting his cheek. "We shall just do it correctly the first time." Although her tone was confident there was a looming doubt hanging over her, a nagging premonition that even the best laid plans often went awry. But she must not think negative thoughts, she told herself. She would do what had to be done and not give way to the idea of failing.

A disturbance at the front gate brought the major and the Deuvalles outside to receive a note and a scarf tied to the rock that had been hurled toward the guards.

As Alexandre read the note, Andrea clutched the pink scarf and lovingly rubbed it against her cheek, a tear trickling from the corner of her eye.

When Alexandre handed the note to Major Bedford, his brows furrowed in concern at the instructions.

Deliver the ransom at eight o'clock. Miss Deuvalle must bring the money and leave it in the mill office. If anyone attempts to follow her, Madame Deuvalle will not live to see another sunrise.

Bedford glanced at Alexandre, his expression stunned

and shocked. " 'Tis far too dangerous for Andrea to go alone."

Andrea peered up at him after she had read the message. "I have no choice, monsieur. If it will save mother then I will go, but not without a pistol." Her tone was firm and insistent.

"Andrea, you may be inviting trouble," Alexandre warned her. "We must not antagonize them."

"I will not use it unless I am forced to it," she assured him. "I will be more confident if I am armed."

"I agree with Andrea," Major Bedford broke in. "She should be allowed to defend herself if the need arises. She has suffered enough at their hands."

Alexandre looked from one determined face to the other and then nodded reluctantly. A troubled expression filled his eyes as he took the scarf from Andrea and walked quietly back to Bedford's quarters for a brandy.

With the money pouch tied behind Major Bedford's personal mount, Andrea climbed onto the brown gelding, leaving Bedford and Deuvalle to stare anxiously after her. With the wind whirling about her Andrea felt more at ease than she had since the moment she arrived at the fort. As she galloped down the path to the mill, she inhaled a deep breath, summoning strength from the thundering steed and the crisp evening air.

When she reached her destination, she untied the money pouch and took time to check to see if it was lined with money or merely strips of paper. A slow smile surfaced on her lips when she saw the funds that would aid in their return to Kentucky and buy the supplies needed to save Boonesborough from attack. While Andrea stood lost in thought, a pair of hands clamped about her waist. She gasped and then relaxed when the familiar fragrance of Damion filled her senses. She turned in his arms, reaching up on tiptoe to plant a surprisingly passionate kiss to his lips.

His brow arched slightly, a rakish smile curving the corners of his mouth upward. "Am I to believe that you missed me, *cherie?*"

His mocking remark turned her affection for him to ice. She squirmed from his embrace and dropped the pouch in his hand, her chin tilting defiantly. "Considering how preoccupied I have been during my stay at the fort where I have been surrounded by a multitude of willing soldiers, I find you to be a bit presumptuous, *mon capitaine*. I offer the same greeting to every man who touches me," she added, just to spite him.

Damion grabbed her to him, urgently seeking her lips, sending a wild tremor surging through her veins. As his hands moved along her back to her hips, Andrea melted against him, aware that she had missed him more than she had realized. Although she had admitted that she loved him, she was determined to think of that emotion in terms of the past, because she knew there was no future for them. This love would not tear her heart in two as it had done to Jeremy. There would be another man someday who would make her forget Damion, one who could return her love, one who could accept her without cynicism. To love Damion was a foolish dream and Andrea tried desperately to convince herself of that while he held her captive in his arms, but it was difficult. He had the power to release her emotions, letting them run wild and free in reckless abandon.

"And did all the others arouse your passions, vixen?" he questioned hoarsely as his hot kisses trailed down her neck to her full breasts. "Were you acting for them or did you give freely?"

Andrea pressed determined hands to the hard wall of his chest, putting more distance between them. "We have more important matters to discuss than my amorous endeavors with the redcoats. And besides, you are the one who ordered me to be as friendly as the situation demanded, remember?" she snapped, her blue-violet eyes flickering in annoyance. "Boonesborough is in danger of being sieged by the Shawnees. We must return to Kentucky as soon as Boone is free."

"How do you know that?" His rugged features hardened, his eyes losing the passionate flame that had consumed them earlier.

"Major Bedford is loose-lipped when he is preoccupied with arousing thoughts. He told me that the colonel has gone to talk with the Shawnee tribal leaders. No doubt they will be well armed with British rifles," she added resentfully. "Both the British and the Shawnees want the settlers to move east and relinquish their claim on the land."

"We must arrive at the settlement in time to prepare for an attack," Damion mused aloud, his brows furrowing thoughtfully.

"Perhaps the money Alexandre confiscated from Hamilton will buy rifles and ammunition to defend the fort." Andrea glanced at the pouch Damion held in his hand.

"Aye." He planted a quick kiss to her lips and then swept her into his arms, depositing her atop the gelding. "Be prepared for tomorrow night," he commanded.

Andrea gazed down at him, a faint smile brushing her lips. "Thank you, Damion," she murmured.

His dark brow elevated in silent question before he

voiced it. "For what?"

"For practically raping me." Andrea giggled at the sound of her remark. Never in her wildest dreams did she imagine herself complimenting a man for abusing her. "It wasn't difficult to relate the incident to Major Bedford."

A wry smile skitted across his mouth as he presented her with an exaggerated bow. " 'Twas my pleasure, madame." As he rose to full stature he slapped the horse's rump, sending him off in a gallop. "Keep your wits about you."

His words were carried off into the wind and Andrea felt a pang of fear as she glanced back to see nothing but swaying shadows. Never in her life had she felt so alone. It was with great determination that she returned to the fort, knowing in the back of her mind that the thought of turning tail and running would have been the safest plan of action.

When Andrea entered the fort, Major Bedford and Alexandre were waiting anxiously for her. Andrea's expression remained sober as Bedford lifted her from the saddle and set her to her feet.

"Are you all right, mademoiselle?" Bedford inquired, a concerned frown on his brows.

"*Oui*," she assured him. "I met with no difficulty, but I did not see Mama or the carriage. I left the money and returned."

"You saw nothing of Celeste?" Alexandre's face seemed tortured, almost haunted. "I was hoping they might assure us that she was alive and well."

"I'm sorry, Papa," Andrea soothed as she tucked her hand in the crook of his arm.

"Perhaps the two of you would like a drink," Bedford

suggested for lack of anything else to say. He knew he could use one and the look on Deuvalle's face assured him that Alexandre could do with one as well.

Alexandre forced a meager smile. *"Merci,* but no," he declined, his voice quivering slightly as his gaze swung back to Andrea, and he drew her closer to him in a protective manner. "I would like to be alone with my daughter."

Bedford nodded mutely and watched father and daughter, arm in arm, take the distance between the gate and Andrea's room in steady strides.

"Did Montclaire have any other instructions for us?" Alexandre questioned after he closed the door and locked it behind them.

"He only cautioned us to be prepared for tomorrow night." After pausing a moment a wry smile crept across her lips. "I took the time to check the pouch and found that you had indeed raised money from my mother's release. I do hope that woman appreciates all the trouble you have gone through for her."

Alexandre chuckled, a wide grin stretching from ear to ear. "I have spent considerable time wondering if the wench is worth the effort I have made to saved her life."

Andrea threw her arms around his neck and planted a quick kiss to his cheek. "You are remarkable," she complimented. "I was almost in tears after I saw that distraught look on your face a moment ago. If I hadn't known you were lying through your teeth, I would have been sobbing deliriously. But as it is, I pity the lieutenant governor whose money you swiped right from his pocket and the British regiment who boarded and protected us. Before long they will find themselves wondering how they could have been so gullible." Andrea released a wicked chortle. "I would love to see the look on Bedford's face when he realizes that he had been played for a fool."

Drawing her arms from his shoulder, André held her hands in his own, his expression becoming solemn. "We have not come out of the worst of this yet, Andrea. I cannot gloat over our success until Boone and the two of us are safely outside these walls."

"You're right. I am being overly confident," Andrea chastised herself. It had been a defensive device, voicing positive thoughts instead of dwelling on the negative ones, ones that came creeping up on her each time she let her guard down. "I've been rather nervous, puttering around here, waiting, planning, wondering." Her lashes swept up to meet his probing gaze. "Quite honestly, all that has kept me from falling to pieces was my ride to the mill."

"I'm sure that was why Montclaire insisted that you bring the ransom," Deuvalle remarked. "I was skeptical about the man at first, but now he has earned my respect. He has cleverly planned each detail. If this mission fails, it will not be because of an oversight on his part. He has calculated every move." A hint of a smile found the curve of his lips. "I greatly admire Montclaire. I don't always understand why he does what he does, but time usually proves his actions to have definite purposes." Alexandre ducked his head, looking a little sheepish. "When he brought you on board the schooner I was ready to resign the mission, thinking he was utterly mad. But as Stratton said, there is method in his madness. He chose you for this task because you are indeed remarkable and very resourceful. You are capable of many deeds that the average woman would never even attempt."

"Like father like daughter," she retorted, playfully pinching his cheek. "I could never have managed this charade without you, you know. You have made it easy to play the role because I have been swept up in your convincing act."

Alexandre grinned as he came to his feet. "Now that we have exchanged compliments, I think I should return to my room so you can see to young Gates."

Her brows furrowed at his last remark. "I'm not particularly fond of deceiving the corporal. He seems a pleasant sort. If it were Bedford I would enjoy bringing him down a notch. He is a bit arrogant and stuffy."

"He's English," Alexandre snorted. "I think perhaps his title has gone to his head. Just be thankful we don't have to contend with Colonel Jensen. Rumor has it that he's a wry old man who is not easily fooled. Jensen may be the one exception to the rule, and he may not have swallowed our story." He strolled toward the door and then glanced back at Andrea. "I will keep an eye out for Bedford so that he will not interrupt you and Gates."

As Andrea approached the corporal, viewing the warm smile that spread across his clean-shaven face, she swallowed her guilt. It left a lump in her throat. Gates did not deserve to be deceived. He would most likely to be the one to receive the brunt of the punishment after the escape. Andrea prayed that it would not be too harsh, but there was little else she could do about it.

"*Bon soir*, monsieur," she murmured, as she edged up beside him.

Gates's greeting was a kiss that nearly stripped her

breath from her lungs. She was surprised by his amorous attack and the chortle that might have burst from her lips was strangled beneath his passionate kiss. Dragging herself away from his embrace, Andrea glanced about her.

"Is there some place we might go that would be more private?" she queried, as she toyed with the buttons of his jacket, a coy smile touching her lips.

Patrick gestured his head toward the supply shack and then scanned the area, hoping that no one would notice that he had left his post. When he had ushered Andrea inside, he took up where he left off. His mouth swooped down on hers, lost to the soft lips that melted like rose petals beneath his kiss.

"You are beautiful," he whispered, his voice graveled with disturbed desire. "You have been on my mind all day. I had hoped that you would come tonight."

"Did you doubt that I would?" She cocked her head to the side, a provocative smile settling on her exquisite features.

Patrick did not bother to reply as he nuzzled against the curve of her neck, tracing a path of hot kisses along her bare shoulder. While he was lost to the heady fragrance that clung to her and the feel of her shapely body molded to his, Andrea surveyed the shadowed room. When she saw what she was looking for, she smiled in satisfaction. As Gates's caresses began to become intimate, she pushed away, bestowing a disapproving frown on the overzealous corporal.

"S' il vous plaît . . . monsieur, non—" she gently rebuked, hoping to discourage him without annoying him.

With a despairing sigh, Patrick dropped his hands away from her breasts and settled them on her waist. "I'm sorry. You must think me to be an uncivilized heathen."

"*Non*, monsieur, but perhaps you are used to being with women who offer you more than I am willing to give at the moment," she added, leaving him with a small ray of hope. "I think perhaps I should go." She untangled herself from his embrace and graced him with a smile that reduced him to duck soup. He stood mesmerized, unable to move as Andrea gracefully exited from the shack.

A sigh escaped his lips as he wandered back to his post, his thoughts so preoccupied that Phelps had to summon him twice to gain his attention.

Andrea awoke the following morning as nervous as a caged cat. Bedford eyed her curiously as she fidgeted in her chair during breakfast. Naturally, he attributed her anxiety to the fact that her mother was still the prisoner of the colonials. He attempted a light discussion with both of the Deuvalles, but they were unreceptive. It was almost a relief when they returned to their quarters since Bedford was running out of conversational subjects.

The afternoon dragged on endlessly for Andrea. After taking a bath to soothe her nerves, she lay down for a nap to tide her through the sleepless night that lay ahead of her. Her dreams were troubled and she woke, hearing her own frightened shriek. A perplexed frown gathered on her brows as she swung her legs over the edge of the bed. An odd sensation flooded over her, shattering her confidence. What if . . . Andrea squeezed back the thought of finding herself behind bars in the stockade, alongside Boone and her newly acquired father. Inhaling a deep breath, Andrea strolled to the mirror to assess her reflection. She tried to summon her composure until she was satisfied with the calm, poised young woman who stared back at her. If only Damion could have been there beside her, to encourage her, to protect her from these worrisome thoughts, she mused disheartenedly. She needed him desperately. But he had thrown her to the wolves, expecting her to outfox them. Just when she thought she had collected her wits, they scattered again as that eerie feeling washed over. No matter how she tried, she could not shake the thought that this plan would meet with disaster.

After waiting at the main entrance for over an hour, Major Bedford offered to send out a scouting party since Madame Deuvalle had not made her appearance.

*"Non,"* Alexandre declared adamantly. "If the thieves spot your soldiers, Celeste might come to harm. We cannot take chances with her life. They agreed to return her tonight, and I have to believe that they have some code of ethics. They have what they wanted." He spun away, wringing his hands in front of him. "We must wait this out."

"Papa, I am going back to my room," Andrea announced. "If the carriage arrives, please notify me."

Alexandre turned back to the major after he watched Andrea hurry across the compound. Her sobbing drifted back to them, and Alexandre watched the major wince uncomfortably, knowing that she was distressed.

"I am sorry that my daughter and I have been such unpleasant company. We can think of nothing but Celeste's return."

"I understand. There is no need to apologize," Bedford murmured, a sympathetic smile touching his lips.

The major heaved a sigh as Deauvalle ambled away. The chances of having the woman returned from the ruthless colonials were slim and none, but he could not bring himself to voice his pessimism. Under different circumstances he would have aggressively pursued Andrea Deuvalle, but she was so preoccupied and standoffish that he did not have the heart to press her. Bedford propped himself against a barrel, waiting the arrival of Madam Deuvalle, if indeed she would be returned at all.

Andrea removed her petticoats so that she would not be inhibited during the escape. With her dagger tucked in her garter, she opened the door, checked the compound, and made her way toward the stockade. The fort was strangely quiet and Andrea could hear her heart thundering in her ears. Her legs were wobbly as she walked toward Corporal Gates. It took little effort for her to throw herself into his arms, accepting the comfort of his embrace.

"I'm so worried about my mother," she breathed, her voice as shaky as her legs. "She has not returned. I don't want to think of it. It is driving me mad." Andrea tugged on his arm, drawing him toward the shack.

Gates followed without complaint, leaving his post without giving it a second thought. When the door was closed behind them, he took her in his arms, drawing her quivering body to his, seeking her trembling lips. It was not Andrea who was going mad, he thought, as his heart flip-flopped and banged against his ribs. It was he who was mad with desire.

"Love me, Patrick," she murmured against his hungry lips. "Take me. I need you desperately. Take the world away."

There was agony in his eyes when he held her away from him and stared deeply into her angelic features. How could he take advantage of this honey-haired beauty, knowing that she was distraught? Hell, how could he not? He had waited a lifetime to take such a desirable woman in his arms and make her his possession. There was a silent plea in those pools of indigo, a need that begged to be appeased. Patrick lowered his head, capturing her lips in a devouring kiss, lost to the feel of her warm body and the heavenly fragrance that was a part of her. Perhaps he would hang for leaving his post, but he didn't care.

Patrick drew her down on the stack of quilts near the object Andrea had spotted on her visit to the shack. And then it was too late. Patrick lost touch with reality in a kiss that he would remember for a long time to come. He was drifting in a world of darkness, unable to find the strength to open his eyes.

Alexandre paced the floor and checked his timepiece for the tenth time in less than a quarter of an hour. He had nearly worn out his vest pocket retrieving and replacing his watch. Finally, he gathered his weapons and stashed them in his coat, drew open the door, and hastily took the distance between his room and the stockade. He waited less than a minute before Andrea appeared from the supply shack, somewhat disheveled, but otherwise unscathed. A smile grazed his lips as he saw the powder horn and musket she cradled in her arms.

"You disposed of Gates?" There was no need for his question, knowing the corporal would not freely relinquish his weapon.

"*Oui*, he has been properly christened with a stone jug. He will have a hellacious headache when he wakes to find himself bound and gagged," she replied with a victorious grin.

Alexandre chuckled, nervous and amused as he glanced at his watch. "You have a notorious reputation for clubbing men over the head and disappearing in the darkness. I heard Montclaire say you once used such methods on him."

Deviltry sparkled in her eyes. " 'Tis a convenient method of ridding myself of unwanted companions."

When Alexandre nodded slightly, their amusement evaporated. They moved around the corner of the stockade, and Andrea positioned herself on the ground so that Phelps could see her when he opened the door.

"Phelps! My daughter has fainted! Help me, *s'il vous plaît!*" Alexandre called, the urgency in his voice bringing Phelps to his feet.

The corporal swung open the door to see Andrea sprawled on the ground. As he knelt down beside her, Alexandre stepped from the side of the stockade and implanted the butt of his flintlock on the back of the man's head. With a groan Phelps crumbled beside Andrea who rolled to her feet to help Alexandre drag the corporal into the shack with Gates. After rummaging through his jacket they found the keys and then hurried to the stockade to release the three prisoners.

The commotion at the front gate brought most of the soldiers to view the carriage that rumbled toward them, the flames lighting the darkness. Bedford ordered several men to gather buckets of water to extinguish the fire before he muttered under his breath, vowing to see the heartless scoundrels hang.

"Should I summon the Deuvalles?" one of the soldiers questioned.

"Lord, no!" Bedford bellowed at him. "Would you want to witness this sight if one of your family was inside a burning coach?"

The young corporal ducked his head and wheeled away to dash to the trough to retrieve water for the fire, wishing he would have had more sense than to ask such a ridiculous question.

While the soldiers tried to extinguish the fire, the Deuvalles, Boone, and the other prisoners made their way out of the stockade. Andrea stepped around the corner and then tossed Boone the musket and powder horn that she had confiscated from Gates. He nodded a silent thanks before moving toward the back gate to find two guards positioned in front of it.

Alexandre glanced back at Andrea, raising a questioning brow. She gave him a wry smile and then darted toward the startled soldiers.

Andrea sobbed hysterically as she stumbled and fell in front of them. "They killed my mother," she choked out before succumbing to another round of wailing.

The soldiers bent down to her, only to be accosted by the prisoners who sprang on them. Andrea scrambled to her feet and darted to the gate to remove the log that secured the exit. She felt the load ease and glanced back to see Boone smiling down at her.

"You've done enough," he murmured, as he stood her aside and swiftly removed the post from the gate.

A shout rang out behind them, and Andrea glanced back to meet the furious gaze of Major Bedford. Suddenly redcoats were swarming toward them, and Andrea remembered what Alexandre had told her. She ran for her life without looking back, closing her mind to the explosion of muskets that seemed to come from all directions.

Her own cry of agony reached her ears when she stepped in a hole and fell face down in the dirt. She looked back to see Bedford charging at her, a menacing sneer curling his lips. Fear constricted in her throat as she struggled to her knees, but she felt as if she were moving in slow motion while the movements of Bedford were accelerated. Andrea choked on a sob. This time there were genuine tears clouding her eyes.

Jeremy pushed away from the table and grabbed his cane. A strange sensation darted through his veins, making the hair on the back of his neck stand up. Tensely, he came to his feet and ambled toward the window, gazing out into the darkness.

"Jeremy?" William arched a wondering brow. One moment they were playing a game of chess and, the next instant, his companion had walked away. "Is something wrong?"

Jeremy drew a deep, shuddering breath, his eyes fastened on the shadows that danced in the moonlight. Only once in his life had he been visited by a haunting premonition. It was the moment before he turned to find the grizzly bear rising up on his hind feet, his jaws dripping in anticipation of the kill. A shudder that drove into his very core seized him, and he clutched the windowsill to keep his feet.

"Jeremy?" William's brow knitted in concern as he watched the color seep from his friend's face. "Are you all right?" He was on his feet, rushing to Drieson in a split second.

His gaze swung back to Stoddard, his expression tortured. "I think I need a breath of fresh air," he managed to say between the furious beats of his heart. Adrenaline was shooting through him, forcing his breath out in ragged spurts.

William grasped his arm and led him toward the door. "What the devil has come over you? You look as white as a ghost."

Jeremy sucked in his breath, feeling suffocated for an instant until the fresh night air revived him. He inhaled carefully, his gaze scanning the darkness, fighting the sensations that come at him again.

"Take me home, Will," he requested, his voice barely audible.

Stoddard wrapped a supporting arm around his waist and urged him toward the dim shaft of light that shone from the window of Jeremy's cabin, wondering what had come over his crippled friend.

When Jeremy had eased down into his chair, he raised a grateful smile to William's apprehensive expression. "Too much brandy," he said quietly.

William doubted that that was the cause of his distress, but Jeremy apparently wanted to keep the problem to himself.

"I will serve nothing stronger than tea tomorrow night," he replied, forcing a smile that was as meager as Jeremy's.

Jeremy nodded agreeably as he eased back in his chair

and stared at the opposite wall. "Until tomorrow."

When William had reached the door, he paused to assure himself that Jeremy was well enough to be alone. "I can stay if—"

"Nay, William. I need to be alone just now," he murmured without glancing in Stoddard's direction.

When he was left to himself, Jeremy expelled his breath and then muttered a curse to his helplessness. Something was wrong with Melissa. He could feel it in his bones, and there wasn't a damned thing he could do about it. Not a damned thing! He would have Zack's head! Jeremy slammed his fist into his hand, cursing the vision of raven hair and steel-gray eyes that materialized before him.

Damion's gaze swept the darkness, his senses alert to the snapping twigs as the fleeing prisoners made their way through the brush to the guerrilla band who waited with extra mounts. As the men appeared from the shadows, his eyes narrowed, studying each one carefully. Fear gripped him as he searched the faces that were captured in the moonlight. He squinted again, surveying the shadows, but there was no one among them. Damn, he growled under his breath.

"Where is Andrea?" His gaze drilled into Davis, cold and accusing.

Davis glanced over his shoulder as he swung onto his steed. "She was beside me a moment ago. I thought she was—"

"You *thought!*" Damion's razor-sharp tone stabbed Davis in the back. "You were responsible for her."

Damion kicked his horse in the flanks, sending him

into a gallop, fighting his way through the thick under-brush that camouflaged them from the fort. A fear, the likes of which he had never experienced, shot through him as he strained to see two figures in the distance.

"You deceitful little bitch!" Bedford's words caught in the wind, taking them to Damion's ears. The vengeance in his voice cracked like a firing musket as he back-handed Andrea across the cheek.

As Damion thundered toward them, his eyes blazed with fury. He yanked his steed to a halt and leaped at Bedford, knocking him to the ground. With one fluid movement he planted his fist in Bedford's jaw. As the major slumped, giving way to unconsciousness, Andrea came to her knees, her head spinning from the blow Bedford had inflicted upon her. Before she could get her bearings, Damion threw her onto the saddle and stepped up behind her.

When his booted foot grazed hers, she gasped in pain. "My ankle," she moaned.

"Dammit, why didn't you call out for help?" Damion growled, as he urged his steed toward the trees.

"Boone was free. That was all that mattered. I had served my purpose," she muttered out of the side of her bleeding mouth.

She wiped the back of her hand over her lips and then clung to the horse's mane as they rode at a reckless clip.

"And Jeremy would have my head if I didn't bring you back."

Just as Damion uttered the last word, a well-aimed shot found its mark and he sagged toward Andrea. She realized that he had been hit when an agonizing groan escaped his lips. As he wrapped his arms around her waist to keep his seat, she took the reins and headed for the underbrush.

"You have been nothing but trouble," Damion ground out as a searing pain shot across his chest.

Andrea fought back the tears that attempted to cloud her eyes and urged the steed toward the men who awaited them. Stratton led the way along the creek, taking them further away from the redcoats who filtered through both gates to pursue the prisoners.

"Boone!" Damion forced out the name in a ragged breath. "Take Andrea with you. I'm in no condition for fast riding. I'll have to hide out and join you later. I caught a musket ball. Heston can take Andrea home."

"Nay," Andrea insisted. "I'll stay behind to care for him."

Boone glanced from one defiant face to the other, admiring the strong will that blazed in both pairs of eyes.

"Andrea, this is no time for one of your fits of temper. Do as I command," Damion muttered as the stabbing pain ascended his arm. He tried to force her from the saddle, but his failing strength made his attempt futile. She wouldn't budge from her seat.

As Andrea reined the flighty steed away from the rest of the men, Boone edged up beside her. "He is right. You better come with us."

"You owe me a favor," Andrea persisted. "I intend to collect on it right now. I must go with him. He cannot survive out here with the redcoats swarming the area. I know where we can take refuge until he is well enough to ride."

"Andrea has proven that she can take care of herself," Davis assured Boone who sat indecisively in the saddle. "We haven't time to waste. If we don't move quickly, the British will be crawling down our necks."

Boone glanced back at the other men who had sided with Davis, all except Heston. He sat staring pensively at Andrea, wanting to take her with him, but knowing that she was Montclaire's only hope for survival.

"Let her go with him," Cory said quietly, and then reined his horse through the shallow creek.

After the other men filed in behind him, Boone focused his somber gaze on Damion. "She is right, my friend. And I cannot force her to travel with us."

As Boone moved away, Damion heaved a defeated sigh that caused a sharp intake of breath.

"Is the pain too great?" she questioned, as she urged the horse toward the open meadow.

"Just point this nag toward safety and get the hell out of here," Damion ordered through gritted teeth.

The reckless pace made him cringe, but he refused to stop until they had put a greater distance between them and the fort. Finally, he feared he could not stand having his insides scrambled without passing out and tumbling from his perch.

"Andrea," he rasped against her ear. "I must rest."

She drew the steed to a halt and, forgetting her own injury, she helped Damion from the saddle to find his linen shirt soaked with blood. "My God! Why didn't you tell me the wound was so serious," she scolded, her brow etched with concern. "You probably left a trail of blood from here to the fort."

Damn, she feared something like this might happen. Damion was paying his dues for threatening that preacher. Andrea blocked out the thought and concentrated on Damion who moaned as he slumped on the ground. Extracting her knife from her garter, she cut the bottom of her skirt to make a bandage for the jagged wound on the back of his left shoulder. After designing a tourniquet, she bound his arm to his chest to prevent any movement that might draw more blood. When she was satisfied with her work, she rummaged through the saddlebag for her buckskin clothes and hastily shrugged them on.

She silently prayed that the guerrilla band had attracted the redcoats' attention away from her and Damion so they could travel at a slower pace. When she had propped Damion back on the horse, she eased up behind him and moved through the thick brush, keeping under cover as much as possible.

Damion muttered under his breath and then glanced back at Andrea, his pain souring his mood. "When I have the strength I am going to take you over my knee and paddle your backside for disobeying my orders."

Andrea patted his pale cheek. "You do that, Captain, just as soon as you feel up to it," she encouraged, her tone carrying the slightest undertaste of sarcasm.

"I intend to. You never were worth a damn at following orders. It seems it is left up to me to pound some sense into you," he muttered before he closesd his eyes and fought the sea of darkness that swam before him.

Andrea felt fear knotting up in the pit of her stomach. Damion seemed so frail and vulnerable as he slumped forward in the saddle, no longer the invincible warrior she remembered. If only he could endure the pain without losing more blood. If only she could transport him to safety to tend to his wounds. Andrea blinked back the tears and guided the steed eastward. Let him live, she breathed, as she lifted her eyes heavenward, letting the tears spill down her bruised and swollen cheeks.

# Chapter Fourteen

Nathan Gibbs struggled from bed when he heard the impatient rap at the door. He managed to pull on his breeches and fasten them before he opened it and peered sleepy-eyed at the small form that was dressed in deerskin. His expression registered shock as he squinted against the bright light of dawn.

"Andrea! What the devil happened?" he gasped, as he glanced over her head to see Damion slumped forward on the saddle, his shirt caked with blood, his face deathly white.

"Damion has been shot," she breathed. "He needs care. Can we impose on you?"

Without bothering to reply, Nathan rushed over to drag Damion's limp body from the saddle. Montclaire had passed out again as he had several times during the night. It was all Andrea and Nathan could do to haul his heavy body into the house.

When they managed to get him in bed, Andrea unwrapped the bandages and groaned when she saw the ugly wound that continued to seep blood. She had not realized the wound was so close to his heart. It had been dark when she first inspected him and time had been short. It was a wonder that he had survived the journey. The tourniquet was all that had saved him from bleeding to death.

"Is there a doctor near here?" she questioned anxiously, never taking her eyes off Damion.

"There is one at the settlement. I'll send Nancy after him," Nathan replied as he rose to his feet and started toward the door. His sister appeared from the hall and he made a quick introduction. "Nancy, this is Andrea and Damion Deuvalle. Go fetch Doc Collier."

"Melissa," she murmured quietly, still picking away the pieces of cloth that clung to the wound.

"What?" Nathan cast her a bemused glance. "Why are you using another name and where is your French accent?" he added when he finally came to his senses.

" 'Tis a long story, Nathan. I'll explain later, but now Damion needs attention. We must boil water and make fresh bandages," she said as she rose from the edge of the bed and found her way to the kitchen.

While Nancy searched for the doctor, Nathan started a fire. Melissa went back outside to retrieve their saddlebags and stash their horse in the barn. When she returned to the kitchen, Nathan waited with a curious frown. He wanted an explanation and he demanded that it come at *that* moment.

"I want to know what is going on. Are you in some sort of trouble?" he queried as he took the buckets from Melissa and poured the water into the kettle that hung in the fireplace.

Melissa stared into his curious face, her countenance sober, her indigo eyes expressionless. "Where do your loyalties lie, Nathan?"

His brows came together in a straight line as he regarded her carefully.

When he made no reply Melissa questioned him again. "Tory or Whig?"

Nathan was uncertain what to say, not knowing which one would please her. Finally he produced an honest answer. "Whig, but I don't know what that has to do with you. I'm beginning to wonder if you are the woman I thought I knew."

A slow smile grazed Melissa's lips as she relaxed and then nodded in agreement. "You don't know me at all, Nathan. Andrea Deuvalle was an alias," she stated simply. "I'm not from France. I am from Kentucky and our mission was to free Boone from the British headquarters at Detroit. Damion was wounded while we were attempting to escape."

Nathan gazed bewilderedly at her while the image that he had formed of Andrea Deuvalle shattered in a thousand pieces and an even more admirable opinion of her began to replace it. She had risked her life for an important cause.

"How the devil did you manage it?" he questioned anxiously.

Melissa glanced over to see that the water had begun to boil and grabbed the bucket of liniment that she had made from the leaves and herbs before coming into the house. She nodded toward the fireplace. "Fetch the water and I will tell you about it while I see to Damion's shoulder."

As Nathan followed behind her, Melissa returned to the bedroom and eased down beside Damion to touch her hand to his forehead. His temperature was soaring, and she was alarmed that his ashen face seemed so calm and motionless, almost as if he were . . . Quickly routing the dreadful thought from her mind, she set to work cleaning the wound.

As Nathan continued to hand her fresh rags that he had dipped in hot water, Melissa heaved a heavy sigh and explained. "My father and I went to the fort, pretending to have been accosted by thieves who had kidnapped my mother."

"Your father and mother?" A perplexed frown gathered on his brows. "But where are they? How does your brother fit into this?"

"There were several men who aided in the escape," she continued quietly. "One of them charaded as my father. We requested the aid of the British while pretending to wait for the kidnappers to return my imaginary mother. We managed to free Boone last night and once we were outside the fort I twisted my ankle—" Melissa halted abruptly and glanced down at her boot. She had been so concerned about Damion that she had forgotten all about her foot. She had walked over a mile, shocked, exhausted, and numb to all except the need to survive.

Nathan met her gaze and then focused his attention on her feet. "Which one?"

"The right."

While Nathan pulled at her boot, Melissa winced in pain. Her ankle was swollen, and he had to cut away her boot to remove it.

"My lord, Melissa," Nathan snorted disgustedly. "It might be broken, and I can see by the look of your face that you overlooked your own injury."

"There was too much on my mind to give it a second thought," she defended with a careless shrug. She pressed her fingers to her throbbing ankle. "It felt better when I had my boot on." Melissa turned back to Damion and ignored Nathan's concern as she continued, "Damion came back for me when I fell and he was shot trying to rescue me."

Nathan stared at her in amazement. She had related the precarious experience as if it were nothing more than a casual stroll in the moonlight, but he could well imagine how dangerous the situation had been, especially if she had been captured. How could her brother have allowed her to become involved in such a dangerous plot? He was as cold and calloused as Nathan had first suspected. Melissa was undoubtedly a remarkable woman or she would not have been able to carry out and survive such an ordeal. The very thought of being in the midst of an entire British regiment unnerved him. One false move, one incorrect statement could have brought their scheme down in shambles around her. Nathan glanced scornfully at Damion who lay pale and lifeless before him. What kind of man was this? How could he have allowed his sister to endure such an experience?

Nancy tapped on the door and looked anxiously to her brother. "The doctor cannot come until later."

Melissa frowned as she peered over her shoulder at the comely lass and then she focused her attention on Damion. There was naught else to do but apply the liniment and stitch the wound. Damion was already on death's doorstep and they couldn't wait any longer. "Bring me a needle and some heavy thread," she ordered urgently. "And I will need more bandages."

As Nancy hurried down the hall, Melissa gritted her teeth determinedly. He must not die! He could not die! When Nancy handed her the needle, Melissa took a deep breath and began stitching the jagged flesh of Damion's shoulder. It was a tedious chore, and by the time she had finished applying more poultice to the tender flesh, she realized that she was completely exhausted. Nathan helped Melissa to her feet, and she flinched when she put weight on her swollen ankle. Swinging her up into his arms, Nathan carried her into Nancy's bedroom and laid her gently on the bed.

"And now for you, mademoiselle," he stated matter-of-factly. "You are going to rest after I bring a cold cloth for your ankle. I'll keep an eye on your brother."

Melissa slowly raised her eyes to Nathan and smiled gratefully. "Thank you. You will have no argument from me. I'm too tired to lift my head from this pillow."

As Nathan peered into the glistening pools of blue-violet and watched her dark, sooty lashes flutter against her cheek, his heart leaped with a warm emotion that took his breath away. Melissa was beautiful, even with her tangled, golden hair lying in scattered disarray about her shoulders. He had adored the delicate, French beauty he had met the previous week, but the fascinating creature who lay in repose had quickly earned his admiration and his love. Aye, that was it, he mused fondly, as he studied her shapely curves and swells that were wrapped in buckhide and fringe. He had never known a woman like her. Melissa was young, vital, and adventurous, not the sort of woman that a man had an opportunity to marry, but the type of goddess that he dreamed of possessing, even if for a moment. She was the unattainable dream that he would have loved to grasp and keep as his own. Perhaps while her brother was recuperating, he would have the opportunity to win her affection and even convince her to stay. Nathan knew that in expecting Melissa to settle

311

down to a tranquil life would be no easy task, but she was worth the effort. And even if he found it impossible to keep her, he would cherish their time together. It was better than never knowing her at all.

"Nathan," she whispered drowsily. "If the doctor comes or Damion wakes, please call me."

He nodded slightly and knelt down beside her as she turned her head to gaze over at him. He moved toward her, placing a tender kiss to her tempting lips, drowning in the intoxicating sweetness that made his thoughts whirl in delight.

"Melissa, I—"

As she pressed her fingers to his lips, a rueful smile curved her mouth. She knew what he was about to say. The tenderness in his green eyes mirrored his emotion, and Melissa halted his words, "Nathan, please . . . go stay with Damion. There is much about me that you do not know and if you did, you would wish to take back what you intended to say just now. Please allow me to rest," she pleaded quietly.

"Nothing can change how I feel about you, Melissa. I know what I want and I have found it in you." He carefully soothed her tangled hair away from her face as his eyes caressed her delicate features. "You are a rare gem, Melissa. You cannot blame me for wishing to keep such a beautiful prize."

Melissa shook her head as her eyes clouded with tears of exhaustion and regret. "Nay, you deserve much more than I can give."

As she reached up to place her hands on either side of his face, a tear trickled down the side of her cheek. "I have nothing to offer you, Nathan."

"But I want no more than you can offer," he insisted.

"Perhaps in time you could learn to—"

"I will only bring you misery. I'm sorry that I came back, but I had to find a place for Damion to stay. Now please go to him," she urged as she rolled to her side, turning her back to him.

Nathan came to his feet, released a disappointed sigh, and ambled out of the room. When he pulled up a chair beside the bed, Damion slowly opened his eyes. Nathan peered into the narrow slits of smoky gray, finding no gentleness mirrored there.

"Where am I?" Damion questioned hoarsely.

"In my home," Nathan replied. "Your sister brought you here and patched you up." He eased back in his chair and studied Damion critically. "She saved your life."

"She is also the one who caused me to catch a musket ball in my shoulder," he muttered disdainfully.

Nathan frowned at his cruel remark. Damion was a heartless cad.

"Where is she?" Damion asked in forced breaths. He was so weak that talking was more of an effort than he had ever dreamed possible.

"She's resting. She asked me to wake her when you roused, but I think she needs some sleep. I do believe that she only managed to bring you here with her strong will and determination," he replied, attempting to praise the brave young woman whom Damion had scorned.

"*Oui*, she has that," Damion admitted, as a ghost of a smile played on his ashen lips. The stubborn wench had disobeyed him, but he had to give her credit for her feat. He was certain that she could confront the devil himself and walk away the victor. The little vixen had a mind of her own and not even Boone or the other men had been able to convince her to go back to Kentucky.

"You can drop the French accent, Mr. Montclaire," Nathan requested dryly. "Melissa told me what happened and who you are."

Damion arched a dark brow and attempted to move to a more comfortable position, but a stabbing pain shot through his shoulder and he winced involuntarily. "What did she tell you?" he questioned, as he sucked in his breath, his chiseled face twisting in agony.

"The truth," Nathan stated flatly.

"Which is . . . " Damion prodded, attempting to draw a definite statement from Gibbs. Why had she confided in this lily-livered chap?

"That you and your sister helped Boone escape from the stockade where you were wounded," he replied as he studied Damion's cold expression.

Damion scowled disgustedly. She should have told him nothing. How could she have been certain that he would not turn them over to the British?

Reading Damion's skeptical thoughts, Nathan continued, "Obviously Melissa trusts me. I am not a British sympathizer and I have no intention of informing the redcoats that you are in my house."

With a grateful nod, Damion forced a shallow smile. "Thank you, Gibbs. I'm afraid I am in no condition to protest if you suddenly decided to do just that."

Nathan took the glass of water from the nightstand and reached behind Damion's dark head, lifting it carefully so that he could drink. "I think you better get some rest yourself, Montclaire," he suggested. As Nathan rose to his feet and ambled toward the door, his brows furrowed thoughtfully. He paused to glance over his shoulder at Damion. "When I first met you, I thought you were foul tempered, overprotective, and only concerned

314

with yourself, but thanks to Melissa's account of the past few days, I have changed my opinion. What you have done is to be admired and what she has done . . . " Nathan's voice trailed off as he slowly shook his head and then met Montclaire's expressionless features. "Your sister is a remarkable woman, but I don't think I could have placed my own sister in such a dangerous situation without my conscience haunting my every thought. If she would have come to harm, I could never have forgiven myself."

Damion was quick to catch the insinuation, but his countenance remained carefully controlled. "Then perhaps your sister does not compare to Lissa. You don't know her as well as you seem to think, *friend*," he added with a hint of sarcasm in his raspy voice.

"I would rather imagine that you gave her little choice in the matter," Nathan snapped, his green eyes flaring to meet the flinty orbs that had begun to smolder angrily.

"Even if I had given her the choice, she would have readily accepted the challenge. Like I said, you don't know her at all."

"That's exactly what she told me, but I intend to find out everything about her while I have the opportunity," Nathan assured him boldly before he exited from the room.

"Damn," Damion muttered under his breath. Was there no man who could resist that minx? He had already envisioned her in the arms of every British soldier at the fort and here was yet another man who wished to possess her. Damion could read the flicker of desire in Nathan's eyes each time he had referred to Melissa. In the past, Damion had never once given a second thought to sharing a woman's affection with another man, but for some

315

reason Melissa was different and he was not sure why. Perhaps it was because she was Jeremy's daughter, or maybe it was the fact that she could not be compared to any woman he had ever met, or because he had allowed himself to know her too well. Whatever the case, he would not permit Nathan to make advances toward her right under her husband's nose. By damned, she would not surrender to a man like a Gibbs if he could help it. He could do nothing about the soldiers, but he could keep an eye on Gibbs. Damion's temper was at a rolling boil and his fever skyrocketed. He was losing contact with reality as the thoughts intermingled in twisted dreams. Soon he was swimming in a blur of confusion, wondering why he cared about the little vixen who remained untamed and invincible. She had survived the ordeal much better than he had and had probably enjoyed enticing all of those redcoats into her bed. Damn that witch! Was there no end to the haunting thoughts? Her image floated about him like a colorful butterfly that alighted for a moment to place a gentle kiss to his lips and then fluttered away to seek new conquests. He watched her go, unable to catch up to her. Each time he crept close, she would take flight, gliding lazily across a meadow of awaiting faces that desired to touch her while outstretched arms sought to hold her, just as he had. None could claim the elusive butterfly. She was far too cunning to be trapped. She had admitted that she loved him, but it was only a part of her game. Each time another man was close, she flew into his arms, responding to his embrace. Her words meant nothing and he could not trust her even now.

Damion's head rolled from side to side as perspiration covered his pale features. He was hot and cold at the same time and shivered with a chill that seemed to wrench his very soul. His mind was tortured and his body was consumed with pain. An agonizing moan escaped his lips and Melissa came awake when she heard him.

As she rolled from the bed, she tested her ankle and found it to be extremely sore. She limped toward the door and braced her arms on the wall as she made her way to Damion's room. When she saw the beads of sweat glistening on his drawn face, a concerned frown furrowed her brows. He looked deathly pale and she gasped in alarm as she carefully eased down beside him.

"Lissa," he murmured in ragged breaths. "Lissa."

"I'm here Damion," she assured him soothingly as she pressed a cold cloth to his forehead and smiled tenderly when he looked to her.

When she gazed into the pools of silver that rippled with pain, Damion raised his right arm and wrapped his lean fingers in her golden hair, pulling her face to his. As Melissa touched his lips, her eyes widened fearfully. He was on fire! The infection had begun its dreaded course, and she quickly drew away to unwrap the bandages.

Damion watched her carefully, noting the weariness in her exquisite face. She seemed so delicate and fragile at the moment. He had the overwhelming urge to take her in his arms to comfort and protect her, but, unfortunately, he was in no condition to console anyone. Of course his conscience had played havoc with his thoughts, he mused pensively, but he wasn't about to tell that to Gibbs. What the hell did he care what Nathan thought of him? Gibbs was the complacent, apathetic kind who was content to sit back and let others do the fighting. He was a coward who would never become involved unless the British were on his doorstep. Only then would Nathan consider raising arms. Damion's musings

317

were interrupted by his own agonizing shriek when Melissa applied the foul-smelling salve to his shoulder. He jerked away from the stinging pain the liniment brought.

"Dammit, woman! If you wanted to kill me, why didn't you just shove me off the saddle somewhere between here and Detroit?" he snapped gruffly, casting her a condemning glower.

Melissa grinned mischievously. Hearing him rant and rave in his usual, razor-sharp tone gave her confidence that he would survive. After all, she thought to herself, it would take a great deal more than a chest and shoulder wound to dispose of a man such as this.

"To leave you alone to die would not have been as gratifying as having you at my mercy so that I could watch you suffer at my own hands," she mocked dryly. Her eyes slid to his face and then focused intently on her chore.

"I should have known it was torture you had in mind for me." His face twisted in pain as Melissa packed more poultice around the stitches. "What is that horrible concoction? The stench is rancid and if that weren't enough, it burns like fire!" he hissed through clenched teeth.

Melissa continued her ministrations as she replied blandly, " 'Tis one of Jeremy's home remedies. I'm surprised he didn't teach you to make it. It may be offensive, but 'tis effective."

Damion grunted and muttered under his breath. Jeremy again, he thought scornfully. That name kept popping up to haunt him. "I should have known Drieson had something to do with it."

Damion reached up to cup her chin in his hand, and Melissa gazed into the pools of stormy gray. "Why did you tell Gibbs about Boone?" he questioned abruptly.

Melissa removed his hand, wrapped the bandage

318

about his shoulder, and sighed weakly. "For several reasons. I thought he had a right to know that he was harboring fugitives, and I was too exhausted to devise another partially believable tale. And besides," she added with a casual shrug," I was tired of deceiving everyone. I had my fill of that at Detroit."

"But you didn't give him the whole truth," Damion reminded her harshly. "You failed to mention to him that we are man and wife."

Staring deeply into his eyes, Melissa paused a moment before replying, "We aren't really. It suits my purpose to have him think that I am your sister," she explained glibly.

Damion cocked a wondering brow. "And just what is your purpose?"

Melissa bestowed a sly smile on him, making her blue-violet eyes sparkle vibrantly. "Nathan is in love with me," she informed him. "I wasn't sure he would allow us to remain here if he knew that I was the wife of such an irascible scoundrel."

With a dark scowl, Damion squirmed beneath the quilts. They were all in love with the witch, every damned one who had crossed her path, except him, of course. He would not fall prey to her bewitching charms. "Then he is a fool," Damion muttered cynically. "And I'm sure he will pay dearly for baring his heart to you."

With a nonchalant shrug, Melissa picked up the glass and offered Damion a drink. "Don't concern yourself with him. You aren't fond of him anyway. What do you care what he suffers?" She tucked the quilt carefully about him and displayed a weary smile. "You must rest."

"Come lie down beside me," Damion requested hoarsely, as his last bit of strength seemed to flow away, leaving him helpless. "If I am condemned to suffer from a witch's potion, the least you can do is allow me to be comforted by your enticing spell."

Melissa tossed her wild hair back over her shoulder, grinned wickedly, and curled her fingers like sharp claws, raking them playfully over his cheek. "Have you no fear for your safety?" she taunted.

A faint smile threatened the corners of his mouth as he drew her close. "I have very little left to lose. I am at your mercy, my cunning witch. Do with me what you will. I am yours, for I have not the strength to fight you."

Melissa placed a kiss to his feverish lips, whispering ruefully, "For a time perhaps, for a short time."

Damion peered into her eyes, seeing a new horizon. He was drawn into their boundless depths, seeking the flecks of gold that splattered in all directions. As he was carried into that forbidden world, blackness surrounded him and he surrendered to its compelling silence.

When Melissa felt him relax, she withdrew, brushing her hand across his face, tracing its distinct lines that often appeared to be carved in stone. Now they were vulnerable. There was no arrogant smirk on his face, nor was there an impassive expression that masked his emotions. Here before her was the gentle man whom she had seen on rare occasions. Beneath that calloused shell was a tender man, capable of compassion. It was not often that she could view the other side of the stone mountain. She stared lovingly at him for a long moment, wishing that by touching him she could transform him into the whole man he had been the previous day. She could endure his cynicism if she could see him as he once was: strong, unyielding, and invincible.

Melissa heaved a whimsical sigh as she ran her hand

through the raven hair that lay across his forehead. If only he had not come back for her, he would not be lying here so lifelessly. It was her fault. She should have been the one to suffer, not Damion. He should have been on his way to Kentucky with Boone and the rest of his men. They needed Damion and here he lay, wounded and helpless, unable to find the strength to lift his head from his pillow. A tear formed in the corner of her eye and slid down her cheek as she pressed a kiss to his unresponsive lips. She would have given the world and all that was in it if Damion would miraculously awake and bless her with one of those blinding smiles that could melt a woman's heart if she wasn't guarding it closely.

## Chapter Fifteen

"Is the patient resting comfortably?" Nathan questioned as he stepped around the corner to see Melissa bending over Damion.

Her gaze slid to Nathan as she twisted around to sit up straight on the edge of the bed. "He's resting, but I doubt that he is comfortable. He's burning up with fever."

"I'll give him a cool rubdown while you bathe and change," he offered. "Nancy prepared the tub for you."

"Thank you, Nathan." Melissa cautiously came to her feet, favoring her swollen ankle.

Nathan closed the distance between them, swept her into his arms, and carried her to her room. As he put her on her feet, she glanced out the window, amazed that darkness had crept upon her. She had slept the entire day and still she was exhausted.

When Nathan left her alone, she stripped from her deerskin garb and sank into the soothing water. Heaving a weary sigh, she leaned back against the rim of the tub, her thoughts wandering as she stared at the opposite wall.

When Damion was well enough to ride, he would take her home and then join Boone. She would be whisked from this adventurous life and deposited in her father's hands. Could she ever be content again, having known the excitement and the hazards that she had faced and overcome these past two months? Could another man take Damion's place, arousing her passions to sensuous heights of ecstasy? Could she be satisfied with the role of the average woman after she had survived in a man's world where life and death were the foremost concern? How could she tell her father of her restlessness? Jeremy might understand what plagued her, but would William? He had expected her to travel to France, rub shoulders with the aristocracy, and return the genteel lady whose main concern was the womanly art of managing a home. "Bah!" Melissa muttered under her breath, her nose wrinkling distastefully at the thought. What was she to do with the rest of her life? Suffer from boredom, dream of adventure, and cry herself to sleep each lonely night, knowing that she would never again be cradled in Damion's protective arms?

Melissa was much too tired and depressed to be having this conversation with herself. And Damion's grave condition weighed heavily on her mind. Today was all that mattered. That is what Damion had told her and she was determined to cling to that philosophy. She would make the most of each day as it came, never expecting it to last forever. And yet, she wondered if perishing at the hands of the British would have been a fitting end. Maybe it would have been better than withering and fading in a vacuum of uselessness.

Her father could manage without her, Damion would quickly forget her, and Jeremy would survive as he always had, with a quiet smile and an accepting nod. To have no purpose was to wade into quicksand, waiting to be swallowed up into the damp darkness.

Melissa discarded her depressing thoughts. She had been wallowing in self-pity long enough. Determinedly she set her mind to the problems at hand. When she had scrubbed herself and washed her hair, she reached for the bucket of cool water that sat beside the tub. It was invigorating and pleasing to her troubled soul.

After searching through the saddlebag, Melissa extracted one of the simple cotton gowns that Damion had packed for her. On the front of the dress, a pin held a chain of gold and a sapphire pendant. Melissa's brows furrowed curiously as she detached the necklace and held it for closer inspection. Was this meant for her? Was it a gift from Damion?

She fastened it around her neck and glanced in the mirror to study her reflection, but the sapphire caught her eye, and she watched it glow in the dim lantern light. It was beautiful, just as the gowns had been that Damion had purchased for her: exquisite, tasteful, and extravagant. As she toyed with the stone, her thoughts transported her back to the night she and Damion had spent together before they traveled to Detroit, the last time he had made love to her. A delightful shiver trailed across her skin. How could she ever forget the feel of his sinewy arms about her, the manly fragrance that encircled her senses, the magic touch that could arouse her to the limits of her sanity? Never! No other man could replace him in her heart.

She was destined to dwell on memories, just as Jeremy had done. Damion would never love her. It was not his way. He would not relinquish his heart, or perhaps she was just not woman enough to gain his trust and devotion, she thought to herself.

Whatever the case, he had merely endured their time together, feeling nothing more than lust and passion. He would have sent her off with Boone with nothing more than a hasty goodbye. Aye, he would have preferred it that way, she mused disheartenedly. He had stashed the necklace in her belongings. It was his way of repaying her for the effort she had made for his cause. She should have left him in Detroit. It would have been best for her. But she had bought precious time, time she could not have spent with him if she had obeyed his orders. She was every kind of fool and she knew it. The longer she remained by his side, loving him more each passing day, the more difficult it would be to leave him.

The tap at the door disrupted her silent reverie. She swept her hair up on her head and hastily pinned it in place before hobbling over to answer the knock. Nathan's gaze ran over her shapely figure, an appreciative smile clinging to his lips. When he noticed the sapphire necklace he lifted it into his hand to carefully examine it.

"This rare gem is almost as lovely as you are, Melissa," he complimented, his voice flowing over her like a tender caress.

"Thank you, Nathan. 'Tis is a gift from Damion."

His brows furrowed over his green eyes. "Your brother who always has a scowl stamped on his face was considerate enough to purchase this expensive gift?" His tone was highly skeptical.

"Damion is not always moody and cantankerous," Melissa defended, a mischievous sparkle in her eyes. "Occasionally, I find him to be only cranky and irascible."

" 'Tis a shame that he is not half as witty and charming as his sister." A broad smile stretched from ear to ear as Nathan bent his head to steal a kiss. "Then perhaps he and I could indulge in a civil conversation."

Melissa sank down on the edge of the bed when Nathan attempted to capture her in his arms and then set to work binding her tender ankle. She sniffed the pleasant aroma that wafted its way into the room. "Something smells very appetizing. Is Nancy preparing dinner?"

" 'Tis ready. I came to call you, but I was sidetracked by a lovely goddess." His eyes took on a hungry look, but Melissa was aware that his main interest wasn't food. He was being overly obvious about his intentions and it made her uneasy.

"I am famished," she declared as she rose to test her foot and, finding that the bandage had eased the pain, she aimed herself toward the door, ignoring his remark and his blatant appraisal.

Melissa was delighted to find Nancy to be pleasant company. Her smile was warm and contagious, putting Melissa at ease. When they had finished their meal, Melissa offered to help with the dishes while Nathan planted himself in a chair by the fire and stared at the flames that curled and danced against the blackened rocks.

"I am sorry to have imposed on you this way, Nancy," she apologized. "I hope we haven't inconvenienced you."

"Not in the least," Nancy assured her with another bright smile. " 'Tis nice to talk with someone my own age." A blush worked its way up her neck as her lashes caressed her cheeks. "You have a very handsome brother. I think I fell in love with him the moment I laid eyes on him."

Melissa couldn't help but giggle at Nancy's dreamy-eyed expression. "Aye, he is an attractive rogue." But then her smile evaporated. "Be wary of him. Guard your heart. He believes in stealing a woman's soul, leaving her with nothing. He does not understand the meaning of love."

A puzzled frown gathered on her brow as she regarded Melissa. "How can you speak of your own brother so harshly?"

Her shoulder lifted in a nonchalant shrug as she continued drying the plate she held in her hand. "I am being truthful. I don't want to see you hurt as others have been." Melissa raised her gaze, holding Nancy's attention. "You may enjoy his company while he is here, but never forget that he will soon be gone," she warned.

"It will be difficult to heed your advice when I look at him," she replied with another lovestruck expression that made Melissa roll her eyes toward the ceiling. "My mind starts wandering off in the wrong direction before I can stop it."

Melissa pensively studied Nancy, seeing the naive simplicity that she had once possessed. It hurt to realize that it had been stolen from her, and she could never return to the woman she had once been.

"Come sit down and give your ankle a rest," Nathan insisted as he strolled into the kitchen, impatient with the length of time it was taking to do the dishes.

When Nathan pried the plate and dish towel from her hands and shuffled her toward the sitting room, Melissa acquainted him with her look of annoyance. "Really, Nathan, you needn't pamper me. My ankle is tightly bound and I hardly feel any pain."

As she attempted to worm from his arms, she glanced up to see Damion propped against the wall, his face deathly pale, but ominously threatening. "Damion," she gasped in alarm. "What are you doing out of bed? You'll tear open your wound."

The menacing scowl that riveted over Nathan made him drop his hands from Melissa's waist. Sparks were flying and Nathan took two retreating steps when he found himself scorched by the fire in Damion's eyes.

"There are two things a man must stand up for," Damion growled in belated reply to Melissa's inquiry. "One is his *sister's* reputation, which is in the process of being soiled by an overzealous lech." His gaze was glued to Nathan, hard and accusing. "And the other is—"

Nancy blushed crimson red, Nathan's face whitewashed, and Melissa bit back a grin as he moved toward Nathan. Judging by his sour mood, she was certain that his next remark was to be off color and overly explicit.

"I think we all know what the other is, Damion." Her patronizing tone did more to antagonize than to soothe him, and she became the recipient of another of

328

his brooding glares. "Let me help you." She wrapped a supporting arm around his waist to steady him.

Nathan sucked in his breath at the thought of Melissa assisting her brother with that particular chore. "I will take care of him," he insisted in a strained voice that lacked eagerness.

Melissa's lashes swept up to see that Damion was still glowering at Nathan. She breathed a sigh of relief when he reluctantly nodded his consent. The angry twitch in his jaw assured her that he was having difficulty controlling his temper. The fact that he was in tremendous pain did nothing to ease his black mood.

Melissa glanced over to see Nancy wilting onto the divan, her face flushed, her expression somewhat awestruck.

"Every time I see him, my knees go weak and my heart flutters as if I could not take another breath." Nancy laughed at her own foolishness. "I cannot seem to help myself."

Melissa could find no jealousy, only sympathy for Nancy's innocence, but still she could not hold her tongue. "You are falling head over heels for the wrong man. Save your devotion for one who deserves you." Her lecture fell on deaf ears. Nancy was entranced by the image that swam before her. The bare-chested man whose finely tuned muscles bulged with each movement was implanted on her brain, and her thoughts were indeed running away with themselves.

When Nathan walked back into the room, his gaze bypassed Melissa, focusing on the fire. "I put Damion back to bed, but he insists that he see you," he stated, a hint of bitterness in his tone.

No doubt Damion's sharp tongue had been working

overtime, Melissa guessed as she silently made her way to Damion's room. When she sank down beside him, his eyes anchored on her, his expression grim.

"Did you and Nathan have words?" she questioned as she unwrapped the bandage to inspect his wound.

"Nay, madame. Only *I* had words," he assured her gruffly. "I told that cowardly ogre to keep his damned hands off you."

As Melissa applied more salve to his shoulder, Damion winced and drew away. "That hurts like hell!" he growled between clenched teeth. "I swear you will be the death of me yet, you and that foul-smelling brew you insist upon smearing all over my chest! I'm certain that damned concoction will burn out the infection along with every inch of my hide!"

" 'Tis almost as foul as your disposition," she taunted, unable to suppress a smile. She knew he was in pain but it was comical to watch him snorting and pouting like a spoiled child.

"Do you think *you* could be more pleasant under these circumstances?" he countered, his tone dripping with sarcasm. "You are out in the parlor playing the lily of the valley while I'm confined to my bed like an outcast weed. Gibbs hovers over you like a lusty gardener, waiting to pluck the dainty little flower and claim it as his own."

Melissa laughed out loud. "Really, Damion. You are exaggerating," she chided between chortles. "Your fever must have fried your brain. I never thought you to be so melodramatic."

"Perhaps you wouldn't find this so amusing if you were the one who was bedfast and I was the one making passes at Nathan's sister." He flashed her another

330

disgruntled frown. "What's the wench's name anyway? We have yet to be introduced."

"Nancy, and she is quite taken with you," she informed him. "But if you persist in behaving like a ruttish boar, she is bound to change her high opinion of you." Melissa slapped a cold cloth on his perspiring brow, pressed a fleeting kiss to his lips, and then attempted to rise, but Damion clamped down on her elbow, prohibiting her escape.

"No matter what Gibbs thinks, you are still my wife. No man touches what is mine if I can help it," Damion assured her, a subtle threat lacing his voice.

Melissa bristled at his remark, her gaze holding a scornful mockery. "You sent me to fend for myself in the British headquarters and you fear that I cannot handle one man?"

"Do you intend to succomb to Gibbs as readily as you surrendered to the redcoats?" he questioned point-blank.

She eyed him levelly. "I yielded nothing more than a necessary kiss."

"What of the stockade guard?" A suspicious frown gathered on his brow, causing the cold cloth to slide off his forehead.

Melissa uncovered his eyes and plastered the cloth above his brow in a dispassionate manner. "Corporal Gates received a blow on the head that rendered him senseless, and that is *all* he was rewarded. You know how I enjoy cracking the skulls of amorous men," she reminded him with a caustic smirk. "I lured him into thinking that I would offer more, but I left him bound, gagged, and unappeased, which is exactly what I am tempted to do with you if you don't stop harassing me."

She bent her gaze to glare at the hand that held her captive.

Damion released his grasp on her arm when his fears were laid to rest. "I underestimated your cunningness once again," he confessed, a half smile hanging on one corner of his mouth. "I should have known that you would not deny yourself the pleasure of making a fool of the man. You seem to delight in transforming men into jackasses. At least I am not the only mule in the pen."

"I have spent so much time with you that I have adopted your cynical attitude toward the opposite sex. Use them, abuse them, and leave them with a pain that they will not quickly forget. And above all, never give them a second thought when you walk away."

Damion studied her lovely face, fascinated by the expressionless mask that disguised emotion. He could not tell if she approved or disapproved of those tactics. She had learned to turn her feelings off and on when the mood suited her or when the situation demanded it.

"At least you will not be the one to suffer," he said quietly. "It is and it will always be survival of the fittest, Lissa. Those who cannot endure will perish."

"And of the two of us, who would you say survived the ordeal with the least amount of suffering?" The barb stuck like a well-aimed arrow. "It seems rather ironic that the master of cynicism lies abed with a hole in his shoulder while his apprentice sustains no more than a swollen ankle." Melissa wasn't sure why she felt vindictive, but the words were out before she could bite them back.

"You would have been dead if I hadn't gone back for

you," he defended, his voice rising testily.

"And you would have perished if I had gone with Boone," she countered, indigo blue clashing with hot silver.

After a long moment, Damion's eyes mellowed. "Why did you stay with me?" he queried in a softer tone.

"Why did you come back for me?" she cross-examined.

"Because Jeremy would have seen me burn in hell if I had allowed his precious . . . " Damion swallowed the word daughter. The fever had dulled his senses, and he was having difficulty guarding his thoughts. ". . . his precious protégé to be captured and tortured by the British," he finished after a slight pause.

Melissa's back stiffened in response to his calloused excuse. "And I remained behind to ensure that Jeremy's devoted friend did not bleed to death and become a hearty meal for a pack of wolves," she sneered as she bolted from the edge of the bed.

"I thought you professed to love me, Lissa," Damion mocked, a ghost of a smile lingering on his lips. "So it was not undying devotion that kept you by my side. I can assume that your confession was only empty words."

"I once professed to love you," she admitted as she wheeled to face him. "But never again, Montclaire. 'Twas foolish of me to think that I could love a man who is made of fire and brimstone."

Damion cocked a curious brow as he watched her eyes flare rebelliously. He wasn't sure what to make of her remark. He could have sworn that at the moment she did despise him. Seeking to cool her fiery temper he

333

changed the subject. He was too weak to fence words with her.

"I see you found your necklace."

As she touched the sapphire stone with her fingertips, she nodded reluctantly. "Aye, thank you, but it wasn't necessary." Her tone was flat and insensitive, not at all what he had expected after buying her such an expensive gift.

"Come here, Lissa," he commanded, his voice quiet and yet compelling. "I have no wish to bicker with you. I am tired and irritable. I admit it. Please. . . just sit with me for a moment. Comfort me. I am unaccustomed to staring up at the world from this position. Being bedridden is hard on my disposition."

Melissa was set to refuse him, but his tone and the silent plea in those silver eyes entranced her. She was lost to the depths of tenderness that glowed up at her. When she sank down beside him, he reached up to touch her face, his thumb brushing across her cheek. Her heart melted all over again when he smiled that lazy smile. Her eyes welled up with a sea of tears that she couldn't blink away.

"I am grateful to you for saving my life, even though I have given you little reason to care. At least Gibbs and I agree on one point. You are a very remarkable woman," he whispered ever so softly.

The lion's fierce roar had become the lamb's quiet lowing. Melissa muffled a sniff as Damion wiped away her tears. "And I am indebted to you for saving mine," she murmured raspily. As his hand wandered down her neck to dip beneath the bodice of her gown, gently cupping her breast, teasing its peak to tautness, Melissa felt a fire kindling in her veins, a fire that burned out of control each time Damion touched her. "And I detest you for stirring a passion that you cannot satisfy." She carefully bent over him, seeking his sensuous lips, drinking freely of the intoxicating brew that had often rendered her senseless.

A spark leaped between them, igniting a hunger that demanded fulfillment. Damion's desire for her was as great as it had ever been, and he cursed himself for wanting her so desperately.

"And you have mercilessly tempted me, knowing full well that the ache in my loins far exceeds the throbbing pain in my shoulder." His hand brushed across her breasts and then trailed across her hips, his heart racing, knowing what awaited him beneath the folds of her gown.

Melissa reached up to rake her fingers through his ebony hair, her gaze surveying each intriguing detail of his face. "The one night that I would have begged you to make love to me, to hold me in your arms, you cannot oblige. I need you tonight Damion," she confessed, her breath ragged with a longing that Melissa could not control. His touch was like wildfire, leaving her burning in anticipation. And yet she knew she would remain unappeased, aching for pleasures that she could not enjoy. "You cannot give me what I need most tonight."

"I could try, my lovely witch." A faint smile threatened the corners of his mouth.

She sensed that he had depleted his strength by venturing out of bed. His eyes were dwindling to a lifeless shade of gray.

"And it could very well be the last thing you attempted to do," she countered, heaving a discouraged sigh as she drew away. "It seems that I am destined to become a frustrated woman."

The voices in the hall brought quick death to their conversation. Melissa planted a hasty kiss to his lips and set his hands from her just before Nathan and a short, round gentleman stepped into the room.

"This is Doc Collier," Nathan announced, his gaze resting solely on Melissa.

The doctor pulled up a chair beside Damion and unwrapped the bandages to inspect the wound. "How did this happen?"

"I was teaching my sister to fire my musket and she missed the damned target," Damion grumbled as he sent Melissa an accusing glare.

Collier glanced over his shoulder as Melissa ducked her head and nodded guiltily. His brows furrowed as he continued to study her. "You actually shot your own brother?"

Melissa nervously wrung her hands in front of her. "Not on purpose, monsieur," she explained, her voice quivering slightly. "The gun discharged while I was trying to steady it against my shoulder. Damion was walking away from the target he had set up for me. I didn't mean to. It all happened so quickly." Tears streamed down her cheeks as her gaze lifted to Damion.

Nathan felt as though he had just taken a seat at the theater. If he didn't know better, he would have sworn that this act was actuality. Melissa looked so guilty and innocent that he pitied the kindly old doctor who was eying Melissa sympathetically.

"Who stitched the wound and applied the poultice?" Collier questioned, as he turned back to the patient and pressed his fingertips to the injured shoulder.

"Lissa." Damion's face twisted in pain, his breath forced and husky. "She's much better at doctoring than hitting targets with a musket."

A crooked smile touched his lips as he twisted around to glance at Melissa. " 'Tis good that you can at least stitch up your mistakes, my dear. If you hadn't provided him with immediate attention, he might not be here to accuse you of this misfortunate deed."

Melissa knelt down by Damion, lovingly brushing her hand over his pale cheek. "I'm so sorry. Can you ever find it in your heart to forgive me? Surely you must know that I would never intentionally harm you. I will never touch a rifle again," she sobbed.

Damion grasped her hand and brought it to his lips as he smiled tenderly at her. "You are forgiven, but when I recover, I intend to teach you to shoot properly. I will even take great pains to ensure that this does not happen again," he murmured.

A concerned frown etched Collier's brow as he touched his palm to Damion's forehead. "Give him this for the pain. It will help him sleep," he instructed as he reached into his bag to extract the laudanum.

As he rose from his chair, he gestured for Melissa and Nathan to follow him into the hall. A feeble smile crept to Damion's lips as they watched the three exit from his room. His energy was drained, and he could not find the strength to call Melissa back to him even when he longed to have her with him. But her image remained, lingering over him until the world of darkness enveloped his senses, leaving him oblivious to all around him.

"Your brother is not through the worst of this," Collier said candidly. "His fever will rise until it burns out the infection. Make him drink when he wakes and keep using the poultice to draw out the contamination and soreness from his wound." He sighed tiredly and then met Melissa's anxious gaze. "If you had waited until I arrived I wouldn't have given him much of a chance of survival, but he is most fortunate that you were there. I will not lie to you. His wound is serious. We can only hope that he has the strength to endure the pain and infection as it runs its course."

Melissa nodded mutely as her eyes strayed back toward Damion's room. Would the doctor have given him any chance at all if he knew that it had been over twelve hours before she was able to tend the wound? Why hadn't Damion been honest with the doctor, she wondered? Because he trusted no one, came the quick answer. If he had his way, Nancy and Nathan would have been led to believe that she had accidentally shot him.

"I'll check in on him in a day or two," Collier offered as he started down the hall. "In the meantime give him cold baths when his fever soars. There is little else we can do for him."

While Nathan escorted the doctor to the door Melissa went back to check on Damion. After replacing the cloth on his forehead she pressed a tender kiss to his unresponsive lips. Impulsively, she grasped his lifeless hand, wishing she could restore his strength by relinquishing hers to him. Tears came easily as she stared at his ashen face, knowing that while he slept he wavered between life and death.

Finally she could stand no more. She needed fresh air. Seeing him as he was drove her mad with worry.

Melissa grabbed a shawl and stepped outside, staring pensively at the darkness that seemed to close in on her.

"Are you all right, Melissa?"

She nearly jumped out of her skin when Nathan's voice intruded on her silent reverie. She was amazed to find him standing so closely behind her.

"I would be much better if Damion were back on his feet," she replied, forcing a shallow smile.

Nathan wrapped his arm about her waist and urged her toward the barn. "Come with me to check the horses. 'Tis not much of a diversion, but perhaps it will help take your mind off your brother for a few minutes."

As they walked into the barn Nathan drew her close to press a kiss to her lips, savoring the honeyed sweetness that took him by surprise. He had not expected such an eager response and it fired his passions to their limits. He had ached to hold her since she had returned, remembering the womanly fragrance that clung to her, the feel of her shapely body molded closely to his.

Melissa was seeking the comfort that she had desperately needed from Damion in the arms of another man. She accepted his kiss, wrapping her arms around his neck as his tongue explored her mouth. She wanted to forget everything that had any resemblance to reality, to lose herself for a few moments before she faced the trials that lay ahead of her. But Nathan's emotions transcended compassion, expecting more than she intended to give.

He drew her closer, clutching at her until she could barely draw a breath. "I want you, Melissa," he breathed raggedly. "I want to make love to you. I want you as my wife." His kiss devoured her, feasting on the soft lips that melted against his. He had to drag himself away to voice his thoughts before they escaped him. "I know Damion dislikes me, but we can be wed before he has the strength to protest."

Again his mouth slanted across hers and he pushed her back to the bed of straw, his hands roaming boldly over her, touching her everywhere. Melissa shrieked indignantly as his body covered hers. When his hand dipped beneath the bodice of her gown she tried to push him away, but he did not intend to be denied.

"Nathan! Stop it!" she protested fiercely. "Let me up this instant!"

"Tell me you want me, as much as I desire you. Tell me," he demanded before his lips captured hers, not allowing her time to reply.

Melissa writhed beneath him until she could grab the knife in her garter. Swiftly she retrieved the blade and pressed the point to his neck, making his head jerk back, his eyes wide in disbelief. "I said let me go or Doc Collier will have to return to stitch up your throat," she hissed.

"Let her go!" came an enraged growl from the entrance of the barn. The fire in Damion's eyes could have set the stable ablaze, but it was directed to Nathan who could feel the penetrating heat of his gaze. "If you ever touch her again, I'll kill you before she even has the chance." His threatening tone cracked like thunder, shattering the stilted silence.

Nathan scrambled to his feet as Melissa rushed to Damion's side to steady him. "You are in no condition to make such a threat," he jeered, his courage strength-

340

ened by Damion's lack of ability to stand on his own two feet without being propped against the door.

Melissa could feel Damion trembling, and she watched in alarm as his face turned deathly pale. When he staggered, she clutched at him, but he was too much for her to handle.

"Nathan!" she cried, her eyes flying to him. "Help me with Damion . . . please!"

The fear in Melissa's expression brought him to his senses, and he stepped toward Damion, bracing himself as Damion collapsed in his arms. Between the two of them they managed to drag Damion's limp body back to bed. Melissa could not fathom where he had found the strength to rise in the first place or how he managed to walk to the barn. He was burning up with fever and his bandages were stained with fresh blood. She forced the laudanum to his mouth, applied the hot salve, changed the dressing on the wound, and gave him a cold rubdown.

Melissa was close to tears during her chores. Damion's breathing was so shallow that she wasn't sure he would survive the ordeal. When she had finished her ministrations, she eased from the bed and wiped the perspiration from her brow. She was exhausted. Never in her life had she worked so frantically and yet so carefully all at the same time.

"I'm sorry, Melissa," Nathan apologized as he stepped from the shadows. "I don't know what came over me. I did not intend to be so forceful. It's just that—"

"All is forgiven," she interrupted without glancing back at him. Her eyes were glued to Damion, as if by never letting him out of her sight she could somehow

341

preserve his life.

"Melissa, I love you." Nathan's voice wavered with emotion.

"Please, Nathan." Her eyes swam with tears and she tried to blink them away so she could keep her attention focused on Damion. "I can think of nothing while the angel of death hovers so closely over him. Please leave us alone."

When she heard Nathan's footsteps fade, she gave in to the tears, unable to hold them back. She fell to her knees, grasping Damion's hand, praying that he would not be taken from her, dying her own slow death as she watched him lying motionless. She could not leave his side. She was afraid to sleep, afraid that she might wake to find him gone.

## *Chapter Sixteen*

The following day was one of intense strain on Melissa. Damion had survived the night, but his fever was soaring and he had become delirious, calling to her frequently. The two times that he had crawled from bed the previous evening had cost him dearly. He mumbled constantly and occasionally his eyes flew open as the words escaped his lips in inarticulate phrases.

Melissa knew that although he was staring directly at her, he couldn't see her at all. She was terrified by his ravings. His life seemed to be passing before him, as if he were reliving each frightening moment that he had ever experienced.

She sat beside him throughout the day, keeping a constant vigil like his guardian angel who watched and waited, wondering if she would see him regain his sanity or observe his soul taking leave of its mortal form.

The day dragged on into endless hours. Damion's words seemed to become clearer, or perhaps it was that Melissa had learned to interpret them. He had called out to his mother, Jeremy and occasionally to her. Melissa sensed that his mother had managed to turn Damion against her, but his ravings were too incoherent for Melissa to understand what had happened. Each time Damion whispered the name Coleen it pained him. His face would twist in anger and frustration before a curse flowed from his lips.

And then suddenly she would hear him call to Jeremy, his voice trembling in panic. She was certain that he was reliving the incident that had nearly taken Jeremy's life. Melissa had not been able to contain Damion when he bolted up in bed, his eyes wild and crazed with a fear that was rarely mirrored in them. She had coaxed him back to his pillow, and he had quieted for awhile after she forced the laudanum down his throat and managed to get him to sip some water.

When he was sleeping soundly, Melissa walked into the kitchen to join Nancy for a few minutes. Nancy wore a dreamy-eyed smile that drew Melissa's curious frown.

"What's the matter with you? You look like the cat that swallowed the canary," Melissa observed, her tone more condemning than teasing. How could Nancy smile when Damion was lying on his deathbed?

"Damion kissed me last night."

Melissa's frown deepened. "When was this?"

"While you and Nathan were outside," she explained. "Damion called to you and I went to his room. It was dark and I sat down on the edge of the bed to calm him. He grabbed me and kissed me like I've never been kissed before. He took my breath away." Nancy's face flushed as her gaze drifted to Melissa for a moment. "When I finally found my voice I asked him what he wanted and then he apologized for

344

embracing me. He mumbled something about thinking I was you. He must have been delirious then, too." A thoughtful frown gathered on her brow. She had been too flustered to consider why Damion would want to kiss his own sister in such a passionate manner until that moment. It was a bit odd. Obviously he didn't know what he was doing or saying.

Melissa bit back a smile. "Aye," she agreed. "He must have been out of his mind. You should have heard some of the strange things he said to me this morning. I am beginning to wonder if he has taken leave of his senses."

"All I know is that he is irresistible, crazed or naught," Nancy insisted. "He can pretend that I am someone else if he wants. I don't think I would mind."

"Nancy!" Melissa chided, sending her a reproachful frown. "If Nathan heard you carrying on like this he would be distressed."

"Nathan is as overprotective with me as Damion is with you," Nancy muttered. "He screens my gentlemen callers and allows us no time alone together. How am I to find a suitable husband when he smothers me like a mother hen?"

Melissa rolled her eyes and chortled to herself. Nancy had seemed shy at first, but Melissa was beginning to realize that when Nathan wasn't within earshot, Nancy was delightfully lively. If she had not been so concerned about Damion she would have enjoyed spending more time with Nancy. But until Damion had weathered the worst of the storm, she was afraid to leave him for more than a few minutes.

That evening as Melissa bathed Damion and applied fresh poultice and dressing to his shoulder, he bolted up in bed and grasped her arm so tightly that she feared he would crush her bones.

"Jeremy!" he screamed in a voice that shook the walls and echoed about them. "Can you hear me? God, don't let him die!"

The look on his face sent a fearful shiver down her spine. "Jeremy is alive," she assured him, attempting to coax him back to bed. "He is fine, Damion. Now you must rest."

Damion struggled against her and Melissa yelled at him as if he were deaf. "Damion! Lie down! Dammit, you will tear your stitches."

Nathan had entered the house in time to hear Damion bellowing at the top of his lungs and Melissa cursing back at him. He hurried into the room and forcefully manhandled Damion while Melissa spooned the laudanum down his throat. She breathed a sigh of relief when Damion closed his wild eyes and sank into a restless sleep.

"I'll sit with him for awhile," Nathan offered as he tucked the hem of his shirt in his breeches after Damion had nearly yanked it off his chest. "I'll tend the horses before it rains and come back to take your place. You look as if you could use a little rest yourself."

Melissa nodded gratefully and displayed a tired smile before she finished replacing the bandages. After Nathan had exited from the room, Damion's eyes fluttered open and he stared at her as if she were something that had just slithered out from under a rock.

"Damn you, Jeremy," he muttered contemptuously. His voice trailed off in an inaudible whisper as he quieted for a moment. And then a scowl settled on his features.

Melissa flinched as the thunder rumbled, shaking the window panes with its fierceness. When she glanced back at Damion she covered her mouth and gasped. His eyes were stone cold as he stared up at her in a deathlike trance. For a moment she thought he had taken his last breath. She could not stand to see him peering up at her like that and she reached out to close his eyes.

His gaze seemed to focus on her, angry and brooding. "Why didn't you tell me?" he muttered sourly, and then tossed his head away as if the sight of Melissa repulsed him. "I don't want the wench. She's not to be trusted. I won't marry."

Melissa knew what he was raving about, and it injured her deeply to realize that he had intensely disliked her, even in the beginning. Her head dropped despairingly as she finished wrapping the bandage over his chest.

"Laura," he murmured, his voice like a gentle caress. "I've waited a lifetime to hear . . . "

She stopped her chore and stared bewilderedly at him. "What about Laura?"

Damion grinned wickedly, his eyes dancing with demented amusement as perspiration trickled from the deep lines on his forehead. "You are a fool, but I won't be. . ." Suddenly his expression sobered, his gaze drilling into Melissa. "Does she know?"

A perplexed frown knitted her brows as she listened intently, hoping to discover what his relationship was to Laura, but he did not mention her name again. Was she one of his lovers? Surely he was not talking about her mother. How could he have known her?

"You cannot force me to wed!" he flared as he clutched at the quilts. "Not even for you."

And then the room became strangely quiet. The only sound to reach Melissa's ears was Damion's labored breathing. After a long moment another rumble of thunder brought Damion to life, as if he were haunted by a ghost whose wailing voice came to him from the wind.

"Three fathers." His head rolled recklessly to the side, a low rumble erupting from his chest. "Jeremy, Will, and now André. You have been blessed."

His words sent Melissa bolting from the edge of the bed, stumbling against the chair in her haste to escape the ghost who rose between her and Damion. As she choked on a sob, she wheeled toward the door and ran headlong into Nathan as he turned the corner. He maneuvered the supper tray to keep from spilling the steaming stew all over the both of them.

Nathan had been eavesdropping and had heard the last of Damion's ravings although he could make no sense of it. But obviously, Melissa had understood him. She was as wild-eyed as Damion. Nathan balanced the tray in one hand and grabbed Melissa's arm as she tried to brush past him.

"Melissa, what is wrong with you? You're as white as a sheet." Concern was mirrored in his eyes as he watched a steady stream of tears flow down her cheeks.

"Jeremy, I will bring her back . . . " Damion's words trailed off as he exhaled.

Melissa glanced back at Damion, a tortured expression on her features. "Jeremy, my God," she rasped before covering her face with her hands.

"You set me up, damn you," Damion growled as his lashes swept up. The look he gave Melissa was worth a thousand words, none of them complimentary, and she winced at the contempt she saw in his eyes. "I don't want her. Take her away. . . ." His madness had exhausted him and his body went limp as Jeremy's name floated from his lips like a curse.

"Who the devil is Jeremy?" Nathan questioned with a muddled frown. "What is he raving about?"

Melissa's gaze circled back to Nathan, peering up at him through tear-rimmed eyes. She opened her mouth to speak and then adamantly shook her head as she twisted from his grasp and ran from the room.

While the storm unleashed its fury on the cottage, Melissa was tossed about by the winds of disillusionment. She buried her head in her pillow and sobbed hysterically, the tension flowing from her body in a sea of tears. She had braved the charade in Detroit, survived the escape, and had kept watch over Damion, caring for him night and day without sleep. But the knowledge she received from Damion's ravings had taken her unaware, and she struggled to grasp the full impact of his words. She had managed to maintain her composure until now. Damion's denial of affection for her cut her to the quick. He had only used her, feeling nothing more than a desire to appease his animal lust. And then there was Jeremy, her mother's lover! Her natural father! Her trusted friend, a man she would have followed to the ends of the earth if he would have requested her companionship.

How did this come about, her mind screamed, as she fought back another onrush of tears.

Melissa raised her head, staring at the darkness as rain pattered against the windowpane. As the lightning cut a jagged streak across the sky, she flinched, feeling as if it had singed her flesh and burned its way to her very core. There was so much she didn't understand, and yet, one point was perfectly clear. Jeremy had sent her to the gates of hell, leaving her to be tortured by the demon who had taken her soul. Jeremy had cunningly incorporated the image of Zack Beaugener into her thinking, intending that she fall in love with the one man she could never have, just as he had fallen in love with the one woman that could never be his own.

Did her father know about Jeremy and her mother? Had William harbored her shame these past twenty years without letting Melissa know that she was not his child? Had he looked at her with regret, haunted by the image that was so similar to Laura? Had William sent her to France because the sight of her and the painful memories she evoked were more than he could endure? Or did he love Laura more than life itself, unaware that she had taken a lover? Could he forgive her anything? Even this?

Melissa had always remembered her mother with fondness. Her soft French accent had been so soothing to Lissa's ears. Laura's voice was always filled with patience and understanding. Perhaps that was why Laura had been so compassionate and forgiving to everyone else, Melissa mused, as she wiped away the tears. How could she condemn others after what she had done? A perplexed frown creased her brow as another thought came to her. She had been certain that her mother loved William. They had seemed devoted to each other. How had Jeremy come into her life? All that Melissa had learned from Damion's ravings were like the pieces of a puzzle, ones that she could not fit together properly. It was too distorted to make sense.

As the thunder rolled over her, Melissa shuddered, feeling her life crumbling about her. She wanted to erase the past few months since she had crossed paths with Zack Beaugener. Once, she had been as naive and innocent as Nancy, full of foolish dreams and fantasies. At least she had found a star to wish upon, a goal on which to set her sights. But now her dreams had been fulfilled, and she wondered if she might have been better off if those fantasies had remained untouched. Dreams were intangible thoughts, clouds of hope, breezes of unending love, meadows of pleasure, something to capture in one's imagination, but once they were within reality's grasp, they lost their mystical pleasure.

Melissa wished to be as she had once been: unaware of passion's intimacy, inexperienced in maneuvering people, and ignorant of adventure and intrigue. But that was impossible. She had changed and she could never go back again. She was no longer an innocent child. Harsh reality had invaded her dream world, shattering the whimsical visions like broken crystal that could never be pieced together again.

Melissa clenched her fists and struck out at her pillow, making it the object of her frustrations. The tormenting thoughts came at her from all directions. How could she ever face her father or Jeremy again? How could she remain with Damion, knowing that he wanted nothing to do with her? And yet, how could she leave him when his life hung in limbo. Even if he cared nothing for her she could not abandon him, loving him the way she did. What was she to do?

"Melissa, Damion is calling for you," Nathan said softly as he stuck his head in her room. She made no move to rise from the bed. "Melissa?" Nathan squinted to see her silhouette in the darkness.

"I'm coming," she murmured, making Nathan strain his ears to catch her muffled reply.

She swung her legs over the edge of the bed and heaved a heavy-hearted sigh. What other surprises were in store for her while she listened to Damion's fevered ramblings? When she walked into his room she was met by Damion's exhausted smile.

"I cannot tell you how disappointed I was to find Gibbs here instead of you when I awoke," he said, his voice hoarse from his constant mumblings.

Melissa eased down beside him and pressed her hand to his forehead, relieved to find that his fever had broken. Perhaps the worst was over, she thought hopefully.

Damion's brow furrowed as he gazed into her red-rimmed eyes, seeing her sooty lashes glistening with tears. "What's wrong, Lissa?" he questioned softly.

"Don't call me that," she snapped, her tone harsher than she had intended. Melissa bit her lip, averting her eyes from his probing stare.

There was something very wrong. The frown settled deeper in Damion's weary features.

"Your fever is gone. I think you will survive," she said flatly, not an ounce of compassion in her voice. "Let me check your shoulder."

Damion watched her intently as she unwrapped the bandages, cleansed the wound, and inspected the tender skin along the edge of the stitches. What the devil had come over her? She seemed different somehow, preoccupied, detached. When she finished her chore, she glanced down at him, her eyes masked with indifference.

"Do you feel up to eating?"

"Perhaps a little," he replied as he reached beneath her chin, forcing her to meet his steady gaze. "What is the matter with you? Has something happened to upset you?"

Melissa removed his hand from her face and lifted her eyes to the window, watching the raindrops trickle down the pane. "A great deal, Damion," she murmured, a faraway look on her face.

"Well?" His impatient tone filtered into her silent musings.

"Well what?" Her gaze slid back to him and then returned to the window, seemingly disinterested in conversation.

"Lissa, for God's sake. I am not up to games. I have just returned from the dead and am too weary for riddles," he snapped irritably. "Has Nathan done something to upset you?" If that scoundrel had dared to touch her again, Damion vowed he would tear that cowardly wretch to pieces with his bare hands—just as soon as he could find the strength to lift his head from his pillow.

"Nay," she insisted, refusing to go into detail. "I will see if Nancy has some broth for you to eat." She attempted to rise, but Damion grasped her arm to detain her, and she flashed him an annoyed frown. "Let go of me."

His hand dropped to his side. "What the hell is

wrong?" he demanded.

Without a word Melissa turned and walked away, leaving him to wonder what had come over her. Why was she behaving so strangely? Damion rolled his eyes toward the ceiling, trying to summon his patience, strangling the harsh words that waited on the tip of his tongue.

When she returned with the broth she offered him a spoonful, but Damion turned up his nose and remained tight-lipped.

An annoyed sigh escaped her lips. "Why aren't you eating? I thought you said you were hungry?"

"I demand to know if Nathan has been molesting you again. If he touched you I swear I'll—"

While his mouth was open, voicing vengeful threats, Melissa stuffed the spoon at him, nearly choking him on his words and his soup.

"I already told you that Nathan has nothing to do with it, and I don't wish to discuss the matter," Melissa informed him curtly. "Now be a good patient and eat your porridge without harassing me. I am in no mood for your childish games."

Damion was too weak to protest, and she was too stubborn to give an explanation unless he forced her. They were at a stalemate, and Damion finally heaved a defeated sigh and sipped his soup. Later, he would pry information from her, he decided.

"Do you need the laudanum to sleep?" she questioned, as she wiped away the broth that had trickled down his chin.

"I'm not sleepy. I feel as though I've slept the entire day away." A hint of a smile found the corners of his mouth, hoping to crumble her defenses with tenderness.

"You did, Montclaire."

The sound of his name on her lips was flat and impersonal. Damion inwardly cringed at her cold tone. He brought her hand to his lips, placing a kiss to her wrist. "Thank you, Lissa."

"For what?" Her chin tilted defiantly, determined not to fall prey to his feigned affection. He wasn't going to sweet-talk her, not ever again. She had heard his innermost thoughts and she could see through his ploy.

"I wouldn't have blamed you if you had left me to die. I have offered you very little in the way of courtesy or gratitude. You deserve better." Damion wrapped his fingers behind her neck, drawing her closer, careful not to scare her away. She was like a frightened bird who would take to her wings if she were threatened. "Kiss me," he requested huskily. "I need to feel your soft lips against mine. The agonizing pain in my shoulder can only be relieved by your gentle touch. Is it too much to ask for you to bestow compassion on a man who is recovering from his bout with death?"

Melissa was caught off guard by this new tactic. Never in the past had he *asked* anything of her. He usually made sharp commands or forcefully took what he wanted from her. She was drawn beneath his spell, losing herself to the delicious taste of his kiss. There was no hope for it. She could never deny him, no matter how hard she fought. Her body yearned for his caresses and his stirring kisses that left her breathless. It was as Nancy had said. Damion could sweep a woman from reality, taking her to a world of heady pleasure, holding her suspended for that timeless instant that defied the consequences. He was the devil's temptation.

It no longer mattered that he didn't truly care for her, only that he could make the world go away, bringing her a pleasure that blocked out troubled thoughts. And yet, as she melted against his sensuous lips, she died a thousands deaths, knowing no one could ever take his place. Damion possessed her soul and she would always be his puppet, needing his touch to live and breathe.

"Hold me," Melissa pleaded, as she nestled against his right shoulder, careful not to cause him more pain than he was suffering. "Don't ask any questions of me. Just hold me. I need you." She closed her eyes, fighting back the tears, enduring the ache of knowing that she could never have him as her own or hear words of love from his lips.

Damion nuzzled his cheek against the top of her head and then pulled the pins from her hair, running his fingers through the sunkissed tendrils of gold that sprayed over his shoulder. He tilted her head back, gazing into her indigo eyes, seeing the tears that lurked so near the surface. His lips brushed lightly across hers, and he moaned as the quiet flow of pleasure meandered through his body, leaving him drifting with the current of desire.

"I wish I could offer you more," he murmured hoarsely. "I want to be a part of you, tasting your passions, taking you with me to that heaven we've shared in the past. And when I want you most, I am denied the satisfaction that I know awaits me in your arms. Is this to be my payment for barely escaping death? The sweet torture of holding you without being able to make love to you?"

Melissa ran her hand over his rugged cheek, wondering if Jeremy had held the same mystical power over her mother that Damion held over her. Was Laura drawn to the same untamed creature that had captured her interest? Melissa squeezed back the thoughts. How could she analyze what transpired between Laura and Jeremy when she couldn't even justify her reasons for clinging to a man who would never return her love?

Her lips parted in response as Damion's passionate kiss deepened to search the recesses of her mouth. For the moment she would not try to think. She would only enjoy the rapturous sensations that Damion's embrace evoked.

Their souls touched, as if reaching out to each other from afar, seeking to unite as one, and yet content to share a secluded pleasure until reality pulled them apart.

After a long moment, Melissa withdrew from his comforting arms and smiled ruefully at him. *"Bon soir, mon ami.* Sleep well."

Those were the same words her mother had whispered to her a lifetime ago. Had Laura uttered that phrase to Jeremy as well? Melissa cried a silent tear as she gazed into Damion's handsome face and then eased from his side. She was so confused, haunted by the past and present. She needed time to collect her thoughts.

"I will sleep well," Damion assured her, his voice showing evidence of his exhaustion. "And in my dreams I will enjoy what reality will not allow."

Melissa snuffed out the lantern and hovered close to him, memorizing each detail of his face. As the flash of lightning filled the room she peered into the glowing pools of silver. "And I shall recall all of the yesterdays

357

that I never thought I would experience," she said softly. "They were worth the price, Damion." Her hushed whisper wavered with emotion before she crept into the shadows.

Being alone in the darkness left Damion with an eerie sensation. Melissa had changed somehow and he could not fathom the cause of the deep sadness in her eyes. It was as if her spirit had been broken. She was subdued, not at all like the fiery vixen he had come to know.

Damion heaved a tired sigh and tried to shift himself to a more comfortable position, but there was none so he stayed where he was, flat on his back. Tomorrow he would question her again. He would make her tell him what had happened, he vowed, just before he drifted off to sleep.

# Chapter Seventeen

Damion awoke the following morning, weak, hungry, and in full command of his senses. It seemed that Melissa's constant vigil had carried him through and he was well on his way to recovery. Although he was unable to move his left arm, the throbbing pain had ceased and he only noticed discomfort when he attempted to seek a different position in bed. He vaguely recalled that Melissa had come to check on him in the early hours before dawn, but between the effect of the laudanum and the exhaustion from the fever, Damion had little recollection of the brief moment that she spent in his room. He had felt her soft lips playing tenderly against his before she disappeared into the shadows.

"Lissa!" he bellowed loudly. He waited an impatient moment and called her again, but he was met with silence.

Nathan stepped around the corner to meet Damion's dark scowl.

"Where's Lissa?" Damion snapped rudely, annoyed

with the unwelcomed sight of Gibbs.

"Gone," Nathan replied in a bland tone.

"Gone?" he repeated incredulously as his heavy brows furrowed over his flinty eyes. "Gone where?"

Nathan shrugged noncommittally as he pulled up a chair beside the bed and seated himself.

"Well, dammit! Where is she?" Damion demanded to know as he threw Gibbs a glare. There was no love lost between the two of them, and Damion made no attempt to be civil or pleasant.

"I thought you might know, after all, you're her brother," Nathan snapped defensively. His dislike for Montclaire was just as obvious as Damion's distaste for him. Nathan readily returned the dark scowl.

Damion met Nathan's frosty green eyes, completely miffed by Melissa's disappearance. "Could she have gone into the settlement?" he questioned in a calmer tone.

Nathan shook his head negatively. "I doubt it. She must have slipped away during the night. Your horse is gone and she took all of her possessions with her."

"What?" he gasped in bewilderment. "Why would she suddenly leave without telling me where she had gone?" His eyes narrowed suspiciously as he focused on Nathan. "Did you try to take advantage of her again?" Melissa had said Nathan hadn't touched her, but he was never sure if she was telling him the truth.

"Nay!" Nathan snorted indignantly. "I didn't touch her. She was upset last night after listening to you rant and rave. She stampeded over me in her haste to leave your room. She was in tears. I would guess that what you said while you were raving like a madman sent her fleeing."

360

Damion frowned thoughtfully, attempting to recall what had happened the previous day, but he drew a blank. Yesterday had come and gone, and he could remember nothing except talking with Melissa late that evening. With a hopeless shake of his head, he sighed despairingly. "I can't recall saying a damned thing," he muttered.

"I overheard part of what you said when I came to bring Melissa's supper tray, but I couldn't make much sense of it."

"Tell me what you heard," Damion requested as he attempted to prop himself up in bed.

Nathan tucked a pillow behind Damion's head and then sank back into his chair, trying to recall the confused phrases Damion had uttered. "The first thing I heard you say was that you would not be forced into marriage. You thought you were talking to someone called Jeremy, but it was Melissa you were growling at," he added, flinging Damion an accusing glance.

Damion's brows shot up and then he anxiously waited for Nathan to continue, afraid that he was not going to enjoy hearing the rest of it.

"And then you said you wouldn't marry, even for Jeremy's sake. You laughed and then muttered something about the wench having three fathers." Nathan paused, attempting to recall the names while Damion swallowed air. "André, I believe was one, Will, and Jeremy," he said nodding thoughtfully. "I think those were the three."

Damion plopped his head back on the pillow and rolled his eyes in disgust. "Sweet mercy," he mumbled under his breath. "What a shocking way for her to discover the truth."

"What?" A muddled frown settled on Nathan's face. Damion had begun to mutter inarticulately again.

"Nothing." Damion waved away the inquiry with an impatient flick of his wrist. "Go on. What else did I say?" He clenched his fists at his side, wishing he could undo the damage and frustrated that he was confined to bed.

"You promised Jeremy that you would bring the woman back to him." Nathan shook his head, another frown gathering on his features. "Can you make any sense of that?" He watched Damion's face turn a whiter shade of pale, wondering if it was from the information or his weakened condition.

"Aye," he muttered disgustedly. "I said plenty and Lissa understood it all."

"I intend to go after her if you can give me any idea where I might find her," Nathan insisted, a determined glint in his eyes. "I plan to make her my wife, with or without your approval. If she agrees to it, we will marry."

Damion's good shoulder lifted in a careless shrug. "You have my permission to follow her, but you won't find her. She is impossible to track," he informed Nathan blandly. "And you will not be able to marry her."

"Why not?" His mouth narrowed in a hard line. "Is it because you dislike me? If that is the reason then I don't buy it. I'm marrying *her*, not *you*."

Damion's lips curved into a mischievous smile. "The reason is simple. She has no use for another husband since that one she has is alive and reasonable well."

Nathan's jaw sagged, but then he frowned when Damion's smile broadened to a face-splitting grin. "I don't believe you. You are trying to dissuade me since you have little use for me."

"Lissa usually leaves it to me to inform her overzealous suitors that she is wed. And you are correct," he agreed. "I have never approved of your amorous designs on her because *I* am her husband." His calm tone changed to a gritted growl, and he watched the look of shock, amazement, and disappointment that whipped across Nathan's face. Damion could not contain a chuckle when he finally found his voice.

"You're her husband?" he rasped when he finally found his voice.

Damion nodded affirmatively. It was strange that he had found such pleasure in telling both Heston and Gibbs that Melissa belonged to him.

"But why have you kept it a secret?" Nathan questioned bemusedly. "Why did you let me act like a fool over a woman I could never claim?"

" 'Tis a long story," Damion said with a slight shrug. "But the reason is not important. The fact remains that she is my wife."

"And I suppose you are not really Damion Montclaire and she isn't Andrea *or* Melissa," he grumbled in annoyance. "I have the distinct feeling that I know as little about her as she claimed, and even less about you." He shot Damion a skeptical glance.

"True," Damion agreed as a crooked smile lifted one side of his bearded face. "I hope you understand why I resented your affection for Lissa. I realize it was rather cruel not to tell you, but for some reason, that was the way she wanted it. You are not the first to fall for her bewitching charms, but I think that you would agree that if our positions were reversed, you would have protested any amorous advances toward her."

Nathan nodded reluctantly. "Aye, but I would have shot you that night in the barn." He exhaled a breath as his gaze swung to Damion, eyeing him accusingly. "And I would also have claimed my position as her husband so that none would dare to take advantage of my wife."

"Melissa can take care of herself, as you well know," Damion retorted, casting a meaningful glance to his companion. "And you cannot begin to understand the whole of it, Gibbs." His quiet voice carried a thread of bitterness that Nathan could not comprehend.

"What are we going to do about Melissa?" he asked anxiously. "Surely we cannot allow her to travel unescorted. After what has happened, she could be in grave danger if the British catch up with her."

"Save your sympathy for the redcoats," Damion suggested with a smirk. "That conniving minx will have the British running in circles. Like I said, you don't know what Lissa is capable of doing. She has left more than one man wondering how she escaped his grasp and, as for the British hunting party, they don't stand a chance of tracking her. Melissa will reach her destination. On that you can depend."

Nathan stared at Montclaire in amazement. How could a man allow his wife to traipse across the wilderness without acting concerned about her welfare, unless he didn't give a damn about what happened to her, Nathan mused scornfully. After hearing Damion's ravings and learning that Melissa was his wife, Nathan came to the conclusion that Montclaire would have preferred to be a bachelor.

He peered at Damion, his green eyes searching the rugged features of Montclaire's face. "You may be married to Melissa, but I wonder if you really care about her. Your casual attitude about her traveling this untamed country alone leaves me with doubts."

Damion's eyes narrowed as his heavy brows furrowed above them. "I don't waste my time worrying about Melissa. It would serve no useful purpose. 'Tis obvious which one of us survived the ordeal at the fort with the least amount of distress," Damion reminded him in a crisp tone. "*I* am bedfast and *she* is long gone. She didn't even bother to inform me that she was leaving. Tell me, Gibbs, who would you venture to say is the better man and what the hell does she care about me if she can leave without a word?"

"But she is only a woman!" Nathan insisted in exasperation.

"Who can hunt and trap game with the best of the mountain men, who can load and shoot a musket and hit a target dead center, who can use a knife as expertly as I can. She has a feminine finesse that deceives any man who looks into those innocent, blue-violet eyes, luring him into thinking that she is helpless and incapable of doing him harm. That, my friend, is what makes that lovely, little spitfire so unique. That beautiful exterior camouflages the sly, conniving witch who can spring on her defenseless prey," Damion added with a knowing smile.

"You make her sound positively wicked." Nathan released a derisive snort as he eased back in his chair and crossed his arms on his chest.

"Well, isn't she?" Damion arched a taunting brow. "Have either of us managed to bend that wild wench to our way of thinking? I ordered her to leave with Boone and my men, but did she go?" Damion questioned sarcastically and then answered his own inquiry. "Nay, she did just as she pleased. Not one of those six men could talk her into obeying my orders. I was injured and physically unable to force her, and the rest of them were too gentlemanly to manhandle her."

"Perhaps what you say is partly true, but I still do not consider her to be so wild and untamed," he insisted stubbornly.

"You have only seen that *other* side of Melissa on one occasion—that night in the barn. If she had found it necessary, she would have slit your throat," Damion assured him. "I know Melissa better than you do. You have yet to tangle with the lady in buckskins who carries a musket in her hand and a dagger in her belt. Do you think I would have turned her loose in a fort with an entire British regiment if I didn't think she would return unscathed?"

"I don't know," Nathan replied with a thoughtful frown. He was well aware that Melissa had come to her own defense, surprising him with her knife, but he could not fully comprehend the woman that Damion had described. "You still have not come right out and said that you care about what happens to her." He shot Damion an accusing glance and squirmed in his chair.

Damion seemed so calloused and unconcerned, Nathan thought to himself as he watched Montclaire prop himself up against the pillow. Montclaire was no ordinary man. He was a calculating machine, and Nathan seriously doubted that he even had a conscience, heart, or soul. He was beginning to wonder if the man was capable of any emotion except anger.

Damion's eyes flickered with flinty sparks, only confusing Gibbs further. "Lissa and I can survive without each other, and she doesn't need me to protect her," he stated as the flicker vanished and his expression became a carefully blank stare.

Nathan was appalled by Damion's insensitive attitude. Melissa deserved better than Montclaire. How could any man *not* fall in love with Melissa? How could a man resist her bewitching charms? It seemed that Montclaire admired and respected her abilities, but he had never mentioned love. Nathan carefully appraised the man who lay before him. His raven hair swirled recklessly about his dark face that had become disguised by a heavy beard. His silver eyes could be as cold as ice or as fiery as an uncontrollable blaze. He was a large, sturdy man who seemed fearless and unfeeling. Even while Damion lay abed, Nathan was not sure that he wanted to tangle with him. Montclaire seemed as wicked as the devil himself, and he would have liked to hear the full story about his marriage to Melissa. Why would she marry such a ruthless man?

"I don't understand you at all," Nathan muttered as he hopelessly shook his head. "If Melissa were my wife, I would shower her with gifts and affection, but you lie casually in bed while she rides off alone in the night with no supplies and no protection. I doubt that you will lose any sleep over the fact that your wife is gone and will not return." He shot Montclaire a reproachful glare. "Not that I could blame her a damned bit."

Damion's brows furrowed, carefully scrutinizing Gibbs. "At the risk of being rude to my gracious host," he began in a voice that hinted at sarcasm, "I will simply say that since you are not her husband, 'tis none of your business how I handle Melissa. After what I told Melissa while I was delirious, I imagine that I am the last person she wants to see right now. The truth that she has discovered weighs heavily on her mind, and until she can sort through it alone, no one will be of any use to her. I cannot follow after her since I cannot stand on my own two feet without fainting, and you would not be able to track her. Just what would you have you me do?" he questioned as he arched a mocking brow.

Nathan shrugged. "As you said, 'tis none of my business. In the future I will attempt to keep my nose out of your affairs." He rose from his chair and turned to leave. Pausing momentarily, he threw a quick glance over his shoulder. "I'll bring you something to eat. You are welcome to stay as long as is needed for you to recuperate, even if Melissa is gone," he added resentfully as he stalked toward the door.

Damion watched Gibbs exit from the room and released a heavy sigh. Nathan would never be able to understand the situation and there was no use attempting to explain. He and Nathan were cut from different types of wood. Nathan was as soft and flexible as a willow, and Damion was as hard and unbending as an oak. If Damion showered that little spitfire with gentleness and allowed her to have her way, she would have him so henpecked he would probably molt twice a year. And of course he was concerned about her, but there wasn't a damned thing he could do. What worried him most was where she had gone. He wasn't certain how she would feel about Jeremy now that she knew the truth. Would she return home or venture elsewhere until she had come to terms with the knowledge? There was a chance that she would travel to Boonesborough. Knowing her taste for adventure, she would rather be in the midst of a battle than to be tucked safely away while others were fighting for a cause. His thoughts were interrupted when Nathan returned with a breakfast tray.

As Nathan set the tray on Montclaire's lap he eyed him sternly. "If you don't love her, then let her go," he urged. "I'm sure there are countless others, including myself, who would treat Melissa with the respect and devotion she deserves."

A stilted silence filled the room as both men critically appraised each other. Damion had heard the same remark from Stratton and it had not set well with him then, nor did it now. "If a man treated Lissa the way that you and every other fool would dare to approach her, he would become her pawn, her slave, and yet another victim of her bewitching charms. He would lose his identity and pride, gaining nothing in the compromise. Lissa is not the type of woman who can truly be tamed or subdued. One night she would just gather her belongings and ride away, fearing nothing or no one, seeking adventure, and loving the freedom upon which she thrives. Perhaps you would make her happy for a time, but eventually you would have to let her go. Forget her, Gibbs. She will only bring you misery," Damion warned in a cynical tone.

Nathan glared at Montclaire and then spun on his heels to hastily exit from the room. Damion didn't want Melissa, but he would not relinquish his claim on her even though he considered her to be nothing but a bundle of trouble. He was a madman, a scoundrel, a demon! Montclaire would keep Melissa tied to him if only to torture every other man who would have attempted to win her heart. Perhaps Melissa was untamable, but she was worth the risk. Damion was the one who deserved to fall in love with her and be left behind. It would serve Damion right to find himself wedged in line behind her suitors, Nathan thought spitefully. Montclaire merited the torture of realizing that even *he* could not subdue Melissa's free spirit.

The association between Nathan and Damion was strained. The following days did nothing to improve the tension. They were at opposite ends of the spectrum, and neither of them had any intention of compromising their positions.

Nancy took over the duties of caring for Damion's wound, and although Nathan had told her that Damion was Melissa's husband, Nancy had difficulty limiting her thoughts to a purely nurse-patient relationship. Her eyes roamed over his handsome face and bare chest each time she walked into his room. Damion was well aware that if he showed the slightest interest, he would meet with no resistance. Nancy was a comely wench and Damion had always been one to enjoy every female who came his way. Perhaps in Nancy's case, Damion was bent on a little revenge of his own. After the way Nathan had hovered over Melissa and ridiculed Damion for the way he handled his wife, he thought Nathan needed a taste of his own medicine. Montclaire played the perfect gentleman when Nancy was about and especially when Nathan was there to witness the scene. Each time Nathan stalked away with his face twisted in a dark scowl, Damion would chuckle wickedly. Although Montclaire and Gibbs were aware of the game, Nancy was oblivious to all except her fascination for Damion.

After a week, Damion began to move about, attempting to use his left arm as much as the pain would allow. He did his share of the chores that he could manage and each time he glanced up, Nancy was watching him with a smile playing on her lips.

One evening while Damion was feeding the horses, he heard the crackling of straw and glanced over his shoulder to see Nancy leaning against the stall behind him. Her long, dark hair lay loosely over her shoulder and her bright, green eyes sparkled in the dim moonlight.

"Good evening," she murmured as a demure smile spread across her face. "How's your arm?" Nancy moved a step closer to the tall, masculine rogue, her heart fluttering wildly at the sight of him.

"Much better," Damion replied before turning back to his chore.

As Nancy sidled up beside him, the fresh, clean fragrance that clung to her tickled his senses, and he paused to lean back against the wooden rail of the stall, carefully surveying her attractive form.

"You look quite lovely tonight," he whispered as he reached up to brush the back of his hand against her flushed cheek.

"Thank you," she sputtered embarrassedly. "I—"

Damion did not allow her to finish her statement as he wrapped his fingers around the nape of her neck, pulling her steadily toward him to kiss her parted lips.

Nancy gingerly looped her arms about his neck, thrilling to the feel of his muscular body pressed to hers.

As he raised his dark head, Nancy gazed up into his silver eyes, lost to their fathomless depths. "Melissa warned me to beware of you," she whispered breathlessly. "She said that you were a devil who had no heart, but I cannot seem to resist the temptation."

"You would take the word of a witch?" He arched a heavy brow as a smile lifted one corner of his mouth upward.

Nancy chuckled at the wicked gleam in his eyes. "If she is a witch then I'm sure you must be the devil she claimed you to be," she concluded.

"Are you afraid of me then?" he questioned in a soft, rich voice that made her quiver with delight.

Damion cupped her chin in his hand, holding her steady gaze and Nancy was mesmerized by his nearness. "Nay, sir." The words that whirled about her mind seemed to float effortlessly from her lips. "Damion, make love to me."

Montclaire's brows arched acutely as he regarded her delicate face. How could he refuse such a pleasurable request? She was young, attractive, willing, and he had not been with a woman since he and Melissa had stayed at the inn.

"Where's your brother?" he questioned, as he drew her into his arms and lowered his head to taste the sweetness of her lips.

Her body trembled with excitement when he kissed her. When he raised his head, she replied shakily, "He had to go to a meeting at the settlement."

Damion drew her full length against him. His hands trailed down her back to her shapely hips while desire began to smother his logic. He lost himself to her sweet lips and the feel of her firm, willing flesh. Nancy melted against his broad chest, reveling in the wild sensation that swept over her as Damion pulled her down to the straw. When he leaned over her, his hands roamed boldly from her abdomen to the swells of her breasts, and he gazed down into her wide green eyes. The emerald pools seemed to change color in the moonlight. They were no longer green, but had mellowed into indigo. Her dark hair had become strands of honey gold that streamed across the straw, intermingling with flaxen highlights that were kissed by the sun. Damion shook his head, attempting to rout the image. He scowled at the haunting vision that had intruded into his private thoughts. That honey-haired witch had cast her spell over him, and she was seeking revenge for all that he had forced her to endure. Damion looked at Nancy again, but it was the vengeful witch he saw.

"What's the matter? Did I do something wrong?" Nancy queried innocently as she gazed at him. "I'm sorry." She didn't know why she was apologizing and was completely baffled by the twisted sneer that curled the handsome rogue's lips.

Damion hopped to his feet and refused to look at her again. "You better go back to the house," he suggested coldly. "I'm leaving in the morning and I have much to do before I retire."

Nancy scrambled to her feet and brushed the straw from her gown. She peered at Damion's broad back in confusion and humiliation. He didn't want her and he had left her with nothing, not even her pride.

"Melissa was right about you," Nancy choked out as

373

angry tears scalded her eyes. "You are a heartless man. At least there is one woman who can resist you. Melissa left *you;* you didn't leave *her.* I only wish that I were as courageous as she is!" The spiteful hiss in her voice settled about his shoulders, and Damion threw her a menacing glare before his eyes swung back to the steed in the stall.

When Nancy dashed from the barn, Damion grumbled under his breath. Damn that witch! The last thing he needed was to be haunted by that indigo-eyed hellcat. Melissa had not been as easy to forget as he had expected, especially when her name was on the lips of everyone with whom he was associated. Montclaire was bound to her, obligated to her because of Jeremy, and responsible for her. After all, she was his wife, wasn't she? A small voice within him rejected the idea and he listened, hoping to convince himself that he owed her nothing more than he had already given. He was defying Jeremy's deceitful scheme, ignoring the bond between Melissa and himself. He wanted no attachments, no ties to inhibit him. Damion thrived on freedom. Lissa had managed to hamper his independence, not because she had forced his fidelity, but because she had managed to preoccupy his thoughts. Dammit, he scowled as he stalked toward the house. He should let go of her, but each time he envisioned her responding to some other, showing the passion that only Damion had discovered, he burned with jealousy. The thought of Heston or Gibbs caressing her alluring body incensed him. If he could lock her safely away in a nunnery his mind would be at ease, at least until she managed to escape. Damion chuckled to himself as he imagined that mischievous little chit housed in a con-

374

vent. How ironic, he mused delightedly. That's what he should do with that ornery misfit, just for spite!

Damion spent a restless night attempting to sleep, but it was slow in coming. He had much on his mind. The vision of Nancy came to him. She had been so warm and willing and he had sent her away. What a fool he had been. Never would he allow that to happen again. Melissa Montclaire could go straight to hell and he could care less. Besides, he thought to himself as he rolled to his side and pulled the pillow over his head, 'twas the devil who was in danger of being burned, not Melissa. She could find a way to make the Prince of Darkness wish he had kept his distance from her.

His breath came out in a rush as he propped the pillow behind his neck, seeking a more comfortable position that would soothe his ruffled ego. Damn that Jeremy! This was all his fault! Drieson had meddled in Damion's affairs and had tied him to the cape of a witch who had spirited off into the night. Was there no end to her haunting memory? Where was the wench? God, if anything happened to that woman Jeremy would skin him alive.

Damion threw back the quilt and strolled to the window, searching the darkness, wishing he knew for certain where Lissa had gone. Stratton's and Gibbs's words kept tugging at his thoughts. "Let her go." Hell, he was trying his damnedest, but the task was more difficult than he had expected. He heaved a tired sigh and eased back into bed, annoyed with himself for allowing Melissa to monopolize his thoughts.

# Part Three

War, hunting, and love have a thousand
pains for one pleasure.

— Spanish Proverb

## Chapter Eighteen

During the following two weeks Melissa had come upon and had carefully avoided two British searching parties and a small band of Shawnees. Since she had no money and very little food, she had sold the only possession of value that she carried with her: the sapphire necklace that Damion had given her. Although her supplies were short and she had to keep a constant watch for trouble, she welcomed the opportunity to sort out her emotions.

She kept picturing Jeremy and her mother together. The thought continued to weigh heavily on her mind. How could Laura allow herself to turn to another man? How long had she known Jeremy? Had they been lovers before she and William married? Where had Laura met Jeremy? The questions flew about her mind in chaotic disarray, and Melissa shut out the thought of Jeremy and Laura in an embrace. It was much too vivid and disturbing.

Occasionally Melissa found herself talking to her steed and she wondered if she was losing her mind.

The gray gelding was a receptive listener, but he offered little in the way of advice. The horse often regarded her as if she had indeed taken leave of her senses. No doubt he was right, she decided, as she rubbed his soft muzzle.

When she stopped at settlements for supplies, she was eyed suspiciously. She did not intend to invite trouble and had left a myriad of trails, hoping to elude anyone who might have attempted to follow her.

Melissa pulled her steed to a halt and glanced down at the fort at Boonesborough as a steady rain hovered about her. She was chilled to the bone. All that she had was the clothes on her back and an extra set of deerskin garb that nearly swallowed her. She had purchased the garments at one of the settlements, but did not take the time to make them fit properly.

Before entering the fort, she pulled her hair up under her cap, changed into the loose-fitting clothes, and smudged dirt on her face, charading as a boy. She had become discouraged with the skeptical glances she had received during her travels and decided that she would draw less attention as a boy than as an unescorted woman.

Boone and the other men who had been her constant companions during their journey to Detroit were busy fortifying the settlement for attack as she walked her horse inside the gate. A smile touched her lips when she saw Heston and Davis talking with Boone. As she sauntered up to them, they turned curious glances to the dirty-faced lad.

"Can I help?" she drawled in a low voice.

Davis's eyes narrowed suspiciously as he surveyed the lad's smudged features. "You look familiar, lad.

Have we met before?"

"Most certainly, Papa," she taunted, her eyes twinkling mischievously.

Davis did a double take and then his jaw sagged. "Well, I'll be damned. Is that you, Andrea?"

Three pair of jaws swung from their hinges, and Melissa giggled at the bewildered looks on their faces. "Nay, the name is Mel," she informed them saucily.

When she pulled the cap from her head, a mass of golden curls tumbled over her shoulders. After she had received a hug from each of the men, Boone frowned thoughtfully.

"Where is Beaugener? I thought you were going to stay with him while he was recuperating. He isn't—"

"He is staying in a small settlement southeast of Detroit. I left without him," she explained casually, hoping to keep the bitterness from seeping into her voice. Melissa had spent the last two weeks trying to put him out of her mind once and for all, but it still hurt to talk about him.

"How bad was he hit?" Cory Heston questioned.

"He sustained a rather serious wound on his left shoulder and chest, but it was beginning to heal when I left. He will be all right," she assured them. " 'Twas a shame the bullet missed his hard heart. I doubt that a powder gun could have penetrated solid rock." There it was again. The bitter remark flew from her lips before she could bite it back.

Her comment brought a chuckle from the four men who tended to agree with her. Zack Montclaire Beaugener was their friend but he had the reputation of being calloused.

"Did you travel alone?" Boone queried, a concerned frown knitting his brow.

"Aye." Melissa smiled and nodded affirmatively.

Boone's gaze swung to the other men who didn't seem surprised that she had traveled across the Northwest Territory unescorted and had arrived unscathed. A wry grin worked its way across his lips. It was little wonder the British had been deceived. There seemed to be no end to this woman's resourcefulness.

Cory tugged on Melissa's arm as he threw a remark over his shoulder and led her away. "I'll find Mel a place to sleep and a bite to eat and join you later."

The grasp on her elbow became a light caress as Cory drew her with him across the muddy square. "Our accommodations are nothing to praise. I'm afraid you will have to sleep in the blacksmith's barn with the rest of us if you insist on charading as a lad." His voice was disturbed as he glanced down at Melissa, his mind wandering back to a time when they had shared tender moments, ones that he had not forgotten. He wanted to take her in his arms and hold her to him, losing himself to the feel of her trim body molded tightly to his.

"I don't mind, Cory. I'm accustomed to sleeping on the hard ground. A pile of straw will seem like a feather bed," she assured him.

Cory paused as they stepped inside the barn and then yielded to the temptation of holding her in his arms. As he reached up to wipe the dirt from her exquisite features, a fond smile appeared on his face. He didn't care if she was dressed in baggy clothes. She was still one of the loveliest women he had ever met.

Melissa accepted his embrace, enjoying the warmth he offered. Cory was a dear friend who truly cared about her, and Zack was far away. Besides, he didn't really give a damn about her. Hadn't he said as much when he was delirious with fever? She had been an unwanted burden to Zack and she knew she had to bury her love for him. Melissa had left him without saying goodbye because that was the way he would have left her—the way he wanted it. Now her love was transforming into anger and bitterness. She knew it was only a defensive tactic to ease the pain, but Melissa couldn't help the way she felt. She only hoped in time that she could forget him completely.

As Cory's mouth swooped down on hers, a weary moan escaped her lips. She closed her eyes, reveling in the tenderness of his embrace. Although no spark made her heart leap with desire there was a fondness that flowed through her veins.

"I haven't forgotten you, Andrea," Cory confessed huskily as he nibbled at the corners of her mouth and then recaptured her lips in a passionate kiss.

"My name is Melissa, but I prefer that you call me Mel," she requested when she finally managed to drag her lips away from his.

"To attach another name to the lovely image that has filled my thoughts will be difficult," he replied as he stared deeply into her indigo eyes. "Melissa . . ." Cory practiced her name, making it sound like a caress.

"Mel," she corrected as she leaned back as far as his encircling arms would allow.

" 'Tis hard to keep up with your aliases," he admitted.

"I have become accustomed to them, but at times I'm not certain who I really am." The smile vanished as she averted her eyes from his intense stare. Melissa had discarded the name of Andrea Deuvalle when she left Nathan's home, hoping to put the past behind her. But her experiences with Damion Montclaire had changed her, and it was difficult to see herself as she had once been.

"You are the lovely, warm woman whom I have been unable to forget. A rose by any other name would smell as sweet," Cory teased as he brushed the back of his hand over her cheek, loving the feel of her velvety skin beneath his touch.

Melissa forced a meager smile, but she could not agree. Zack had easily forgotten her and, no doubt, when he was well enough, Nancy Gibbs would become the object of his affection. Nancy was too love struck to keep her distance from that devilish rogue.

"Shall we find you something to eat?" Cory questioned, drawing her from her silent reverie. "You must be starved." When she nodded mutely, he placed a quick kiss to her lips and led her back outside. "We'll see what they have to offer at the tavern, but it doesn't compare to your cooking."

Melissa was through making comparisons. She was trying to accept things for what they were instead of labeling them better or worse. Her only concern was to adapt and learn to be content with life. But it was difficult after her experience with Zack. He had turned her world upside down and then left her to pick up the pieces.


Melissa worked tirelessly beside the men, securing the fort for the inevitable attack. Much had been done, but there was much left to do if the settlers were to survive a siege. Boone had already built blockhouses, put out rain barrels for a water supply since they would be unable to sneak out to the nearby spring where they usually acquired water for the families and livestock. A few wells had also been dug in preparation, but it seemed the list of chores was endless. Although part of the underbrush had been cut away from the walls of the fort to prevent the Indians from using it as cover, it was impossible to clear the entire area.

After Boone returned with a scouting party he reported that he had seen the force of Shawnees who had gathered for the siege. He ordered all the rifles to be cleaned, more bullets molded, and all the livestock to be brought back inside the walls. There had not been enough hours in the day to complete all the tasks, and Melissa began to wonder if it would all be in vain.

The five men who had traveled with her to Detroit had urged her to leave before the Indians arrived but they were met with stubborn defiance.

"You know I do not intend to leave and if you try to send me away, I will return," she declared, her gaze sweeping the solemn group that had congregated around her.

"Now, Melissa," Davis began in a coaxing tone. " 'Tis true that we are shorthanded and could use another good marksman, but Beaugener would never forgive any of us if you met with harm." A wry smile appeared on his lips. "The man has a short fuse on his temper and I, for one, do not wish to be around when he explodes. I know who will catch the blame for letting you stay."

"What I do is none of Beaugener's business." She

drew herself up in front of them, her feet widespread, her fists clenched on her hips, her chin tilting determinedly. "You trusted me in the British fort with only one man as protection. Now will you send me away when I'm surrounded by able-bodied men? Are you implying that I fare better alone?"

"You're being unfair," Cory protested. "The Indians will come well prepared for this attack and besides, 'tis not your home you're defending."

Melissa eyed him levelly. " 'Tis not your home either, Heston, nor yours, Davis. But you choose to stay and so do I." She whirled around to find Boone standing behind her, his arms crossed on his chest. "Have you come to side with the rest of them?" she questioned in a challenging tone.

"This is not your battle," he reminded her in a calm voice. "When the fighting begins, there will be no time for us to keep a watchful eye on you, Melissa."

"I need no special attention, nor do I expect it. I can handle a musket and knife as well as the next man," she defended.

"And if you should perish here, what shall we tell Beaugener?" His dark brow arched, subtly reminding her of her abandoned husband.

"You will not have to answer to him. I am my own responsibility, not his." Melissa stood her ground, refusing to back down to anyone, not even Boone.

Daniel peered over the top of her head, meeting the sober-faced men who stood behind her. A brittle silence hovered in the air for a long moment.

"She stays," Daniel commanded. "If Beaugener were here, I doubt that even he could convince her to go." His eyes came to rest on Melissa once again. "We

386

need good marksmen and I have heard that you are handy with a rifle. We appreciate your patriotism."

Suddenly a wry smile spread across his lips as his gaze wandered boldly over her buckskin garb.

Although Melissa was puzzled by his blatant interest in her, she voiced her allegiance to his cause. "I will do all I can." When the smile on Boone's face became a splitting grin, Melissa frowned curiously. "Why are you looking at me like that?" she questioned point-blank.

Boone chuckled and gestured to her attire. "I just had an idea that might make the Shawnee think twice before they attack us. We will dress all of the women in men's clothes and walk them past the gate. Maybe we can convince the Indians that our numbers are greater than they had first thought." With that, he spun on his heels and walked across the square to give the order.

At ten o'clock the following morning the Indians appeared on the ridge overlooking Boonesborough, a British flag waving in the breeze. Chief Blackfish sent a message to the fort, requesting to parley with Boone. Melissa watched anxiously as Daniel walked out to the chief who ordered that the settlers evacuate the fort. Boone informed him that they had no intention of giving up their homes, even though they were outnumbered six to one.

Melissa and the other men and women continued to file past the gate, hoping to convince the Shawnees that Boone had gathered reinforcements. Dummies had even been positioned along the walls to deceive them. The settlers had resorted to every tactic of delusion, but once the Indians realized that they had been tricked, the Shawnee war cry resounded among the braves.

A cloudburst of bullets exploded around the fort as Daniel made his way back inside the walls. He received two minor wounds before he managed to take cover, and Melissa experienced the same fear that had gripped her the night Damion had been shot at Detroit.

She discovered what it meant to fight for her life when bullets and arrows rained down around her. Determinedly, she swallowed the lump of fear and raised her musket to the onrush of braves that came at them from all directions.

Boonesborough was built in a valley and it only took a moment for the Indians to surround them, shooting down from the hilltops and underbrush that had not been cut away. It didn't take Melissa long to realize that they were sitting ducks who were at the mercy of the Shawnees. The settlers couldn't retreat and it was too late to surrender. All they could do was defend themselves.

All that the settlers had on their side was the weather. The nightly rains dampened the cabins that had been set afire with flaming arrows. The fort did not burn to the ground as the Indians had hoped, and it infuriated them further that the settlers held their ground, knowing they were far outnumbered.

On the eleventh day, Melissa raised weary eyes to the dawn, finding no Indians in sight. Her elation was dampened when Boone warned them that it might be a trick. They sat for several hours, watching and waiting, before sending out a scouting party. When the men returned with the news that Blackfish and his braves had abandoned the attack, a cry of cheer echoed around the walls of the fort.

Melissa found herself swept into Cory's arms and whirled around until her head was spinning. He showered her with kisses, hugged her close, and then stood her to her feet.

"I'm taking you home, young lady," he informed her as he grasped her arm and led her to her horse. "The Indians are heading north to attack the other settlements and we will be needed elsewhere. But first I am going to stash you away for safe keeping until I can come back for you."

Melissa's brows furrowed as Cory dragged her along behind him. "Coming back for me? What are you talking about?"

Cory set her up on her horse and then grinned at her. "Now that I have found you again, I don't intend to let you go."

Her breath came out in a rush when she grasped his meaning. "Cory, I can't—" She swallowed the rest of her sentence when Stratton and Davis edged up beside them.

"We're going with you," Stratton announced as he winked at Melissa. His motive was twofold. He wanted to assure that Melissa was delivered safely, and he felt the need to keep an eye on Heston. He had become too infatuated with Melissa the past few days. Zack Beaugener would be breathing fire if he discovered that Heston had staked a claim on this captivating young woman.

"I am going alone," she insisted. "You are needed at the northern settlements and I will not detain you, any of you." Her eyes narrowed meaningfully on Cory. "I am quite capable of finding my own way home."

Melissa reined her horse toward the gate, but all three men followed at her heels. When Davis pulled her horse to a halt to argue the point, a lone rider appeared on the hill and then slowly edged down the slope toward them. As he moved up beside them, his rugged face was set in a carefully guarded stare that missed nothing, but showed no changing expression.

"Beaugener," Stratton greeted as Zack focused his full attention on the grimy-faced lad in baggy clothes.

Melissa's heart did a flip-flop when she met Zack's eyes, although she was doing her damnedest to feel nothing. Seeing him as he had been the night he found her in the shack brought back too many forbidden memories. His face was covered with a heavy beard once again, his eyes, the stern, penetrating silver they had been before he was wounded. The vulnerability was gone and Melissa knew that he didn't need her now that he had fully recovered.

When Zack finally settled his gaze on Heston, he was met with an angry glare.

"You certainly took your sweet time about getting here. You're about ten days late," he snapped, frustrated that Zack had showed up in the first place, and especially with such perfect timing.

Zack did not bother to retort to the snide remark. Instead, he went right to the heart of the matter. "I'm taking the lady home . . . alone."

"No one is taking me anywhere! I can manage on

390

my own," she snapped in stubborn insistence.

Zack flashed her a silencing frown and then rested his eyes on Stratton. "Take the men and ride north. I'll catch up to you as soon as I can."

As the men filed by, Melissa placed a farewell kiss to their cheeks, feeling as though a part of her life was being snatched away from her.

"I'll be back," Cory assured her, his blue eyes skimming across her face, wanting to say more, but then he didn't need to. Melissa knew what he was thinking.

"Come on, vixen," Zack muttered.

He had ridden hard the past few days, pushing himself to the limit, hoping to arrive before the attack, but he had not come in time to aid the settlers. His arm had healed, but it was still weak, and the constant strain of the rigorous journey left it throbbing. He was irritated that Melissa had traveled to the fort, infuriated that the men had not sent her on her way, and incensed with Heston's remark that he would return for her.

"What the hell did you offer my men not to send you home?" Zack questioned as he watched his men ride away.

Melissa's eyes were alive with indignation. "Maybe the same thing Nancy offered you to keep you there a few days longer than necessary," she flared. The pleasure of seeing him again was quickly smothered by his insult.

A devilish grin hung on one corner of his mouth as his gaze swung over to her. "You haven't changed a damned bit, have you?" Zack released a derisive snort as he grabbed her reins and led her along behind him. "I had wondered if the Indians captured you whether they would have cut out that sharp tongue of yours."

His remark set her teeth on edge and she glanced at his broad back. "My journey to Boonesborough was a peaceful one since I did not have to endure your sarcasm. You may join your men, Beaugener." His name flew from her lips in a hiss. "I do not require your services."

"Not any of them?" He arched a heavy brow as he glanced back at her, watching the steam rise from the collar of her jacket. "As your husband I thought perhaps there was at least *one* service that might interest you."

Furious crimson made fast work of staining her cheeks. "None of them!" she insisted adamantly. "And you are *not* my husband!"

Zack nudged his steed to a faster gait, pulling Melissa along behind him. "I said I was taking you home and that is just what I intend to do so you might as well learn to live with it."

Melissa grumbled under breath and yanked at the reins, but Zack refused to release them. "Damn you," she thundered. "You are not going to lead me home!"

Zack drew his steed to a halt, released an impatient sigh, and then twisted around in his saddle. "I'm tired and I am in no mood to chase you across the country."

"I won't try to escape from you," she assured him, but as usual Zack put no faith in her promise.

"You must think I'm every kind of fool," he said with a smirk.

"Aye," she agreed. "But I am giving you my word this day that I will not attempt to flee from you. I only want to handle my own horse."

A skeptical frown gathered on his brow as he regarded her for an indecisive moment and then he

tossed her the reins. "I expect you to keep your word
. . . for once."

Melissa settled herself in the saddle and followed
after him, making a mental list of insults to fling at
him. When they had their next argument, and there
would be another, she thought to herself, she would be
well armed.

Their ride was slow and quiet. It seemed they had
nothing more to say to each other. When they stopped
for the night, Melissa welcomed the opportunity to
climb down from her steed. It had been a long, tense
day and she was ready for sleep.

After Melissa prepared their meal, she shook out her
bedroll and stretched leisurely upon it, moaning wearily as she squirmed to find a comfortable position.
Zack watched her every move, but did not utter a word
until she had settled herself beneath the quilt.

"Did you have a rough time of it, Lissa?" he questioned quietly, surprising her with the sincerity of his
tone.

Melissa looked up to see him towering over her, just
as she had the night he had found her in the cabin.
Why did she keep thinking of that night? She wanted
to forget those two days ever existed. " 'Tis not easy to
watch men fall and die, knowing that you were the one
who took their lives," she murmured.

Zack squatted down on his haunches, but she
frowned suspiciously and scooted a safe distance away.
"I feared that you would go to the fort. I could have
told you what to expect, but you didn't even bother to
inform me that you were leaving." He reached into his
pocket and dangled the gold chain in front of her. "You
left this behind," he said, his eyes narrowing in annoy-

ance. "This was an expensive gift, Lissa. I did not give it to you so that you could sell it for little or nothing."

"I needed supplies and that was all I had of worth to trade," she defended.

As he fastened the necklace around her throat, his hand brushed against her breast, sending a passionate spark bridging the gap between them. Melissa tried to still the rapid beat of her heart, but it had already run away with itself. It was useless, she thought despairingly. His touch was magic, making her skin tingle and ache for more.

"Next time you need money, take mine, but keep the necklace," he ordered huskily.

Melissa thought for a moment that he intended to kiss her and she was determined not to fall prey to his tender ploy. She presented her back to him, refusing to gaze into those spellbinding silver eyes. "I didn't know you were so sentimental and I doubt that there will be a next time."

Her words hung in the air like a separating partition. She was trying to tell him that it was over and done without coming right out and saying it. And for the life of her she didn't know why she was trying to be tactful.

Zack dropped his head apologetically and when he spoke, his voice was soft and sympathetic. "I know why you left me." When Melissa peered back at him he continued, "Nathan overheard what I said and told me what I was raving about." His breath came out in a rush. "I'm sorry, Lissa. I never meant to tell you, and I don't think Jeremy intended for you to know the truth."

When he reached out to touch her cheek, she pulled

away. "I learned several interesting facts that night," she said coldly.

Melissa was afraid to let him touch her again. He could make her emotions churn like a volcano that was dangerously close to eruption. It would have been easy to throw herself in his arms, hoping to forget the terrifying experience she had endured at Boonesborough. But she had to stand alone, keeping a tight rein on her unsettled feelings. She turned away from him, fighting back the tears that scalded her eyes. Playing the role of the tough, calloused lad at the fort had taken its toll on her composure. She felt the need to be loved and protected, and she would have turned to anyone but Zack for compassion.

As Zack reached beneath the quilt, his hands roamed boldly over her. "Melissa . . ."

"Leave me alone! I told you I wanted nothing to do with you and I meant it," she flared, unrestrained tears streaming down her smudged cheeks.

Zack pulled the handkerchief from his pocket and gently wiped away the tears and grime. "I have never had to resort to rape to satisfy my desire for a woman. Most of them came willingly, and occasionally uninvited," he taunted, knowing his remark would incense her, and it did. A wry smile played on his lips as he met her condemning glare. "However, I must admit that the idea of rape becomes more appealing each time I recall the alluring body that lies beneath those fur quilts and buckskin clothes."

Melissa pulled the blankets tightly beneath her chin, as if the meager protection would prohibit intrusion. "Then go ravish some poor, defenseless maid," she spat harshly. "There might be some hereabout who would not find you so disgusting once the deed was done. You may even persuade some wench to yield willingly, but I know you too well and I would continue to despise you." The hiss in her voice reminded Zack of a snake that was about to sink her fangs in human flesh. "You have stripped me of my pride, must you take my clothes as well?" she questioned sarcastically. "I have had enough fighting these past few days and I haven't much strength to struggle with you. But I promise you, Zack Beaugener, if you try to take me you will find no pleasure in it. I will curse your name each time you touch me and it will be a fight to the bitter end."

He was at his wit's end, unsure of how to deal with Melissa. She had not seemed happy to see him that afternoon and she had presented him with a cold shoulder during their journey. Finally he decided to drop the subject. He could never rape her. He had only made the threat, knowing that was all it was. She was Jeremy's flesh and blood and he could not abuse her. After all, he had sent her to hell and back already. Besides, they were both exhausted. Tomorrow would be a better day for dealing with Melissa.

As he rose to his feet, Melissa strangled the words that would have called him back to comfort and protect her. What was wrong with her? One moment she was insulting him, warning him to keep his distance, and in the next breath, she was ready to beg him to hold her close.

"Where are you going?" she questioned, straining to see him walk silently away.

"To the stream for a *cold* bath," he muttered as the swaying shadows swallowed him, leaving Melissa feeling alone and frightened.

She closed her eyes, begging for sleep, and when it came she welcomed it with open arms. But her exhaustion and the haunting events of the past few weeks came at her in a nightmare. The faces of the men who had fallen during the siege tortured her thoughts. And then it was her own face she recognized among those who had died during the battle. She was screaming hysterically as their blood mingled with hers. Melissa fought to find her feet, afraid that she would be left for dead. Someone was shaking her, refusing to let her go, holding her to the ground, keeping her among the mangled corpses.

"Lissa, wake up. Dammit! Lissa!" Zack bellowed as he soundly shook her again.

Her lashes swept up as beads of perspiration formed on her brow. When she realized where she was and whose strong arms were holding her, she choked on a sob. Zack was looking at her with concern. He was out of breath, bare chested, his hair still dripping with water.

Melissa threw her arms about his neck and nestled against his solid frame. "Oh Zack, it was horrible," she cried, gasping to force out the words. "I was watching myself fall and die with the others. I was afraid, Zack, so afraid they would leave me behind. . . ." Her voice trailed off in broken syllables as she clutched him closer, her body trembling uncontrollably.

Zack encircled her in his arms, nuzzling his chin against the top of her head, surprised by another side of Melissa that he had never seen. He had watched her stand up against impossible odds, defying defeat. He had seen her come alive with passion, feeling her warm and willing in his embrace, but this shattered, disillusioned child drew upon his strength and emotions.

" 'Tis not easy to watch men die, friend or foe," he whispered soothingly. "It never gets easier, Lissa. I would have kept you from the experience if I could."

She was crying quietly now, trying to regain her composure, but it was yet another battle. "I'm sorry, Zack," she said, her voice wavering. "I'm sorry for being weak."

Zack reached beneath her chin and raised her quivering lips to his, finding no words to comfort her. He was no good at sympathy or consolation, nor had he ever tried to be. And the one time in his life when he would have attempted it, he found himself speechless. His kiss was giving, not taking, showing Melissa a strange tenderness that she had not expected from him.

Was this the same, cold, uncaring man that she had abandoned? Was this the devilish rogue who only sought to satisfy his desires? Although she was troubled and confused, she responded, taking what he offered, melting in the protective arms that shut out the world of harsh reality.

"Love me, Zack," she requested in sobbing breaths. "I need you tonight. Help me forget. . . ."

As his lips descended on hers in another slow, deliberate kiss, he lay back on the pallet, drawing her with him. He pulled the buckskin clothes from her body, his eyes boldly caressing her flesh before his hands leisurely followed the path of his gaze. The moonlight glistened on her skin, mesmerizing him, making him ache with a need that had hindered his thoughts for the long weeks that they had been apart. He had been certain that he could recall everything about her, but he found that he was sadly mistaken. Melissa was even lovelier than he remembered. Her face was so delicate, so angelic. Her body was perfection, like a goddess that men only found in their dreams.

For a time he was content just to stare at her, watching the sparkle in her blue-violet eyes, letting his hand trail over her hip, remembering the many faces that he had seen in their months together. His hand lifted and tunneled through the flaxen hair on the side of her face and he smiled to himself. She was breathtakingly beautiful. There were no defiant sparks in her eyes, no belligerent tilt to her chin. She was no longer the cunning witch whose sharp claws slashed his flesh, cutting him with vindictive remarks. Now she was the gentle angel whose tender touch could evoke a contented purr from a mountain lion. At times she had the power to inflict pain and occasionally, she could heal the wound with her light caress. His eyes took on a mellowed gray hue as he continued to touch her, loving the feel of silky skin beneath his hands, wanting her, and yet oddly satisfied just being with her.

His caresses were setting her on fire. Melissa yearned for him to take her, to become a part of her, giving of his strength. But tonight he had unbelievable patience instead of the hungry urgency that she had remembered. His hand cupped her breast and he lowered his head, his mouth capturing their taut peaks, teasing her until she moaned in undescribable pleasure. A wildfire exploded within her, sending her blood coursing her veins like smoldering lava. Her need for him filled her senses, driving her to the limits of her sanity.

Their lovemaking had been a part of the past that lay in repose like a sleeping mountain until the inner fire became too great to contain. Melissa was unsure she could endure the sweet torture of his caresses. She couldn't breathe. She couldn't think. She could only feel, aroused to lofty heights that left her to wonder if this was another fantastic dream, more pleasant than the one that had awakened her.

As his searching hands found the soft flesh of her thighs, she clutched him to her, unable to get close enough to the fire that burned her inside and out, abandoning her pride.

As Zack lifted himself above her, she drew him to her, boldly caressing him, wanting him to touch the same stars that were within her grasp. She guided him to her, needing him more than life itself, consumed by the desires she had tried desperately to forget. But it was impossible. The feel of body molded to hers, sharing an intimacy that she had only known in his arms, was branded on her mind.

As her fingers dug into the rippling muscles of his back, he plunged deeply within her, satisfying the maddening passion that held her suspended. Zack pulled her closer, burying his head against her shoulder as the rumbling volcano of emotions exploded like thunder that shook the earth. And then he sought her lips, impatiently wanting to touch all of her. He savored and devoured her mouth as they moved together, pleasure streaming like molten lava, consuming all in its path, leaving no part of them unaffected. Their souls were forged by the intensifying heat and took flight, soaring above the smoldering coals. On pinioned wings they glided toward the far horizon, content and secure in their lofty flight.

*"Ma cher ami,"* Zack murmured hoarsely before his mouth captured hers once again, finding no resistance as their breath blended into one.

Tears streamed down her cheeks as she surrendered all that was hers to give. Melissa clung to him, feeling herself spiraling to dizzying heights as a wild budding ecstasy took her higher and higher. The words that forced their way to her lips were strangled beneath his scalding kiss. And yet, she knew that she could not speak them. He did not need her love. He had her heart and had completely possessed her body and soul, but there would be no vows of devotion. She would deny her love for this powerful man who could bend her to his will until the end of eternity. There was another ache gnawing at her consciousness, one that tore at her heart, sending her spirit plunging from its precarious perch. Zack would never love her.

She had promised herself that she would never submit to him again, and yet, she had shamelessly begged him to make love to her. Her cheeks flushed with humiliation, recalling how she had abandoned all restraints, boldly touching him, urging him to ravish her as if she were some common trollop who could never resist seeking her own pleasure.

Zack felt the tears on his chest and rolled beside her, taking her in his arms as he frowned in confusion. She had taken him to heaven, giving him unequaled pleasure and yet, she cried. He was bewildered by the vulnerable woman who lay in his arms.

"What's wrong, Lissa?" he questioned raspily as he wiped away her tears.

Melissa shook her head, refusing to answer, avoiding the penetrating silver eyes that sought to draw the truth from her soul.

Cupping her chin in his hand, he lifted her tear-stained face, but her lashes swept down to shield her from his gaze. "Answer me," he commanded softly. "Why are you crying?"

"It doesn't matter," she murmured, muffling a sniff.

"It does to me." A demure smile crept to his lips as he traced his fingertips over her kiss-swollen mouth. "I have never been able to read that remarkable mind of yours. I cannot fathom what has caused the tears."

"Perhaps they are tears of pleasure," she said evasively, keeping her eyes averted from his face.

Zack cocked a skeptical brow. "And perhaps not."

When she tried to squirm away, his grip tightened. "Please don't question me now," she pleaded, biting back another round of tears. "Just let me sleep in your arms. Protect me from those horrible nightmares. I have survived this past week, but not without losing part of myself to those who will never see another sunrise." Finally her eyes met his, silently appealing. "Just hold me. Is it so much to ask?"

With a reluctant nod, Zack wrapped his arm about her waist, pulling her back against the rock wall of his chest. *"Bon soir, ma cherie,"* he whispered against the hollow of her neck.

While Zack drifted off to sleep, Melissa lay awake, searching the depths of her soul. She had slept long enough to be wide awake, just as she had at the fort when the crack of rifles ceased for a time. She stared up at the sky, watching the diamonds that sparkled above her. How remote and distant they seemed now. Only minutes before she had held them within her grasp. A rueful smile touched her lips, knowing that she would never touch them again.

Melissa edged away from Zack's embrace and collected her scattered clothes. She had to leave him. He was needed in the North. His cause was more important than delivering her home. And Melissa couldn't say goodbye to him. It was better this way, she told herself as she silently gathered her belongings. They would part as they had met, like two souls passing in the night, uniting for one brief moment before pursuing their courses.

Melissa rode through the night, intent on her destination. After her experiences the past week, she was ready to return home to her father and Jeremy. She had finally come to terms with the knowledge she had received in Detroit. At first she had been bitter and disillusioned, but with time, she had come to accept the fact that Jeremy was her natural father. How could her mother *not* have fallen in love with Jeremy, she had asked herself. He was gentle, compassionate, witty . . . she could have spent the entire night describing his admirable qualities. There was nothing about Jeremy that she could criticize, except that he had cared too much for Laura and that he could never truly release his claim on her, loving her through the years, never allowing her memory to fade. And then there was William, whose qualities equally matched Jeremy's. He was tender, understanding, capable of unselfish love. Laura must have loved both of them, just as Melissa did, but Laura was forced to make a choice. William could offer her a home and security while Jeremy offered her an adventure in an untamed land, and no doubt, a love as wild and romantic as Zack had offered Melissa. Laura had been gently bred, unprepared for the rugged life upon which Jeremy thrived.

Tears sprang from Melissa's eyes, realizing the hell that her mother had endured. What torture it must have been to live, torn between the love of two men. And no one would, could ever know the agony Jeremy had suffered, loving a woman who was married to another man, knowing that she cared for both men, watching his daughter grow without being able to claim her as his child. And what of William? Did he know that Laura had borne another man's child? Had he lived with yet another kind of torture?

Melissa heaved a heavy sigh. Damion was right when he said she had been blessed. She loved both fathers dearly. They had taught her a great deal in their own special ways, unselfishly giving their time and love to her.

There were many questions that still plagued her, but at least she had begun to understand what might have happened in love's eternal triangle. She could not despise her mother. Laura had known two, unending loves, but had been confined to enjoy only one of them while Melissa had discovered first love's pain, determined to deny the emotions that wrecked her heart.

Zackery Montclaire Beaugener was not a man who could be conquered by love as William and Jeremy had been. Melissa was destined to follow in Jeremy's footsteps. She would have to learn to be content with a lesser man, remembering the passion she had once shared with Zack. Melissa choked on a sob. Could she ever forget? The answer came quickly. Nay, time could not heal all wounds. She was doomed, just as Jeremy had been, loving a memory. Jeremy had hoped to bring her unsuffering love when he threw Melissa and Zack together, but he had only succeeded in allowing history to repeat itself. Melissa ran her hand over her abdomen and blinked back the tears. What would her father and Jeremy say when she informed them that they were to be grandfathers? How could she explain the past few months to her father so that he would understand?

Her gaze swept the shadows of the night, feeling frightened for the first time in months, expecting some hideous form to leap at her. And yet, perhaps it would have been easier to perish than to endure what lay ahead of her. Aye, history had repeated itself in the second generation, she thought dismally. And she must learn to accept her destiny.

## Chapter Nineteen

Zack awoke as the first rays of dawn sprinkled across the meadow. He reached out to pull Melissa against him, but the bundle beside him was only quilts. Prying one eye open, he scanned the campsite, half expecting her to be kindling a fire to make his breakfast as she had often done while they traveled across the Northwest Territory. When the realization that she was nowhere to be seen finally filtered into his drowsy thoughts, he rolled to his feet to grab for his clothes.

"Damn that deceiving witch!" he bellowed furiously as he wrapped the quilt about him and stalked over to the leather bag that lay on the ground.

When he had flung open the pouch, he muttered another curse to Melissa's name, a curse that sliced through the crisp morning air like a double-edged knife. Zack's features turned to stone as his gaze swept the countryside, burning a path that could have ignited the entire area in a raging blaze. That ornery wench! She had left him with a bedroll, a few supplies, and the bag of coins he had brought with him. He had no horse, not a stitch of clothes, nothing but a fur quilt and a pair of moccasins!

She had spirited off into the night while he slept like a trusting child. Dear God, what was happening to him? How could he have been so addle-witted as to believe she had would not try to escape?

Zack gathered what little she had left him, wrapped the quilt about him, looking like an oversized Indian squaw, and stomped off across the meadow, inventing new curses for every angry step he took. That woman had made him look the fool more times than he cared to count. When he got his hands on her, she would regret this last bit of mischief, he vowed to himself. Never again would he trust her. Never again could he allow her to sleep without staking her to something that could not be uprooted in the middle of the night— like a tree, he decided, his face twisting in a furious scowl.

Something she had said the previous afternoon hit him like a hard slap in the face, and he turned his curses on himself for not realizing what she had meant. But then, she had intended that he misinterpret her pledge. Damn her! "I give you my word *this day* that I will not try to escape," she had said. He should have known that when the day ended she would flee. That sly, cunning, underhanded . . . damn!

That woman would continue to haunt him until he managed to completely subdue her, not only in bed, but in every facet of their relationship, which, judging by his past dealings with that little firebrand, would be precisely one hundred years from never!

Zack thoughtfully considered his choices, trying to

compose himself, but it was damned hard, considering his blood was boiling through his veins. He could admit defeat and turn back to follow his men, facing their amused gazes when they saw him strolling into the fort, disguised as one of the enemy's wives, or he could pursue that wench, kidnap her from her home, and recreate some medieval method of torture to break her spirit and singe her flesh. At the moment he was highly entertaining the idea of torture. After the way she had humiliated him, she deserved to scream in agony and beg for his mercy. Nay, she would die before she pleaded forgiveness, he predicted. Lissa would never admit defeat. He would have to find some way to reach her soul without leaving a mark, but what? Zack had a long walk ahead of him, and he was determined to find an answer by the time he caught up to that mischievous little witch.

Of all the women he had known, Melissa continued to baffle him. She was unlike the ones he could take to bed and then toss aside. Even when he held other women in his arms, she had come to haunt him. Her appearance was bewitching, her pride unconquerable, her spirit undaunted. She was an instinctive creature of the wilderness, a lioness that could be tamed with passion, but no man could ever really bring her under control. She could be purring the instant before a man would feel her bite. Melissa had been trained by the same man who had taught him to survive, but obviously, Jeremy had devoted more time to his beloved daughter than to his adopted son. Damn that Jeremy! This was all his fault, Zack grumbled resentfully as he stalked across the Kentucky countryside.

Jeremy had created a misfit. In a man's world, one

woman should not reign supreme! And yet, she had traveled with a guerrilla band, living as they had without complaint. She had outmaneuvered an entire British regiment, crossed the Northwest Territory alone, fought against impossible odds, and had survived it all with no more than a sprained ankle. Was there no end to that vixen's capabilities? Hell yes! Zack intended to put the wench in her place. By damned, he would do just that if it was the last thing he ever did.

Now *she* was the prey and *he* was the hunter. It seemed their relationship had always been reversed, and Zack had an aversion to being on the receiving end. He was his own master and it burned him to the quick to follow in her footsteps, and damned if that wasn't what he was doing!

A wicked smile parted his lips as he adjusted his quilt. Not even Boone's freedom could be as gratifying as bringing Melissa Stoddard to heel. Revenge would taste sweet and he had become obsessed with conquering her.

Melissa gazed down at the settlement that lay nestled in the valley. It had been over four months since she had left her father in Norfolk. So much had happened to change her life. She had enjoyed the adventures that had once been hers in the fascinating stories that Jeremy had related to her. But now that was over and done. Eventually, these vivid memories would fade, becoming part of the past.

She had faced a rogue with silver eyes and jet-black hair, had released Boone, right from under the noses of the British, tracked her way through the untamed wilderness, and survived an Indian attack. There had been no stone left unturned. And it had been worth the struggle, she mused thoughtfully. She had served her country. It was enough. It had to be, she told herself.

Again her thoughts turned to Nancy Gibbs, as they had on several occasions. She was a young woman, dreaming of the knight in shining armor who would come to carry her away. That had once been a part of Melissa's childhood fantasy, but there were no gallant knights, no coats of armor, and no mystical castles. Harsh reality had invaded her dreams, and she could not help but wonder if Damion Montclaire had shattered Nancy's dream or given it substance. Nancy had carelessly fallen for Damion's magnetic charms, and Melissa was left to wonder if he had destroyed her. Perhaps Nancy would carry the same scar that slashed across Melissa's heart. Melissa pitied Nancy if she had not heeded the warning to keep her distance from Damion.

He was as untamed as the wind, wild and raging, occasionally calm and serene, but constantly changing and moving. He could never remain in one place for any length of time. He was a restless breeze that could touch one's face with tender warmth or the chill of an arctic wind.

It had been difficult for Melissa to leave Zack's protective embrace, but she knew in her heart that it was for the best. He needed to be with his men. He was dedicated to his cause, and she had given him the freedom he wanted. She had made it easy on him and herself. He would be annoyed with her, but after all she had suffered at his hands, she could not resist humiliating him one last time. Soon she would be safe at home, resuming the life she had known and Zack would be only a memory.

Melissa heaved a hopeless sigh, knowing that Zack would always be following at her heels, riding the riderless steed that she led along behind her. And then an evil grin lifted the corners of her mouth. At least the devil would be in his true form, not disguised as a man. She had all of his clothes tucked in her saddle bag. It was not difficult to imagine the curse that would send the birds to their wings when he discovered that she had left him without a stitch. She would have loved to see the fury in those silver eyes as long as she wasn't in the direct line of fire.

Her wicked chuckle rang through the air as she nudged her horse down the winding path. Sweet revenge, she breathed as she tossed her golden mane over her shoulder and ducked beneath the low-hanging branches that reached out to snare her. In her own way she had conquered him. Zack would remember her. His recollections would not be pleasant, but he would remember her just the same. And when the panther growled, his silver eyes blazing like torches, it would be *her* face that rose before him, haunting and infuriating him. Let him rave, she thought spitefully. When the demon panther howled like a banshee in the night, it would not frighten her. It would only delight her!

Another thought came to her, one that dissolved her pleasure. She could never forget Zack for she carried his child. But at least she could give their baby all the love that she would have freely given Zack. She could watch the child grow, teaching him to be like his father. Melissa would raise him to know the meaning of love and compassion. Perhaps she had won out over Zack after all. She would bear his flesh and blood, making him the man Zack would never be—a man who possessed a heart and understood the meaning of love.

Melissa reached Martin's Fork late at night after pressing hard for over two weeks. When she arrived, she went straight to her father's room, only to find him gone. After moving through the shadows she slipped into Jeremy's house and tiptoed toward his bed, standing over him, watching his aging face in calm repose as the moonlight streamed in from the open window.

The gentle side of Jeremy, she mused, as her gaze lingered on his scarred face. This was the part that Laura had loved while the call of the wild drew them apart. After spending so much time with Zack, Melissa could understand how her mother had suffered, loving a vagabond, just as Melissa had.

There was no hatred for the lost lovers who had conceived her, no outrage for Laura and Jeremy who had shared a special love before going their separate ways. Melissa could understand how they had suffered and she sympathized with them.

As she continued to study Jeremy, his eyes fluttered open and he gasped in disbelief when he peered into the shadowed face that hovered above him. The name floated from his lips, thinking his lost love had returned from the dead.

"Laura." His voice was like a gentle caress.

A sad smile brushed across her lips as she eased

down beside him. "Nay, I'm afraid 'tis only Melissa. Hello, Father," she whispered.

Jeremy's arms dropped to his side and his face paled, the scar on his cheek turning deathly white. His drowsiness fled as he searched her face, knowing that Melissa was alive and well and knew the truth that had haunted him for over twenty years.

"So he told you," he murmured, wishing he could hold her to him, but afraid of being rejected.

Melissa reached out to trace her fingertips over the scar as she gazed into his pained blue eyes, seeing her own reflection in them. There were golden flecks encircling those pools of sapphire. Sapphire . . . it reminded her of the necklace Zack had given to her, and she touched the gem that hung around her throat. Only now did she see the reason for the necklace and the resemblance between father and daughter. The truth was clear.

"Why?" Jeremy questioned as he wrapped her hand in his own and brought it to his lips. "I never wanted you to suffer, knowing the truth about your mother and me. Why did he tell you?"

"Zack didn't even know that he had told me. He was delirious with fever and pain after he was wounded in Detroit. He had no control over his thoughts or words," she explained.

"I'm sorry, Melissa. Your mother and I had vowed that our child would never have to live with what happened." The agony in his voice was like a choked sob and her heart went out to him.

"Jeremy," she began, meeting his tortured gaze. "You and Mother endured a lifetime of pain. I cannot condemn you, either of you. I love you as I always

413

have. What happened twenty years ago cannot dissolve my devotion to you."

A relieved smile crossed his battered face. "I don't think I could have survived if I lost your love, Lissa," he whispered as he drew her to him, nuzzling against the top of her head. "I let my love for Laura grow in you. You are the bond between us that can never be destroyed."

Melissa nestled in his arms, her eyes clouding with tears. "I will never leave you. Never!" she sobbed. "Papa, you and I belong together."

"But I'm afraid you must." Jeremy cupped her chin and raised her face to his. "Much has happened while you were away. When I saw you standing there, I thought I had seen a ghost, not only your mother's but yours as well."

Melissa brushed away the tears and frowned at his strange remark. "What is wrong? Where is Papa? He is all right, isn't he?" Her voice wavered fearfully. Jeremy seemed to have the weight of the world balanced on his shoulders.

"William is alive, but he lives with a grief that has confused his thinking."

Her frown deepened. "I don't understand. You're talking in riddles."

Jeremy drew a long, shuddering breath. "He thinks you're dead."

"What?" she gasped. "Why should he think that? Zack left him a letter in Norfolk. He told me so."

"But someone else came to convince him that you did not survive your mission. When the ship arrived in France, Captain Stephens told Lelia about the message. She sailed to the colonies to ensure that William was well. The captain remained here for over a week, hoping that you would return. He seemed very anxious to see you again." He paused to arch a curious brow. "I had the feeling that the young captain had become enamored with you." Jeremy searched her face for some sign that the fondness was returned, but Melissa had learned to mask her emotions when it met her whim, and Jeremy was met by a carefully blank stare.

"Go on," Melissa urged impatiently.

"After Stephens left, Lelia began placing doubts in William's mind about your welfare. She insisted that she hire a man to discover what had happened to you. I tried to convince William that you were safe if you were with Montclaire, but Lelia kept voicing her pessimism and that made him restless and uneasy."

Jeremy sighed as he clasped Melissa's hand in his, meeting her anxious gaze. "Your aunt is a wealthy woman and I am sure that she paid her informant a goodly sum to return a few weeks later to announce that you had perished. The story he gave your father was that Montclaire and his associates were massacred by Indians and that no one survived."

"What?" Melissa nearly choked on her breath. "Why would she do such a thing to Papa? Damn that woman!"

"I'm afraid you don't know your aunt very well," Jeremy muttered, his eyes narrowing into angry slits. "When Laura and I began seeing each other, Lelia provided an alibi. She and Laura would leave together and then Laura would come with me. But it was Lelia's jealousy for her sister that spurred her actions. She was willing to do anything to keep William and Laura apart. And when the day came that William

415

turned his attention to Laura, Lelia was infuriated. She never forgave your mother for stealing William from her, not that it was your mother's fault, but Lelia blamed her just the same.

"That was why I was hesitant about allowing you to travel to France. I never trusted that woman. I was afraid she intended to take her vengeance out on you, especially since you and Laura bear such a striking resemblance. I had the uneasy feeling that she meant to do you harm. William could not see that. He was plagued with his own guilt for what had happened. He could never view Lelia with a critical eye."

"But where has Papa gone?" Melissa inquired after Jeremy had explained why she had been the recipient of Lelia's hateful glares.

"Lelia convinced him that they should marry and return to France, at least until the war is over. I doubt that she intends to return, fearing that you might split them apart. They left for Norfolk about a week ago. William resisted the idea, hoping that you would miraculously appear, but finally he gave in to Lelia." Jeremy sighed hopelessly. "The woman has William in her clutches while he mourns for you. Nothing matters to him anymore. All that he ever loved was gone, and he allowed Lelia to have her way."

Jeremy peered into her alarmed face, his brow arching curiously. "Where is Zack? I was hoping that he could travel to Norfolk with you."

"Zack went back to join his men. The Shawness have gone north to raid the other settlements," she murmured, preoccupied with her own thoughts.

"Then I will have to go with you," Jeremy insisted, pleased with the idea.

416

"I appreciate the offer but I will need to travel cross-country. I will make better time alone," Melissa replied, letting him down as she graced him with a persuasive smile. Unfortunately, Jeremy would not yield.

"Nay, you will not go alone," Jeremy commanded sternly.

Melissa arched a haughty brow as she cocked her head to the side, her expression slightly mocking. "Just how do you suppose I managed to arrive here from Detroit, Jeremy? I told you Zack had been wounded. I left him at a settlement and continued without him."

"You did what?" Jeremy gasped incredulously, wishing he had not heard her correctly, but certain that his ears did not deceive him. He sat straight up in bed, bracing his arms on either side of himself. "Melissa! That was a foolish thing to do. You could have perished, just as Lelia had hoped."

"Now, Jeremy, calm yourself," she coaxed, her eyes twinkling mischievously. "You're behaving like an overprotective father. After all, you are the one who taught me to travel the wilderness. Do you doubt your ability . . . and mine?"

Jeremy sputtered helplessly. "Nay, but I never expected you to journey alone," he defended. "I expected Zack to protect you."

"I do not need his protection," she informed him, her tone carrying a hint of annoyance. "I don't need him at all."

A dubious frown etched his brow, noting the rebellion flicker in her eyes. "You and Zack still have not buried the hatchet?"

"Aye, we buried it," she assured him bitterly. "In each other's backs. We are too much alike and yet in some ways we are worlds apart."

"You are both stubborn and independent," Jeremy added, a sly smile parting his lips.

Melissa nodded reluctantly. "Aye, and because of that we bring out the worst in each other."

Jeremy would have dearly loved to hear each and every episode, but Melissa was not one to divulge much information on the subject of Zack. All she offered were simple yeas and nays to his questions.

"Did Zack refuse to accompany you home?" Jeremy pried when his thoughts returned to the present.

"Nay, *I* refused to allow him to accompany me."

"And he agreed?" Jeremy was surprised that Zack would permit her to return without an escort, even if they continued to bicker and quarrel. Zack was a man of obligations and he didn't take them lightly.

"He had no say in the matter. I left him during the night with only a quilt and a pair of moccasins so that it would be difficult for him to follow me," she explained with a casual shrug. Her mind was on her father, not on Zack.

Jeremy choked on his breath and then a wide grin stretched from ear to ear. Zack would never allow her to have the last laugh and he would never release her until he had the final word. What Jeremy had carefully planned had taken a delightful new twist. Unknowingly, Melissa had challenged Zack to pursue her, and he would never be content until he caught up with her.

"Then I would imagine Zack is fit to be tied," he predicted with a merry chuckle.

"I would have done that, too, but I was without a rope," she assured him, a mischievous smile pursing her lips as she bent her gaze to Jeremy who was still all grins.

"And through it all you have come to love him, haven't you?" he concluded.

The smile evaporated from her weary features and she hesitated a long moment before replying, "Aye, I did for a time, but Zack could not return my affection. He does not know the meaning of the word and I have seen the last of him. 'Tis over and done. He has never trusted me, and this last bit of mischief will sever the frail bond between us."

"Zack is afraid of love, Melissa," Jeremy explained, his expression sobering as he met her rueful gaze. "The Indians do not frighten him, nor the British, but love does. His mother abandoned him to run away with another man, and his father refused to live without her. He died of a broken heart, leaving Zack to fend for himself at a tender, vulnerable age. Phillipe Beaugener was not a well man to begin with. When Coleen left him, he lost all desire to live. Zack was terribly hurt by his mother, and he saw his father destroyed by a woman. He watched me mourn for a love I was never able to enjoy. He has seen the bitterness and destruction love can bring, but he refuses to admit that it does not always have to be that way."

Her heart was moved to pity for Zack. Jeremy was right. Zack had not been surrounded with the type of happiness she had known. He saw love as pain and sorrow. And yet, no one could convince him to change because he was too stubborn and set in his ways.

"I feel sorry for him," she murmured. "He is destined to live without a woman's love. But at least he knows the bond of friendship. He cares deeply for you, Jeremy." Melissa managed a faint smile. "You alone have his devotion. Boone and the others have his respect, but your friendship is valued above all else. At least Zack has allowed himself one intangible bond."

"And perhaps that one will open the door to others," he mused aloud. "In time he will learn that love is not meant as a curse."

Melissa doubted his words for she, too, had become cynical of the love between a man and a woman. "Zack cannot change and perhaps he has a point," she said thoughtfully. "If you give your heart away then you are vulnerable. At least Zack doesn't suffer, nor is he tortured by memories. I have learned to live each day as it comes and keep the past buried. He warned me not to fall in love with him, but I was foolish. Never again will I make that mistake."

A troubled frown knitted Jeremy's brow. "You will change you mind one day," he insisted.

"Nay." Her chin tilted stubbornly. "I do not wish to be hurt again. If Zack can survive without love, then so can I."

After pressing a fond kiss to Jeremy's forehead, she eased from his side to collect her belongings and supplies for her trip. When she returned to tell him goodbye, he tried to persuade her to travel by coach so that he could accompany her. But Melissa would not change her mind and Jeremy reluctantly watched her go. If Zack could not deter her from having her own way, how could he hold a tight rein on Melissa, Jeremy asked himself. Besides, she had already proven that she was capable of managing on her own.

Melissa nudged her palomino stallion into a canter, hoping she could locate her father before he sailed, saving him the agony of thinking she had perished. She could never forgive Lelia for making him suffer, and she would make certain that her father knew of Lelia's deceit, even if she had to follow them all the way to France, she vowed, as she galloped off across the countryside.

Melissa had been afraid to tell Jeremy about the child she carried, certain that he would not have permitted her to make the journey. And she could not bear to see the look on his face when he learned that history had indeed repeated itself. Later she would tell him, she decided, when she had time to talk at length. But for now, it was her secret.

## Chapter Twenty

Zack barreled through the door, letting it crash against the wall, sending a stream of dust trickling from the woodwork above him. It drifted about him like a cloud, and Jeremy wasn't quite certain if it was dust that hovered around Zack or a puff of smoke since he was sure his younger friend was breathing fire.

"Where is she?" Zack demanded to know, his face darkening in a scowl, his silver eyes spewing irritation.

Jeremy had to bite his lower lip to keep from cackling. Zack looked as sour as a lemon and as poorly dressed as a pauper. The buttons popped from the undersized shirt with each angry breath Zack inhaled, and the tattered sleeves did not even reach his wrists. His high-water breeches fit as tightly as his own skin, and Jeremy was certain he would split his seams as he stalked into the cabin. It took a great deal of composure for Jeremy to sit calmly while he was inwardly chuckling at the ridiculous picture this rough-edged frontiersman presented in his ragged clothes.

"Where is who?" Jeremy inquired as he set his teacup on the table and eased back in his chair, still fighting the urge to bust out laughing.

Zack quickly closed the distance between them to tower over his friend like a fuming dragon. "You know damned well who I mean so you can drop the naivete," he commanded, a distinctly unpleasant edge to his voice. "Where is that conniving little minx?"

"If that disrespectful term refers to my lovely daughter, she isn't here," Jeremy informed him as he scooped up his cup and continued to survey Zack from over the rim.

"Obviously not," Zack mocked, his tone sarcastic and growing more impatient as he listened to the clock's methodic tick, alerting him that he was wasting precious time. "Now where is that little termagant?"

"Would you care for a cup of tea?" Jeremy offered as he struggled to his feet and grabbed for his cane. "You look as if you could use a drink."

"Nay, dammit. I want that wench!" Zack thundered, his eyes flashing like lightning, warning Jeremy that he had been pushed to his limits.

"She's gone," Jeremy replied as he gazed at the furious man who hovered over him.

Zack's ebony hair lay in disarray, his beard untrimmed, and the menacing glare of his hard features was more threatening than Jeremy remembered.

"Why don't you sit down and relax a bit, Zack," he suggested in a patronizing tone. "You won't find her."

Zack stalked across the room and threw open the cupboard. He grabbed a bottle of brandy and a glass before planting himself in the chair beside Jeremy. Aye, he could use a drink and a moment of relaxation, he decided. His journey had not been a pleasant one and he sorely lacked rest.

"Since when did you begin dressing as a homestead farmer?" Jeremy questioned, his amused gaze sweeping the tight-fitting shirt and breeches that had been made from feed sacks. "Is this another of your disguises, Montclaire-Beaugener, or have you assumed yet another name to fit this new lifestyle?"

Zack shot him a scornful glare and chugged his drink. "I began dressing as a homesteader when that ornery misfit stole all my clothes and left me stark naked. But I'm sure you knew the answer to that before you asked," he muttered sourly. "That witch was probably cackling when she related the story to you."

"She told me she took your clothes and your horse," he said blandly. "But Melissa said very little about these last four months. All I could pry out of her was that you were wounded at Detroit and that she had taken your belongings and had come home."

"She managed to hit the high points to make me like a witless soldier and an utter fool," Zack growled, refusing to meet Jeremy's beaming smile.

"I hope those were not your two best efforts," Jeremy taunted wickedly. "If that is the case, our country is in grave danger of being overrun with redskins and redcoats."

"I am sick to death of running a distant second to that incorrigible little witch," Zack muttered half aloud.

"Am I to understand that Melissa is the colonial heroine?" He arched a dark brow, its angle mocking. But it was a wasted effort. Zack would not look at him.

"To all but me and the British troops at Detroit," he snorted derisively. "The British want her head on a silver platter after what she did to them. The major at the fort has already gone head-hunting, but he will have to wait his turn in line. I intend to torture her to within an inch of her life."

Jeremy's shoulder lifted in a shrug. "Ah well," he began, sighing heavily. "A man raises his child, sends her out into the world to make friends, and all she collects is enemies. What is a man to do?" The laughter in his voice gave Zack no amusement.

"The British will never live down what she did. And after what she had done to me, I'm seriously contemplating turning traitor and handing that chit over to them when I have had my revenge."

"What could Melissa possibly have done to the redcoats? I wonder if perhaps you are exaggerating," Jeremy said skeptically.

"She and one of my men who impersonated her father went into the fort to free Boone. Most of the credit goes to Melissa. Her companion only added substance to her charade as a French countess." Zack focused his attention on Jeremy, waiting for him to explode which he did.

"What?" Jeremy's blue eyes flared in outrage and his fist hit the table, sloshing tea on his cuff. "How dare you thrust my daughter into such a precarious situation! *I* am the one who should have *your* head. Dammit, man, what the hell were you thinking of?" His face reddened, his angry gaze penetrating both layers of Zack's thick skin.

"Boone," he answered simply as he eased back in his seat.

"Then if she effected Boone's release, how the devil were you wounded?" he questioned caustically.

"Melissa turned her ankle when she was trying to flee from the fort. When I went back to retrieve her, I caught a bullet. All she suffered was a swollen foot," he explained bitterly. "She managed to haul me to safety and then stitched me back together. After she discovered that you were her father she left me without a word and traveled to Boonesborough to join Boone and my men." He paused a moment, noting that Jeremy did not seem surprised to hear that Melissa knew the truth about her parentage. Obviously, Melissa had confronted him with her knowledge.

"Melissa fought at Boonesborough?" Jeremy sucked in his breath and held it until he expelled his next question. "Why the hell didn't they send her away? She had no business there."

Zack's heavy brow arched mockingly as he peered into Jeremy's wide eyes. "And just whom do you know who could convince that little firebrand to do anything except what she intended to do?" Zack snorted distastefully. "No one." He answered his own question and then muttered under his breath. "She fought alongside Boone and my men. When I finally caught up to them, the siege had ended and Melissa sneaked off during the night."

Jeremy stared at him for a long moment and Zack knew that he was indeed a lucky man that Melissa had survived the entire ordeal; otherwise, Jeremy would have torn him to shreds. Jeremy always did have the strength of five men when he was angered, Zack remembered. And *angry* would have been a mild description of his tempermant if Melissa would have met with catastrophe.

"Did you marry her as I requested?" he questioned

pointedly.

Zack cast him a hasty, sidelong glance as he sipped his brandy. "Aye. 'Twas what you wanted so I obliged . . . for your sake," he was quick to add.

A suspicious frown gathered on Jeremy's brow. "As Beaugener or Montclaire?" he persisted.

Zack finished the last of his drink in one gulp. "Montclaire."

Again his fist pounded the table, and Zack was aware that Jeremy was having difficulty containing himself. His blue eyes were flaring with sparks. "That does not satisfy me and you know it!"

"But that was all I intended to offer. You will have to settle for a compromise," he insisted, his jaw set in determination. "And more than that vixen deserves in the first place. As a matter of fact, I almost had to break her arm to make her say the vows. She wanted nothing to do with the marriage or me."

"So you placed her in the same category as your mother by giving her the name of Montclaire," Jeremy accused, his frown holding contempt. "If Melissa would have known how you felt about Coleen, she would have been insulted to share the same name."

"She was insulted just sharing it with *me*," Zack assured him tartly. "I could hardly control her throughout the ceremony. She was breathing fire and the clergyman who married us probably regrets the day he laid eyes on either of us."

Jeremy could not suppress a chuckle, envisioning the scene, but his amusement died. Melissa was still not legally married to Zack, and perhaps she never would be unless he somehow managed to persuade Zack that he could not live without Melissa. But how?

Jeremy sat quietly for a moment and then eyed Zack levelly.

"Well, my friend. I suppose it no longer matters." He shrugged slightly, drawing a curious frown from Zack. "It seems that I have failed as a matchmaker. I will make no more attempts to intervene in either of your lives. You are free to pursue your other obligations. Melissa has a difficult time ahead of her and too much on her mind to bicker with you. She told me that the two of you were not compatible, and I have resigned myself to the fact that my daughter and my adopted son will never truly be man and wife. I am sorry, Zack. If I have caused you undue stress by tossing Melissa at you, I hope you can forgive me. I should never have meddled in your life. I suppose Melissa must turn to another man, just as Laura turned to William."

Now what was he up to? Zack frowned suspiciously. What had Melissa told him that had changed his attitude?

Stormy pools of gray locked with carefully masked blue eyes. "Where is she, Jeremy?" His question was slow and deliberate, demanding a straight answer, but he was not to be given one.

"She does not want you to know. She doesn't want to see you again." Jeremy stressed the point again that Melissa had washed her hands of Zack. "I promised not to interfere and I do not intend to. I owe her that much after all I put her through. She didn't even allow me to travel with her when she left. From now on she travels alone, because she says that is the way she prefers it." His breath came out slowly as he glanced at the opposite wall. "I suppose you were right. No one can change her mind once she had made a decision."

A bemused frown slashed across Zack's bearded face. Where could she have gone? To the mountains? To France? Did she inform Jeremy that she despised him, too, and wanted nothing more to do with him either? Were her whispered words of love a ploy as he had first suspected. His thoughts were whirling in rapid circles, haphazardly linking with whatever answer happened to float past.

"Did she tell you that she was in love with me?" Zack blurted out, surprising Jeremy and himself with his bluntness.

"Did she tell you that she was in love with you?" Jeremy countered, arching a graying brow, his gaze calmly assessing.

"Aye," he answered with a firm shake of his raven head. "Once."

"And she told me that the two of you were finished and that she would never see you again. It would be next to impossible to get Lissa to change her mind now," Jeremy replied, noting the spark that flickered in Zack's eyes. He was turning Zack every which way but loose, enjoying every minute of it! "Besides, it would serve no purpose. You don't love her and Melissa doesn't like to fight lost causes. She must have sampled the taste of victory at Boonesborough." Jeremy lightly flicked his wrist and then clasped his hands around his cup as he glanced at Zack. "You are off the hook. I will make no more demands on you, and Melissa expects nothing of you. You should be a happy man. Will you be leaving soon?" The question hit Zack below the belt, as if he were being brushed aside, discarded like a moccasin with a hole in its sole.

Melissa no longer loved him? She never wanted to see him again? She had run away from her father and Jeremy? And Jeremy was ready for him to take his leave? Nothing was making sense. What had gotten into that wench? Had her heart turned to stone? Had she denied feeling for anyone? Well, dammit, he wanted to see her for himself! He wanted his revenge and by damned he would have it! He would have a few choice comments to make to that spitfire. Few, hell! Zack decided, giving the matter more thought. He had a few thousand choice words aching to be voice!

"Where is Stoddard? I want to speak with him," Zack demanded.

"He's gone, too." Jeremy's casualness was creeping beneath Zack's skin, just as he had anticipated.

"Did he go with Melissa?" Zack prodded, itching for information.

"Nay. He is traveling with Melissa's aunt to France. William thinks Melissa is dead."

"Whattt?" The news hit him like a hard slap in the face, leaving his jaw swinging from its hinges. "Who the hell told him that?"

"Lelia apparently paid someone to concoct the story and return to William with that information. Stoddard did not take it well and he blames Montclaire. Fortunately, he does not know whom he despises. I didn't dare tell him you were one in the same for fear that he'd hate me, too," Jeremy added with a meaningful glance that seemed to accuse Zack for the unfortunate incident. "That would have been the last straw for Stoddard. His whole world would have crumbled down around him."

Zack growled disgustedly as he reached for the bot-

430

tle of brandy. "You better tell me all that has happened since I kidnapped Melissa," he suggested, certain that he wasn't going to like what he was about to hear.

Jeremy sighed weakly, collected his thoughts, and then gave Zack a precise account of the past four months, making a special point to inform him that Stephens had come looking for Melissa.

The fact that Melissa was never without an audience did much to stir Zack's jealousy. He had been the first to taste her passions, and it galled him to know that he could name more than a handful of men who would be delighted to take his place.

"You know where she is and I demand to know . . . now," Zack insisted, his gaze narrowing threateningly on Jeremy.

"I cannot tell you that. Melissa would never forgive me." Jeremy set his chin stubbornly, meeting Zack's stormy gray eyes.

There were several loose ends to be tied and the line on his patience had been stretched thin. Wherever she was, she had a head start and Zack was losing precious time. He grabbed a handful of Jeremy's shirt, twisting it tightly about his neck, pulling him close, their faces only inches apart. "Where's Melissa? Did she follow Stoddard or did she take to the mountains to elude me?" The deadly hiss in his voice would have wilted a lesser man, but Jeremy had already stared death in the face and had no fear of it.

Jeremy's blue eyes turned stone cold, the scar on his face taut. "You have had your revenge for the trap I set for you. You took my own flesh and blood, my daughter, as your mistress for these past six months and you would not give her your name. You used her to free

431

Boone, knowing she might have perished. You told her that I was her father when I never wanted her to suffer with that knowledge. And because of you, she learned the horror of killing men and watching them die an agonizing death. You have destroyed a young woman's dreams and you even tamed her heart for a time. How much more torture do you intend to extract from her?" he growled, his face twisting in a sneer.

" 'Twas *your* fault that this happened at all!" Zack accused, his voice rumbling like thunder.

"But only a man with a heart of ice would have been so cruel to make an innocent young girl endure a lifetime of suffering in half a year!" Jeremy countered, his words slashing like a double-edged sword. "Don't try to make me the culprit. You are the one to blame and you damned well know it!"

"Only a sadistic father would send his untouched daughter into the arms of a man who had never in his life refused a beautiful woman's charms." Zack parried in an intimidating tone.

"And what kind of friend would continue to misuse the daughter of his devoted companion, indeed, his adopted father who taught him practically all he knows?" Jeremy argued, his eyes narrowing to hard slits, his lips thinning into a grim line.

"I gave her my name!" Zack defended, and then slammed his jaw shut to prevent bellowing Jeremy's face. Damned if he knew why he was being courteous. Jeremy didn't deserve it!

"You gave her nothing." Jeremy emphasized every word with such potency that Zack had to retreat, releasing the shirt that he had clenched in his fist.

"I gave her my trust and she turned on me."

"If you would have offered your love she would have protected you with her own life. But nay," he spat contemptuously. "You denied her that. You have shamed her, smothering her desire to give herself to another man. Her protective armor is so heavy that no lance can penetrate it now. Many men will attempt to claim her heart, but she will have nothing to do with any of them. You have turned her soul to stone, Beaugener. I hope you're proud of yourself." He lowered his voice, but still his tone was laced with hostility.

"She left you in the night, expecting you to follow your men. It was her way of telling you that you are under no obligation. She was turning you loose before you turned on her again." Jeremy's eyes anchored on Zack, and he paused a moment so that the full impact of his following words fell like a hard blow to the jaw. "You have lost her, Zack. She has given you that precious freedom that you have always craved and she demands nothing of you. In the future, when you come to the settlement to visit me, I want you to steer clear of Melissa. I made a grave mistake by sending you to track her. I openly admit it and I will not be blamed for her suffering again." A thoughtful frown creased his brow as he traced the jagged scar across his face. "Even if you found yourself in love with her I don't think she would listen. She may never allow her heart to be broken again. Melissa has a natural instinct to survive, and she will do it without love if she must, just as you have done."

Zack stared at him long and hard, a brittle silence hanging over the room. "Where is she?" he demanded gruffly.

"Go to hell, Beaugener," Jeremy snapped back at

him. He was laying it on thick, pushing Zack to the point that he was oblivious to everything but the challenge of finding Melissa, holding her just out of his reach as if he were dangling a carrot in front of a mule. Aye, it was wicked, but there were times when deceit was justified, he rationalized.

Again, Zack was aware of the methodic tick of the clock on the mantel. No other sound reached his ears as his thoughts turned each stone that Jeremy had placed in front of him. If Melissa wanted nothing more to do with him then she had gone to search for her father, he concluded. She would be intent on having him know that Lelia had purposefully lied to him. Although Jeremy had not broken his promise to tell Zack where Melissa had gone, he had offered enough information to lead Zack to her.

A sly smile crept to his lips, his eyes glowing like silver. Jeremy's expression matched the younger man's, and he lifted his cup in a silent toast before taking a sip.

"You would never have taken Melissa from that ship and found a way to keep her with you, nor would you have followed her home if you didn't truly care about her," he predicted and then shrugged leisurely. "I'm sure you told yourself that you were merely fulfilling an obligation to me, but that wasn't the real reason, was it, Zack?" Jeremy regarded him with a knowing smile. "You found, as I did, that some women cannot be disregarded, no matter how hard you try to forget them. You know Melissa is in your blood, the only one who has ever captured and held your interest."

"Damn you, old man," Zack muttered, but there was no hatefulness in his tone. "I think you must sit around, devising new ways to torment me."

As Zack rose to full stature and ambled to the door, Jeremy twisted around in his chair to watch him go.

"Zack?" Jeremy's voice was soft as his gaze lifted to study the muscular man who filled the open door. "If by chance you see my daughter, tell her that I love her," he requested, a half-smile draped on one corner of his mouth.

Pausing to lean on the doorknob, Zack glanced back at the crippled form of a man whose face was slashed with a long, jagged scar and whose body was covered with the claw marks of a bear. Jeremy had endured many trials and yet, bitterness had never twisted his thoughts. Zack had called him father and friend because he respected Jeremy and admired his ability to adapt to all situations, no matter how difficult the obstacles.

"Jeremy, I . . ." His words trailed off when he met the warmth of sunrays sparkling in Jeremy's blue eyes, uncertain what he had intended to say. Finally he nodded his consent. "I'll tell her . . . *if* I see her."

As Zack disappeared from sight, Jeremy heaved a sigh. Zack's battle had only begun. Melissa was not likely to forget her vow to keep her distance from Zack. She would be suspicious, wary, and determined to find her father. At least Zack could accompany her . . . if he could track her. Perhaps neither of them would admit that they cared for each other, but they would be together again. A disturbing thought crossed his mind and he frowned in concern. If Melissa was sought by the British, she could be in grave danger if she showed her face in Norfolk. The British would pay a handsome price to make an example of her. Whether she realized it or not, she might need Zack.

Jeremy struggled from his chair and tucked the keys to the tavern in his pocket before limping toward the door. He needed something to occupy him, something to divert him from worrying about Melissa.

Zack stepped back inside Jeremy's cabin, finding it empty. Perhaps it was better this way, he thought, as he hurriedly wrote Jeremy a note and propped it against the teacup. The words came easier on paper than they would have from his lips. Silently, Zack closed the door behind him and then mounted his steed, his gaze focusing to the east, watching the sun make a slow ascent into the sky. He would find Melissa, he told himself determinedly as he dug his heels in the horse's flanks and galloped toward the sunrise.

# Chapter Twenty One

Riding hard, doing without much needed sleep, Zack pursued his prey. After several days he began to wonder if she had met with trouble. He had passed two British regiments, cautiously avoiding them. Perhaps he should have taken a closer look, he thought, as he watched the smoke from their campfire curl into the sky. Melissa was wanted by the redcoats. Although they searched for Andrea Deuvalle, her rare beauty was impossible to disguise, no matter what name she used. Her description would be easy to give and quickly recognized. Nathan had informed him that Major Bedford and several other men from the fort had been ordered to search for her. They could be anywhere. The thought made him uneasy, and he circled back to the camp to have a second look.

After two weeks of riding without catching sight of Melissa, Zack was considering retracking. Either she had sprouted wings and had flown to Norfolk or he had taken a different route.

And then something darted through the trees and he focused his attention on the streak of gold that disappeared among the shadows of the forest. A wicked smile surfaced on his lips as he envisioned coming face to face with that little firebrand. But he would not be hasty this time, he decided. He would stalk her, keeping his distance, waiting for the right moment to spring on her.

That evening he hid in the brush, watching as she started a small campfire. His gaze swept the area, carefully noting the distance between the fire, the bedroll, and her palomino stallion. He was not about to walk in and risk being shot. Melissa would use her rifle and ask questions later, just as he would have done.

It took a great deal of patience to sit quietly in the underbrush, seeing her strip from her clothes and sink into the stream to bathe. His vengeance was overshadowed by a rising desire, a thirst so unquenchable that even the stream of water could not have appeased it. Her skin, dancing with droplets of silver in the moonlight, seemed to beg for his touch, and he found himself remembering the feel of that satiny flesh beneath his searching caress. As she walked back to the bank, smoothing the wet tendrils from her face, Zack swallowed hard, wishing he could take to the cold stream to ease the ache in his loins. Damn, but she was bewitching, like a sea nymph rising from the depths to cast her spell on mortal man. Nay, Major Bedford would have no trouble describing her to a scouting party. It was like seeing an angel. Only a blind man would miss each exquisite detail about her.

After Melissa had stepped into her clothes and walked back to camp, Zack made his way around to view her from another angle. He watched her pause occasionally, like a wary doe that sniffed the air for the scent of man, her ears pricked to the sound of danger. Dressed in brown buckhide breeches and a shirt, the comparison could not have suited her better, he mused, as he continued to keep his eyes fixed on her.

Melissa quietly ate her meal, doused the fire, and then crawled beneath the quilts, her bones and muscles weary from the tenseness that plagued her throughout the long days. She had no rest since she had left the settlement near Detroit. That and the fact that she carried a child were taking a heavy toll on her strength. At times she was certain that she would wake to find that her body refused to move. But she must continue, she told herself determinedly. She had to find her father. Nothing else mattered until he knew that she was safe and that Lelia had deceived him.

After Zack watched her stretch out on the ground, he crept down to the stream to bathe. The cold water was invigorating and he could not suppress the smile of anticipation that curved his lips. Tonight he would have his revenge. He had waited an eternity to snare his lovely prey.

Zack waited almost an hour, ensuring that Melissa was asleep before he edged up to her, pushed her musket aside, and positioned himself above her. He aimed his rifle at her and then lowered the barrel to stab her in the side.

Melissa came awake with a frightened start, peering into a pair of silver eyes that flared diabolically. He towered above her like Satan himself, his ebony hair glistening in the moonlight. His bearded face was dark and foreboding and there was a wicked smile on his lips.

Melissa gulped hard and practically choked as her heart catapulted to her throat. This was a nightmare, she told herself. Zack wasn't standing above her. It was only that the memories she had buried had surfaced to intermingle with her exhaustion.

"So we finally meet again." His threatening tone made her flinch, assuring her that it was no dream but fearful reality. "Get up, but move very slowly."

Reluctantly, she gathered her feet beneath her, knowing that Zack would have delighted in pulling the trigger if she had not immediately obeyed.

"What are you doing here?" she questioned, bracing herself with a courage that was only skin deep. Melissa surprised herself by speaking the words without her voice quivering.

"I have been stalking my prey," he snorted derisively. " 'Tis revenge I seek." He laughed a low, devilish laugh that sent a fearful tremor skipping down her spine.

Her lashes swept up to meet those sparkling pools of silver. That always irritated her, she mused. She had to look up to him. It was humiliating. She could never look him square in the eye without tilting her head. What a time to consider that, Melissa thought foolishly. Here she stood, facing a man who thirsted for blood, and she was annoyed that she wasn't a foot taller.

Zack cocked a wondering brow as the faintest hint of a smile bordered her lips. She had not backed cowardly away, nor had her eyes registered fear, except in that first moment when she awoke. And, holding true to the form that she never backed down from a fight or an argument, she tilted a stubborn chin, assuring him that she wasn't about to start now.

"What form of torture do you have in mind for me this time, Beaugener?" She questioned brazenly.

Zack retrieved a short rope from his pocket and dangled it in front of her. "My first impulse was to tie this around your lovely neck, but I have decided to save that until later," he informed her, his tone heavily laden with sarcasm. "Turn around."

Melissa's eyes spewed defiance and her chin tilted a notch higher. "Why don't you just kill me and be done with it," she suggested. "I am in no mood for your fiendish games."

Zack's arm snaked out to spin her around and then he tied her hands behind her back. "Doing away with you without allowing you to suffer would give me no pleasure. I have dreamed of this moment and I do not intend for it to end quickly."

"Zack, listen to me," she implored, a hint of urgency in her voice. "I know you think I deserve to be tortured after what I did, but I have an important matter to attend to in Norfolk. I will do as you wish if you will only allow me to go to my father. He is on his way to France and he thinks I'm dead. I don't want him to sail without knowing the truth."

He scoffed as he twisted her around to meet his unsympathetic gaze. "How convenient for me. I can dispose of you since it seems that you are no longer among the living. Why allow the poor man to think he had seen a ghost?" His voice was laced with mockery, his eyes scorning everything about her. "The shock might kill him."

"Damn you!" Melissa stormed at him in outrage. "Do you hate me so much that you would allow my father to go on believing that I am dead? The woman he intends to marry has cruelly deceived him. You are heartless! How could you be so cold and unfeeling? My father has done nothing to you. Why should he suffer?" Her indigo eyes blazed like torches. "I demand that you release me!"

Zack grabbed her elbow and dragged her toward a tree, seemingly unmoved by her plea of desperation. After shoving her against the rough bark, he tied her securely in place, moving his hands deliberately across her alluring body, searching for the dagger she always carried. When he came up empty-handed, he reached down the side of her boot to feel the handle of the knife. A wicked smile tightened his lips as he pulled it from concealment.

Lightly scraping the blade across her throat, he propped his arm above her head and moved closer, his lean body pressing against hers, their faces only inches apart.

"There have been many times this month that I have visualized this scene," he informed her, a heavy threat in his voice. The knife pricked her skin, but still she did not bat an eye. "Imagine how humiliating it was for me to travel cross country cloaked in a fur quilt and leather moccasins. I cursed your name and your image with every step I took, obsessed with slashing you to shreds with your own dagger."

"Then for God's sake, do it!" she spat viciously, her gaze mirroring the hatred she felt for him at that moment. "As you said, Papa think's I'm dead so I may as well be. Go ahead. Kill both of us!" Melissa bit her lips so fiercely that she could taste blood. Why had she said that? She had vowed never to tell Zack that she carried his child.

"Both?" His brow quirked, regarding her curiously.

"Me and my father," she replied, hoping that he could see through a remark that had double meaning. "He thinks he has lost the last of his own flesh and blood. First mother and now me. He will not survive a year." Melissa was relieved when he let the matter drop.

"I will dispose of you in good time. I am in no hurry," he assured her. "I have harbored my feelings for you much too long to let the moment flee before I enjoy complete satisfaction."

Suddenly, as if he was repulsed by the physical contact, he released her and stalked into the darkness. Did he plan to inform the British patrols that he held her captive? Or did he intend to start a fire beneath her feet and watch her burn alive? Who could know what ran through that scoundrel's mind? Melissa hopelessly shook her head. All she knew was that the madman was hell-bent on revenge.

It seemed an hour had passed while she impatiently waited, stewing over her fate. Finally he reappeared to eat his meal, care for his horse, and repack his supplies. And then he walked off into the shadows. Melissa shifted her weight to her left foot, giving her right leg a rest, and sighed wearily. The crackling of grass beside her nearly caused her to jump out of her skin. If only she had, she would have been able to escape, she thought to herself. Her gaze fastened on Zack as he checked the ropes to ensure that she was still

443

securely tied.

"Zack, please. . . ." The word was difficult to force from her lips, and Zack turned from his chore to peer at her, a wry smile catching the corners of his mouth.

"You surprise me, Melissa. I didn't realize that word was a part of your vocabulary," he mocked.

He was making this torturous, she mused angrily. Zack was delighting in harassing her, testing her patience, letting her steam and stew, wondering what he intended to do with her. He was so damned stubborn that she could talk until she was blue in the face and still she would see nothing for her efforts to appeal to his softer side. But, of course, a rock was void of softness, she thought bitterly.

Melissa dropped her head and heaved a disheartened sigh. "Zack, I seek to bargain with you."

He released a derisive snort and then strolled over to tether his horse beside the palomino. "The last bargain I made with you got me nothing more than a knot on the head, and it cost me a day's tracking to retrieve you again," he recalled, his tone harsh. "Nay, vixen. No bargains. Nothing you could offer means a damned thing to me."

Her lashes swept up as Zack moved silently back to her. his eyes holding cynical amusement. "I will do anything you ask of me if you will only allow me to see my father first."

"Anything?" Zack questioned sarcastically. A hollow smile rippled across his lips and then vanished. "Slay my enemies? Spread yourself beneath me and my friends when we seek pleasure? Serve as my slave, claiming that I am your master? Steal and lie for me if I command it? Any . . . one . . . thing, minx, or

444

everything?" His words carried such a bite that Melissa flinched as if he had sunk his fangs in her flesh. Zack laughed bitterly. "You are very clever with words. You can twist them to suit your own meaning while I am led to believe something totally different. Now which is it you offer?" His silver eyes flared with mistrust as his gaze boldly ran the length of her and then doubled back to her face. Melissa drew herself up from her slumped position and spat out the words before she choked on them. "Any and all that you command, Beaugener." His name rushed from her lips like a witch's curse, and he winced at the spiteful sound that cracked the silence.

Jeremy was right. Melissa's coat or armor was thick with hatred. If he hadn't been so obsessed with seeing the look on her face when he caught and trapped her, he would have returned to his men, allowing her memory to fade. Somehow he would penetrate that defensive shell, he told himself. Somehow he would find her weakness.

"For how long? A day? A week? Until you have the opportunity to escape?" he queried, arching a heavy brow.

Melissa was nearing the end of her patience. It took finely tempered tolerance to proceed with his detailed interrogation, but she was determined to see it through if she could gain from it. There was much at stake and she would agree to almost anything.

"I will not leave you until you permit it, or until you grow tired of me," she choked out begrudgingly.

Zack listened with amused patience and then he reached up to brush his calloused hand over her cheek, but she turned her head away, afraid of his touch,

445

afraid she would melt as she always had.

His eyes hardened like cold granite. "Melissa, look at me," he snapped gruffly.

She refused his sharp command, determined that, for once in her life, she would not yield to him.

"Melissa!" His mouth thinned in a grim line. "I said look at me, damn you!"

Reluctantly, her lashes swept up, her eyes sparkling with a hatred that flashed like lightning. His gaze locked with hers, silently attempting to draw her under his spell. Again he reached out to caress her cheek and again she jerked back like a wild animal that had been chained, but unwilling to accept a man's touch. Zack had difficulty controlling his outrage when he witnessed the rebellious tilt of her chin, the stubborn profile of her face as she looked the opposite direction.

"Look at me." His demand was softer now, but there was an undertone of anger.

Summoning her composure, she met his penetrating gaze, her lips quivering as he lowered his eyes to follow the curve of her mouth. When his hand touched her cheek for the third time, she stilled the urge to retreat, repulsed by his attempt to subdue her like some undomesticated beast, annoyed that she could not separate her mind from her body, transporting her soul a safe distance from him. As he lightly caressed her cheek and then brushed his fingertip over her lips, she fought to ignore the warm tingle that crept across her skin. His hand trailed down her neck to unlace the leather ties across her breasts. When her shirt gaped, his hand dipped lower to fondle the full swells that he had longed to touch, to rediscover the feel of her creamy flesh beneath his caress.

From beneath the long, dark lashes a glint of silver peered at her. He was trying to arouse the sleeping passion that he had once been able to evoke from her, but Melissa would not surrender, even if it meant enduring the tortures of hell. As his hand wandered to the band of her breeches, Melissa caught her breath, feeling the fire begin to burn, a familiar fire that she had never been able to extinguish until it had run its course. She dared not breathe, trying to resist, hoping that no emotion had flickered in her eyes.

"Do we have a bargain, Beaugener?" she questioned tightly, her voice threaded with impatience.

Zack's lingering hand ascended to cup her breast, teasing its peak to tautness, while his free hand slid over hips, bringing her body in close contact with his. The heat that radiated from him scorched every inch of her flesh, evaporating the chill of the damp night. Melissa was hot and breathless, cursing herself for allowing the erotic sensations to tear at her resistance. She looked up to meet his rakish smile, watching the darkness of his hair absorb the moonlight, inhaling the musky male fragrance that was beginning to wrap itself around her senses. He continued his caresses for what seemed an eternity, and Melissa fought to control her churning emotions, determined not to let her outward appearance show what a devastating effect he was having on her.

Zack leaned full length against her, his hot kisses trailing along the hollow of her neck, keeping her pinned between him and the tree. His breath was warm against her ear. The fires of desire assaulting her with every technique he had mastered over the years and a few new ones that he had invented for just this moment.

Melissa strained against the binding ropes, her body involuntarily arching to fit them together like two pieces of a puzzle. She swallowed the rising passion that worked its way up her entire body, her breaths coming in erratic spurts. Her senses were reeling in the bittersweet torture of his nearness, crumbling her defenses.

And then he drew away only far enough to stare deeply into her eyes, eyes that had begun to sparkle with a desire that she was desperately trying to conceal.

"My beautiful vixen," he rasped as his fingers tunneled through the gold tendrils on the sides of her face. "Your charms could move mountains, and this alluring body of yours tempts every man who dares look upon you. You can drain my strength with your fiery passions, and you can entrance me with the sound of your seductive voice." His lips covered hers, drinking of the intoxicating taste of her kiss, their breath intermingling as one, and then he withdrew, holding her spellbound with the liquid silver fire in his eyes. Another smile trailed across his mouth, an expression of scornful mockery. "But we have no bargain, my enticing witch. You offer empty promises. You have tricked me once too often for me to trust you again."

And then he released her, leaving her trembling from the chill on flesh that had been fired with warmth the moment before. He never bothered to cast her a second glance, and Melissa felt her restrained anger unleashed like the winds of an approaching storm.

"Damn you!" she thundered at his broad backside, her gaze drilling into him like poison-tipped arrows.

"Damn you to hell!" Her body stiffened in rage, her cheeks flushed with fury, as he wheeled to face her curse.

"I have been condemned to hell these past six months, thanks to you," he shot back at her, the glint of steel in his eyes so intense that Melissa could feel the flaming slivers penetrate her skin.

"I had nothing to do with that. I didn't ask you to track me into the mountains," she defended hatefully. "I did not call for you to rescue me at the fort. You had Boone and I knew that you would feel no regret if I perished. It would have been a relief to be rid of me. Only your pride was pricked because you could not deliver me safely to Jeremy, like the gallant knight." The underlying sarcasm in her voice cut him to the quick, and he clenched his fists at his side, suppressing the urge to stalk back to her and wrap his fingers around her neck. "I rebelled against the marriage and I refused to let you bring me home. I have not brought you this living hell, Beaugener. You brought it on yourself because of that inflated male ego of yours." Her gaze slid down his virile form before she flung her head, staring off into the darkness. "You are the one who dragged me to the river, Stix, and shoved me in, never bothering to ask if I could swim. You left me there to drown, hoping the jaws of hell would open to swallow me. I was already wading knee-deep in a wedding I adamantly protested and, if that weren't enough, I was left in the midst of wave upon wave of British soldiers. And where were you?" Her gaze circled back to him, smoldering with contempt. "You were sitting by a campfire, enjoying your freedom, leaving me to fend for myself, hoping I would die a slow, agonizing death. All you cared about was that Boone was free. You didn't give a damn what happened to me. The hell I survived was far worse than yours."

"You loved the adventure. You delighted in the intrigue," he countered, his tone sharp and intimidating. "You even professed to love me. And then when my back was turned, you gave your affection to every man within ten feet of you. I'm sure you let Heston discover your passions at Boonesborough and only God knows who else sampled your charms. You only kept your distance from them on the journey to Detroit because I was watching over you. And when I was not close at hand you probably slept with every damned one of my men!"

Melissa gasped in indignation, infuriated by his accusations. "You made me your whore and you would have had me surrender to the entire British force at Detroit if necessary! Why shouldn't I choose my own lovers? You choose yours. You would have taken that dark-haired wench at the inn if I hadn't picked the inopportune moment to summon you. And what about poor, innocent Nancy Gibbs?" She cocked her head to the side, her gaze making a slow descent from the top of his head to the toes of his moccasins. "Did you find some perverted pleasure in deflowering another virgin, stripping her of her dignity?"

"Did you delight in sleeping with all of my men?" he flared, taking a bold step toward her.

"Every bit as much as you thrilled to the attempt of taking some wench right under my nose!" she countered.

"But I didn't have the chance. You interrupted me."

"Adultry is in the thought as well as the deed," she reminded him, giving quick death to his defense.

"I could have gone with her, but I didn't. I came to you instead," he snapped. "And for the life of me I don't know why I did."

"Because you were afraid I would flee and your mission would meet with failure. You needed me to serve your purpose," she accused bitterly. "Otherwise, you would have added that doxy to your list of conquered prizes."

"I came back to you because I regretted what I intended to do."

The sincerity in his tone drew her suspicious glance, but she knew better than to fall for that ploy. "You only regretted that I discovered your unfaithfulness. And what of Nancy Gibbs?" she questioned, arching a mocking brow. "I suppose she threw herself at you, overpowering you."

"Aye, that she did," he agreed, his anger dwindling to mild amusement as he watched Melissa strain against the ropes, her breasts coming dangerously close to spilling with every angry breath she took.

She sneered at the ridiculousness of his reply. "Do you really expect me to believe that Nancy forced you against your will?"

"Did you sleep with Heston?" Zack questioned abruptly, his irritation igniting again, despite the delectable temptation that had distracted him.

"Did you seduce Nancy?" She answered his question with her question.

Zack stared at her for a long moment, deep in thought. Would it have mattered if she had succumbed to Heston or the other men? Could he condemn her for seeking comfort during the frightening experience at Boonesborough? Could he forgive her, even when he had sampled the charms of more women that he dared to count? The answer was slow in coming and he knew it was unfair. But he did not want to be one of many men where she was concerned. Perhaps he didn't really want to know about Heston and the others. There were times when it was far better to be ignorant of the truth and this was one of those times, Zack thought to himself.

Even though Zack was hesitant to know about Heston, Melissa was determined to learn about Nancy Gibbs. She regarded him curiously, unable to read the thoughts that flashed in his eyes. Why had he refused to reply?"

"Did you make love to Nancy?" she persisted. "I want the truth, Zack."

Zack looked her straight in the eye, his gaze sober. "Nay," he said quietly. "She offered herself to me, even after she learned that we were man and wife. I sent her away."

He presented his back to Melissa and shook out his bedroll while she stared bewilderedly at him. Had he really cast Nancy aside? And if he had, why? Zack was never one to refuse a woman. Zack Beaugener denying his lusty passions? It was inconceivable. Melissa watched him remove his powder horn from his shoulder, lay his musket beside his pallet, and pull the buckskin shirt from his chest.

The rippling muscles of his back and arms flexed and relaxed as he settled himself on his bed. She studied his virile form as she always had, in awe of the power and strength he possessed. Again she was reminded of the sleek, black panther that crouched to spring on his prey. The sturdiness of his frame and the sinewy muscles of his body made him seem invincible. The thick raven hair and heavy beard that encircled those gleaming pools of silver gave him an animalistic appearance. Aye, he had come to destroy her, she mused bitterly. He was bent on revenge and she was his captured prey who would soon be devoured and cast aside for the buzzards. How could she ever have professed to love this calloused man? It was true that she had always been attracted to him. Maybe it was because he seemed so wild and free, a daring challenge. But love? Melissa hopelessly shook her head, wondering why she still harbored this strange emotion for him.

"You would leave me tied to this tree for the night?" she questioned incredulously when she realized that he intended to remain where he was, stretched leisurely beneath the quilt.

Zack propped himself up on an elbow, a wicked curl to his sensuous lips. "Would you leave me in the middle of the night with no horse and not a stitch of clothes?"

Melissa flinched when she met his disdainful glare. Her head dropped, staring at the plush grass beneath her feet. She had done it and he would do it, she mused despairingly. "I cannot sleep like this. At least allow me to sit," she pleaded, her tone deflated.

Zack eyed her warily. Was this another charade or had she been subdued? It brought some small consolation to see her humbled.

"What are you willing to yield to sleep in a more comfortable position?" He eased back on his pallet and clasped his hands behind his head as his attention swung back to her.

His eyes narrowed in annoyance when she intercepted his taunting smile. "Not what you have in mind," she snapped stubbornly. "I would prefer to remain tied to the stake than to suffer your repulsive touch."

"Repulsive?" He sent her a skeptical frown. "I thought you enjoyed my caresses, vixen. I have seen your wildest passions and don't try to deny it."

"No more." Melissa put out a defiant chin. "I can think of many others I would rather embrace."

Zack rolled to his feet and swaggered toward her. When he stood directly in front of her, he placed his hands on either side of her and leaned dangerously close. "Such as Captain Stephens?"

Melissa felt suffocated by his nearness, her breath rattling in her chest before it managed to climb into her throat. "Aye. Rorick has the power to arouse me," she assured him, surprising herself with the deliberateness of her voice.

"Corey Heston?" He fired the name at her.

"As many times in one night as he could rise to the occasion," she shot back, her tone carrying a spiteful hiss.

"Nathan Gibbs?" His voice was low and venomous, the hard features of his face set in a scowl.

"I wish I had never stopped him that night in the barn."

"And the redcoats? Would you spread yourself beneath them just to spite me?" he jeered.

"I would yield to every last one of them . . . willingly," Melissa insisted, meeting his hateful glare.

Melissa knew that any moment he would strike her.

His face was red with rage, his eyes smouldering furiously. The muscles of his bare arms bulged as he dug his fingers into the bark of the tree, and she was well aware that it could have been her neck. And then his hand did clamp about her throat, but she raised a fearless gaze, calmly awaiting her fate, defying him to the end.

Zack had been pushed to his limit, but when he peered into the sea of dark blue that sparkled with gold, like the sun glistening on the water's surface, he eased his grip on her. She was staring death in face, just as Jeremy had, but her chin tilted proudly, prepared for what was to come without begging for his mercy.

She watched the flame of contempt dwindle and she raised a curious brow and his hands fanned across the sides of her face, his thumbs brushing over her cheeks. He studied her thoughtfully for a long moment and then he gave her a smile.

"Perhaps when I am finished with you, I'll turn you over to the British. There is a reward for your capture. They also seek revenge for the way you humiliated them."

Her eyes widened apprehensively and Zack nodded confirmation. "Aye. They are willing to pay a handsome sum for that lovely hide of yours." His finger trailed across the soft curve of her lips as another mocking smile settled in his features. "I could have the reward and you could have the entire British army for your pleasure. No doubt, that would make you happy."

"You wouldn't dare!" Even before the words were out she knew that he would. She wouldn't put anything past that devil!

Zack smoothed the golden strands away from her face, his grin stretching from ear to ear. "I might if you provoke me. I even return vagabond daughters to their fathers if the price is right," he reminded her with a throaty laugh.

"Zack, please. All that concerns me is finding my father before it is too late. I don't—"

Zack cut her short to voice his remark. "And all I care about is revenge for all the times you have infuriated and humiliated me."

Melissa was tired and angry. Although she attempted to fight back the tears, they began to cloud her eyes. Zack's brows furrowed, flinging her an unsympathetic glance.

"That won't work either, Lissa," he informed her, his tone cold and uncaring. "The last time we met I kissed away your tears and comforted you. My thanks was that you left me in the middle of the night, laughing at your own cleverness. I fell for that ploy once, but never again.

Zack wheeled away and stretched out on his pallet, refusing to be taken in by the tears that trickled down her cheeks.

"I promise that I won't run away," she murmured, her gaze falling to the ground, along with her spirits. "Don't leave me tied here."

His attention circled back to her, looking at her with nothing less than contempt. "I don't trust you. You can endure one night of discomfort. I survived more than two days without clothing before I found a man who consented to sell me his ill-fitting garb."

Melissa's head jerked up and she sliced him a cold glare. "You better pray that I don't find a way to free myself." Her voice was acid with anger. "For if I do, I swear you will die in your sleep."

Undaunted by her threat, Zack propped up on an elbow and arched a mocking brow. "Am I to fear that you will strip me of my breeches as well?" Sarcasm dripped from the lower side of his half smile, and Melissa strained against the ropes, wishing she could have slapped that haughty smirk off of his face.

"Nay," she hissed. "I will be too intent on cutting your hard heart from your chest."

His shoulder lifted in an unconcerned shrug. "At least I will not be laid bare again. Some men prefer not to die with their boots on, but I have an aversion to leaving this world without my breeches," he commented as he squirmed beneath the quilt and settled himself for a night's sleep.

Melissa muttered in exasperation and then leaned her head back against the tree that was to be her pillow. If he let his guard down, she would escape him, but not before she watched him suffer for the way he was humiliating her, she vowed to herself.

# Chapter Twenty Two

The night caught and captured eternity while Melissa remained staked and bound with ropes. Each time she dozed, her head scraped against the rough bark. She woke, cursing Zack's demented cruelty. Finally she could stand no more and she screamed his name, bringing him to his knees, crouched for an oncoming attack.

The corded muscles of his neck and arms tensed as he swung the musket to his shoulder, searching the shadows. He was met with silence. Finally, he glanced back at Melissa, annoyed that she had scared ten years off of his life.

"What the hell's wrong with you? Do you intend to have the British crawling all over us?" he growled sourly.

"I must see to my needs," she informed him, her tone as unpleasant as his.

Zack grumbled at being disturbed. It was the first peaceful night's sleep he had enjoyed in weeks. Reluctantly, he rose to his feet and walked over to untie her. After he unloosened the rope from the tree and led her away, his fingers clamped into her arm, ensuring that her hands were still tied behind her back. Melissa turned every shade of red when he unfastened the strings to her breeches and pushed the deerskin garb down from her hips. Damn him! He intended to shame her, totally, completely, stripping her of every ounce of pride.

"At least turn your back!" she ordered sharply.

Zack gave his raven head a negative shake. "You may as well resign yourself to the fact that you will have no privacy. I will not turn my back on you," he assured her.

"Zack Beaugener, I will find a way to make you rue the day we ever laid eyes on each other!" she spat, her anger so intense that it was tying her stomach in knots. If she could only get her hands on him. A myriad of vengeful thoughts sprung to mind, and Melissa would have dearly loved to pursue each and every one of them.

Amusement glistened in his eyes as he watched another wave of crimson red work its way up from her neck. "I already regret it. You have raked me with those sharp claws of yours, continuously drawing blood. 'Tis a wonder that I have managed to survive this long."

When Melissa drew herself up in front of him again, Zack stepped close to tie the strings of her breeches, his hand brushing across her abdomen, taunting her unmercifully. Melissa could stand not one more moment of his harassment. While he was preoccupied, she lifted her knee, catching him in the groin, and sidestepped as he doubled over, grimacing in pain. Zack reached for her, grabbing a handful of hair, brutally yanking her back to him before she could escape.

"You'll pay dearly for that!" he sneered as he dragged her, kicking and fighting, to the pallet and shoved her to the ground. His hard body covered hers, forcing the wind out of her. Zack planted himself on her belly, glaring down at her, his eyes flamed with such intensity that Melissa could feel the heat of his gaze scorching her flesh.

"You think me cruel and heartless?" His lips curled in a menacing smile. "You are about to learn the true meaning of those words."

Zack ripped open her shirt, leaving the soft mounds of her breasts bare to his devouring gaze. Melissa was certain that he intended to rape her as he yanked her shirt away and twisted her hair about his hand like a rope, forcing her to endure his kiss. His lips opened on hers, his tongue plundering the recesses of her mouth, savagely taking what he wanted while she lay helplessly pinned beneath the weight of his body. Melissa knew that she could go on despising him, hating him for his abusive treatment. But then suddenly, he became the patient lover, his kisses awaiting a response, his hand clasping the back of her neck, soothing away the tension that had claimed her the moment before. It was to be another form of torture, she mused, one more devastating than being devoured and quickly taken in the heat of his passion.

As he scooted beside her, laying a muscular leg over her thighs to prohibit her struggling, his mouth covered one pink peak and then the other, his tongue teasing them to tautness. Melissa squeezed her eyes shut, trying to ignore the erotic shiver that flew down her spine, fiercely clinging to her vow of remaining unaffected.

His hand weaved over her breasts and then roamed over her abdomen, dipping beneath the loosened waistband of her breeches and then ascended to her breasts, not once, but over and over again, until the arousing massage left her plaint and responsive to his skillful touch. His hot kisses abandoned the swells of her breasts, following the sensuous trail his hand had blazed across her skin. Melissa caught her breath, painfully aware that her resistance had fled from the path of fire his touch had evoked. All was lost. The familiar need of his lovemaking made her blood boil with a desire that defied logic, melting what was left of her defenses.

Her senses reeled, spinning in chaos, alert only to the manly fragrance that was so much a part of him and to the feel of his hard body pressed closely to hers. The warmth of his flesh on hers seared her skin, branding her as his possession. When he had slipped the buckskin breeches from her hips, his caresses began again, more boldly than before, leaving Melissa to wonder if she could endure the sweet torture of wild sensations that made her heart run away with itself.

His caresses wandered to the softness of her thighs, his seeking hands starting yet another fire that burned its way to her soul. Her body involuntarily arched to meet his probing hands, and then she shamelessly yielded, knowing that the bittersweet magic of his touch had completely destroyed the last of her resistance.

She was quivering beneath the delicious feel of his hands roaming intimately over her body. She wanted to clutch him to her, holding tightly to the only stable force within her grasp as the world slid out from under her. But her hands were bound and she was forced to endure the torturous rapture that flooded over her like a tidal wave, rocking her, tossing her along with wave after wave of wild, indescribable sensations that tore at her sanity.

"Zack. . . ." His name escaped her lips as her head rolled from side to side, wishing she could appease the maddening ache that was slowly consuming every inch of her body.

His mouth swooped down on hers, drawing the last of her breath from her lungs, leaving her suspended, while his caresses searched and claimed each sensitive point, sending her soaring to yet another climactic summit of rapture. Again, Melissa closed her eyes, but the image of the sleek, black panther leaped at her thoughts, refusing to release her from his spell. The glowing pools of silver poured across her skin like a fiery river while his hands fanned along her hips, weaving a path that drove her insane with desire.

"Do you want me?" Zack questioned, his voice heavy with disturbed passion.

Although he had whispered in her ear, he seemed a thousand miles away. She was bobbing on an endless sea, unable to see the distant shore, dying a slow, agonizing death. And just when Melissa thought she had relinquished her will to live, his mouth descended on hers, giving her new life, his warm breath reviving her.

"Take me," she gasped as another wild tremor sent her spiraling.

"Tell me you want me, Lissa," he demanded as he nibbled at the corners of her mouth.

His method of torture was worse than death, and Melissa despised him and herself for the unquenchable passion he had ignited within her. But the words flowed from her lips before she could bite them back, answering his command.

"Zack, love me. I want you."

As his hips slid between her thighs, he held himself above her, taunting her, waiting for her to look up at him. Her lashes swept up, glistening with hot tears. Indigo eyes locked with flaming silver as his lips slanted across hers, making her his complete possession. The rapid beat

462

of his heart thundered against her naked breasts as he lowered himself to her. He plunged deeply within her, satisfying the overwhelming need that had consumed their flesh, driving, seeking ultimate depths of intimacy until their souls had forged as one. And then the maddening hunger died as they soared above the smoldering embers, winging their way to rapture's pinnacle, seeing a new world on the far horizon. Their flight caught and captured eternity, leaving them exhausted when they finally drifted back to reality.

As Zack shuddered above her, he clutched her closer, nuzzling his head against the curve of her neck. He drew a long, ragged breath and then rolled beside her. When he gathered her into his arms, she stiffened, angry with herself for the way she had responded to him. Zack reached beneath her chin, turning her face to his, searching the eyes that were rimmed with tears and glowing with the dying flame of passion.

"Do you despise me so much that you can deny the pleasures we have always found in each other's arms?" His voice was like a soft caress before his lips moved lightly over hers.

"I despise the satanic power you have over my body. I know I cannot resist you, but I hate you because you are a coward," she blurted out and then choked on a sob.

"A coward?" he repeated incredulously. His brows furrowed in a long line over his eyes as he drew away to meet her gaze. "I have been called many scandalous names in my life, but never a coward."

"But that is what you are," she insisted. "You are courageous when you face impossible odds that require physical strength, invincible when others would perish. But when the situation pertains to affairs of the heart,

463

you are suspicious and fearful." Her narrowed gaze was coldly accusing. "You are afraid to care, afraid to trust, afraid of being hurt. You guard your heart as if it were fragile crystal."

"I have learned to be wary and cautious," Zack defended. "Wounds of the flesh mend and leave their scars, but a broken heart may never heal. I will only gamble my heart when I find a woman who earns my respect, a woman who can understand me and love me for the way I am. Only a fool offers his love to someone who would speak of affection and then vanish into the night."

"And you never stayed long enough in one place to know if you could feel more than physical desire for a woman," she countered in an intimidating tone. "You seek a shallow existence, satiating your lusts and searching for nothing more."

"Because I have never found a woman who possessed more than an appetizing body, who fascinated and intrigued me with her resourcefulness, who could survive in my world." He paused a moment and addressed her a faint smile. "That is, until I went in search of the one woman I never expected to find."

The color drained from her cheeks as she listened to words that lured her into false hope. Was this another form of torture? she wondered.

"I found a woman of unequaled beauty, who was as cunning as the wiliest fox, one whose passions matched mine." His eyes glowed with a strange warmth that was unfamiliar to Melissa. "I was no longer the hunter, but the prey. I fought to escape from the memories that chained me to you. Each woman I took in my arms in my attempt to forget you fell short of my expectations. I came for you even after I told Jeremy that I refused. I struggled against myself, ignoring you, denying myself the pleasure that I knew you could bring. When Nancy Gibbs came to me, offering what no other man had claimed, I knew that I had lost the battle," he confessed as his hand brushed across her cheek, memorizing her exquisite features. "Her open arms beckoned me. Her green eyes smiled willingly. But when I reached out to her, her face became yours, her eyes mellowed into haunting indigo, and her hair became a stream of honey gold. I wanted you, not her, and I sent her away."

Melissa regarded him suspiciously. This did not sound like the man she knew. This was not Zack Beaugener, the calloused frontiersman who took what he wanted, feeling nothing more than a moment's passion, guarding his innermost thoughts. Nor was this Damion Montclaire, the arrogant rogue who sought to charm a woman into submission. "Is this another ploy?" Her brows furrowed into a cynical frown. "What is it you want, for me to effect the escape of another of your comrades?" Melissa scoffed at him. "I am no longer a fool, Zack. I once offered you my love and you would not accept it. I was innocent of all men and you made me your whore. Never again will I fall prey to that weakness. You are wasting your time trying to lure me into another of your traps.

"I once thought I could offer you my love, even when you had no interest in accepting it, but that brought another kind of torture, one that was not quickly forgotten. You will not sweet-talk your way into my heart again and use me for another mission. I have not yet healed from the first painful wounds. And you will not destroy me for I intend to survive, no matter how many pounds of flesh you try to extract from me."

Zack heaved a sigh, knowing that Jeremy had read her

well. She was immune to his words. She had been burned and was hesitant of standing too close to the fire. When she tried to squirm for release, Zack laid his leg across her hips and then reached around to untie her hands.

"No more games, Lissa," he assured her solemnly. "I have played them with you in the past, but they did nothing to save me from your bewitching charms. I didn't want to love you because I feared spending the rest of my life like Jeremy, remembering a dream that could never become reality. Nor did I wish to wither and die like my father when my mother abandoned him.

"But now I am gambling my heart." His gaze scanned her creamy flesh, and then he glanced down at the rope that he laid between them, assuring her that she was no longer his prisoner.

Again his eyes focused on her. "I love you, Lissa. You fill up my senses, that sight and feel of you . . ." His voice trailed off as he traced the gentle curve of her lips, wishing he could lose himself to the delicious taste of her kisses. The words were difficult to produce because he had never said them before. He felt strange and awkward and Melissa wasn't helping matters. She just kept staring at him, refusing to believe that he spoke from his heart. "I admire your determination. I adore that fiery temper of yours that brings me both anger and amusement."

He was no good at this, he thought disgustedly. So much for tender words. Zack decided to speak what he was feeling. "I will continue to crave that delicious body of yours until my last dying breath. But I will not come as your slave to kneel at your feet. I come as your companion. I cannot change the kind of man I am, nor do I intend to try. I will fight your battles for you, defend your honor, and challenge any man who tries to take you from me."

Zack cupped her face in his hands, his gaze locked with hers, watching the bewildered expression that surfaced on her features. "If you try to escape me again I will track you to the ends of the earth. You may flee from me, evade me for a time, but when you look behind you, I'll be there, waiting to come to you in the stillness of the night. I will stalk you wherever you go, becoming your constant shadow. No man will have the chance to win your heart because I will forbid it. You will learn to love me again or you will never again know love." The glint of steel in his eyes assured Melissa that he voiced no idle threats. "I will never let you go, Lissa. I love you."

A smile blossomed on her lips. This was the man she had known and loved, the stubborn, unyielding black knight who possessed a satanic power over her, the skillful rogue who had taught her the meaning of passion, and the fearless hunter who blazed trails that she would forever follow. Her heart swelled with so much joy that she knew it would burst as she gazed up at him with an adoring smile. She reached out to smooth the thick ebony hair across his forehead. She wanted no knight in shining armor, no submissive slave, and no gentleman cloaked in elegant garments. All she had ever wanted was this dark warrior who had taken her from hell to heaven with his confession of love.

"From the first time I awoke to find you towering over me I knew I was no longer the mistress of my own fate. My life was yours, my heart belonged to you, and my soul was cast upon the silver sea that I had seen in your eyes." Melissa flashed him another warm smile as her hand trickled over his broad chest, watching the hard muscles flex and then relax beneath her touch. "No man has known me as you have, Zack, for no man can exorcise the hungering spirit that has consumed my being. I have turned them all away, pledging myself to one man and his destiny." Her hand curled around his neck pulling his face to hers to place a light kiss to his waiting lips. "I do love you, Zack, and I cannot escape the power you hold over me. There is no haven that could shelter me from this spirit that possesses me. I love you above all others and I shall forever."

As their lips touched again, a bond of fire forged their souls together and their love blossomed to create its own design. Their admission of defeat was their victory, their forteited hearts were receptive to the overwhelming sensations that inflamed them. Wrapped in each others' arms they soared to passion's towering pinnacle, thriving in a universe that only lovers could view. Melissa had never known such contentment. She was gliding like an eagle and the wind beneath her wings was the breath of love, a love that she never dreamed she could capture. It consumed and sustained her, leaving her wanting for nothing more than to share the world of being held in Zack's arms.

Whatever they must face, they would endure together. Whatever powers attempted to fling them apart would meet with united strength. Their wild, sweet love had made them invincable, and Melissa was gripped by the spine-tingling sensation that together they were indestructable.

Zack folded Melissa deeply in his embrace and breathed a ragged breath, amazed by the emotions that sizzled their way to his very core. "Don't ever stop loving me, Lissa," he murmured hoarsely as he nibbled at her ear. "I have no wish to endure the pain that could tear my heart in two now that I have experienced the pleasure loving you can give." He tilted her head back, sending a cascade of honey gold tumbling over his shoulder. "The first time I stared into those indigo eyes that sparkled with gold, I knew I was on the threshold of a new horizon. The sun seems to rise and set in your eyes." A demure smile hovered on his lips as his arm encircled her waist. "Jeremy would have had me yield to the inevitable much sooner, but I could not surrender without a fight. I could have saved myself many torturous nights if I would have accepted my fate and walked into the world of paradise I have seen in your eyes."

Melissa giggled giddishly, her laughter wafting its way through the midnight air. "And each time you seek to escape, I shall mark false trails that lead you in circles, bringing you back to me."

"You would delight in watching me track witches and winged horses up trees again, wouldn't you?" he teased, his smile melting her heart, leaving it dripping on the inside of her chest.

"Aye, my love. And there will be no doubt in your mind that my palomino stallion and I can fly," she murmured, her voice quivering with emotion.

"There never was any doubt, my enchanting witch," Zack rasped, his eyes beginning to burn with a fire that he wondered if he could ever extinguish when he was lying beside her. "But now I can follow you. My love for you have performed miracles."

"Aye, a miracle," she agreed, deciding to take the opportune moment to tell him of the child she carried, but his mouth urgently possessed hers.

She swallowed the confession as they tasted passion's intoxicating brew, drinking their full of the heady pleasures of loving and being loved.

As she nestled in his arms in the aftermath of love, Zack smiled quietly to himself. He had once thought love to be a prison of intangible chains and tortures that left the man's soul to bleed, but he was engulfed by a strange sense of freedom and contentment, one that he never dreamed existed. Jeremy had his wish and Zack had a bird's-eye view of heaven. He had pledged his love to the one woman who was gentle enough to touch his heart and strong enough to possess it for all eternity.

## Chapter Twenty Three

As dawn's first light streamed across the horizon Melissa raised heavily lidded eyes and glanced over at Zack. A satisfied smile brimmed her lips as she reached out to trace her fingertips over his mouth. His dark lashes fluttered open to see her leaning over him and he returned her drowsy smile.

Melissa caught her breath when she noticed the tender expression in the pools of silver. There was no threatening flicker in them. She was gazing at an endless sea that shimmered in the moonlight, a sea that was void of angry waves, rippling gently with the breath of love.

A rakish smile curved the corners of his mouth upward as he slid his hand around her back, molding them together. "I had the strangest dream last night."

"Oh?" She cocked a wondering brow as she glanced up at him.

"I had captured a goddess, an angel that hovered so close to the ground. 'Twas a night that I shall long remember," he rasped as his leg slid between hers, press-

471

ing her to her back. "I wonder if the same dream will visit me at dawn."

Melissa dodged his intended kiss, holding him at bay with small but determined hands pressed to his chest. "We must catch up with my father." Every moment we tarry puts us farther apart," she insisted.

Zack heaved a disappointed sigh. Only for love would he deny himself the pleasure he sought. She had changed him, he thought to himself. If Jeremy could see them now he would be doubling over in laughter, but then he probably was already. The note that Zack had propped against the teacup would have brought a self-satisfied grin to Jeremy's lips. "If I see your daughter, I will tell her that I love her . . . over and over again until I have swept away her doubts." And love her he did, so totally that he could never gaze into her eyes without being overwhelmed by an emotion that blazed a path to his very soul.

"Very well," he conceded as he willfully dragged himself away from her. "We will ride, but don't expect me to keep my hands from you when we stop for the night. I have never been an overly patient man, especially when it comes to bewitching women."

Melissa flashed him a provocative smile as her hands weaved across the dark matting on his chest. "When we stop for the night, I doubt that I will be thinking of sleep."

Zack swallowed his words as he drew her to her feet, noting the faraway look that was reflected in her eyes. She was again thinking of her father, and she would never be truly content until she had found him. Zack felt a smoldering anger for the woman who had cruelly deceived William Stoddard. The woman would receive

472

her just reward for what she had done, he vowed to himself, as he swept Melissa into his arms and sat her atop her palomino stallion.

Each day that passed without catching sight of Stoddard wore on Melissa's nerves. She was restless and preoccupied, and Zack knew that he would never truly have her as his own until they faced Stoddard with the truth.

The day before they were to arrive in Norfolk, Melissa insisted that they continue through the night, but Zack refused to push the horses. They were exhausted from the hard days of traveling and so was Zack.

"If we don't rest our mounts, we'll be carrying then on *our* backs," he muttered sourly. "And I, for one, do not relish the thought!"

"Then you stay behind and I will go on alone," Melissa suggested, her gaze searching the area ahead of them, just as it had for days on end. "I cannot rest until I know if Papa has left for France."

Zack released a disgruntled sigh as he nudged his reluctant steed. "We will ride to Norfolk, but if this nag drops in his tracks, then I intend to go no further either!"

Melissa leaned over to place a kiss to his rugged cheek. "Thank you, Zack," she said appreciatively. "If we find Papa, then I will become your slave, obeying your commands without complaint."

Zack cocked a skeptical brow. "I have no need of a slave. All I desire is a willing wench to warm my soft feather bed."

"Whatever you wish," she conceded with a weary smile.

"Don't be so agreeable," Zack grumbled. "It makes me suspicious."

As he moved ahead of her, Melissa studied his muscular frame. She had asked a great deal of him the past few days, and he had complied to all of her requests. The day would come when she could show her devotion and tell him of the child, when they would have time to talk instead of falling into an exhausted sleep after making love beneath the ceiling of stars. But first she had to find her father.

Leila and William had returned from the theater late that night. William could barely recall the play, his thoughts wandering from Laura to Melissa. It had been difficult to accept the fact that his daughter had perished, just as it had been agony to realize that he had lost his wife those many years ago. Lelia has been his strength throughout the ordeal, and although he could never truly love her, he had agreed to marry her, hoping to find consolation, companionship through the lonely years that lay ahead of him.

Leila was right, he mused, as he stared off into the darkness. He needed a change of scenery to help him forget. When he stepped down and then turned to assist her from the carriage, he heard the thundering of hooves and glanced up to see the golden palomino galloping toward him, its rider's hair streaming across her shoulders in disarray. William's heart skipped a beat and his knees buckled under him as he watched the approaching steed.

"My God," he breathed, as his hands dropped away from Lelia's waist, leaving her fumbling to maintain her balance.

When Melissa caught sight of her father, she reined her stallion to an abrupt halt and dashed into his waiting arms.

Lelia's face went white with rage as she gazed into the bewitching features that had haunted her for an eternity. It was as if she had seen a ghost of her sister materialize from the darkness to steal William away from her again. She clutched the carriage door to keep her feet, swaying, gasping for breath. And then vengeance burned like the fires of hell when she noticed the loving expression on William's face, a look that had tormented her for over twenty years. It was that same devotion that he had offered Laura during their wedding. Lelia's body trembled with fury, hating the memories that came at her from all directions, despising the young woman who was her mother's image.

"Lissa," William whimpered as he brushed his hands over the wild tresses that flowed down her back. "I thought you were dead. All these months—"

"I know, Papa." Melissa's gaze swung to her aunt, drilling accusingly into the woman who braced herself against the carriage.

"Come inside and tell me what all has happened. There is so much I do not understand," William insisted, urging Melissa along beside him, afraid to release her now that he had found her again, completely forgetting the violet-eyed woman who had been his constant companion the past few months.

When Melissa glanced back to the coach, Lelia was

nowhere to be seen, and Melissa found herself wishing that Lelia would flee, never to return. The grief she had inflicted on William was unforgivable.

"Did you travel here alone?" William inquired, along with a rash of questions that had haunted him. "Where have you been? Why were we told that you were dead? And what of the mission? I—"

Melissa pressed her fingertips to his lips, silencing him so she could answer at least one of his many questions. "Captain Montclaire escorted me, but he went to his home to have our room prepared for the night," she explained.

"*Your* room?" William's brown eyes narrowed disapprovingly.

Melissa grinned at his concerned expression. "Montclaire is my husband. We were married four months ago."

"What?" His breath came out in a rush, as if she had knocked the wind out of him. "But you only met him four months ago. Why would you marry a man you had only met?"

Her amused chortle only confused him further. " 'Tis a long story, Papa. And the hour is late. I will explain it all to you tomorrow," she assured him before pressing a loving kiss to his cheek.

"Tomorrow?" he repeated bewilderedly. "I cannot wait! You return from the dead, tell me that you are wed and that I must endure the night before you give an explanation?"

"I'm afraid that you must," she said softly. "I promised Montclaire that I would go with him as soon as I had seen you. We can discuss all of this tomorrow after the wedding."

"The wedding?" he gasped and then quickly closed the distance between him and the chair, collapsing into it. If it had been another step away he would have crumbled to the floor. His mind was playing tricks on him. "Melissa, what the devil is going on? I thought you said you were already married. You're not making any sense, or I am losing my mind?"

She knelt down beside him, bringing his limp hand to her lips. "I am married, but tomorrow I am marrying another man and you will be there to give me away." She giggled as she watched William's face turn a whiter shade of pale.

"But how—"

Melissa rose to her feet and wheeled around when she felt a presence behind her. The smile on Lelia's face drew her suspicious frown. The woman appeared too self-satisfied and it made Melissa uneasy.

"I am so relieved that you are alive and well, Melissa," Lelia said, her honeyed-tone causing Melissa's frown to settle deeper.

"I'll just bet you are," she scoffed before stepping around Lelia, careful not to brush against her, repulsed by the sight of her.

Willian remained where he was, his jaw sagging, his eyes wide and disbelieving. Lelia's request for him to walk her to her room jolted him from his pensive musings and he came unsteadily to his feet.

When Lelia was alone in her chamber, a demented chuckle floated in the darkness. Melissa would disappear as quickly as she had appeared. After William and Melissa had ignored her, Lelia hurried down the street in desperation, devising a way to dispose of Melissa once and for all. Luck had been with her when she ran headlong into a man who had been standing inconspicuously in the shadows. In frantic breaths she concocted her story, begging for the man to aid her, explaining that the younger woman was plotting to kill her. Lelia had extracted a pouch of coins from her purse and offered it to him.

"I don't care what you do with her or where you take her, but I want her dead before she destroys me!" Lelia ordered, her violet eyes sparking with deranged madness.

The evil chuckle that floated from the man's lips sent an eerie shiver down Lelia's spine. There was something frightening about him, as if he delighted in vindictivness.

"It will be my pleasure," the man assured her, his voice low and raspy. "You have saved me a great deal of trouble, madam."

He stepped to the street and swung up on his dark steed and then reined toward the alley to await his victim. Another low rumble erupted from his massive chest, and Lelia glanced up at the dark face that towered over her, swallowing the lump that had collected in her throat. The devilish smile on his lips assured her that he would not only do as she had requested, but that it would bring him excessive pleasure. If she had not been so desperate she would have feared for her own life.

Lelia slumped back on her pillow, squeezing back the thought of his evil smile, wondering if Melissa was at this moment confronting the man Lelia had found hiding in the shadows. She knew there would be no mistake this time. William would be by her side forever! Her lifelong dream would come true. Laura had stolen William away and Melissa had kept him from her. And her own hasty marriage in France had separated them for long years. But now they were all out of the way, and she and William would be together. Lelia had suffered torturous eternity for her love to be fulfilled, but it had been worth the wait and she would pay any price to keep her beloved William.

Melissa's eyes radiated happiness as she watched the handsome rogue who reined up beside her. She leaned across to hug his neck, showering him with adoring kisses. Zack swept her into his lap and chuckled in amusement as he settled her in front of him on the saddle. It was as if a heavy yoke had been lifted from her shoulders. She was reckless and carefree once again.

"Take me home, sir," she requested as she nestled in his protective arms.

Zack pressed a tender kiss to the slim column of her neck, his breath warm against her skin. "Did you tell Stoddard that you were spending the night with a strange man?" he questioned.

"Nay, I told him I would be sleeping with my husband. He had enough of a shock for one night," she replied as her hand curled along the side of his face.

He took the palomino's reins and urged his steed toward his mansion, passing the dark alleyways of Norfolk's main street, keeping to the shadows that swayed in the dim moonlight. "If you think you will be sleeping, *cherie*, you are sorely mistaken."

Melissa returned the seductive smile. "And which rogue will I find in my bed, Beaugener or Montclaire?"

"Which would you prefer?" His dark brows arched curiously.

Melissa frowned, thoughtfully considering his question. "I think perhaps the clean-shaven, dashing sea captain would be a pleasant change. I have grown tired of that bearded frontiersman of late," she taunted.

"He no longer satisfies you, vixen?" Zack's silver-gray eyes danced with mischief.

"I have never really forgotten Montclaire," she assured him. "The first time I laid eyes on him, he took my breath away. I could only stand and stare at his handsome face."

When Zack halted his steed, he effortlessly set Melissa to her feet, and tossed the reins to the groomsman who appeared at the door of the stables. As they paused at the top of the spiral staircase, Zack gestured toward the door to the right. Melissa walked into the room and gasped in delight. Before her waited a steaming bath. At the foot of the bed sat the trunk that she had left on the schooner. Upon the blue velvet bedspread lay a nightgown of white, trimmed in gold. When she glanced back to speak to Zack he was gone. She smiled to herself, closed the door, and hurriedly stripped from her buckskins.

Melissa sank down in the tub and eased back, allowing the perfumed water to soothe away her tension. After her bath she donned the gossamer gown and stretched leisurely on the bed, reveling in the peacefulness that had suddenly flooded over her. She had everything. the world lay at her feet. What woman could wish for more?

Zack opened the door, his gaze focusing on the alluring young woman who lay seductively on her side, a cape of honey-gold cascading over her shoulder. When she glanced up, her breath caught in her throat, her eyes sweeping his clean-shaven face, the face of Damion Montclaire. Suddenly, she recalled the first time she had seen him as he swaggered across the deck of the schooner. She felt that same wild flutter in her heart as he eased down beside her.

A provocative smile pursed her lips as her hand made a leisurely ascent over the dark hair on his chest. "I've missed you, Montclaire," she breathed, silently summoning him to her as her lips parted in invitation.

It was given and quickly accepted. His mouth slanted across hers, their breath intermingling as one before he drew far enough away to lose himself in the love that glowed in her eyes. "And I have never forgotten the siren who stood at the helm, her hair blowing in the breeze, her shapely body framed by the vastness of the sea."

The white gown, so quickly donned, was immediately discarded. Zack ran his hand over her perfect flesh, loving the feel of her, the sight of her, everything about her. And then suddenly, a thoughtful frown crossed his brow.

"How is it that you have survived and flourished on the meager rations we've been eating of late? I have dwindled to skin and bone." A playful smile curved his lips. "Has this witch been sampling a potion that she has kept hidden from me?"

A warm blush worked its way to her cheeks as his hand roamed over her abdomen. "If I become grossly overweight will you continue to love me as you have confessed?"

Zack eyed her suspiciously. "Do you intend to stuff yourself so there will be more of you for me to love?"

A demure smile crept to the corners of her mouth. "Or perhaps there will be two of us for you to love."

He sat there staring quizzically at her until her insinuation finally soaked in. And then he jerked his hand away from her as if he had been stung, an angry frown replacing what had moments before a tender smile. Melissa bit her lip, hurt by the condemnation in his eyes. Perhaps he did not want a child, she thought disheartenedly. Melissa had foolishly thought she had the world at her feet, but that illusion was shattered when Zack stood up and paced the room.

"How could you?" He wheeled to face her, his jaw twitching as he forced out the words.

"How could *I*?" Melissa grabbed for her gown and hastily shrugged it on. "You had as much to do with this child as I did," she countered, her tone as angry as his.

Zack muttered under his breath and then flashed her another annoyed frown. "Why didn't you tell me about this earlier? You allowed me to stake you to a tree for the night, throw you to the ground, and you have pushed yourself to the point of exhaustion," he accused as he stalked back to her, wagging a lean finger in her face. "Dammit, Melissa, that is my child you have been abusing and from now on you will behave like a mother-to-be!"

Relief spread across her face as his arms came around her waist, and she smiled secretively, wondering how long before he would be unable to curve his hands around her midsection.

"Then you are not upset that you are to be a father?"

"Upset?" Zack's grin stretched from ear to ear. "Madam, I could not be more delighted." But then he frowned thoughtfully, giving the matter a bit more consideration. "And then again . . . " When Melissa cocked a curious brow, his smile returned. "I would be more elated if we had a houseful."

Melissa slid her arms about his shoulders, gazing into those fathomless pools of silver. "I love you," she murmured softly. "We shall fill the world with Beaugeners, and each of them will have their father's eyes, that mysterious shade of gray that holds men and women spellbound."

Zack groaned with pleasure as his arms tightened about her, crushing her to him with an urgency that had driven him since the first time he had seen her in his mountain cabin. "And I love you, Melissa," he whispered as he nuzzled against the top of her head. "I never thought I could say those words to anyone and mean them with both my heart and soul."

Melissa's eyes clouded with tears of joy. "Love me," she pleaded. "Always love me. I don't think I could live without you now that I know the happiness I have found with you."

The winds of desire rushed through the terrace doors as they clung together, surrendering to the raging passion that sent them spiraling in a darkened world. There was no hesitation as they whispered their love for each other. They were swept up in a breathless tempest, living and dying in the sweet ecstasy that their lovemaking brought.

As the storm clouds parted, a gentle breeze of love

touched their perspiring skin. The rapid beats of their hearts slowed their frantic paces, their harmonic rhythm lulling them into tranquil dreams. Contentment drew a ragged breath as Melissa and Zack lay entangled in each other's arms, enjoying the pleasures of a love that had endured the worst of times and had blossomed to share the best of times.

A mysterious smile played on Lelia's lips as she waited beside William in the hotel lobby. But Stoddard was too preoccupied to notice. His gaze was glued to the door, anxiously awaiting the arrival of his daughter and along with her, the explanation that he had spent a sleepless night anticipating.

But Lissa would not walk through that door, Lelia thought to herself. William would have to suffer the loss again, but that would only bring him closer to her. No one would ever take William away from her again. She had waited too long, surviving only on memories.

The door eased open to reveal Melissa and Zack. Both Lelia and William gasped at the sight of the handsome gentleman whose muscular frame filled the entrance. It only took William an instant to recognize the silver-gray eyes and dark features of Zack Beaugener. There was no heavy beard or buckskin clothes, only the rugged face and elegant clothes that had been tailor-made to his his well-proportioned body.

Lelia's guttural moan drew William's attention, and he dragged his eyes off of the couple to see what distressed Lelia. Her face was as white as a sheet, her violet eyes darkening to furious purple. A demented madness claimed her, vengeance churning like an angry whirlwind. The moment she gazed into the slaty eyes, seeing the devilish gleam in them, she wanted to scream in rage. The man she had met the previous evening wore a heavy beard and a cold smile. She did not mistake the mockery in Zack's grin as he came steadily toward her, as if he held her secret, torturing her until he found the opportune moment to destroy all that she had planned for over twenty years. He was the same man she had met on the street, the man she had paid to dispose of Melissa. Damn her luck! Damn them all!

"Papa, this is my husband, Damion Montclaire," Melissa introduced.

Again the color seeped from Lelia's cheeks and she clutched at William's arm for support, as if the world was sliding out from beneath her, and she intended to cling to the most important thing in her life.

"Montclaire?" William questioned bewilderedly. "But I thought your name was—"

Melissa sent him a silencing frown and then anchored her accusing gaze on her aunt who still clung fiercely to William.

"Madam," Montclaire began, nodding slightly to Lelia. From his pocket he retrieved the pouch of coins, pried her hand from William's arm, and dropped the money in her palm. "I fear I must decline your offer." The sarcasm in his words made Lelia wince as if he had slapped her across the face. "You have paid me well to kill Melissa, but I intend to keep my wife."

"What?" William's head swiveled around to glare at Lelia.

"I was outside waiting to escort Melissa home last

485

night and this woman approached me, requesting that I dispose of her niece. Since she didn't know who I was, I let her believe I would follow through with her command. She lied to you about Melissa perishing in an attack. And no doubt, she paid her informer to give you the news of Melissa's death." Montclaire's condemning gaze scorched Lelia with such intensity that she staggered back. "Jeremy warned me not to trust her so I came back last night to ensure that Melissa came to no harm."

Lelia's violet eyes came alive with a crazed madness as she retreated from the accusing glares. The tiny thread that held her sanity for twenty years was severed when William turned on her, his face twisted with disgust. She jerked the handgun from her purse and aimed it directly at Melissa, but it wasn't that she saw. It was Laura.

"You cannot have him, *ma soeur,*" she raged, a wild, frantic hysteria in her voice. "You took him from me once, but never again, Laura. Never again, do you hear me? I have waited too long. I survived these years of torture, knowing he was holding you in his arms. *Mon Dieu,* how I despise you! My own sister! You knew that I loved him and you delighted in stealing him from me, didn't you? You always had everything. Your beauty, your poise. You used your body to capture him. I could hear you laughing at me each night that I lay alone in my bed. But you cannot have him now." The deep purple in her eyes glowed, smoldering with the years of hatred that had burned like cancer. "He is mine!" The barrel of the gun was aimed at Melissa's chest and not a one among them doubted that she intended to pull the trigger.

The threesome stood motionless after listening to Lelia's demented ravings. She had gone mad and any sudden movement would bring her wrath down on Melissa. Lelia was too close to miss her target.

Zack trembled in fury, and it was all he could do to contain himself. If anything happened to Melissa he would tear this woman to shreds with his bare hands, he vowed to himself. His jaw twitched angrily, his features stone cold, but he was helpless to come to his wife's defense.

"Lelia, what is going on here?" Rorick Stephens stepped inside the foyer to see the woman holding the gun. And then his attention swung to the golden-haired woman who had her back to him. "Melissa?" he choked in disbelief.

The familiar voice filtered through Lelia's tortured thoughts. When she glanced up, Zack sprung at her, but Lelia saw him coming and squeezed the trigger before Zack could grab the gun.

The world spun furiously a split second after the pistol exploded, shattering the silence. Melissa heard the enraged growl of the black panther but she could not answer. A vast darkness swam before her, beckoning her to drift on the endless sea that reflected the silver glow of moonlight. Melissa tried to draw a breath but it never came. And then there was nothing but a dark, interrupted silence. . . .

## Chapter Twenty Four

Zack braved a glance over his shoulder, holding his breath, afraid that Lelia had accomplished her deed. Out of the corner of his eye he had seen Rorick diving at Melissa. Zack hopped to his feet and hurried to Melissa as Rorick scooped her from the floor, her head dropping lifelessly from his shoulder, her golden hair streaming over his arm.

"God, don't take her from me when I've only found her again," Rorick murmured.

He pressed a tender kiss to her unresponsive lips, as if he were the handsome prince whose magic embrace could bring sleeping beauty back to life. Zack stiffened in irritation as he watched Rorick's mouth linger on Melissa's. And then his anger burned a hot, blue flame when the kiss broke her deathlike trance. It cut him to the quick that it was not *his* kiss that roused her to consciousness.

Melissa moaned groggily, feeling the warmth of a man's chest. Thinking it was Zack, she wrapped her arms around his neck and nestled in his protective embrace. Although Zack breathed a relieved sigh that Melissa was alive and he was grateful that Stephens had managed to knock Melissa from the bullet's path, seeing her in another man's arms transformed him into a jealous, green-eyed monster.

"Stephens!" he bellowed, his voice booming through the lobby like a clap of thunder. "Unhand my wife!"

Rorick jumped as if he had been lashed with a whip and then turned to meet Zack's furious glower. Melissa was snatched from his arms and he just stood there, frozen to the spot, the color draining from his face like a bucket of water that had sprung a leak.

"Your wife?" Rorick squeaked when he finally found his tongue.

Zack focused his attention on Melissa, carefully searching for a wound. He examined the knot on the side of her head, sustained when she had hit the floor, and then he offered a faint smile to the captain, his voice softer now. "Aye, my wife," he affirmed. "My thanks Stephens. If not for you, Lissa would not be alive."

"Melissa's eyes fluttered open, roused by the sound of Zack's rich voice. Her gaze circled the room and then she frowned. "Where is Lelia?"

The three men searched the faces of the people who had gathered during the commotion, but there was no sign of Lelia.

"She harbored a hate for the wrong person all these years," William mused aloud, a guilt-ridden expression on his features. "I treated her shamelessly and she continued to blame Laura." His eyes settled on his daughter. "Are you all right, child?"

Zack clutched her tighter as she nodded to her father. Only now did he fully realize how William and Jeremy felt about Laura, the woman who had touched both of their lives. And he knew how dangerously close he had come to losing the only woman he had ever loved. When Melissa smiled up at him, hiding none of her feelings, his heart melted. If anything ever happened to this beautiful vixen, he would surely go as mad as Lelia. The strong ties he felt for Melissa solidified as he gazed into the pools of indigo that glistened with sunrays.

"Lissa, do you feel up to the wedding ceremony?" he whispered, his voice quivering with emotion.

"I thought you said she was your wife," Rorick interrupted, a suspicious frown gathering on his brows.

Melissa threw him a mischievous smile. "I am, Captain, but I am marrying Zack Beaugener this afternoon," she explained.

"What the sweet loving hell is going on?" Rorick grumbled in exaspiration. First he entered the lobby to find Lelia holding a gun on Melissa, ranting like a lunatic, calling Melissa by another name. And now Melissa insisted that she was marrying again after she just affirmed that she was married already. He was beginning to wonder if the entire family was a little touched in the head. "How many husbands do you have?"

"I shall have two before the day is out," she giggled as her lashes swept up to meet Zack's loving smile. "And I think perhaps two will be enough."

Rorick's breath came out in a rush. "But you can't—"

"Don't ask her any more questions," William interjected, cutting Rorick short. "I am not in the mood to

490

hear any more of her twisted explanations. I think the bump on her head has scrambled her brain!"

Melissa ignored her father's taunting remark, her eyes anchored on Zack. "Are you certain that this is what you want? I promised myself in the beginning that I would not hold you to any bonds that you could not willingly accept. But if we marry, I expect you to honor the vows."

His answer was in his smile, but he chose to voice it, assuring that she would not be dragging him to the alter. "I have never been more certain of anything in my life, *cherie.*" His lips hovered on hers as he gently set her to her feet and then tossed Stoddard and Stephens a quick glance. "Come along, gentlemen. We shall need two witnesses."

Zack had made a point to seek out the same clergyman who had performed the ceremony on board his schooner, hoping to set the man's mind at ease since he feared that he had made a tragic mistake the first time. The clergyman was not at all pleased to see him and misinterpreted the request, believing that the crazed captain intended to take yet another wife. But when Zack returned with Melissa, the preacher breathed a sigh of relief. This time there was no hesitancy in her voice, no hostility in her eyes, only the glow of love, and he was happy they had finally come to terms.

Zack tossed his cravat over the back of the chair and

absently unbuttoned his waistcoat, his gaze lingering on the open window. A quiet smile pursed his lips, remembering the loving expression on Melissa's face when she spoke the vows. And then he chortled to himself, recalling how he had shuffled the guests from his house. Melissa accused him of being rude, but he could not wait to get her alone. Melissa had conquered his untamed heart. She was in his blood, filling him so completely that he was left to wonder if all men who fell hopelessly in love experienced the same indescribable sensations that consumed him. Nay, he decided, after giving the matter a moment's consideration. No other love could burn as brightly as the emotion he had pent up inside him.

"Are you satisfied?" he questioned as he pivoted toward Melissa, his gaze devouring her with enough heat to melt the moon and leave it dripping on the night sky.

Melissa cocked a curious brow. "Satisfied with what?"

"You have acquired both my names, you have stolen my heart, and my fortune lays at your feet. 'Tis it enough to content a woman like you for a lifetime?" He certainly hoped so since he had offered her all he had to give.

An impish grin settled in her exquisite features as she shrugged the white-laced gown from her shoulders, held it up in the air, and then let it drop in a careless heap on the floor. "Nay, my handsome rogue." Her seductive whisper sent a wild tingle darting down his spine and then ricocheting through his limbs. "After all, what is in a name? And you cannot extract your heart to place in my hands. Nor can your fortune buy what I desire."

His dark brow quirked, noting the suggestive gleam in her eyes and the provocative way she sauntered toward him. "I am left to wonder if mortal man can appease you, witch," he murmured as he lifted a stray gold curl and then let it drop on her shoulder.

"Only one," she insisted as she shed her chemise and stood shamelessly before him.

Her willing smile had him burning like a flaming torch. She was all woman, every perfect inch of her and she was his.

Zack hooked his arm around her waist, drawing her full length against him, letting her feel his desire for her. His caresses wandered to her breast and then ascended to her creamy cheek. He was captivated by the liquid pools that rippled with passion.

"Lissa . . . " He drew a shuddering breath as he buried his head in the soft tendrils that cascaded over her shoulder. "Do you have any idea how devastatingly beautiful you are?" When he touched her his heart hammered against his ribs, threatening to beat him to death before he could appease this overwhelming need to lose himself in the sight and feel of her.

Melissa leaned back as far as his captive arms would allow, a mischievous smile parting her lips. "Nay, but if you tell me, your every wish will be my command."

A low chuckle escaped his lips as he pressed a kiss to her forehead. "You never were worth a damn when it came to following orders. Why should I suddenly believe that you have changed, *cher ami?*"

The playfulness vanished, her gaze mirroring an emotion so pure and sweet that Zack trembled beneath her warm regard. "Because I love you," she assured him softly.

Zack cupped her face in his hands, holding her spellbound. "I don't know what lies ahead of us in these troubled times, but I do know that I will dare to love only once in my life. Without you I would become an empty shell, void of emotion. You are my reason for being, my breath of life, Lissa. You make me laugh and smile, bringing a happiness I never realized existed until you came into my life. I cannot imagine an existence without you. I was ready to kill Lelia when I thought she had hurt you. And I still think I would have even after I realized that you had survived. But she vanished into thin air, and no one has seen her. I hope she threw herself into the ocean," he muttered.

Melissa drew away to gaze up at him, lost to that captivating glint of silver in his eyes. There was a rare quality of gentleness in this powerful man, an emotion that was directed only to her. She was oddly content to bask in the warmth of his smile. Whatever dangers he faced, she would be by his side, loving him as deeply as he loved her, protecting him and encouraging him each step of the way.

As their lips touched Melissa melted in his arms. She was hopelessly lost, her body responding to his touch as it always had, freely, wildly, answering his passion with desires that simmered just beneath the surface. They had captured the sunrise, consumed by its fire. They were of one heart and soul, sharing a love to span eternity.

In the aftermath of love, Zack propped his arms on either side of her, gazing down into indigo eyes that radiated with happiness. He only thought his desires had been appeased until he felt another surge of warmth invade his body. Just staring at her left him with a craving that left him wondering if he could ever be appeased for any length of time.

"I have found heaven in your arms," he whispered, his voice heavy with renewed passion. "Take me there again."

Melissa tossed him an impish grin as she smoothed the tossled raven hair across his forehead. "I fear you have in insatiable appetite, but I have never been able to refuse you, nor can I now."

A low rumble erupted from his massive chest and a rakish smile hovered on his lips, showing even white teeth. He held himself above her, the muscles of his arms flexing and then relaxing as he came to her, still unable to get close enough to the flame that burned him inside and out.

"See that you don't, my love," he commanded softly. "I do not like to be denied, nor do I ever intend to be when it comes to loving you."

A provocative smile grazed her lips before he kissed it away. She had no intention of refusing the man who claimed her soul. "Nor will you ever be," she assured him just before his mouth captured hers again, taking her breath away and then giving her new life, a life that knew no beginning or end in the encompassing circle of his loving arms.

# A Note To The Reader

The events of 1778 are as they appear in history, with one exception. Daniel Boone was not freed in Detroit, but actually escaped on his own while traveling back from the British headquarters with the Shawnees who escorted him to Boonesborough. He had convinced Lieutenant Governor Hamilton that he would persuade the settlers to abandon the fort.

For the sake of the romantic adventure, Boone escaped a few days earlier than the history books show. In no way would I discredit his resourcefulness and accomplishments.

The siege of Boonesborough is an accurate account of the incident, even down to the detail of women dressing as men to convince the Shawnees that they had gathered reinforcements.

It is through the intriguing adventures of men like Daniel Boone and women such as Molly Hays and Deborah Samson who outfoxed the British that it becomes possible to imagine the feats of heroes and heroines in fiction. They are believable because our forefathers have lived the adventures, giving us fascinating ideas for plots. My thanks to all those legendary heroes and heroines.